THE CHIEF RESIDENT

ISBN: 978-0-9890713-2-1

THE CHIEF RESIDENT

A NOVEL

By

Michael Banas

Chapter One
THE CHIEF RESIDENT

Dr. Phillip Drummer was chief surgical resident at the Philadelphia General Hospital, and in charge of the case. It was late Friday night and standing beside him was surgical intern Westbrook, holding a scalpel in his trembling left upper extremity. Westbrook was a portly intern cursed with ten sausage fingers that did not work well together.

"Ah, maybe we should call in Doctor Johnson?" asked Westbrook as he peered into the teenager's abdomen, sweat drenching his surgical hat. He had just made the emergent incision minutes ago.

"Don't be ridiculous," said Phil while holding a suction device in the wound, eerily hissing away the patient's bright red blood. "You're doing great, this is a slam dunk, just stay clear of the artery. See it there?"

"I think so," said Westbrook. "Is that it?"

"Yep," said Phil. "Now just take your time, slowly dissect out the appendix, it's the swollen structure right in front of you."

"I appreciate you letting me do this," said Westbrook. "I was worried internship was going to end without having done a single surgery on my own."

"You're way ahead of the game," said Drummer, "I did my first appendix on the last day of my internship, in this very room."

"Time flies when you are having fun," said the chief anesthesia resident as his head appeared from below the sterile sheet covering the patient's upper torso. His attending physician was also absent, rumored to be somewhere in the hospital. "Where are you heading next year Phil?"

"Applying for a few fellowship positions," said Phil as he carefully held a retractor, protecting an artery precariously close to the Metzenbaum scissors darting back and forth in Westbrook's hand.

"What's that?" asked Westbrook as he squinted into the wound.

"Just some fat," said Phil. "We are in no hurry Otto, just take your time. We have all night."

Just then the door of operating room number five opened and in walked fellow fifth year resident Rick Polk, wearing surgical scrubs and a pair of bedroom slippers. He was holding a folded copy of the *Philadelphia Chronicle* under his arm.

"Yo, Yo," said Rick. "What's happening?"

"Acute appendix," said Phil while still protecting the artery. "Taking Otto through his first case. What brings you up here?"

"How's he doing?

"Great," said Phil trying to instill some confidence in the intern, who over the past year exhibited no innate surgical prowess. "A real pro."

"See one, do one, teach one," said the anesthesia resident. "Isn't that the surgical motto?"

"Couldn't sleep," said Polk. "Nothing good on T.V., so I thought I would take a walk. Quiet in the neighborhood but then I saw Doc Johnson asleep in the lounge. "

Rick Polk had spent the last five years dwelling either within residency housing or the main hospital itself. He had already surpassed the record set by Kenny "The Mole" Frederickson, who after three years of living in the PGH had to move out because of a sudden commitment called marriage. It was rumored that Frederickson wept bitterly on his honeymoon, missing the drab hospital confines with a suburban condo bearing down upon his soul. Rick was not about to let that happen, having already reached cult status and just six months away from graduation. If he went the distance his name would live in perpetuity, besides a PGH record that could never be broken. He sensed immortality.

"Where you staying now?" asked the anesthesia resident, while scanning a series of monitors.

"Moved down to a subterranean lair a few months ago," said Polk. "Next to the Maintenance Department. My man Maurice set me up in some unused space, really quiet but no cable, only the local channels and they come in fuzzy. You have to take the freight elevator to get down there."

"Watch out for the pumper at the base of the appendix," said Phil. "See it pulsating?"

"Got my own private bathroom facility, fixed it up really nice," continued Polk. "It has a high handicap commode. When I'm on that throne I feel like a gargoyle perched on the ledge of a building."

"Sounds nice," said the anesthesia resident. "I'll have to visit it some day."

"Ah crap," yelled Westbrook as bright red blood pulsated up into the wound. "I don't know..."

"You hit the artery Otto," screamed Phil. "You hit the artery!"

Blood instantaneously shot upward onto the gowns of Phil and intern Westbrook, who recoiled reflexively from the burst. Phil drove the suction tip into the depths of the wound, hoping the artery was a small peripheral bleeder, but it was not. He shook his head in disgust and rapidly packed the small wound with bandage sponges. A quick look up at the anesthesia monitor noted the patient's blood pressure to be stable. Without prompting Rick Polk was gowned and gloved by the scrub nurse and knocked Westbrook away from the table. The two residents then went to work on the bleeder, with a combined skill set developed over the past five years. Polk clamped the lacerated arterial ends with a series of hemostats and held them still, while Phil applied a quick series of sutures in slide knot fashion. Polk removed the hemostats and to the relief of everyone, the bleeding stopped. Both surgeons cautiously inspected the surrounding surgical field for any further signs of iatrogenic injury. No additional damage was seen.

"I'm sorry," said Otto Westbrook. "I'm really sorry."

"You have to be extra careful around that artery Otto," said Phil. "Concentrate! You have a young patient on the table."

"Yes, yes I understand," replied the trembling intern. "I'm sorry."

"It's alright, no problem," said Phil, aware of raising his voice to the underling. "It happens to the best of us. Just learn from your mistake. O.K.? That artery at the base of the appendix is a snake in the grass. Never forget it's there, alright?"

"Yes," said a relieved intern Westbrook. "I will never forget it, never. Thanks chief."

"My slippers!" yelled Polk. "You've ruined my slippers!"

The surgical team looked down upon Polk's feet as he stepped back from the table and peeled off his gown.

Blood speckled his hospital issued slippers. In mock disgust he looked back up at the team shaking his head.

"No good deed goes unpunished," said the anesthesia resident. "That should be the motto of any residency program."

Phil Drummer rapidly completed the case while teaching the intern the final steps of an appendectomy. He let the intern close the wound. A weary eyed Doctor Johnson then strolled into the surgical suite, having been aroused by Polk on his way back home.

"How's it going team?" mumbled Johnson, scratching his lower back while approaching the surgical field. He held a surgical mask up to his mouth, signifying the visit was going to be brief. His eyes were heavy, with saggy, wrinkled skin hanging beneath. "Any problems?"

"No sir," said Phil. "Doctor Westbrook here just completed his first appendectomy, skin to skin."

"Westbrook?" asked Johnson in jest as he stood on his tiptoes to momentarily scan the operative field, his only contribution to the case. "Really, and the patient is still alive?"

"I've never seen one done better," said Phil with a smile and quick glance at the intern.

"Alright, seems like everything is under control right Drummer?" said Doc Johnson, already taking a step towards the door.

"Closing the last layer," said Phil. "Stable and no significant complications."

"Great, I'll go and talk to the parents," said Johnson as he shuffled towards the door. "What's the kid's name?"

"Parker," said the anesthesia resident.

Just before Dr. Johnson reached for the door he paused, while staring at the floor. It appeared that his brain seized up for a few seconds before he turned his arthritic frame completely around to look at Phil.

"Hey Drummer, remember the time I took you through your first appendectomy four years ago?"

"Yes. Yes I do Doctor Johnson," said Phil, surprised that the old timer remembered the event. "It was here in this very room. Pete Larson was the chief resident. How could I forget?"

"Ah the good old days," said Johnson trying to recall his own first appendectomy a half a century ago. "You've come a long way Drummer. Keep up the good work, you've got what it takes kid."

"Thank you Doctor Johnson. Thank you very much."

"By the way, does anybody know why Doctor Polk's slippers were covered with bright red blood?" asked the wily senior surgeon. "He left a trail outside like a wounded animal."

Absolute silence gripped the room. No one moved. Johnson allowed the uncomfortable pause to continue for several seconds.

"I didn't think so," said Johnson as he turned to leave the room. "I didn't think so. Goodnight gentlemen."

Chapter Two
GRAND ROUNDS

Surgical Grand Rounds at the Philadelphia General Hospital was a steadfast tradition, occurring on the last Friday of each month for the past 140 years. Attendance was mandatory for everyone, with an exact 11 AM start. The venue was the capacious and drab Franklin Auditorium, in need of a renovation since 1970. The one hour session consisted of a single authoritative speaker presenting a topic in his or her field of expertise, followed by a scholarly discussion. Per academic protocol the department chairs and full professors occupied the first several rows of the auditorium, followed by a mass of healthcare providers in descending pecking order. Phil and Rick Polk sat midsection in the auditorium, next to fellow fifth year resident Cathy Finley. The three had been together since orientation day five years ago.

"This is going to be good," said Polk, an eager look in his eyes. The single page agenda in his hand listed the Grand Rounds speaker as "Frederick Riles II, M.D., Chairman, Department of General Surgery." The topic was "Post Surgical Abdominal Adhesions – The Science and Expanding Role of Lysovage."

A noisy rumble of excitement filled the hall as the start time approached. Then in faint overhead fashion, the hospital page operator could be heard saying, "Grand Rounds are commencing now, in the Franklin Auditorium, first floor Kirby Pavilion." The lights above immediately dimmed, hushing the crowd.

Rick looked at his colleagues and whispered, "Thirty minutes, I give it no more than thirty minutes," pointing to his watch.

A short, bald and slightly obese middle-aged physician then wobbled up towards the podium. He wore a long white lab coat bearing the name of Dr. Stein, Department of Obstetrics and Gynecology. Dr. Stein was the coordinator of Grand Rounds and a long time friend of Dr. Riles, the two having roomed together in medical school. He welcomed everyone to Franklin Auditorium and began to introduce the guest speaker. The name of Dr. Frederick Riles II was followed by a laundry list of impeccable credentials and accomplishments that could only exist in the world of academia. Superlative adjectives described his passion for surgery, research and education. By the time the revered Bostonian stood to approach the podium an innocent bystander may have been led to believe the savior of mankind had arisen.

After setting the microphone's height and adjusting his papers, Riles cleared his throat and thanked Dr. Stein for the kind introduction. Looking up towards the assemblage he smiled, exposing a trademark set of blazing white porcelain ivories, seemingly too large for his mouth.

What followed was a masterful presentation covering the basic science, current research and clinical indications of Lysovage, or LSV. Lysovage was developed to combat intra-abdominal and pelvic adhesions that can occur after common surgical procedures, such as an appendix or gall bladder removal.

"Adhesions are abnormal connections of fibrous tissue between normal intra-abdominal surfaces, which occur in upwards of 60-80% of patients after abdominal surgery," said Riles to the crowd. The chairman had been involved with the development of Lysovage since its inception. "When adhesions occur the small and large intestines become tethered to one another or nearby organs. Normal bowel movements are disturbed and an irregular twisting motion of the bowel develops, which leads to pain and at times a complete bowel obstruction. Adhesions are one of the most common causes of abdominal pain."

Dr. Riles then cited one academic paper after another that proved LSV's efficacy in the laboratory. He had authored or co-authored all the articles.

"Our clinical trials at the PGH show great promise," said the speaker. "The trials are nearing completion, to be followed by FDA approval, and release of the drug to the public. I'm optimistic the approval process can be granted within a three-year time frame."

After some additional details he opened the floor to questions.

"Yes, a question from Doctor Johnson," said Riles with a smile upon completion of his pitch.

"Very interesting work Dr. Riles," said old Doc Johnson as he stood up to speak, his body seemingly fighting gravity in the process. "By looking around it appears that I may be the most senior surgeon here, and I've been battling postoperative adhesions for decades. You lost me a little bit on how the drug is delivered, can you please recap that portion of the talk?"

"Certainly," said Riles as he reversed a series of slide photographs on a large screen suspended from the auditorium rafters. "Here is the delivery route, via two small laparoscopic incisions." The slide showed a standard laparoscopy technique, common to any general surgeon except those of Dr. Johnson's era. "LSV comes in powder form in a standard four gram dose, sterilized of course." He clicked to another slide showing a dry white powder in a small clear glass vial. "The LSV is simply mixed together with standard saline solution. Once the diagnostic portion of the laparoscopy is complete and adhesions are confirmed, then any air or gas is vented from the peritoneum, followed by administration of the Lysovage saline mixture, usually about 100 cc total for a standard size adult patient. The laparoscope is then removed and the wounds are closed."

"Then what?" asked Johnson.

"LSV selectively targets dense, fibrous inflammatory tissue and breaks down its structure at a molecular level," said Riles with a nod of his head.

"Interesting," said Johnson.

"Yes, another question from the second row," said Riles.

"How does LVS differentiate between a pathologic adhesion and normal tissue?" asked a junior attending physician. "Certainly it cannot disturb or breakdown normal tissue, as the outcome would be disastrous."

"Good question, and the drug is LSV not LVS," said Riles. "As you may well know, adhesions occur when inflammation causes local deposition of fibrin. Fibrin is a profibrotic compound that induces fibrosis. We have proven that adhesions are due to the inability of the fibrinolytic system to degrade fibrin."

"Again, I would like to know how LSV, if I've pronounced it correctly Dr. Riles, can tell between normal tissue and abnormal tissue?" asked the junior attending.

"We've determined at the molecular level that adhesions are constantly turning over, they are not static," said Riles. "Lysovage is what I like to call a "designer" fibrinolytic medication, that only recognizes the active turnover and production of fibrin, which in the peritoneal cavity is only occurring on or within the adhesions. It will impact and effectively degrade this process, thus destroying the adhesive mechanism. Simply put, it spares the remaining normal tissue in the peritoneal cavity, because no fibrin exists on their surface."

"We are using this stuff here?" asked Johnson. "At the PGH?"

"Yes," said Riles with a smile and nod of his head. "The first half of clinical trials began in Boston, during my tenure there, the second half here at the PGH for the past two years."

"I've never heard of it, who else is using this in the department?"

"I am," said a young and confident voice from the third row. "From my experience LSV works, and works well."

A young surgeon then stood up and turned towards the audience, quite confident in his stance. His height was six foot two inches tall and he had short cropped blonde hair, with a hint of a gel wave in the front. He wore glasses that added to his professorial appearance yet didn't deter from a pair of deep blue eyes. Despite wearing a long white lab coat his physique stood out in a strong athletic fashion. A bright blue fashionable tie complemented his Italian tailored pants, and gold cufflinks shimmered from his wrist. Those sitting within ten feet of his body appreciated cologne emanating from his skin that was both feminine and manly. The hearts of several women and men in the auditorium skipped a beat. His name was Dr. Stuart Greyson.

"Over the past three years I've had the honor of being a part of the clinical trial process," continued Greyson, taking off his glasses for effect. "The clinical results have been spectacular. I believe that Dr. Riles and his laboratory are on the verge of a far-reaching breakthrough, that will reverberate within the walls of this great institution for some time." He slowly reached into his pocket and pulled out a single glass vial of Lysovage, raising it above his head. "Behold Lysovage, the game changer!"

A wave of excitement rumbled through the auditorium, as the handsome attending physician continued to nod his head up and down. Behind him stood Riles on the podium, giddy with anticipation.

Rick Polk leaned towards his fellow residents and held out his hand while saying, "Wait for it now, wait for it."

Then, as if on cue, a single hand rose from the far right side of the first row. Riles seemed to ignore the hand initially, yet had to acknowledge it in the absence of other questions.

"Yes, a question from my esteemed colleague," said Riles.

Dr. Richard Knight arose methodically from his chair while turning a bit to his left to face the speaker. He held a white Styrofoam cup of coffee in his left hand, and slowly cleared his throat before speaking. Phil noticed a slight touch of gray in his hair, accentuated by the bright overhead stage lights.

"Dr. Riles let me first compliment you on your presentation and the stunning scientific trail that you have blazed on this topic," said Knight in a matter of fact tone. "What you have presented is groundbreaking material that I know has already generated a significant amount of excitement in the field of General Surgery."

"Thank you Dr. Knight," said an appreciative Dr. Riles.

"The scientific papers you have presented are undeniable," said Knight who then paused. "However I would like to know how your clinical trials are set up and when complete, what level of evidence they will reflect?"

The second half of the question caught Riles a bit off guard, yet he responded with confidence. Over the next several minutes he described the ongoing clinical trials at the PGH, which involved diagnostic laparoscopies performed on patients who were randomized into two control groups–one that received Lysovage and the second a placebo. A repeat laparoscopy was then performed two months later, at which time tissue samples were obtained from previously seen adhesion sites and normal surrounding tissue. The biopsied tissue samples were sent to pathology for review and analysis. To date the study was eighty percent complete, with statistical significance approaching.

"Dr. Riles my question is whether the surgeons are blinded to the study also?" asked Knight. The term "blinded" meant that within the study protocol, the treating surgeon would have no knowledge as to whether or not they were using the real LSV or a placebo.

"Yes," said Riles with a hint of reservation. "I mean, the study was set up by a hospital review committee in Boston, with an assist from the statistics department. "

Knight then slowly turned his frame towards the third row with a nod of his head. Phil noted a characteristic look in his eyes, a twinkle that signified a pending verbal comment guaranteed to produce angst within the recipient. He inhaled before speaking with a frown and nod of his head.

"Dr. Greyson, you seem quite confident in your anecdotal experience with this so called LSV. How so if you were blinded to which medicine was being injected into the patient's abdomen?"

"Way obvious," retorted Greyson with a cocksure tone while rising up from his seat. "I mean during the second look laparoscopy the adhesions that I saw previously were gone. It was obvious as to which patients got the real medicine as compared to those who got none." The young physician then spontaneously tossed the vial of Lysovage in underhand fashion to Knight two rows away, which he caught in reflexive fashion. "You're holding the future of medicine in your hand Dr. Knight. How does it feel?"

"I see," said Knight without acknowledging the junior staff member's showmanship. "Dr. Polk, can you please tell the audience the importance of a clinical study, and its ultimate level of evidence?"

Rick Polk had a Butterscotch Twinkie stuffed in his mouth. He immediately stood up while rapidly swallowing his snack. He took a quick slug of water from a plastic bottle that Phil thrust into his hand.

"Ah, excuse me Dr. Knight, can you please repeat the question," mumbled Polk. "I didn't hear it all."

"Answer the question Dr. Polk," said Knight.

"Yes sir," said Polk as he swallowed the remainder of the confectionery treat. The fifth year resident then succinctly reviewed the importance of a clinical studies' ultimate level of evidence. He correctly stated that five levels of evidence existed, with level one being the preferred. A level one study involved patients randomized by a computer into treatment plans carried out by surgeons who had no knowledge of what treatment the patients were receiving. This was the definition of a "double blind" study, which carried the most clout in the scientific community in regards to ultimate outcome.

"Do you know what is the most common level of evidence presented in the scientific literature over the past ten years, Dr. Polk?"

"Level two," was the guess.

"Level four, if you can believe that," said Knight, now addressing the entire audience. "Over the past five years there has been an appropriate attempt by all scientific communities to produce data that is valid and reproducible. Data produced by a scientific method categorized as level one evidence." Knight then turned back towards Dr. Riles.

"Excellent point Dr. Knight," said Riles. "Excellent point."

"Dr. Polk unfortunately omitted to disclose the final key component of a level one study," said Knight. "That the pathologists reading the biopsies are also unaware of what medication the patient received. Only then, will the results of a study be worthy of level one evidence." After making this final point he sat down.

"Most definitely," said Riles, thankful for no further questions from the senior attending. "Wonderful points Dr. Knight. Are there any other questions from the audience?"

"Yea, are we getting lunch soon?" asked Doc Johnson with a burst of laughter. "You've lost me on this level of science stuff and something sure smells good."

"Ha, ha, ha," laughed Riles loudly. "If there are no other questions then yes Doctor Johnson, we are getting lunch, compliments of Union Park Biotech, whose representatives have set up a delicious luncheon in the foyer area. I will certainly be available during the luncheon to answer any further questions. Thank you for your time and interest. Surgical Grand Rounds are now over."

Chapter Three
AN ACUTE ABDOMEN

Phil took the pass on the right wing in stride and dribbled towards the hoop. A slick crossover move dispatched Maurice in ankle breaking fashion, leaving the path to the basket uncontested. Despite not having played collegiate basketball in nine years the senior resident took flight and dunked the basketball in tomahawk fashion.

"Ooooohhhh!" screamed the scant crowd in unison, laughing mostly at Maurice who claimed he slipped on a wet floor spot. The dunk gave the Vital Organs a one-point halftime lead.

"Nice move Drummer," said Maurice with a smile and strut towards the sideline "Next time I'll meet you at the rim."

"In your dreams Mo," said Phil heading towards the old-fashioned water fountain, tucked into the recess of a wall in the small gymnasium. The water arcing out of the rusty spigot was warm and refreshing.

Maurice Rhett was captain of the Sweepers, better known in the medical center basketball league as "Maintenance." They were the undisputed kingpins of the basketball league, having beaten Phil and his teammates in the championship game the last three seasons in a row.

Maurice was thirty-nine years old and had a slight potbelly, but at times flashed a brilliance that landed him on the Philadelphia Big Five all star team twenty years prior. He was the glue that held Maintenance together, which consisted of a hodgepodge of locals working in the hospital's Physical Plant department.

The venue was the old South Wing gym, constructed seventy-five years ago as part of the Psychiatry Department, sitting within the PGH complex itself. The gym was a classic "shoe box" court with a wall just a few feet behind the basket and enough room on one sideline for two old wooden benches to sit. Around the second floor of the gym circled a balcony, whose walls were painted with the likes of famed NBA players with Philadelphia roots. It was halftime of their first meeting that season and Phil was set on bringing the coveted championship to the Surgery Department, along with a team picture that would hang in the Kirby Pavilion forever.

The Vital Organs consisted of Phil, Rick Polk, Jackie "Skywalker" Rhimes, Troy "Sweet Carolina" Huckabee and Michael "Hoosier Daddy" Boyce. Boyce was a first year intern in the program from the basketball crazy state of Indiana, and had a skill set that Phil knew would help capture the elusive title that year.

"I'm gassed," cried a red faced Rick Polk as he lay supine on the sideline, sweat pouring from his brow. "We need a pre-season to get in shape."

"Nice half," said Phil to Boyce, "Just keep shooting, your jump shot is going to carry us to the title."

"These guys can fly," said Boyce.

"Three of them are wearing jeans," said Jackie. "I think they are still on work shift."

"Yo Drummer," said Maurice, "Where did you get that boy from Indiana?"

"I believe that was a rhetorical question," said Huckabee.

"He like the Birdman."

"Blue chipper from the Hoosier state," said Phil. "He's just warming up Mo, you haven't seen anything yet."

"Ha, ha," cackled the captain of Maintenance. "I'm gonna put a youngin on him the second half Drummer. Shut him down."

The third quarter was a hard fought battle with a play-off atmosphere, as both teams exchanged the lead several times. It was after Phil hit a silky smooth jump shot from the wing that he heard his pager go off, stuffed deep within a gym bag lying on the floor.

"Oh no," cried Polk. "We have no subs."

"Oh, yes," said Mo Rhett.

Phil indeed had to depart the gym in emergent fashion, sending the Vital Organs to a bitter defeat that evening. A middle-aged patient with an acute abdomen was in the emergency room and heading to the O.R. immediately. Doc Johnson called upon his team of Phil and Otto Westbrook to assist in the case.

Ms. Julia Rudenko was a thirty six year old Ukraine immigrant and mother of three. Her youngest child was a four year-old beauty named Sasha who was born by Cesarean section. Three years ago Julia developed abdominal adhesions after childbirth and subsequently had a laparoscopy before voluntarily enrolling into the Lysovage study. Her decision was largely based upon the recommendation of her surgeon, who happened to be the department chairman at the PGH. A computer randomly enrolled her into the LSV study and she underwent a second laparoscopy seeking relief from painful adhesions. She had no idea as to what medication she received, if any. However she was quite sure of the unbearable pain centered just below her umbilicus that morning which prompted a trip to the

PGH emergency room. Her surgeon, Dr. Riles was away that week, lecturing in The Netherlands on the benefits of Lysovage.

"How about we do a laparoscopy first," said Drummer to his attending as he prepped out the patient's abdomen. He knew quite well what the answer would be.

"Don't waste your time," said Doctor Johnson. "Her gut is laden with adhesions. Besides the laparoscope in an instrument of the devil himself."

"She is a patient enrolled in Dr. Riles' LSV study," said Phil as he drew out a long incision directly down the midline of abdomen. "I wonder if she got the real stuff or a placebo?"

"Probably some sugar water," said Johnson. "Otherwise according to Dr. Riles and Greyson, she would be magically cured."

"Sounds like pretty amazing stuff," said Phil after sensing Johnson's sarcastic tone. "The LSV I mean."

"Listen Drummer, I've been around long enough to see the next great thing come and go a hundred times. As a general rule if something sounds too good to be true, it is. Never forget that. Now let's go, it's getting late."

Phil then took a scalpel to the abdomen of Julia Rudenko and within minutes the trio had her abdomen splayed wide open, exposing a scene of peculiar carnage.

"What the hell?" said Johnson. "Looks like her abdomen was burned."

Phil rapidly inspected the patient's bowels and no perforations were seen. Her appendix was normal and the liver and gall bladder appeared benign. No ulcerations were noted throughout her stomach area.

"No free air or fecal material," said Phil. "Looks like a torch was lit insider her though."

Over the next twenty minutes the surgical team inspected every internal organ of the patient, yet failed to identify any perforation. Nothing was found that could explain her clinical picture, which prompted the emergent trip to the O.R.

"I've never seen anything like it," said Johnson. "I mean she had an acute abdomen, no doubt we had to open her up."

"It was a classic acute abdomen. What should we do know?" asked Phil.

Johnson just paused and continued to stare into the wound, occasionally lifting a portion of the patient's bowel, hoping to see some pathology. He suddenly recalled the words of his mentor, long deceased, telling him to never close a patient's abdomen without documenting an emergent reason to have been there.

"Here," said Johnson pointing into the wound. "I believe I see a small perforation in her duodenum."

"Where?"

"Right here Drummer," said the senior attending. "It's small."

"I don't see it," said Phil.

"Neither do I," said Westbrook.

"Give me a stitch," said Johnson to the scrub nurse impatiently.

The scrub nurse slapped a suture ligation into the arthritic hand of Doc Johnson who then rapidly placed a single superficial stitch into the outer mucosa of the patient's duodenum. After Phil cut the knot the attending surgeon immediately stepped back from the wound.

"Looks like we got here just in time," said Johnson as he peeled off his gloves. "Admit her to the surgical ICU tonight Dr. Drummer and keep a close eye on her. Understood?"

"Yes sir," said Phil as he prepared to close up the abdomen with intern Westbrook.

"Take a few sample biopsies from her abdomen wall before you close," said Doc Johnson. "And I will dictate the operative report."

"Got it," said Phil.

The senior attending then departed the scene, heading home to his apartment just six blocks away. He lived alone there for the past thirty years, ever since his wife passed away.

After tucking Julia Rudenko into the SICU, Phil Drummer took a pensive walk through the Penn Campus, towards the Greycliff. It was a cold, cloudless January night in the city. A stiff wind strangely gusted steam rising up from the noisy subway line below. His heart and soul were heavy in thought, wondering what was to become of the next six months. In a strange way he did not want to leave the confines of the Philadelphia General. As he approached the Greycliff he couldn't bear to look up at his seventh floor apartment, knowing it would be dark. The foyer of the apartment complex was empty, as was the noisy elevator ride upstairs. Sadness seemed to overwhelm him as he walked the long hallway towards his apartment door. He was startled to see Troy Huckabee's door open and head poke out with a smile.

"We had them Phil, we had them," said Troy with a smile.

"I know. I'm sorry I had to leave Troy."

"Maurice knows it too, this is our year."

Phil just shook his head and smiled, happy with the friendship that had formed over the years with his neighbor from North Carolina.

"Good night Troy," said Phil quietly.

"Night Phil, if you need any company just give a holler, alright?"

"Thanks Troy, I appreciate it," said Phil as he entered his apartment.

As the door slammed behind him Phil just stood in the dark, unsure if he had enough energy to continue inward. The harsh silence was only broken by the rhythmic tick-tick-tick of a clock on the kitchen counter. He tossed a backpack of books into the corner of the hallway, stepping towards the living room. Lights from the city below guided him across the flat into the single bedroom. The chief resident then kicked off his shoes and dropped supine onto the bed, not bothering to remove his surgical scrubs. Exhaustion sent his mind into a semiconscious trance, as he stared at the ceiling above.

He heard a whistle from the old train tracks that ran behind his childhood home, knowing it could not be true. The freight train passed by at exactly 2 A.M., blowing its horn in anticipation of the river trestle ahead. He pictured the second floor of the old double block where he and his brother shared a room, the family estate where mom and dad slept just down the hall. Silence echoed in his ears as he took several deep breaths, trying to calm his emotions. The warmth of the old coal furnace his dad cherished was soothing, as was the pungent sulfur smell. He waited for the second blare of the train, a short toot as it began a trek over the Susquehanna. His left shoulder twitched at that moment, allowing reality to penetrate the scene. It was only then that his mind conceded a stunning visual of Jenna–her lips and face so beautiful and serene.

Chapter Four
NURSE HUDSON

Lucy Hudson was head nurse of the PGH general surgery floor. Twenty-five years ago she walked onto the ward fresh out of nursing school, vowing to stay for a year prior to moving to California with her boyfriend. Her beau however vanished along with the past quarter century, leaving her a bit worn yet much wiser. Two failed marriages left her with three children and a bad taste for slick talking physicians, or in her case former husbands. Lucy was five foot six, and a touch overweight, yet still possessed a frame that caught the attention of any male nearby. She wore surgical scrub pants with a tee-shirt top, usually long sleeved during the winter. Her hair was a highlighted beige blonde with some true brown roots, frequently held together in a twisted bun. Soft blue eyes matched a cute nose that sat atop a set of full lips. Just below her pretty face was the only good thing her second husband left her–a pair of breast implants that balanced her torso with a full-bodied posterior. Clog shoes occasionally added two inches to her height. She had a bit of a potty mouth, a byproduct of talking to surgeons on a daily basis. Yet despite her pleasing display it was a unique mannerism that set her apart, an ability to get close to a person with a savory allure, generally involving bodily contact. Nurse Hudson had to be close to you in conversation, making her overall package intoxicating to the common man.

"Nurse Hudson," said Phil. "A pleasure to see you. Would you care to make rounds?"

"With you Dr. Drummer, anytime," said Nurse Hudson with a pleasing voice that matched her face. She thought very highly of the young chief resident.

Phil and intern Westbrook had just arrived on the general surgery floor along with two female medical students eager to learn. Doc Johnson mandated that his team round every afternoon in his absence.

The tenth floor of the Kirby Pavilion housed post-operative general surgery patients for the past century. It was a traditional patient floor with a nursing hub in the center, surrounded by a rectangular series of rooms, having a maximum capacity of sixty patients. Two long corridors ran parallel to the nursing station, which was flanked by clear glass panels, attempting to control the cacophony from within. Amid the station was a hodgepodge of health care workers including nurses, physical therapists, nursing assistants, social workers, pharmacists, and physicians. The countertops were littered with a series of computer screens, each occupied by a worker, justifying their meaningful use. Peculiar to the nursing station was energetic youth, the hallmark of any tertiary care medical center in the middle of a major city. Nurse Hudson was at least fifteen years older than her closest coworker in age, a testimony to her staying power and love for the game. The only hospital employee her senior was unit clerk Wilma Williams, who had been at the PGH since turning nineteen years old. Wilma was a trusted hospital employee who occupied the same chair at the same station for the past thirty-three years, only calling off twice for the birth of her children.

"They're getting younger and younger," said Wilma as she looked at the medical students while shaking her head. Besides her mouth the only other portion of Wilma's body that moved throughout the work shift was her right arm, which answered the phone and occasionally tapped a keyboard before her. Outside of these simple motions her body never moved from the chair, a tribute to her job description. When not speaking or answering the phone, Wilma just stared forward in a peaceful trance, occasionally humming a gospel tune. She was always present and overtime was her best friend. Everyone loved Wilma Williams.

"Let's see," said Nurse Hudson to Phil as she looked down upon a computer printout sheet. "Doctor Johnson only has two people on the floor, Mr. Martin went home earlier today." She then looked up at Phil with a smile.

The group headed into room 1034 where a single white male named Stanley Jankowski sat upon the bed's edge. He was in his late seventies with a slight frame and a spirited set of eyes. Upon seeing the medical team he said, "jak sie masz?"

"Excuse me Mr. Jankowski?" asked Phil.

"How are you?" asked the patient. "Jak sie masz?" is Polish for how are you?"

"Quite well," said Phil with a smile, "How are you?"

"Much better today," said the patient with a smile. "Thanks to Dr. Polk."

Two days earlier Mr. Jankowski had a kielbasa dinner charged with homemade horseradish that set his innards afire. Within an hour the concoction blew a hole in the wall of his stomach that prompted an ambulance ride to the E.R. Doctors Johnson and Polk emergently opened his abdomen to repair the perforation. Polk was on call that night and immediately befriended the patient.

"Let's take a look at the incision," said Phil as he prompted the patient to lie supine on his bed.

Intern Westbrook then circled around the bed to remove the dressing as the two female students gathered near. Nurse Hudson remained close to Phil's left side.

"Looks good," said Westbrook upon removing the dressing to expose a long midline incision. He then pulled a stethoscope out of his white coat and placed it into his ears and then upon the patient's abdomen.

"What's he listening for Kayla?" asked Phil as he looked at the medical student closest to Westbrook.

"I'm Kaylee, she is Kayla," said the student quietly.

"I'm sorry," said Phil. "You two really look alike. I'm sorry."

Both third year students then giggled in a nervous way, sending their straight blonde, shoulder cropped hair dancing. "I know, I know. People always get us confused."

"O.K. then Kaylee," said Phil distinctly. "What is intern Westbrook listening for?"

Silence.

"Come on now," said Phil. "What's the term for audible bowel sounds that signify the return of peristalsis?"

"Audible bowel sounds...." said Kaylee as she pulled out her cell phone to search for an answer. "Audible bowel sounds...."

"No, no," said Phil. "Put that phone away. Memory, use the memory banks in your head. The word is somewhere in your cranium. Think."

Silence.

"Borborygmi," said Phil. "Borborygmi."

Both medical students then laughed at the funny sounding word, having no recall of the term from a lecture one year ago.

"Commit it to memory," said Phil. "Borborygmi–it signifies a functioning bowel that will allow Mr. Jankowski to leave the hospital soon."

"Good bowel sounds," said Westbrook as he snapped the stethoscope off his head and tucked it away.

"You know I drove a beer truck for forty years," said Mr. Jankowski. "I know every barroom in the city."

"Really," said Phil as he reached down towards the patient's abdomen to help hold on a new dressing. Intern Westbrook then fumbled in his pockets for tape.

"Yes siree, never got in one accident. I'm proud of that."

"No tape," said Westbrook as he bolted around the bed and headed to the supply room.

"Let me help you," said Nurse Hudson as she leaned forward to hold the dressing, intertwining her right arm below Phil's extended left.

"What beer company?" asked Phil while appreciating firm contact from Nurse Hudson's upper frame, accentuated by her forward lean.

"Schmidt's beer," said Jankowski with a big smile. "Schmidt's of Philadelphia."

"My dad used to drink that," said Hudson with a smile and look upwards at Phil, her hair falling in front of one blue eye.

"The beer that made Philadelphia famous," said Phil.

"No, no," said Jankowski. "One beautiful beer," was their saying. "Schmidt's, one beautiful beer!" Nostalgia filled his face.

Intern Westbrook then walked back into the room with surgical tape and began applying it to the dressing. Nurse Hudson slowly moved her arm back and forth to smooth the dressing, much to the delight of Phil, who held steady.

"Great," said Phil standing erect with the head nurse. "Start passing some gas today Mr. Jankowski and tomorrow we will let you go home."

"Dziekuje," said the Pole with a smile.

"Your welcome," said Phil leading the group out of the room. They then turned left and headed down to room 1043, where Julia Rudenko sat in a chair, two days status post her emergent surgery.

"Hello Ms. Rudenko. How are you today?" asked Phil.

"Very well," said the patient with a strong eastern European accent. "May I go home?"

"Perhaps tomorrow morning," said Phil. "If it's O.K. with Doctor Johnson. How is your stomach feeling?"

"Better. May I go home?"

Phil was always amazed as to how a patient's ethnic background affected their management of pain. Ms. Rudenko had a very high pain threshold.

"Tomorrow," he said with a calm voice. "I'm sure tomorrow will be fine."

"Where is Doctor Riles?" asked the patient.

"Actually in Europe," said Phil. "He will be out of the country for some time. Lecturing in Europe."

"A smart man, no?"

"Yes, very smart," said Phil while placing a stethoscope on the patient's back. "Take a deep breath Ms. Rudenko."

"What's he listening for?" asked Westbrook to the students.

"Borborygmi," said Kayla and Kaylee in unison.

"No," said Westbrook. "Her breath sounds, making sure her lungs are clear."

"Very nice," said Phil while stepping back. "Let's plan for tomorrow, O.K.?"

"Yes, thank you doctor."

The team departed the room and circled the corridor back to the nursing station. Phil began discussing some simple orders with Nurse Hudson whose attention remained undivided. It was then that a booming voice was heard from behind.

"Good afternoon ladies," yelled Dr. Stuart Greyson as he turned the corner with a smile. "Who wants to round with the young, handsome doctor?"

No one answered.

"How about these two students?" asked Greyson while looking at Phil. "Can you spare them Dr. Drummer?"

"Sure," said Phil. "We just finished rounding."

"Nurse Hudson," said Greyson. "No go around would be complete without you. Yes? Care to round?"

"Shift change," said Hudson with a smile and shake of her head. "Have to coordinate the shift change, sorry."

"No problem," said Greyson while continuing to stare at the young female students. "I'm sure I can teach these two young ladies something."

He then turned about with the two innocent medical students in tow.

"What are your names?" asked Greyson as they left the station.

"Kayla and Kaylee."

"Whoa, sounds like the name of a movie I watched last night," said the young attending with a smirk and turn of the corner.

Phil thanked Nurse Hudson and walked towards unit clerk Williams. The hustle of a nursing shift change abounded. He asked Wilma to print out a copy of Julia Rudenko's surgical pathology report, which she did. A printer atop her desk quickly spat out the request. Phil took the report and rolled it up into his right hand. He turned to leave the station, somehow humming a gospel tune. It was then that he saw her for the first time, amid of group of fellow nurses, entering the ward. Her facial features were perfection as their gazes momentarily met, excitement in her eyes. Her name was Caroline.

Chapter Five
PRINCE IGOR

It was a cold, cloudless night as the private jet began its descent into the Philadelphia International Airport. The City of Brotherly Love skyline was a welcome site to the weary travelers. On board was Dr. Riles, his wife and representatives of Union Park Biotech, having just completed a ten-day European junket. The trip involved a series of lectures throughout the continent, at major teaching universities. The speaker was Dr. Riles and the topic was Lysovage. The journey was funded by Union Park including room and board at five star hotels, world-class meals, sightseeing and shopping – all gratis. The tour was a smashing success and an exhaustive bliss filled the plane's dimmed compartment.

Frederick Riles II sat beside his wife and looked out of the small window as the aircraft banked over the Walt Whitman Bridge. He remembered the first time his father brought him to Philadelphia, a young child so eager to see the sites. The original Dr. Frederick Riles was giving a speech at a medical convention that weekend and Frederick's mom took him to visit Independence Hall. He remembered a sweltering hot May afternoon and a long line to just enter the historic site. A man who smelled like cigars gave a talk while wearing a white wig and period specific costume, sweat pouring from his brow. The hall was musty and poorly ventilated causing young Frederick to pass out midway through the speech. He cried after the event, wanting to go to the Philadelphia Zoo, but dad expected him back at the hotel along with an academic discussion of what was learned. His parents went out to dinner that night, leaving young Frederick in the hands of a nanny, who watched cable television and talked on the phone all night. He sat on the sill of a large hotel window that evening, looking down upon the sites of Broad Street. City Hall sat before him, with William Penn perched atop the rotunda. His gaze caught a peculiar angle of Mr. Penn that evening, playing a cruel trick on the young boy's eye. He appreciated an angle well known to Philadelphians that caused the scroll in William's hand to resemble his extended manhood, on display for everyone to see.

"Beautiful skyline," said Vic Fanicci.

"Gorgeous," said Riles. "I'm looking for William Penn on City Hall but can't make it out."

"City Hall used to be the tallest building in the state through the 1930's," said Fanicci, a native Philadelphian. "Was the tallest in the city until 1984, when they allowed skyscrapers to rise up around it."

Victor Fanicci was Union Park Biotech's senior vice-president of the Northeastern United States, having joined the company thirty years ago. He grew up in a humble row house in South Philadelphia, his parents second generation Italian. His dad worked as a Naval Yard welder while mom ran a produce stand at the Italian Market. Victor helped out at the market, rising early before school to gather fruit from local warehouses and prepare the stand. Afternoons found him back at the market with mom and too many relatives to count. An above average intelligence earned a scholarship at St. Joe's Preparatory

School followed by college at Drexel. An M.B.A. from The Wharton School completed his Philadelphia education and his first employer was Union Park. What followed was a slow steady rise up the food chain of the company, fueled by hard work and a commitment to their products – namely pharmaceuticals.

The LSV Project was his golden egg, a gift from above that comes across a Union Park's executive desk once in a lifetime. Since the project's inception fifteen years ago Vic Fanicci was present among the managing team's upper echelon. As co-manager of investing Rounds A and B he amassed a total of 28 million dollars for Union Park and the project. This success led to a promotion to clinical director, a position he managed well until last year. The untimely death of his boss, confidant and mentor catapulted him into the number one slot – principal investigator. His rise to the top was already lucrative, heavy with bonus payouts that were incentive based. However, what sat over the rainbow was a prize that Union Park legends were made of, awash with cash and stock options massive enough to impact future generations. The end was so very near, only pending final clinical trials and subsequent FDA approval. Who would have guessed it thought Fanicci, a poor kid from South Philly making it big.

"What a wonderful trip, thank you Victor," said Mrs. Riles.

"It was our pleasure," said Vic. "I hope you enjoyed it."

"I most definitely did, and thank you Vanessa," said Mrs. Riles with a smile, looking back at the seat behind Fanicci.

"It was my pleasure," said the dark haired beauty sitting behind the principal investigator. She extended her manicured hand forward to touch the arm of Mrs. Riles, with silver bracelets from Barcelona shining. "Loved the shopping girlfriend," was her next line as the pilot prepared the cabin for landing.

After touchdown a limousine whisked Dr. Riles and his wife off the tarmac, a trunk loaded with contraband. Their route cut through downtown Philadelphia towards the Washington Square flat they owned. As the limo navigated Broad Street Dr. Riles gawked upwards at William Penn, trying to reproduce the quirky angle that his childhood memory bore. His wife silently stared out the window as the vehicle sped past the Academy of Music. The large playbill out front announced *Prince Igor* in large red letters, which meant nothing to her.

The atmosphere inside the Academy of Music was electric. Ongoing was the final act of Alexander Borodin's *Prince Igor*, and sitting in the Presidential Box above the stage was Dr. Richard Knight. It was the opera's first showing in Philadelphia since an 1890 premiere in St. Petersburg, thanks to Dr. Knight. Over the past five years the surgeon devoted a massive amount of his time in bringing the production to fruition. He initially lobbied the Academy Trustees to approve Borodin's magnum opus and then spearheaded a fund raising campaign that culminated in the production before him. Ongoing beneath his gaze was the riveting reunion of Yaroslavna and Igor, lovers reunited and signing with joy. Church bells began to ring.

"So beautiful," said the female voice softly to his right side. "So very beautiful Richard."

Knight then looked upon the first few rows of the opera house, keenly aware of the dignitaries present, a true slice of society's elite. Their eyes fixated upon the joyous celebration of Igor's return as the Russian chorus sang, "God heard our prayers." He looked forward to a reception in the Academy's Great Hall that evening, anxious to meet the prima donna with Tatar features whose voice was radiant. The production in his opinion was a masterpiece, sure to generate rave reviews.

Knight then looked up at the ornate ceiling of the venue, thinking of Borodin. He was a chemist who composed only in his free time, yet became a member of Russia's "Mighty Handful" or "The Five." A group of composers dedicated to a specific Russian music that reflected the charm and pageantry of their motherland. Their music rejected the standard of western European conservatory training. The Five were leaders of a Romantic Nationalist movement–mavericks, the avant-garde of their time. Knight looked down at the Opera scorecard, which summarized Borodin's life, highlighted by an advocacy of women's rights and their education, having founded the School of Medicine for Women in St. Petersburg. Knight recalled visiting his grave in St. Petersburg, where he took a photo beside his bronze bust. He wondered what his legacy would be, and how he would be remembered.

Suddenly his right forearm twitched followed by a rolling tremble in his fingers. The uncontrollable tic was becoming more frequent, a result of neurologic damage from the car accident years ago. The neurologists had no cure, only hope that it would not progress. He tried to ignore the flutter, which abated yet returned. Knight then felt the soft hand of his partner being placed upon his extremity, calming the twinge with a soothing rub. The grip was firm and reassuring, bringing solace to his troubled heart. She was his anchor in life he thought, an angel that almost got away. What was he thinking?

"Bravo! Bravo!" screamed the crowd as the opera ended. A riotous roar echoed through the great hall. Knight stood to his feet in applause, the floor beneath him trembling. "Bravo! Bravo!"

Kudos passed through the ranks of the Russian troupe followed by a thunderous roar for the conductor and orchestra. The maestro bowed to the audience several times and diverted their adulation to the musician's before him. Then the moment arrived, and the maestro looked upwards to the Presidential Box, extending his hand towards Dr. Knight in homage of his contribution.

The entire audience turned slightly to the right in honor of the man that brought *Prince Igor* to the Academy. The applause was deafening. Knight extended both arms downward towards the conductor and troupe, praising and thanking them aloud. The standing ovation continued in his glory, prompting Knight to raise his left arm to the crowd and place his right around his spouse, who raised her right. Their image together was stunning, the moment magic. He looked to his right to see the graceful woman trembling in his arm, just as beautiful as their wedding day thirty-five years ago.

"I love you," said Knight above the roar. "I love you."

A young female attendant then stepped into the box with a dozen long stem red roses and placed them in Mrs. Knight's arms, tears rolling down her cheek.

"Hurrah, Hurrah! Bravo!"

"I love you too Richard," said his wife. "I love you too."

Chapter Six
GRAVE MATTERS

Jonathan Mitchell took pride in being the Philadelphia General Hospital's Chief Executive Officer. A native Bostonian, he took the appointment several years ago after his good friend Dr. Frederick Riles II endorsed him. Both he and Riles worked together for years in the Boston health system. Their departure from New England was considered a blow to the medical community, a loss of two stalwarts in the field. Mitchell himself was a life long hospital administrator, being one of the few college majors in the field thirty years ago, well ahead of the curve.

Mitchell was tall at six foot three inches and slightly balding. He wore outdated wire rimmed glasses and despite his compensation package, dressed average. He walked with a bit of a limp, complements of a degenerative right hip condition, not yet ready for replacement. Mitchell delegated vast power to his subordinates with ease. He was not a detail man and preferred to look at the broader picture, confident that any mistake could be rectified by a system chock-full of cash.

CEO Mitchell took a peculiar pride in trying to know every worker in the hospital, which was a daunting task since the PGH was the biggest employer in the Delaware

Valley. He addressed every person in a hospital corridor, frequently calling them out by first name. Conversation was his trademark along with a firm handshake, hearty slap on the shoulder and witty line. Unlike most hospital CEOs he was actually respected by the majority of employees, a tribute to his communication skills. Like all hospital administrators Jonathan Mitchell enjoyed one thing – meetings. His entire adult working life centered about a conference table and the art of conversation.

"Not another God damn meeting," growled Doc Johnson upon entering the cramped conference room of the General Surgery department. "I have nothing more to say."

CEO Mitchell mandated a meeting with all department professors every other month, to "take the pulse" of the medical center.

"Good morning doctors," said Mitchell as he stepped into the room just behind Doc Johnson. Sitting at the table were Drs. Knight, Riles, Johnson and Stone, the only full professors currently on staff.

"John, good morning," bellowed chairman Riles as he stood up with a smile.

I brief discussion then broke out among the group, typical of any mundane conference. Topics of local sports, interests and family were touched upon, before Mitchell recalibrated the meeting upon medical center issues. From that point forward the conversation occurred between Chairman Riles and CEO Mitchell, with Doc Johnson being a conscientious objector and Knight and Stone attentive yet mum.

"Is everything set for the annual department shin-dig?" asked Mitchell. "The same venue I presume?"

"Yes, everything is set," said Riles. "And I must say the party is much appreciated by all staff workers within the department."

"The casino?"

"Yes," said Riles. "We booked The Emerald Room this year, a bit larger than last year's room."

"Were the floor nurses invited?" asked Dr. Stone sharply. "They were miffed last year by not being invited."

"Yes," said Riles. "I think it appropriate we invite them, which of course is the reason for the larger room."

"How much?" asked Mitchell.

"Total package, food, band, alcohol – forty thousand."

"Well worth it," said Mitchell always happy to spend the health system's money. "The casino has kept us on their workman's compensation panel which covers the party cost ten fold."

The conversation then changed to a blunt discussion regarding the department's associate surgical professors, totaling six surgeons in all.

"Any trouble in the ranks?" asked Mitchell.

"Dr. Strauss is demanding a raise," said Riles. "Threatening to leave if he doesn't get one. Has an offer from Temple."

"Is he a producer?" asked the CEO.

"Barely covering his salary," said Riles. "Great surgeon but no cash cow."

Mitchell then looked around the table asking if anyone had a strong objection to letting Dr. Strauss go. No one objected.

"Stick to the academic line regarding his salary," said Mitchell. "You know the routine, fast track to full professor by age forty-five. If he leaves then so be it."

"What about Greyson?" said Dr. Knight, who sat opposite Riles, holding a Styrofoam cup of black coffee in his left hand. "Any more complaints?" Knight kept his gaze upon the table, not making eye contact with Riles.

"None," said Riles. "At least not since our last meeting."

"Did you talk to him about that Grand Rounds stunt?" asked Knight. "Very unprofessional."

"Yes," said Riles. "It won't happen again."

"Fred, I'm counting on you to keep him in check," said Jonathan Mitchell. "In today's society lewd comments and sexual innuendos are verboten." Mitchell slowly rolled his thumb and index finger together before stating, "If anyone needs to keep him in check Frederick, it's you. He will listen to you, at least I hope."

Riles went silent realizing that it was he who recruited the brash young surgeon to the PGH, against the strong objections of Dr. Knight. Since arriving on the staff two years ago a series of sexual harassment complaints had been filed against Greyson, all from female hospital employees regarding inappropriate comments. However, no allegations rose to the level of a disciplinary action.

"A short leash," said Knight. "Keep him on a short leash."

"How are the chief residents this year?" asked Mitchell to change the subject. "Any keepers?"

A discussion then ensued regarding all four chief residents who were posed to graduate in a few months. It was well known that Cathy Finley already accepted a prestigious position in New York City. A decision was made not to recruit Jackie Rhimes, who although a great resident, was considered a risk to any surgical group.

"Drummer is a keeper," said Dr. Riles. "Great set of hands, works well with others and has a solid knowledge base."

"Agree," said Stone. "Don't let him get away."

CEO Mitchell then scanned the group, not bothering to ask Doc Johnson who simply would not respond in protest. He was cautiously aware of the history between Dr. Knight and the resident, but had to seek his opinion.

"Richard, any thoughts on Dr. Drummer and his future here at the PGH?"

"One of the best residents I've seen in nearly thirty years," said Knight without hesitation. "My highest recommendation."

"Very well," said Mitchell with a smile. "Perhaps he can replace Strauss. Frederick, how about you and I take young Dr. Drummer out to dinner over the next few weeks, make him an offer?"

"What about Polk?" asked Knight.

"Ah, Dr. Polk," said Mitchell. "Isn't he the resident we've been trying to flush out of the hospital over the past several months?"

"Yes," said Riles. "I believe his last place of residence has been vacated. It was somewhere near the morgue."

"He's not gone," said Stone. "Rumor has it that he moved elsewhere in the physical plant. The guy is like a tunnel rat."

"Let him go," said Knight. "In six months it will be over."

"Richard, we've discussed this before," said Mitchell. "Legal informs me of a host of problems in regards to someone taking up residence in the hospital."

"Great resident," said Chairman Riles. "Everyone seems to love him, but I'm not sure he is academic material."

"Agree," said Stone.

"I disagree," said Knight. "The guy lives and breathes surgery. Intelligent, dedicated and always present. He's a terrific resident, has been from day one. Let's just keep him in mind."

Silence ensued for several seconds allowing Knight to realize he was in the minority. He looked at Doc Johnson who enjoyed Polk's company, but the crusty old surgeon refused to speak.

"How's the LSV Project going?" asked Mitchell with ten minutes of meeting time left. He noticed Doc Johnson checking his wristwatch.

"Fantastic," said Riles. "Just got back from a delightful trip to Europe where our data was quite well received."

"And the clinical trials?" asked Mitchell.

"Going well," continued Riles. "Results are very promising. Very promising. We should be presenting the final data at our national meeting in one year."

"Good for you," said Dr. Stone. "Maybe I'll start using the stuff. By the way that was a fantastic grand rounds presentation."

"Thank you," said Riles with a slow nod of his head, chin protruded.

CEO Mitchell allowed a few seconds to pass, yet Dr. Knight refused to chime in on the project. He cleared his throat and went to speak, but suddenly was cut off by Doc Johnson, breaking his self -imposed gag order.

"I just operated on one of your trial patients," said Johnson. "Don't forget to include her in the results."

"Excuse me," said Riles.

"When you were overseas," said Johnson. "Middle aged woman whose gut looked like a blow torch lit it up."

"A study patient? Why wasn't I informed of this?" asked Riles. "I mean… this is news to me. What was her name? What happened, what was the presentation?"

"I can't recall her name. A Russian woman I believe. Had a hole in her duodenum. Her peritoneal cavity looked like something I've never seen before."

"Dr. Johnson, I would appreciate you telling me if one of my study patients has had a maloccurrence. It's critical to our data collection process and the integrity of the final results. This is a landmark study in progress, with world wide implications."

"I just informed you," said Johnson.

Dr. Riles' blood pressure was rapidly on the rise, quite aware that both Doc Johnson and Knight were skeptical of his LSV Project. Since his arrival in Philadelphia he considered the two remnants of the old PGH corps of surgeons, not amendable to change. His mistrust of Knight went back to their troubled residency days together, which only complicated the situation.

"Polk and I saved her," said Johnson with a smirk. "And by the way I believe Dr. Polk is a keeper too. He's the type of resident we all were a long time ago, before this whole medicine industry destroyed our souls."

"Well I will need her name and medical record number immediately," said Riles. "I consider your delay in informing me of this event unacceptable and unprofessional," barked Riles.

"Maybe it was just a bad batch of that lye-whatever you call it that was squirted inside her."

"It's called Lysovage," said Riles sharply. "Lysovage."

"Gentlemen please, please," said CEO Mitchell with a raise of his hand. "Frederick, it's just one patient. Our electronic med record system will provide you with all the patient's information with a single click of the keyboard. Everybody just calm down."

Dr. Riles got up from his chair and stormed out of the room, as did Doc Johnson, happy the session was over. The old-timer simply despised his chairman as much as he did meetings.

Later that evening, Phil Drummer was unaware of his pending offer to join the surgical staff of the PGH. He had more somber matters at hand. The cemetery sat on a ridge, overlooking the valley below, surrounded by a chain link fence that had seen better days. A dirt path led him through rusty gates towards a large cross directly ahead. To his right and left were tombstones old and new, broadcasting the surnames of those below. A gravesite to his right was fresh, with slightly wilted roses upon the uneven sod, a crow standing watch. Gravel beneath his shoes broke the silence as he approached the large cross marking the graveyard center. Before the crucifix was an altar made of stone that triggered memories of the ceremony exactly one year ago – a cold, crisp sunny day. He slowly turned to his right and viewed the dwarf pine shrub marking his destination–sacred ground. There were no tears, just sadness.

He went down upon a single knee in front of the grave, oblivious to the damp soil beneath. While bowing his head a series of prayers were spoken quietly, in a manner learned as a child. Only then did he allow his gaze to respectfully rise forward and stare directly upon the marker, still with disbelief. Evening dew glistened off the chiseled letters of granite, which for all of eternity would proclaim the Drummer name.

His dad always wanted Jozef to mark his resting site, a name that his mother called him as a child. So it was, and to his right rested Martha, his beloved spouse. Mom and dad were gone.

Joseph Drummer died of an apparent cerebral aneurism, suddenly and without warning, while sitting at home, alone in his favorite chair. A concerned neighbor found him deceased the following day with a rosary in his hand and a picture of his wife at his side. Phil had spoken to him over the phone three days earlier and recalled his final words before saying goodbye, prompting him to take good care of himself.

At his funeral reception a cleric promised Phil that both his mother and father would be closer to him after death, a concept he did not understand at the time. Yet what the preacher man said was true. He spoke to his parents often and they spoke back, louder and sweeter than ever, guiding him through each day. They were alive in spirit.

"Phil," said a voice behind him.

Turning about he saw his older brother Joe, who made the journey in from Poughkeepsie, New York. Together the two brothers paid silent homage to their parents resting below them, proud of their Drummer name.

Chapter Seven
THE TORPEDO ROOM

Frederick Riles II possessed average surgical skills on a good day, a steadfast Riles' family tradition. He knew his limitations and stayed within their margins of safety, never pushing the surgical envelope. The department chairman deftly slid all complex cases to his junior partners, allowing him to concentrate on simple laparoscopic procedures and the Lysovage Project. Hence his moniker among the associate professors – "The Teflon Doc."

"Now we will instill the Lysovage mixture, or perhaps just a placebo," said Riles to the crowd surrounding him. On hand were two visiting surgeons from California, chief resident Rhimes, an intern, two medical students, Vic Fanicci and a reporter for the *Philadelphia Chronicle*.

Riles took the saline mixture from the scrub nurse and held it up in regal fashion. He held the concoction slightly towards the surgical lights, peering into the vial as if performing a final quality assurance test. He shook his head in a positive fashion before attaching the syringe onto the laparoscope, and then plunged the mixture into the abdomen of the experimental patient.

"Why don't you know if it's the real stuff?" asked the beat reporter for The *Chronicle*, thankful he hadn't passed out by this point of the surgery.

"It's a double blind study," said the professor. "The highest level of evidence to support experimental data."

"No one knows," said Fanicci. "Not the patient, Dr. Riles or the pathologist reading the results. Only the computer and a team of statistical analysts are privy to such information."

"I've seen an occasional ad in our newspaper asking patients to contact the PGH if they've had a history of post surgical adhesions. Is that your ad?"

"Yes," responded Riles and Fanicci in unison.

"Are the patient's compensated for enrolling in the study?"

"Yes," said Fanicci. "Standard operational protocol for an investigative study of this magnitude."

"May I ask how much?"

Riles and Fanicci paused and briefly looked at each other. The reporter noting Riles to give a subtle nod of his head prior to an answer.

"Five hundred dollars," said the Union Park Biotech representative.

"Doesn't that skew your results?

"Absolutely not," retorted Riles with authority as he pulled the laparoscope out of the patient's innards. He held his hand out for a suture driver, which the nurse slapped into his hand. "A post-surgical adhesion is a post-surgical adhesion. The results of the study are not based on a patient's satisfaction or subjective pain relief, only the ability of LSV to selectively break down adhesions, on a molecular level."

"How are the results so far?"

"We are not aware of exact results," said Riles. "I can only get summary information from the project leader who is standing at my side."

"Excellent so far," said Fanicci. "I believe the study will be statistically significant and support the benefits of LSV in patients with post surgical adhesions."

"How far along is the study?"

"We are on the verge of wrapping it up," said the representative with an upward bob of his body, causing him to momentarily stand on his toes. "It's been a long ten year process, but the end is near."

Just then the door opened and in strutted Dr. Greyson, holding a surgical mask up to his mouth. He took a close stance directly behind the two female medical students, each with blonde hair and eyes that made telling them apart difficult.

"How's it going?" asked Greyson, appreciating a whiff of perfume from the students.

"Excellent Stuart," said the chairman. "No complications."

An introduction was then made between Greyson and the gang of observers.

"Listen," said Greyson to the reporter. "Off the record this is amazing stuff, it's going to change the landscape of medicine and the way surgeons approach adhesions. Trust me. I've seen it work."

"I'm already blown away," said the reporter trying to remain unbiased. "Are your patients part of the study protocol?"

"You bet," said the junior professor. "The second look laparoscopy clearly shows who received the real deal. LSV busts up adhesions in dramatic fashion."

"Which needs to be confirmed by some pathologist reading the biopsy, correct?" asked the reporter.

"I've got another LSV case starting next door," said Greyson. "Care to join me?"

"Sure," said the enthusiastic troupe together.

"How about our young medical students here, Kayla and Kaylee?" asked Greyson. "I'll even let you scrub in and drive the scope around a bit. Show you some real anatomy."

"Great. Sure," said the young women.

The horde then followed Greyson out the door, across the hall and into the adjacent room.

"Academic medicine, always looking for a better way," said Riles as he peeled off his gloves. "What are your thoughts Dr. Rhimes? You've been quiet all day." The professor peeled off his gloves and shot them in rubber band like fashion across the room, missing the waste bin by several feet.

"I'm going to wait for the final results," said Rhimes confidently as he helped tape the dressing on the patient's tiny incisions. "Then and only then can I make an educated decision."

Chairman Riles did not bother to ask another question, realizing in five months Jack Rhimes would be gone, another benefit of academic medicine. He picked up the patient's chart and left the room, not noticing the elderly nurse leaning downward to pick up his bloody gloves.

Eight hours later in the exact same room, Phil Drummer was taping the dressing on another LSV patient, yet the incision was much bigger. Forty eight year old Greta Crane hit the emergency room two hours prior with signs of an acute abdomen, on the watch of Doc Johnson. She was five weeks out from getting the Lysovage elixir infused into her visceral cavity. Their exploratory surgery found similar findings as those of Ms. Rudenko, just weeks earlier.

"Still no answer," said Doc Johnson, as he hung up the phone in the room. "The guy wants me to notify him ASAP when one of his study patients takes ill, yet he never answers."

"The Teflon Doc," mumbled the old anesthesiologist at the table head.

"I'll keep trying him all night," said Drummer, now helping to slide the postoperative patient onto a hospital gurney.

"Designer medication my ass," said Johnson with a howl. "They should send that stuff over to the Vet school, to help euthanize the animals."

"I'll get her to the SICU tonight," said Phil trying to calm the surgeon's tirade. "Will keep a close eye on her."

"Probably was outlawed by the Geneva Convention," barked Johnson. "Maybe a mustard gas derivative!"

Phil spoke no more, allowing the surgeon to vent as he wheeled the patient to the recovery room.

"We'll be reading about his data alright, in the medical malpractice annals, after they bankrupt the hospital!"

After writing a series of postoperative orders the chief resident walked down a corridor and summoned a hospital elevator. It was ten o'clock in the evening, and the freight car took him to the subbasement, or LL-5 button on the grid. He entered a sector of the hospital, which at such a late hour, was barren. Scuffed hallways were littered with full and empty cardboard boxes, an occasional forklift blocking his route. Near the end of the hall Phil turned right and took a final stairwell one floor deeper, into the inner bowels of the hospital itself. Through the fire door he turned left into a dimly lit narrow passageway, his destination a few steps away. The door was simply marked "Torpedo Room," and without knocking he entered.

Phil immediately espied the room's inhabitant, Rick Polk, looking at a computer, with a familiar looking man beside him frantically pointing at the screen.

"There, there! There I am!" yelled the fidgety little man.

"No way," yelled Polk. "That is you! Stan the man!"

"It's still good," said Maurice Rhett who was sitting on the couch sipping a beer. "Mmmm, refreshing."

Polk and his guest turned around to see Phil, the elderly man wearing a Schmidt's hat and faded gray work shirt with the name "Stan" embroidered on the left upper chest pocket. Phil immediately recognized him as Stanley Jankowski.

"Jak sie masz?" said the Pole with a smile.

"What the hell is going on?" asked Phil.

"Stanley had a cameo appearance in a Schmidt's commercial in the 1970s," said Polk. "He's famous."

"Schmidt's–one beautiful beer," sang the Youtube clip as it ended.

"Hooked us up with some Schmidt's," said Mo.

"Schmidt's of Philadelphia? Is that what it says on that beer label Mo?"

"Stan the Beer Truck Man," said the maintenance foreman. "Never got in an accident."

"What are you talking about?" said Phil. "That brewery went out of business decades ago. They don't make that stuff anymore."

"Exactly," said Polk. "That's where Stan comes in. The guy is a genius."

"When I heard the line would be shutting down in a few days I bootlegged a few truck loads of the brew," said Stan.

"I'm a bootlegger Jerry," said Polk loading some beer bottles into a mini-refrigerator, referring to the popular *Seinfeld* episode where Jerry bootlegged movies.

"Exactly six full truckloads in all, hell the company was bankrupt, no one cared. I got a few boxes of hats too."

"What?" said Phil.

"My whole basement is stacked with cases of beer," said Jankowski. "The coolness of the cellar keeps it fresh."

"Are you guys nuts?" said Phil. "That stuff can't be still good." He noticed two cases of sixteen ounce returnable bottles on the ground. "That must taste like...."

"Stan knows the beer industry," said Polk defensively. "Was involved in the brewery process for years. A real brew master."

"I don't recommend drinking that stuff," said Phil.

"Sit down Drummer," said Maurice. "You're uptight man, relax. Have a beer, it tastes good to me."

"Maurice, don't drink that..."

"Hey does anybody remember the Miss Schmidt's Philly contest?" asked Maurice.

"I met her once," said Stan. "Miss Philly, the cute blonde from the baseball stadium. Have a picture of her with all the truck drivers."

"They always picked the white girl," said Mo. "Never the sister."

Phil just sat down in disbelief as the bizarre scene continued to unfold before him. The door opened and in walked Jackie Rhimes.

"Skywalker," said Mo while pointing a finger at Rhimes.

"Have a beer Jack", said Polk.

"Hey, Schmidt's, my dad used to drink that stuff," said Rhimes while slapping Mo's extended hand. "One beautiful beer."

"Oh my God," said Phil slowly. "Nothing good can happen from this. You guys are going to get sick, trust me. Will need your stomachs pumped."

After Rick filled up his refrigerator with beer bottles he flipped on a small television set sitting on a crate. The Torpedo Room was aptly named, resembling the tight quarters of a submarine, with low overhead clearance and exposed pipes and ductwork. A deep hum emanated from behind the walls, suggesting a nearby engine room. Polk had relocated to the area with the help of Maurice. He tuned in the Philadelphia 76ers game whose reception was fuzzy at best. Rhimes began a discussion about the upcoming department party, scheduled in two weeks.

"I hope that hot new nurse from the floor shows up," said Rhimes. "Now that's a fine Philly girl."

"Who? What's her name?" asked Polk.

"Caroline," said Rhimes.

"Don't spell it."

"C-a-r-o-l-i-n-e." said Rhimes. "Tall, gorgeous, tight body. Have you seen her Phil?"

"If it's the girl Nurse Hudson pointed out to me then yes I have."

"Juicy Lucy Nurse Hudson," said Rhimes. "J-U-I..."

"Yo Phil," said Maurice. "I'm sorry to hear about your old girlfriend man."

An uncomfortable pause took hold of the room, interrupted only by the static coming from the T.V., the local team losing again.

"Thanks Mo," said Phil remembering the dress Jenna wore to last year's party. It was a snug fuchsia dress. She never wore it again.

"She was one fine lady. I mean fine."

"Thanks Mo."

"Phil, can I say something about Jenna?" said Rhimes. "With all due respect."

"Sure."

"We all loved the girl and we all feel your pain, but it may be time to move on. You've given it enough time."

Phil paused and shook his head. He then looked at his best friend, Rick Polk.

"I would agree," said Polk. "I miss her too. She was the best, but life goes on my friend."

"Drummer, half the nurses in this joint want to have your baby," said Maurice. "You got the pick of the litter."

"Wow, I never thought of it that way Mo, thanks for the perspective."

"Phil, we are your best friends, just trying to help. We worry about your mental well being at times," said Rhimes. "You're just not you."

"I'll think about it," said Phil. "Thanks guys."

"Let's make the department casino party your debut?" said Rhimes. "Every nurse in the joint is going to be there."

"The pick of the litter," said Mo. "You get the pick of the litter."

"Maybe," said Phil. "Maybe."

"C-a-r-o-l-i-n-e," said Rhimes. "Caroline."

Let's celebrate with another round," said Stan the Beer Truck Man. "It's on me!"

Chapter Eight
A FLY IN THE OINTMENT

"My stomach still hurts," said Ms. Rudenko to her surgeon. "Very painful."

To her right, staring into a computer screen was Dr. Riles. It was Ms. Rudenko's first follow-up appointment since being discharged from the hospital, at her side was Sasha, holding her head to her mother's abdomen.

"What is wrong doctor?"

"By the looks of the operative report you perforated your duodenum," said Riles, continuing to stare at the screen. "Do you have a history of ulcers?"

"I don't know," said Rudenko. "You are my doctor."

"Yes, well the pathology report is somewhat benign Julia. I believe you had a duodenal ulcer that perforated acutely. I don't believe it had anything to do with the LSV."

The patient did not speak while holding her young child's head and stroking it softly. Her surgeon continued to stare at the computer.

"We will still need to take another look inside," said Riles. "As part of the clinical trial protocol."

The patient gave no response, but seemed ill at ease regarding the suggestion of more surgery.

"Any questions Julia?"

"Dr. Johnson told me no more surgery," said the patient. "Absolutely no more."

"Well that is Dr. Johnson's opinion, but he is no longer involved in your care. I believe that another laparoscopic procedure will be necessary in the future, to take the necessary biopsies, as part of the study you signed up for."

A gentle knock occurred on the exam room door, followed by a nurse poking her head inside the room.

"Excuse me Dr. Riles, but there is an important phone call."

Riles left the room without excusing himself. On the phone was Doc Johnson.

"I've been trying to get you for twelve hours," barked Johnson.

"Yes, well my cell battery was dead and I left my beeper at home. Had a long administrative meeting this A.M."

"Another one of your LVS patients hit the ER last night, acute abdomen scenario."

"Why didn't anyone call me?" asked Riles.

"We did, multiple times before and after the case," said Johnson. "I just told you that."

"Who was the patient? What was the presentation?"

Doc Johnson proceeded to summarize the case presentation and surgical findings of Greta Crane, including the peculiar findings in her abdomen.

"Same picture as your other study patient," said Johnson. "Looked like a five alarm fire in her gut. Grossly inflamed organs and peritoneal tissue, some loss of mucosa from the outer bowel walls."

"What floor is she on?"

"Tenth. Are you sure that stuff is safe, Frederick?"

"Of course I am," barked Riles sharply. "Two patients do not make a study Doctor Johnson. Lysovage has been safely used in thousands of patients, with a very low complication rate."

"Must have been a bad batch," said Johnson, who then hung up the phone.

Riles was upset, now having two patients with reportable complications. Under duress he saw three more patients prior to an office nurse informing him that Ms. Rudenko and her young daughter were still in an exam room, waiting patiently for him.

"Dr. Riles, when will I get the money for the study?" asked Julia Rudenko respectfully. "My husband is sick. He was hurt at work and we have to pay the rent, buy food."

"You haven't gotten the money yet?" asked Riles incredulously. "I will see that you are promptly paid," said Riles. "Perhaps we can increase the reimbursement, after the repeat surgery that I recommend."

"I don't understand?"

"Julia listen," said Riles pulling up a chair. "It is critically important that we check out your inside one more time. We have to know how the medicine worked. Do you understand?"

"Will the pain go away?"

"Maybe, but the only way to know is by trying. Nurse Jones will be in with the surgical consent. In the mean time I will talk to the project director regarding the money owed to you. O.K?"

The Ukrainian did not respond.

"Very good, see you then Julia," said Riles upon leaving the room. "Call me with any questions."

Later that evening Dr. Riles called the private cell of Vic Fanicci, a number shared among four elite members of the project. It was a hotline, available 24/7 for any matters regarding Lysovage.

"Frederick, good evening," said Fanicci. "How's my favorite surgeon?"

"Not so good," said Riles. " A fly in the ointment. We had a second complication yesterday regarding Lysovage, another acute abdomen requiring emergency surgery."

"I see," said the Union Park representative now getting out of bed. "Tell me about it."

Riles updated him on the patient, another female with similar findings to the first, and both involving Dr. Johnson.

"Johnson again?" asked Fanicci. "Maybe he is pulling the trigger early on these reoperations."

"Claims they are clear cut emergencies," said Riles. "He's a curmudgeon, but a good surgeon. I have to believe him."

"If I remember correctly Johnson and a Dr. Knight are a bit skeptical of our product."

"That's an understatement," said Riles. "Johnson because of his surly personality, Knight because he hates me for too many reasons."

"How bad of a hate?"

"A hate that goes back decades," said Riles. "Back to our training days together when quite frankly he botched a case and blamed me."

"Should we worry about him?"

"No, let me handle him. I am the chairman and have the upper hand. There is a bit of jealousy here too Vic. Knight is seeing the benefits of LSV without his name attached to any academic publications regarding it."

"And the royalties," said Vic. "The royalties."

"I'm sure that has entered his mind."

"Listen Doc, what is the name of the second patient? I'll talk to the crew back in Boston and breakdown their profile. Perhaps that will help."

"Sure," said Riles somewhat relieved that the salesman was acting upon his concerns. He learned to trust Fanicci over the years.

"Greta Crane," said Riles. "Her name was Greta Crane, that's C-r-a-n-e."

"Thanks Doc," said Fanicci sensing impatience from the female lying next to him, the call having interrupted a very personal matter between the two.

"Oh by the way," said Riles suddenly remembering, "Ms. Rudenko needs to be paid for her involvement in the project promptly. She was the first recent complication, or should I say reoperation. You remember her, a Ukrainian immigrant."

"No I don't remember her. But the guidelines clearly state they are reimbursed after the clinical trial is complete," said Fanicci.

"Trust me, pay her now," said Riles. "She is a bit upset and dragging her feet about a reoperation. I would even suggest you double the reimbursement."

"No problem," said Victor, sensing his romantic moment was slipping away, which at his age was a real concern. He wanted to ask Riles about the pathology report, but only cared about the arm reaching around his torso, compelling him to terminate the call.

"I'll get a thousand dollars to her by tomorrow. Good night doctor, everything will be fine, get some sleep," said Vic Fanicci with a tap of the cell screen.

"Troubles?" said the soft voice behind him.

"Nothing that can't be cured by the magical touch of a woman," said Fanicci with a laugh. "Do you know such a woman?"

"Have I ever failed you?" asked Vanessa Rose with a pout. "Ever?"

Thirty minutes later Fanicci was again out of bed and powering up his laptop. While looking out the window at the Philadelphia skyline, a sense of entitlement surrounded him, as did the fresh aroma of female pheromones. From memory he keyed in a series of five numerical and alphabet strokes, which delivered to his eyes the glorious data of the LSV project. It was a document that only he and one other company representative had privy to. The South Philly product keyed in the names of Rudenko and Crane, followed by a cross reference to their numerical codes. He studied their profiles, medications and past medical history. Nothing of particular concern stood out to his eye. Their surgeries were uneventful and the operative descriptions of their adhesions classic in presentation. He chocked up their complications to pure chance, a vagary of the numbers, sure to be forgotten among the landslide of success. No reason for alarm.

Within a minute he logged off and snuggled next to the body of his girlfriend of three years. She was a fellow Union Park employee who worked her way up the project ladder in both action and deeds. A hot little number from Taos, New Mexico whose official title was "personal assistant to the project director." She was pure arm candy, at least fifteen years younger, but who cared thought Fanicci, he deserved some perks. Life was too short was his justification, remembering how young his older brother had died. Why him and not me? Sleep became impossible. He thought of his ex-wife and the children.

Paranoia prompted him to climb out of bed and head back to the computer, once again accessing the project's data. Something was bothering him as he again scanned the files of Julia Rudenko and Greta Crane. Why had the Lysovage caused apparent widespread damage, prompting emergency surgery? Up until this late point in the project he could not recall such a complication. Was it a red flag or just bad luck? Then a peculiar thought entered his mind, prompting a series of rapid keyboard strikes. It was only when the computer produced more information that a queer feeling seized his mind.

Chapter Nine
POKHARA

It was a cold, rainy morning in the Gandaki valley when Maya Rai opened her eyes, thankful that the pain in her stomach had eased. The six year-old orphan had taken ill three weeks ago with signs and symptoms of typhoid fever which was endemic in the region. For two weeks she suffered through headaches, fever and diarrhea until a Good Samaritan dropped her off at the local medical mission, where she received antibiotics and hydration. The treatment saved her life.

The young Nepali girl looked upwards at the caring face fixated upon her, having never seen blue eyes or blonde hair before. She then appreciated the warmth of a hand moving a stethoscope across her chest, a sense of calm from the physical contact.

"Maya, my sweet Maya. You gave us such a scare," said Jennifer. "Oh it's so good to see you alert."

The child smiled upon receiving a warm hug from her caretaker as a steady rain pelted the thatched roof above. Jennifer pulled another blanket over the patient while feeling her forehead.

"The fever has finally broken young lady. I hope that tummy is feeling better. How about some rice?"

"Hurray!" said an approaching male voice behind Jennifer. "Little Maya is going to make it."

"Oh look at how beautiful she is," said Jenna. "Her eyes are just gorgeous."

"Dhan'yavada," said the little girl with a weak voice. "Dhan'yavada."

"You're welcome my little precious," said Jennifer, stroking the child's hair gently off her forehead. "You're welcome."

"Good job Jen, now get some sleep. You've been up all night with this young one," said the mission's medical director. "I'll keep a close eye on her this morning."

"There is just something special about this girl," said Jenna while standing up and sensing fatigue. "Promise to keep a close eye on her?"

"Yes," said Doctor Albright emphatically. "Now get some sleep Ranier. Doctor's orders!"

The UMC medical mission was approximately forty miles outside the city limits of Pokhara, in central Nepal. The clinic itself was a makeshift hospital, consisting of thirty beds and six large open-air treatment wards, each with a central fire pit. Construction of the facility took over fifteen years with the first five concentrating on infrastructure, including the need for running water, as more than one third of all households in Nepal had no toilet or running water. The mission was operated by an international entity known as The Unlimited Medical Corps, or UMC. Their goal was to provide basic medical care to the women and children of a country struggling with high levels of hunger and poverty. Nepal health services were lacking in comparison to international standards. Diseases were prevalent including high levels of gastrointestinal disorders, intestinal parasites, leprosy and tuberculosis. Malnutrition was also high and maternal-child health care low.

The UMC mission was situated at an altitude of 1000 meters, surrounded by three of the ten highest mountains in the world. Travelers accessed the facility via a precarious bus ride from Pokhara, along a dirt highway that bisected several steep mountainsides. The bus ran back and forth from Pokhara every other day with frequent cancellations due to weather conditions and mechanical breakdowns. A series of rural villages bordered the UMC mission, providing a population base to care for. Volunteer physicians and health care workers from around the world staffed the facility, including those from the PGH. Each care worker signed up for a minimum three-month tour of duty, with the option to continue on for a full year.

Jennifer walked across a dirt road littered with puddles to her apartment across the street. The three level flat was home for the past seven months. A cow stood in a pasture staring at Jennifer as she passed.

"Good morning Thelma," said Jennifer to the animal before passing by a group of children huddled beneath a roof playing carrom. Once inside the building she climbed a set of creaky steps to the second floor, towards a room shared with a nurse from the Philadelphia General.

"Good morning," said Jen to her roommate, Sara Black. "Just getting up?"

"Yes, I usually do get up in the morning," said her roommate. "Where have you been young lady?"

"Out shopping at the mall," said Jennifer as she kicked off her shoes and dropped onto her bed. "Macy's is having a killer sale on lingerie, buy one get one free. "

"Yea right," said Sara. "Oh to be back in civilization again." Sara was finishing up her third month at the clinic, and had no plans to continue on with her humanitarian career.

"Tomorrow a few of us are heading down to Pokhara," said Sara. "Got to get back onto the internet for a few hours. I'm getting the shakes, delirium tremors I believe. Any interest?" Their current geographic location had no internet or cell service within thirty miles in any direction.

"Nah," said Jenna. "Life off the grid is pretty darn good, once you get used to it. If you stayed for another three months your withdrawal symptoms would ease." Jennifer had not looked at a computer or visited a social networking site in over five months, part of her self imposed introspective purge. She never felt so liberated.

"I doubt it," said Sara. "I need a good dose of Facebook."

"Have a great shift," said Jenna as her roommate left to cross the street. "Keep an eye on Maya." She then stretched out her body and took a deep breath. A window to the left caught a glimpse of a snow-covered peak off in the distance. Some heavy clouds surrounded the summit. The window was slightly ajar, allowing a breeze and the steady pitter-patter of rain to enter. In the distance the devotional bells of an ancient Hindu temple rang, calling her brain to silent meditation.

Her journey towards Nepal began innocently one year ago, while in a traffic jam on the Schuylkill Expressway just outside Philadelphia. While staring at a billboard advertising jewelry, she informed Phil that Stacey Ricketts got engaged the prior evening, after a two-year romance with a young attorney. The wedding would be the following year.

"That's nice," was the terse response from the driver.

Maybe it was the brevity of the reply that prompted a retort, or perhaps the tension of a prolonged standstill on the roadway. Jennifer often thought what would have happened if she kept quiet.

"Don't you think that's special?" was the spark that ignited the fireball. "I mean for Stacey, to get engaged."

"I didn't say it wasn't special," said Phil. "I said that's nice."

"You don't have to get angry about it Phil, I'm just happy for Stacey. She was so lonely for such a long time."

"Send her a text from me," said Phil as he watched a slow moving car cut in front of him, jockeying for position in the gridlock. "Tell her good luck and I think the whole situation is special – love and kisses, Phil."

"That's not nice Phil, Stacey is my best friend."

Silence ensued for roughly three minutes while a rage began to swell inside her female soul.

"Look at this idiot in front of me," said Phil. "I don't understand why people weave back and forth when traffic is moving so slow. We should have taken the last exit. I knew it!"

"She helped me when I really needed a friend," said Jenna coldly. "If it wasn't for her, we wouldn't be together."

"Oh, really," said Phil, now realizing where Jenna was headed. Despite a never-ending heartfelt series of apologies, Phil's infidelity remained her trump card, with no known counter.

"Yes really," said Jenna staring directly ahead at the back end of an eighteen-wheeler. Rain began to fall on the windshield. "She kept me sane while you sorted out your priorities. Remember those days?"

"Great. Well then she is responsible for us sitting in this eternal traffic jam," said Phil smartly. "P.S.–thanks for getting us back together so we could enjoy this quality time – love Phil. No better yet, sign it Sucker on the Sure Kill Expressway."

Approximately thirty seconds of stillness passed before Jen's boiling point was reached. She took a deep breath and Phil sensed an escalation at hand. He tried to speak but his mind froze.

"I don't think it's unreasonable to be happy for a girl that just got engaged," said Jen. "Why you wouldn't think that is nice, I don't know."

"Jen, what I...."

"You never cared for my friends. I mean is it a sin to get engaged Phil? Can't Stacey be happy?"

"I didn't say...."

"I put up with your friends all the time Phil. A bunch of adolescents who fool around and think everything is a joke. Making fun of everybody."

"Jen, please."

"That's the problem Phil, you and your cronies are just passing through, always looking ahead to the next year, the next hospital, the next year of training. Life is always ahead of you."

"Jen, you are overreacting," said Phil, now in damage control mode.

"Well this is my life Phil, and I'm not passing through. This is it, and it doesn't get any better."

"Jen, can we talk about something else?"

"No! You've got a commitment problem Phil, and it's now my problem. A big problem that I have to deal with, and quite frankly I don't appreciate it."

Phil went silent, now feeling the force of the commitment card, which by the laws of nature trumped the infidelity factor. He became a bit short of breath.

"That's the problem," said Jen. "It's so obvious now. Commitment. You can't commit."

"Jen, what are you talking about?"

"You know what? I've had it with this traffic jam and I've had it with this relationship," said Jen with fierce defiance. "I'm out. Nobody is going to dictate what I do in life."

"Jen, please. Relax."

She opened the passenger door and stepped out, aware that traffic was at a dead standstill. Her dramatic exit took a path directly in front of the car and across the stationary line of traffic in the adjacent lane. Phil noticed two children in the back of a van yelling to their parents about the apparent mad woman crossing the highway. He began to roll down his window in an attempt to control the meltdown, only to see his girlfriend of four years step over a guardrail and disappear down an embankment thick with shrubs, never to be seen again that day.

A week later Jen attended a luncheon at the PGH sponsored by the hospital's Department of Travel Medicine. The guest lecture was their department head, Dr. Thomas Albright. His topic was "Providing Basic Medical Care to an Impoverished Country – My Ten Year Experience in Nepal." Jen took interest in the medical mission and after much thought, volunteered to participate. Three months after the Schuylkill Expressway debacle, she left for Nepal, never regretting her decision.

A dog barking across the street suddenly brought her back to reality, blinking her weary eyes. She noticed some black insects crawling up a wall opposite her bed, not uncommon in the flat. She turned over to face a nightstand beside her bed with sparse personal belongings atop. A spontaneous movement took her hand across the tabletop to grasp a single acorn perched near the edge, then back to her torso. She began to slowly rub the oak nut, smooth from handling.

The acorn was a product of Phil and Jennifer's first dinner date over four years ago. She came into possession of it while walking home with Phil that evening down a cobblestoned center city alley. Out of nowhere from above, an acorn dropped and bounced off Phil's shoulder. While laughing he picked up the white oak souvenir and dubbed it their "lucky acorn," while handing it to Jen. She placed it in her pocket and since then kept the charm, being quite superstitious. It was the one personal object that she brought to Nepal that connected her to Phil.

She left on reasonably good terms with Phil, their emotions calmed after the spat. Both parties agreed that some time apart to recalibrate priorities was in order, hopeful that what they had together was salvageable. Jen felt a communication black out was critical to the process, giving each person time to think. At first, time apart was devastatingly lonely, resulting in some expected depression and a series of sleepless nights. But then the inner calm of the third world country brought peace to Jennifer, and tincture of time healed her wounds. She immersed herself in work and the gratitude she received in return was medicine for her soul. Without hesitation she opted for a one-year extension on her tour. Her last communication to Phil was a short email sent from a hotel in Pokhara five months ago, notifying him of her decision. She signed her name with a tear in her eye "with everlasting love – Jennifer."

As she rolled the acorn back and forth a gaze towards the mountains noted the clouds to be parting, suggesting a sunny day. To the left of the highest mountain peak was the moon, still visible in the daylight. As she drifted asleep she thought of Phil, wondering if he too was looking at the celestial body above.

Chapter Ten
CAROLINE

At that very moment, approximately nine hours and forty five minutes earlier by international time standards, Phil was indeed looking at not one, but two celestial spheres directly before him. His body was pinned between the side bumper of a Saab 900 and the front bumpers of Nurse Lucy Hudson. The Saab was a byproduct of her first divorce and the orbs between her waist and beautiful face the second. She had just pulled her lips back from Phil's with a purr that reeked of satisfaction.

"Oh that one was for me," said Nurse Hudson slowly, her eyes closed. "Ohhh."

Phil had innocently escorted Nurse Hudson out to the casino's parking lot, the manly thing to do at such a late hour. Alcohol played a roll in the decision process as did a peculiar feeling that Nurse Hudson stirred within him. The seasoned veteran wasted no time in pinning the chief resident against the vehicle with a sensual kiss that caught him off guard. Stunned from the first, he willingly accepted the second with a bodily contact suggesting more to come.

"Wow," said Hudson still holding on to her prize. "Thanks Dr. Drummer, that brings back some good memories."

"Memories?" asked Phil, still looking down upon the nurse's face, the second kiss still reverberating throughout his body.

"I'm sorry but I just wanted to remember what it felt like," said Hudson. "To have the handsome resident in my arms and to press his lips onto mine. I thought I had forgotten the feeling, but you brought it back Phillip, and it tasted good."

"Worth the wait?"

She pressed more firmly against his body and proceeded to refresh her memory one more passionate time before pulling back just a touch.

"Mmmm, definitely worth the wait," said Hudson. "Better than I thought."

They just looked at each other as Nurse Hudson let out a sigh of satisfaction, her hands still upon the young doctor. Phil had no idea what was coming next.

"Thanks Dr. Drummer, but I have to go," said Hudson. "Early shift tomorrow."

Phil just stared at her in disbelief.

"Listen Phil, I'm way past your time, too much baggage," said Hudson. "But take my advice young man, enjoy the ride. It won't last for long. Tomorrow you are going to wake up and be a forty-five year old."

"What ride?" asked Phil, sensing their impromptu contact was over.

"Youth, innocence, love, the whole package," said Hudson as she patted him on the cheek. "You're so perfect you don't even know it. But trust me, enjoy it, because it never lasts."

They just stared at each other for a few more seconds before Hudson kissed him on his cheek and then wiped the red lipstick off with her fingertips.

"Thanks. I really needed that," said Hudson. "You made me feel special again. Good night doctor." She then sidestepped Phil, slipped into her Saab and sped out of the parking lot, leaving him alone. With a shake of his head he walked back towards the casino and departmental party, still in full swing.

The Emerald Room was one of five banquet halls inside the Three Nations Casino, which sat beside the Delaware River. The casino was run by ninth generation descendants of a Manayunk Indian Tribe rumored to have lived on the sacred grounds of the venue. In reality no such tribe existed until gambling was allowed in the state of Pennsylvania. Once permitted a group of savvy businessmen from Dubai gathered three members from a local ironworkers union and created the Three Tribes of The Manayunk Nation, a name shortened by a marketing firm to Three Nations. The lucky workers were dubbed the last known survivors of the peaceful tribe that once lived along the banks of the Delaware, fishing and trading goods with our nation's forefathers. Their sacred homeland was by chance located on an abandoned pier several blocks from downtown Philadelphia with a population base of five million. The Nation was granted historical charter via a series of bribes to local politicians followed by a license to build a casino. A construction company owned by the state senator was awarded the bid to build the facility, bringing the whole corruption full circle. The three ironworkers received a modest salary for their time and facial features, allowing vast fortunes to be made by the businessmen, complements of Philadelphia's working class.

The Emerald Room was extensive and ornate, with bejeweled chandeliers hanging from above and alcohol flowing throughout. A patron only had to walk a maximum of twenty steps in any direction before hitting a liquor bar. Scantily clad cocktail waitresses assured the absolute distribution of alcohol, catering to less mobile customers with a smile. Situated along each wall were long buffet tables, laden with food groups from around the world. Chefs manned stations while carving beef and lamb covered with succulent sauce. The dessert station was massive and constantly restocked with fresh baked cakes, pastries and pies.

"I think I'm getting the gout," said Rick Polk while shoveling down another cannoli, an alcoholic drink in his left hand. "Big toe is acting up, too much rich food."

"Where's Drummer?" asked Jack Rhimes. "I saw him leaving with Juicy Lucy about twenty minutes ago."

Just then Phil entered the room and headed towards the duo, running a gauntlet of surgical department employees and casino workers. While passing through the mob he brushed past Dr. Riles who was talking to Stuart Greyson, overhearing a singular line.

"If your wife is sick, don't you think you should be home with her?" said the department chairman incredulously. Phil failed to appreciate the response.

Phil then bumped into Dr. Knight and his spouse, both sober and checking out the nearest exit, as if ready to leave.

"Good evening Dr. and Mrs. Knight," said Phil. "How are you this evening?"

"Wonderful Dr. Drummer," said Knight in terse fashion. "Hard to believe another departmental party is here."

"I enjoyed Dr. Riles speech," said Phil fumbling for a topic, unaware of the remaining red lipstick on his cheek.

"Richard, is this the young man that will be joining your department next year?" asked Mrs. Knight.

Brief silence ensued as Knight stared incredulously at his wife. Phil waited for a response from the attending.

"Perhaps dear, he is part of a great graduating class. We are looking at all of them as potential members of the staff."

"It would be an honor to even be considered for such a position," said Phil putting the faux pas to rest. "An honor, Dr. Knight."

"I believe we've met before Dr. Drummer," said Mrs. Knight. "One evening after Richard and I had dinner in Manayunk."

"Yes, I do remember that," said Phil.

"Oh where is the time going? Seems like yesterday," said Mrs. Knight.

"Well we have to be going," said Knight checking his watch. "Early case tomorrow morning. Let's go dear."

"Good night Dr. and Mrs. Knight," said Phil, sensing a peculiar angst in the speech of his mentor.

"Drummer," said Knight before leaving. "Tell Polk to take it easy on the booze, I'm counting on him to first assist in the morning. Got it?"

"Yes sir," said Phil. "Consider it done."

Phil made his way across the room to join his friends, delivering the message to Polk in regards to his alcohol consumption. It was then that Jackie pointed out Nurse Caroline Ell who had arrived to the festivities late with a single friend.

"Your coming out party young man," said Rhimes with a slap on Phil's back. "I'm so proud of you son."

"Remember what Mo talked about," said Polk. "The pick of the litter."

Phil thought long and hard about the advice from his friends. In his mind the embrace by Nurse Hudson was not of his doing, and therefore considered an innocent good night cordial. Since Jenna left town his slate was clean yet lonely, in honor of the woman he still loved.

"Hey there goes Kayla and Kaylee!" said Rhimes while looking over Polk's shoulder. "Who invited them?"

"I don't know, but let's check it out," said Polk enthusiastically. "Kayla loves me, or wait is it Kaylee?"

The two friends then bolted away from Phil, alone with his thoughts, and wondering what to do next. His mind began to calculate the time difference between Philadelphia and Nepal, wondering if Jennifer had woken up yet.

"Hi Phil," said a female voice behind him.

Turning about he looked directly at Nurse Caroline Ell, whose girlfriend was heading to the bar for some spirits.

"Hi Caroline," said Phil, already introduced to the nurse previously at the hospital by Hudson.

Nurse Ell defined natural beauty. At five foot eleven inches tall her waist to hip ratio was a perfect 0.7 and not an ounce of fat resided on her frame. Her facial features were perfectly symmetric with smooth skin and clear cheekbones. Full pouty lips added to the mix, as did a set of deep blue eyes. Thick jet-black hair completed the masterpiece, cut to shoulder level with a slight curl. Phil stared directly at her, a bit in awe.

Ell was a recent graduate of Villanova where she excelled in track and field, especially the 400 meter race. She was born and raised in a small town one hour east of Pittsburgh, the youngest of four daughters. A tomboy by nature she excelled in sports, which landed her an athletic scholarship to the Main Line school, where she majored in nursing. She went by the name of Cara.

"We just got off shift at the PGH," said Caroline while noticing the rouge on Phil's face. Through the hospital grapevine she was aware of Phil's long time girlfriend and her current soul searching mission in the Himalayas. She was also aware of Jennifer's beauty and feminine prowess.

"How's it going?" asked Phil. "Is Nurse Hudson showing you the ropes?"

"Oh yea, she is so great," said Cara. "I'm learning a lot from her, the things they don't teach in the classroom."

"A great nurse," said Phil. "Someone who knows how to handle everything."

Cara just shook her head up and down in a moment of awkward silence between the two.

"Dr. Drummer," said the booming voice of Dr. Riles behind Phil, prompting him to turn about. "I'd like you to meet Mr. Victor Fanicci, of Union Park Biotech."

"Ah yes, please to meet you," said Phil while stepping backwards to include Caroline in the group. He shook hands with the slick looking middle-aged gentlemen with an expensive Italian suit. Next to him was a stunning woman with an hour-glass figure wearing a skin tight dress that sparkled.

"Dr. Drummer is one of our star chief residents," said Riles with a smile and flash of his teeth. "We expect great things of him in the future."

"Perhaps LSV material?" asked Fanicci with a coy smile, obviously aware of Phil's possible future membership on the PGH staff.

"Hello doctor, my name is Vanessa," said Ms. Rose while extending her hand to Phil, interrupting the discussion. "I am Mr. Fanicci's personal assistant."

"A pleasure," said Phil with a smile, sensing danger upon touching the beautiful woman's hand. "I'd like all of you to meet Caroline Ell, a wonderful new nurse at the PGH. She works on the general surgery floor."

During the exchange of greetings, Phil appreciated a brash look upon Vanessa's face as she surveyed the young nurse. She had perfectly manicured nails that slowly rotated a swizzle stick within a glass.

"Doctor Drummer," said Fanicci, "Chairman Riles tells me that you are a gifted surgeon, and we at Union Park Biotech are always looking for young talent surgeons to represent our product."

"It seems like an exciting product," said Phil, the words of Doc Johnson echoing in his mind. "Dr. Greyson swears by it."

"Ah Dr. Greyson, a very, very talented surgeon who we are delighted to have involved in the project. Excellent surgeon."

Phil noticed Dr. Riles to be swaying back and forth of his feet, in obvious glee while watching the LSV pitchman ply his trade.

"Perhaps you can join Ms. Rose and I for dinner some night," said Fanicci. "To discuss the LSV project and its future?"

"Well, I'm not sure that..."

"Philip, to be invited into the inner circle of the Lysovage project is a real honor," said Riles. "As your chairman it's an offer that I would advise you strongly consider. LSV is going to change the face of surgery in the near future."

"What do you say Dr. Drummer?" asked Fanicci with an extended hand. "I would also like to invite your beautiful date here to attend the dinner with us. Caroline correct?"

"Yes, but please call me Cara."

"What a beautiful name," said Fanicci. "Cara, would you please honor us with your presence at dinner, along with Dr. Drummer?"

"Ah, maybe but..."

"Yes, yes! As his chairman I will accept the invitation," said Riles with a head nod and corny wave of his hands.

"It's too good an offer to pass by Phillip. You'll thank me in the future."

"Wonderful!" said Fanicci. "I know a little Italian restaurant in center city that is out of this world. The seafood risotto is to die for."

"Great," said Phil trying to digest the surreal events in progress.

"How about two weeks from this Friday," said Fanicci. "Say about 6 PM. I'll have a car pick you up."

"Oh no, that's OK," said Phil. "I, I mean we, can just take the train downtown."

"Don't be silly," said Fanicci with a wide smile. "Vanessa will take your cell phone numbers and coordinate the whole night. You won't regret this Dr. Drummer. Trust me. A product like Lysovage only comes around once in a lifetime."

After a firm handshake to seal the deal, the Union Park gang vanished into the crowd as quickly as they appeared. Mission accomplished.

"What just happened?" asked Phil with a dumbfounded look upon his face.

"I have no idea," said Caroline. "But I believe you and I have a dinner date in two weeks. I hope you like Italian food."

"Hey Phil" yelled Jackie Rhimes with a hurried approach from the left. "Two things, first Rick hit the jackpot on a slot machine, the money is still pouring out."

"What!"

"Second, Doc Johnson just sent out an alert to find you. There's another acute abdomen in the emergency room and he needs you back at the PGH stat!"

Chapter Eleven
THE KNIGHT WATCH

Operating room number four was the sole domain of Richard Roman Knight, chief of cardiothoracic surgery at the Philadelphia General Hospital. Despite the events of four years ago his reputation remained stellar, his name always found on the short list of *Best Physicians* in the greater Philadelphia area. His standards remained high along with a quest for surgical perfection. Outwardly, his physical appearance commanded respect and attention, suggestive of a sound and vibrant middle-aged man, yet the motor vehicle accident from years ago left him with some serious functional sequelae.

Fatigue was one problem as was a slight loss of whole body strength, both secondary to his brainstem injury and thoracic fractures. Abdominal pain was another, due to the adhesions that formed after his small bowel laceration and subsequent resection. The pain was so severe that he considered a surgical procedure a year ago to break up the adhesions, yet never consented to the operation. Easing his surgical schedule allowed him to cope with the fatigue factor, and his mental toughness dealt with the pain. However the one post-traumatic residual with no antidote was the tremor that haunted his right upper extremity. Its presence was unpredictable, at times triggered by stress and fatigue but usually spontaneous in nature. Most worrisome in regards to the dominant arm quiver was its frequency, recently a daily event. Knight disguised the tremor by occasionally tucking his arm into a pant's pocket or firmly gripping an object nearby. However deep down inside he knew that further progression of the malady would end his surgical career, a consequence that would deliver absolute devastation to his life.

"Out late last night?" asked Knight to chief resident Polk who stood opposite the table, an elderly man's chest exposed and open between them.

"No sir," said Polk. "Early to bed and early to rise, makes a man healthy, wealthy, and wise." Polk was assisting Knight, and scheduled to finish his training under his tutelage.

"Who coined that term Doctor Polk?"

"Abe Lincoln, during the Gettysburg Address," said Polk with confidence.

"That was Ben Franklin," said scrub Nurse Ella Frey. "Everybody knows that. Philadelphia's own Mr. Benjamin Franklin."

"Honest Ben," said Polk.

"Speaking of Philadelphia's finest, I had a Schmidt's beer yesterday evening," said Knight. "Schmidt's, can you believe that?"

"Schmidt's? I didn't think they still made that stuff," said a male perfusionist in the room, sitting next to a heart-lung machine that was keeping the patient alive. "They shut down in the 1980s."

"My brother and a few of my uncles worked at the Schmidt's brewery," said Ella. "Down at North Liberty and Kensington. Always came home with a belly full of beer."

"They had a tap room on site," said the circulating male nurse. "I grew up next to the brewery. It was a shack about the size of this room, unheated with a keg of beer in the middle and benches surrounding it. Open twenty four seven, every day of the year including holidays."

"Tap room?" asked Knight.

"Yea. All the workers drank there for free and a good portion of the surrounding neighborhood did," said the nurse. "It was a part of becoming a man, sneaking into the tap room as a young teenage and having a few sips of beer with your dad or uncle."

"I rarely drink beer," said Knight as he expertly sutured a coronary graft into place, looking through a pair of magnifying glasses. "But just seeing that old label triggered some good memories of my high school and college days."

"Everybody drank Schmidt's back in the seventies and eighties," said Ella. "Every tavern in town had it."

"Where did you get it? " asked the perfusionist.

"Out at the Three Nation Casino," said Knight. "Had some sort of a kiosk in the corner, limited supply."

Polk remained silent, taking in the glory and adulation before taking credit for the coup. He and Jackie had masterminded the event, which for several hours flew beneath the casino's security radar.

"Even had an old worker there in his uniform. Name was Stan. Said he drove a beer truck for over thirty years, never got in an accident."

"Wow," said the circulating nurse. "Maybe it's making a comeback."

"How did it taste? Like you remembered?"

"Quite frankly it tasted like rotten piss water," said Knight with a growl. "Ruined my night, had to leave early. Nasty stuff."

Polk kept quiet.

“Maybe your taste is different?” asked the circulating nurse. “I couldn’t eat or drink half of the crap I shoveled down back in the college days.”

“I don’t thing so,” said Knight. “The stuff was rancid.”

“Maybe they have a different recipe,” said Ella.

At that moment and unexpected and violent tremor struck Knight’s right forearm, causing his hand to noticeably shake. Nurse Frey and Polk were privy to the ongoing problem and adhered to the age-old surgical adage of “what happens at sea stays at sea.” They spoke to no one else about it. The team paused as Knight stepped back to regain his composure, a needle driver and fine thread suture in his hand.

“‘Schmidt’s, one beautiful beer’ was there saying.”

Knight inhaled deeply while staring at his right hand in anger, as if about to scold a child. The rolling tremble continued through all of his digits for several more seconds during which he pressed his forearm against the patient’s body. The maneuver seemed to calm the attack. Once steadied, he attempted to proceed with suturing the final bypass graft, but the flutter persisted and he could not.

“Here,” he said to Polk while passing him the needle drive. “Let’s see if you’ve learned anything over the past five years.” After releasing the suture material to Polk he forcefully pressed his right hand onto the surgical field to control the tremor. Dr. Polk took the fine suture material, squinted at it carefully and then began to secure the graft.

Just then the door opened and in walked Doc Johnson. He appeared more fatigued than his usual self, fighting gravity with every step.

“Up all night with another magical mystical lyso-whatever you call it patient last night Richard. Looked like someone poured five alarm chili into the poor guy’s gut.”

"I heard," said Knight while keeping a close eye on Polk, aware that the patient on the table was the CEO of a well-known local charitable organization.

"Why me, why do they all come in on my shift?" asked Johnson. "Our chairman is always in Rome or Paris or up at the Casino hob-knobbing it while his patients are howling in the E.R. from pain."

"Bad luck," said Knight.

"Something is wrong with that stuff Richard," said the grouchy surgeon. "This just isn't right and quite frankly I don't want any part of it, or the collateral damage associated with the quackery."

"I'm not exactly sure what we can do," said Knight. "I'm assuming the whole project was cleared by the hospital's advisory board."

"I think we should bring it up to the administration," said Johnson. "The CEO, board of trustees, whomever. Something is amiss. We can't let this go by."

Knight paused, recalling his similar sentiments just four years ago surrounding the perceived delay in action by the hospital bigwigs, leading to the death of several patients. His right hand trembled again. He knew Doctor Johnson was right, and they were the two most senior surgeons at the Philadelphia General. It was their watch. They had a moral obligation to speak up quickly.

"Not on my watch!" said Knight. "Let's bring it up to administration as soon as possible. If I'm not mistaken that's a total of three patients you've seen over the past few weeks."

"Yes," said Johnson. "I agree, let's demand some action and accountability."

"Done," said Polk, proud of his suture job.

"You let Polk sew up a bypass graft?" asked Johnson.

"Yea, great job. Polk's a keeper," said Knight.

"A bee keeper maybe, or even a zoo keeper," barked Johnson. "I've seen the kid suture before and believe me, once that patient sneezes that graft is gonna blow."

A healthy laughter filled the room thanks to the old timer's sense of humor. The case finished shortly afterwards without complication.

The following evening an emergency meeting occurred within the office of CEO John Mitchell. Present was Mitchell, Chairman Riles, Dr. Greyson and Victor Fanicci. The matter involved a certified letter of concern authored by Knight and Johnson to the hospital CEO regarding the safety of LSV, demanding an official action and response.

"He has always despised the project," said Riles. "Hated it from day one."

"Perhaps," said Mitchell. "But my concern is this letter in hand stating three patients enrolled in the LSV study have sustained a significant complication, raising questions as to the safety of the product itself. The two men who have signed the letter are full professors of the department of surgery and have been around the block a few times. I must respect their concerns."

"LSV is very safe," said Greyson. "That's why I'm part of this study."

"Why are no other doctors involved?" asked Mitchell. "I mean why are just two surgeons using the stuff here?"

"Doc Johnson is a dinosaur," said Greyson with a brash attitude. "The other general surgeons are just too cautious, too conservative. Trust me, in due time they will be lining up to use the product."

"We may have a new young surgeon on board very shortly," said Riles, hinting at the potential of Phil Drummer's offer.

"Jonathan, the history on LSV is one of safety. There are minor side effects which are not unusual, but major complications, no," said Fanicci while holding a binder full of project results. "I have all the data here for your review."

"Victor, Victor please," said the CEO. "I do not have the time or medical background to digest that stack of test results. I need input from these two surgeons regarding LSV in order to report back to the hospital advisory board in charge of clinical trials. Is LSV safe?"

"Yes," said Riles and Greyson in unison.

"Then why the three complications?"

"Bad luck," said Greyson. "It's that simple. Look at the data over time."

"John, I've been at this project for fifteen years," said Riles. "This is my life's work. Do you think I would be pumping an unsafe product into patients? I have research data to strongly support every step of the LSV approval process so far. Quite frankly this whole subject is quite insulting. A personal attack on my professional credibility."

"Frederick, take it easy. I know the product is safe. But I need some stronger justification to take back to the board. Bad luck doesn't fly when a hospital's reputation is on the line."

Silence gripped the room, each man searching for an answer, eyes down.

"Alright," said Fanicci. "It's a violation of study protocol but I believe now is the time to disclose some information. Information that may put the whole matter to rest."

"Disclose what?"

"I've taken the opportunity to review all of the data regarding the three patients who required emergent surgery," said Fanicci. All three were patients of Dr. Riles."

"Obviously they were my patients," said Riles.

"I've checked and cross checked their computer randomization into the study."

"And..." said Riles.

"Believe it or not all three incidents involved patients that received a placebo," said Fanicci with a wide grin on his face. "None of them received Lysovage.

"Fascinating," blurted Riles, his voice notably excited.

"What are the odds of that?" said Greyson.

"Enlighten me further," said CEO Mitchell.

"Sugar water," said the Union Park representative. "A placebo is basically nothing, part of a standard clinical trial. In this case it's just a mixture of saline and a salt mixture. Harmless."

"Basically normal saline solution," said Riles with a smile and shake of his head. "The stuff we run through the abdomen during every laparoscopy."

"Exactly," said Fanicci. "So these complications cannot be from LSV. They are absolutely unrelated."

"Wonderful," said Riles with a raise of his hands. "Amen."

"Interesting," said Mitchell. "Clear cut response as far as I can see. The board shouldn't have a problem with that."

"So in reality it was just bad luck," said Greyson. "I was right."

"We were at a dead end," said Fanicci. "I was hoping an explanation would be available that still protected the integrity of a double blinded study, but none was in sight."

"Great," said Mitchell. "I'll draft a response to both the board and Drs. Knight and Johnson."

"Can I proof it before you send it out?" asked Riles.

"Sure I'll send you a rough draft," said the CEO.

The meeting adjourned and the parties arose with firm handshakes.

"John, will you be attending the Union Park VIP cruise in Boston this year?" asked Fanicci.

"Hell yes," said Mitchell. "Same yacht?"

"Even bigger this year," said Fanicci. "Twelve hours out on Boston harbor, with lobster tails the size of baseball bats."

"Always a wonderful time," said Riles. "This must be my eight or ninth year in a row."

"Is Vanessa coming this year?" asked Greyson.

"You bet," said Fanicci. "Along with a few of her girlfriends. I expect the same top shelf alcohol on board. Should be a good time gentlemen. I have a block of rooms reserved for you right on the harbor plaza."

"You know I miss Boston," said CEO Mitchell. "That's still my home."

"Me too," said Riles. "Philly is cold, gritty. There is no love here."

"It all started there," said Fanicci. "Remember our first meeting together? We had no idea if the clinical trials were going to be approved."

"Had to beg the advisory board."

"The end is near gentlemen," said Riles. "The end is so damn near. I can taste it."

Chapter Twelve
A DAY WITH STUART

Dr. Stuart Greyson was thirty-eight years old. He was born and raised on the Isle of Manhattan, the product of a business mogul and his third wife. With no siblings he grew up in a sterile high-rise apartment under the watchful eye of a nanny who ultimately became his stepmother. Copious amounts of money landed him at a boarding school in New England by age fifteen, followed by an Ivy League education and medical school. Throughout the process Stuart maintained his mother's good looks and father's libido, never lacking for a female friend. A coveted surgical residency landed him in Boston where he came under the training of Frederick Riles II. While in Boston he met an enchanting young female named Mia at a hospital fundraiser who ultimately became his wife. She too was from a well to do family.

After accepting an offer to join the Philadelphia General Hospital staff the Greysons bought a cute mansion in the Gladwyne suburb of Philadelphia, reachable via combined wealth. They struggled at first but within two years an addition was constructed onto the manor along with the installation of a built in swimming pool. A recently added stand alone three-car garage brought the young couple up to neighborhood standards.

Mia Greyson was as equally attractive as her husband. Together they made an immediate impact upon the social scene in Philadelphia, he the young heartthrob surgeon and she the beautiful wife, so concerned about society as a whole. Days were filled with works of good deeds and nights spent about town enjoying everything a major metropolis had to offer. The Greysons were the envy of the neighborhood, young and beautiful with excellent cash flow.

However over the past two years a matter of concern entered Camelot, that being the inability of the twosome to conceive a child. Mia was thirty-six years old and for the past two years unable to successfully bring a fetus to term despite conventional methods. Currently in process was an in-vitro fertilization program under the direction of the PGH's gynecology department. Although horribly expensive, both partners were fully committed to bringing about a newborn to carry on the Greyson name.

"How are you feeling?" asked Stuart while eating breakfast and staring at the sport's page. His wife was moving rapidly about the kitchen that morning, preparing for departure.

"Great," said Mia. "Ultrasound today. And remember your services may be necessary at any moment." She had just completed a round of hormones that ripened her eggs and hopefully started the process of ovulation.

"Standing by to assist and fertilize," said Stuart with a half salute above the newspaper. "That's been my motto since about age fifteen."

"Just keep your cell phone on," said Mia, bending forward and delivering a kiss on his cheek. "If a donation is needed, we will call. Love you."

"Love you too," said Greyson, his eyes upon the NBA box score in the paper. "Good luck. Lay and egg."

A red Porsche with black interior rapidly delivered Dr. Greyson to the Philadelphia General that morning. An uncharacteristically warm spring day allowed him to ride with the top down. A smile on his face signaled an exciting day ahead, full of activities. His surgical schedule included two Lysovage patients and two gall bladder removals, taking up three hours of his time. Late morning found him in the office, seeing a few post-surgical patients.

Lunchtime found the young doctor at a popular downtown restaurant with his financial advisor, a meeting he had recently set up to discuss some matters of concern. The financial guru was an old friend of his father's, having already made more money than he could spend, but kept himself in the game for reasons of sanity.

"Donald, thanks for meeting me on such short notice," said Stuart with a handshake and firm smile. "I really appreciate it."

"Stuart please," said Donald Cabot. "We are like family, remember I once dated your mother, years before she met your father." Cabot was the consummate financial advisor, well dressed and glib. "How is your mom doing?"

"Great," said Greyson. "She is in Italy now, or maybe France. I'm not sure."

The maître d' then escorted the couple to a side table with a window view of Chestnut Street. A single flower in a clear vase sat between them.

"How's Mia?" asked Cabot while scanning the lunch menu. "I saw her picture in the newspaper the other day, beautiful woman. How does she keep that figure?"

"Great," said Greyson. "Happy and busy. She keeps herself very active. Runs a lot, she works out constantly."

"I see," said Cabot with a fatherly look above a set of reading glasses perched upon the bridge of his nose. "Any little Greysons in the near future?" asked Cabot. "As your financial advisor I need to know. We can hide a ton of money in the little one's trust fund."

"We are thinking about it," said Greyson. "Thinking about it. Hey you should try the roasted chicken sandwich, I had it last week, great stuff."

Cabot did indeed take the advice of his client and ordered the chicken sandwich, served with some asparagus spears and fruit. It was near the end of the meal when serious conversation began between the two.

"It's about the Lysovage stock options," said Greyson after completing his smoked salmon club. "Running into some potential problems. Some possible changes."

"What's the problem?" asked Cabot while motioning for the waitress to refill his drink. "A no-brainer, fifteen percent of the stock block was going to be your share, before the IPO. Right?"

"A little internal shake-up," said Greyson. "Within the pharmaceutical company that is. My share may be going down to about five percent, or less."

"Why? I mean that's a ton of money Stuart, you don't need an advisor to tell you that. We're talking millions of dollars."

"Has to do with the wording of the clinical trial protocol and who the primary investigators are," said Greyson with a wave of his hand. "Apparently a document predated the protocol commencement date which set exact percentage distribution to all parties involved. Remember I came in a bit late into the game, after my residency training ended. Apparently my share is an arbitrary number that is tough to pin down."

"You need a good attorney for that," said Cabot. "I know a real bulldog when it comes to the market and corporate law, can give you his number."

"My question to you is what happens to stock options in a marriage, considering the two endpoints of a marriage?"

"What do you mean by endpoints?"

"Death or divorce," said Greyson. "Fifty-fifty now a days, take your pick."

"Listen to me Stuart, I promised your father to always remind you to never, ever get divorced. Fifty percent of your empire is gone with a stroke of the pen."

"Then he should be bankrupt," said Stuart with a chuckle. "Been divorced so many times I've lost count."

"That's why the old man only owns three homes now," said the advisor. "His ex-wives took all the other estates. The poor bastard."

"Actually he technically owns four," said Greyson. "I just happen to be living in one."

"Listen to me," said Cabot while lowering his voice and looking around. "Do not get divorced. I repeat, do not get divorced. What's going on Stuart, a problem?"

"No, no. No problem. Just asking a hypothetical. If Mia and I own stock options together as man and wife, and then divorce, what happens to the options both pre and post IPO?"

"An attorney," said Cabot with a shake of his head and hand wave. "Stuart, you need an attorney and perhaps a marriage counselor. Maybe talk to your father, he's been through it all before."

"Right, advice from a guy who shagged more women over a lifetime than any man deserves. For Christ sake, he should be in some sort of a sex addict rehab clinic."

"Modern medicine has certainly extended his illustrious career," said Cabot while sliding the business card of his attorney friend across the table. "I saw him with a hottie the other day, young enough to be your sister. He's not going down without a fight."

"When did life become so complicated?" asked Greyson with a shake of his head and look out the window, watching the common man walk by.

"Stuart my good boy, anyone would kill to be in your shoes. Stay the course young man. You have everything in front of you. Look at me for Christ's sake, it's all in the rear view mirror. Blink your eyes and it's over."

Two minutes of silence went by during which time Donald Cabot had a third drink and stared at the waitress' figure down the aisle. She was middle-aged with a strangely attractive portly frame, not wearing a wedding band. He checked his watch, aware of another appointment across town in an hour, perhaps time for one more drink.

"Your right," said Stuart with a purse of his lips and bob of the head, coming out of his funk. "I'm Dr. Stuart Greyson, associate professor of general surgery at the Philadelphia General hospital. Life is good. It doesn't get any better."

"That's my boy!" said Cabot. "Keep telling yourself that and make the call."

Stuart took the business card off the table and studied the attorney's name. With a smile he looked at Cabot and placed the card in his upper left shirt pocket, then dabbed his lips with a napkin.

"Now listen," said Cabot. "I shouldn't be telling you this because I can be arrested, but I've recently become privy to a deal down in the Cayman Islands that is too good to be true. Can make enough dough to put Stuart Jr. through college ten times. Are you interested?"

"Talk to me Donald," said Greyson with a wild look in his eyes. "Talk to me."

Early afternoon found Greyson back at the PGH, strictly for administrative purposes. By four o'clock in the afternoon he was in a West Philadelphia athletic club, pushing some weights, his sculpted body smiling back in the mirror. A hot sauna eased his fatigued muscles followed by a shower. A two-block stroll east took him to happy hour at a trendy pub, packed with people of his ilk. He was meeting the recently befriended reporter from the *Chronicle* to further discuss the Lysovage project and its future. A light dinner followed, complements of the fourth estate.

Six o'clock found the young doctor strolling confidently into the lobby of the Marriott, which sat opposite the PGH. The hotel was connected to the PGH via an above the street crosswalk, conveniently located for visiting family members to stay. Being a frequent patron of the facility the doorman tipped his index finger in salute. Once inside he nonchalantly scanned the foyer, easily spotting her bleach blonde hair in a ponytail across the way. A subtle nod set the plan in action.

Over the years he learned to easily spot the interested medical student. She was the one whose smile was just a bit broader and skirt a bit tighter, occasionally acknowledging his double entendre. They were easy prey, in awe of a young attending showing some interest in their earthly existence. Today's selection particularly interested him, having a friend with a quirky physical resemblance that made telling them apart difficult. It was such a fascination that he looked for in a potential bedmate.

The elevator ride took him up alone to the top floor. He always reserved the Betsy Ross Suite looking east which provided the most fantastic view of the Philadelphia skyline. The vista was breathtaking, including a most peculiar angle of William Penn a top city hall. After opening the drapes he set the room temperature and freshened up. Exactly ten minutes later a knock on the door admitted the luscious guest of honor, followed by a champagne toast. What then transpired was a byproduct of Stuart

Greyson's genetic composition, mutated by generations of natural selection and honed by his father's perversion. The promiscuous student knew what was in store, but was caught off guard by the expanse and extent of the spectacle. The tryst was over in about thirty sordid minutes.

"You're one sick man," said the third year student holding a sheet up to her neckline, anger in her eyes. "Absolutely sick!"

"What do you mean?" said Greyson, standing next to window and getting dressed. "That was great. Didn't you like it?"

"You need help. What just happened is not normal."

"Ah come on, it was the first time, we just need a few more sessions to learn each other's moves. Get comfortable with each other."

"No way," said the female student jumping out of bed and quickly putting on her underwear. "There isn't going to be another time. Trust me."

"Listen," said Greyson with a step towards the young woman. "We just need some more quality time together, perhaps next week."

"Stay away from me," said the student while quickly putting on her clothes and shoes, then stepping towards the door, a tear in her eye. "Just please stay away from me."

"I can explain," said Greyson. "It's just that I've been going through some difficult...."

"Do not come near me!" said the woman with a scowl and backward step towards the door. "I've never been violated like that before. Never! You're a weird man!"

"Please, Kaylee I'm sorry," said Greyson as the student opened the door and began to exit. "Please let's talk it out. Kaylee!"

"It's Kayla! My name is Kayla!" screamed the student with a slam of the door in anger. "Kayla!" was the howl from the hallway, followed by silence.

Greyson was home by eight o'clock that evening, his alibi another late case in the operating room. His wife had bad news from the gynecologist and by ten o'clock they were both in bed, staring at the ceiling, wondering where their young lives were headed.

Chapter Thirteen
THE OFFER

"WHAT WAS THAT?" asked Phil.

"What?" said Polk. "I didn't hear anything."

"Meow."

"That. Was that a meow I just heard?"

The two were sitting in the Torpedo Room on Friday night, having just finished a day's work. Phil was wasting an hour before heading downtown for a dinner date.

"Meow, meow."

"Rick, do you have a cat down here?"

Before Polk could respond a jet-black kitten with a splash of white beneath its chin appeared from underneath a couch. The feline arched its bony back upon seeing Phil.

"Now I've seen it all," said Phil. "Are you nuts?"

"Shhhh," said Polk. "You're scaring my little precious."

The kitten then walked over to Phil and began rubbing its head against his leg with a slight purr. A small bell attached to its collar pinged.

"She loves you," said Polk. "My little baby."

"What? Where? How does this happen Rick? How does a cat end up in the Torpedo Room?"

"I found her abandoned about three blocks from here," said Polk. "She followed me home."

“Rick, you live in a hospital. A stray can’t follow you home!”

“Well she did. Try to guess her name?”

Phil just shook his head in disbelief. The cat then began playing with a beer cap on the floor, disappearing beneath the couch.

“The Liberty Bell. Her name is the Liberty Bell,” said Polk. “Get it? Philadelphia and the Liberty Bell.”

“Yea, I get it Rick.”

Just then the door opened and in walked Maurice, just off his own work shift and planning to watch the ball game with Polk. The cat immediately shot out from beneath the couch, darting across the room. Maurice didn’t flinch.

“Whoa, a rat,” said Mo.

“Mo, close the door,” said Polk. “The Liberty Bell is an indoor cat.”

“A cat? Looked like a puny rat to me. What up Drummer?”

Mo headed to the fridge and popped open a beer. He informed the two doctors that the sub-basement of the hospital was infested with mice and a few rats, saying that the Liberty Bell would be good for pest control.

“Don’t declaw her,” said Mo. “She’ll be a better hunter with the claws. Lethal.”

“I would never declaw a cat,” said Polk, while pointing to a scratching post he bought earlier in the day. “Got her a post.”

“Where’s the litter box?” asked Phil.

“Tucked away on the other side of the wall,” said Polk. “Some sort of a boiler room next door, she can get through a crawl space over there.”

Phil continued to shake his head, avoiding reason with the two. He deferred on a beer and watched the first quarter of the basketball game before departing for his dinner date.

It was a warm spring evening outdoors and the walk took him five blocks from the hospital to a trendy eatery named Firenze. Fifteen years earlier it was located twenty blocks west and called Flo's Diner after its owner. Flo was a hard working mother of seven who loved to cook and opened the eatery after encouragement by her relatives. The small restaurant became an immediate success and catered to a growing fan base, migrating to West Philly after five star reviews. Soon the small corner shop could not handle the masses and a local group of businessmen convinced Flo into moving east towards the Penn campus. She agreed, as long as the diner maintained her namesake. A marketing firm along with a smooth talking attorney convinced the proud owner to modify the name to Florence's and ultimately Firenze. The food was the same, but the trendy name and atmosphere easily justified a thirty percent markup on all entrees. Flo still owned fifty one percent of the complex and worked in the kitchen nightly, cooking up her signature meals.

"I'll have the Chicken Grand-Mere," said John Mitchell. "It's my favorite here."

"Very good choice," said the waiter who then looked at Dr. Riles. "And you sir?"

"Is the Mahi-Mahi fresh?" asked Riles.

"Why yes sir, it is."

"I mean fresh like over the past twenty four hours fresh? I don't enjoy Mahi-Mahi that has been sitting on ice for more than forty-eight hours. Too tough for my liking."

"Well sir, I can't exactly tell you when it was caught, but other customers have thoroughly enjoyed it today."

"Well if you don't know then I will have the Chipotle Grilled Salmon with Pineapple-Avocado Salsa. Is the salmon farm raised or wild?"

"We have the wild salmon option but that price is market based, not the menu price," said the waiter.

"North Pacific salmon?"

"I believe so, yes sir."

"I'll take it," said Riles who never passed up an opportunity to dine on the tab of CEO Mitchell. "And please make sure it is cooked by indirect heat methods only."

"Why yes sir, I'll talk to the chef personally," said the waiter. "A most excellent choice. And you sir?"

"I'll have Flo's Special, the pierogi and kielbasa combo, with horseradish," said Phil. "Sounds like a Sunday dinner back home."

"My favorite," said the waiter. "Thank you gentlemen, I'll be back with your appetizers shortly."

"And waiter, one more thing," said Riles. "Do you have Schmidt's beer on tap? That would go wonderfully with the appetizer."

"Schmidt's? I'm sorry sir, we do not have such a beer."

"Good God Fred, that brewery shut down decades ago. They don't sell that any more," said Mitchell.

"Actually I heard it's coming back," said Riles. "Even selling it at the casino."

"Oh really," said Mitchell.

"I've never heard of it," said the waiter. "Is it an import?"

"No, no of course not," said Riles. "A local brew. I suggest you put it on your menu."

"Yes sir," said the waiter. "I will notify the manager."

The three sat at a corner table on the second floor of a building overlooking Market Street. The table was positioned a bit away from the other patrons allowing personal conversation to flow easily. Riles began the discussion by embellishing the wonders of academic medicine and all it stood for. Next CEO Mitchell touched upon the changing landscape of medicine and the power of numbers, stating the PGH was the "big boat" a young surgeon needed to be on to assure financial survival. Riles finally made the offer, a two-year contract for Phil to join the staff at the PGH, starting in July. From the sounds of the chairman, it was an opportunity that no sound minded person would ever pass up.

"Wow, I'm just overwhelmed," said Phil. "An honor, thank you Dr. Riles and CEO Mitchell." Like any new graduate from a training program, Phil had no questions to ask. After being treated like a second-class citizen for the past nine years and living just a click above the national poverty line, any job offer was a blessing. Unfortunately before he could speak the beauty of the moment was spoiled by an avalanche of clauses brought up by the two elder statesmen.

"The base salary again is $150,000," said Mitchell. "The standard base for all associate professors starting out."

"Wow, I don't know what to say but thank you." Back home in Phil's old neighborhood no person within a ten-mile radius made half that amount of money.

"Of course you have to generate revenue over $300,000 to justify the base," said Mitchell. "Sometimes the first year is tough to generate that type of income. It may take a while to build a practice."

"And if I don't?"

"Then the base salary is adjusted downward, standard protocol," said Mitchell. "We have the accountants take care of it all so you don't have to worry."

"I see."

"That's revenue solely billed and collected under your name," said Riles. "It does not take into account revenue generated from your referrals to PGH's ancillary services."

"Ancillary services. I'm not sure what that means?"

"The Philadelphia General generates a significant amount of revenue from your patients going to physical therapy, occupational therapy, our laboratories and radiology department," said Riles.

"And the MRI unit," said Mitchell with a businessman's smile. "The magnet that keeps us all together. We can't officially put it into your contract but the expectation is that you keep all your patient's and their imaging studies within our system."

"Of course."

"What happens when I generate more than $300,000?" asked Phil feeling a bit cynical.

"All the better," said Riles. "Many surgeons do and that money goes into a special chairman's fund." While saying the word "chairman" he held up his fingers in quotation fashion. "At the end of the year the excess funds are distributed to the staff based on the discretion of the department chairman."

"It's a policy of all departments," said Mitchell. "The chairman can then reward certain physicians based on his or her understanding of the entire staff dynamics."

"I see."

"Philip, we have chosen you as one of the best," said Riles. "This is a win-win situation for all of us. To top it off you will receive two weeks of full paid vacation and we will put you on the fast track to full professor by the age of forty-five."

Nurse Hudson's warning shot right into his cranium, alerting him of waking up some day and being forty-five years old. He thought of how good she felt in his arms, and why he was thinking such a thought at this moment.

"Of course we have to bring up one more detail," said Mitchell with a lift of both hands as if bracing Phil for bad news. "A legal term called a restrictive covenant that every physician in the system, including full professors must abide by."

"A restrictive covenant?"

"Yes," said Riles looking behind himself impatiently for his food to arrive. "Once we market you, build your practice and promote your name, we can't allow you to take your services elsewhere and compete against us."

"Take my services elsewhere? I don't understand?"

"As an example let's say you are unhappy at the PGH and resign, then go across town to Temple and reopen your practice," said Mitchell. "Certainly your patients would find you and leave the PGH system. It would be a loss of business for our system."

"They can't follow me somewhere else?"

"It's not that they can't follow you," said Mitchell. "It's that legally in today's world of competition, we can't allow you to practice nearby."

"It only applies if you ever leave us," added Riles. "Which is highly unlikely."

"Wow," said Phil. "I guess I have a lot to think about. What exactly is the covenant?"

"Two years and fifty miles from any PGH owned hospital, clinic or ancillary service center," said Mitchell while shaking his head up and down. "So if you leave, you cannot join any practice within a fifty mile radius of any of our facilities."

"For a total of two full years," chimed in Riles.

"That's a big area," replied Phil.

"Dr. Drummer, all of our medical physicians have the same covenant. It's non-negotiable. I can say with confidence that any contract you sign from this point forward will have a restrictive covenant clause."

"What if I break the clause? I mean I love Philadelphia."

"You can buy the clause out by paying two full years of base salary, or be prosecuted to the fullest extent of the law," continued Mitchell. "The covenants do hold up well in court."

"Listen Phillip, the contract I have for you is cookie-cutter stuff. The wording in your contract is basically the same as mine," said Riles. "We've thrown a lot of stuff at you this evening, perhaps too much. But the bottom line is we want you. The academic position being offered doesn't come around too often, and I hope you realize that."

"I do. I do," said Phil.

Dr. Riles then pulled out a crumpled manila envelope from a leather case that he brought to the dinner. The envelope looked like it was run over by a vehicle. He slid it on the table to Phil.

"Here is the contract young man," said the chairman with a smile.

"Congratulations. We will give you one month to decide. I'm confident you will make the right decision."

"Thank you Dr. Riles. Thank you Mr. Mitchell." Phil looked at the envelope, which had the name "Drummer" written upon it.

"You're welcome son," said Mitchell. "Of course you can have an attorney look at it. I know the names of a few that can help."

"Thank you. I'll keep that in mind."

"Finally," said Riles impatiently. "Here comes the food. What took so long?"

The dinner was then laid before the trio and after further questions regarding the salmon, the banquet commenced. Flo's special was fantastic and brought back great memories to Phil.

"I keep in close touch with Dr. Albright in Nepal," said Mitchell out of the blue. "He tells me things are going great out there."

Phil just looked at the CEO, not knowing where he was going with the comment. He didn't respond.

"The man is a saint," said Riles. "I attended his lecture. To return to the squalor of that country year after year is commendable."

A significant moment of silence passed among the group, aware of the sensitive topic at hand.

"I mentioned to Dr. Albright that I was having dinner with you this evening Philip," said Mitchell. "He wanted me to specifically pass on the fact that a Ms. Ranier is doing marvelous. A wonderful physician assistant who is making a major impact in the community."

"That's wonderful news," said Phil suddenly appreciating a queer feeling in his stomach.

"She signed on for a full year and he is trying to convince her to be a regular in his brigade."

"Wonderful," said Riles. "I applaud those people who make the commitment... trying to help the less fortunate."

"He specifically stated that she has a natural ability to connect with the populace in Nepal. A "gift" is the exact word he used. Quite a complement coming from Dr. Albright, who as you know doesn't dispense kudos on a regular basis."

"He is a very serious physician," said Riles chewing on his salmon. "A true professional. A tribute to the medical staff here at the PGH."

"That's great," said Phil to the CEO. "If you happen to talk to Dr. Albright again, please send my regards to Jennifer. Wish her well throughout the remainder of her stay."

"I will do that Phillip," said Mitchell in a fatherly tone. "I'm sure she will appreciate the message. As you may know, it can get lonely being away from home for so long."

Phil didn't respond, uncomfortable with the ongoing topic. His silence signified the end of the conversation in regards to Nepal.

At about the midpoint of the meal Riles then brought up the LSV project, informing the duo that as of yesterday the clinical trials were complete, having generated enough numbers to produce results that were statistically significant. He stated that it was now just a matter of crunching the numbers, analyzing the data and disseminating the information to the medical world. Optimism poured out of his being.

"I hear that you have been approached by the project director," said Mitchell to Phil. "That in and of itself is quite remarkable."

"Yes I have," said Phil. "Exciting stuff."

"I encourage you to talk to Dr. Greyson," said Riles. "He got on board with LSV immediately upon joining the staff here, and has never regretted it."

"An amazing surgeon," said Mitchell. "A wonderful example for all young surgeons coming out of training."

"Phillip, I'm aware of the meeting pending with Mr. Fanicci," said Riles. "And I just want to educate you on one important benefit of getting involved with Lysovage."

"What's that?"

"A little thing we call stock options," said Riles. "I'm not going to go into much detail but all surgeons who agree to utilize the medicine in their practice will be offered premarket stock options."

"Those are stocks, awarded at a much lower rate, available to young surgeons such as yourself," said Mitchell. "Before they are available to the masses in an initial public offering."

"The window to get involved is closing rapidly," said Riles. "We anticipate an IPO in approximately one year.

So getting involved quickly will offer you the benefit of these pre-market options."

"Yet another opportunity for you here at the PGH," said Mitchell.

"Oh, to be young again," said Riles. "Everything is in front of you, waiting to be taken."

It was then that Phil's cell phone rang. The screen informed him that the operating room was calling. Phil answered and on the other end of the line was a scrub nurse requesting his immediate services. He heard a significant amount of commotion in the background along with Doc Johnson's voice barking out orders. The crotchety old surgeon then got on the phone, telling Phil he had yet another LSV patient gone bad, again a patient of Dr. Riles.

"He's there with you now?" screamed Johnson in disbelief after being informed of the dinner. "Has his beeper or cell phone gone off over the past hour? I've been trying to get him since this old gal hit the E.R."

"No it hasn't," said Phil sheepishly.

"Well you can tell the Teflon Doc that his patient, thee Mrs. Biddleton, of the Philadelphia Biddleton family, is critically ill and about to be cut open. Now get over here stat!"

Phil notified his chairman of the news and was told to report to the hospital immediately. He was to deliver the message that Dr. Riles would be arriving as soon as humanly possible. The young doctor then sprinted back to the PGH. While putting on his scrubs he heard the overhead operator paging the cardiac arrest team to the operating room.

"Code C.A., operating room number four!" screeched the overhead voice. "Code C.A., operating room number four!"

Upon entering the room he witnessed a chaotic scene with Dr. Johnson standing at the midsection of the patient, who was lying prone on the surgical table. It appeared that no incision had been made yet. The face of the elderly female patient on the table was still and blue.

"I said continue the god-damn code!" yelled Johnson to the anesthesiologist and gang of care workers surrounding him. No one in the room moved.

"It's right here," said the circulating nurse who was standing next to the anesthesiologist. She held up the patient's chart to show the front page of a legal document attached.

"Doc Johnson, it truly is a Do Not Resuscitate form," said the anesthesiologist. "It's a full health care directive saying no mechanical intubation or heroic efforts shall be used in the event of a cardiac arrest. She's a D.N.R."

"You were just about to put the tube down the patient's throat. Intubate her you idiot, or she will die!"

"Doc, she has an agonal heart rhythm," said the gas passer firmly. "Her EKG is basically flat lined. Anything beyond this point will be heroic."

"Put the tube down her throat!" screamed Johnson. "Or we will have an intraoperative fatality on our hands!"

"No," said a second attending from the anesthesiology department who was also at the head of the table. "We are not going to be held liable for intubating a patient against her wishes. She's a D.N.R., it's that simple."

Old Doc Johnson then erupted into a tirade that only surgeons of his generation could deliver. Profanities flowed off his tongue like common pronouns in his outcry to intubate the dead patient. He demanded a representative from the legal department report stat to the room, knowing full well it would never happen. He cursed the creators of Lysovage and the product itself, calling it a plague upon humanity. As the rant continued the crowd slowly began to thin out as the corpse cooled down. Soon it was only Phil and two nurses left in the room, with Johnson still dressed in his full surgical attire, standing beside the deceased in disbelief.

"Where's your chairman?" said Johnson.

"I don't know," said Phil. "I don't know."

Back at Firenze Dr. Riles had just finished off a most delightful dessert. The Tulipes with Raspberry Sorbet was scrumptious and complemented his entrée quite well. He then requested a glass of Port wine, to satisfy his palate.

Chapter Fourteen
THE POST-MORTEM EXAM

A CONCERNED DISTANT relative and dermatologist from Nevada convinced the local Biddleton family that an autopsy was in order. The corpse was naked and prone on a cold stainless steel table, surrounded by health care workers and bright overhead lights. Dr. Jane Falcon stood mid-torso with a scalpel in her hands, already half way through the post-mortem exam. Up until that point the pathologist was underwhelmed by the findings, yet confident that the cadaver's abdomen would solve the mystery of her rapid demise. With nonsurgical skills she placed the lancet directly beneath the xiphoid process of the deceased and applied a firm downward pressure. The penetration of the blade into the peritoneal cavity produced a dull audible pop, similar to the burst of a limp balloon. The pathologist slid the scalpel down the midline of the abdomen until the firm pubic bone halted her jagged progress. Two cups of coffee that morning caused her right hand to tremble, resulting in a serrated cut. She then placed a large self-retaining retractor into the abdominal cavity and began to ratchet the instrument open, exposing the entire peritoneum.

"Oh my god!" said Doc Johnson as he leaned forward to look inside. "The other three patients had exactly the same presentation, like a blow torch went off inside."

"I've never seen anything like it," said Dr. Knight with a shake of his head, still holding a coffee cup in his left hand. "Never."

"Very impressive," said Falcon. "Obviously a diffuse inflammatory process was involved here, encompassing the entire peritoneal cavity." The pathologist then placed both of her hands into the remains of the departed and began to move her innards about in a gross inspection manner. While doing so the exterior membrane of the bowels began to slough off, producing slime on her gloves.

"Look at that," said Johnson. "The outer wall of the bowel is peeling off. Like the skin of a burn victim."

"Was this a Lysovage patient?" asked Knight.

"I'm not privy to that information," said Dr. Riles who up until that point remained silent. He too was shocked by the extent of the carnage before him, yet remained calm in response.

"Well you better be," barked Johnson. "I've spoken to the family and they are hot! Demanding answers."

"This unfortunate patient was a D.N.R.," said Riles. "She could have been saved but was allowed to expire as per her legal wish."

"Tell that to the legal team about to crawl up my ass," said Johnson.

"Please Dr. Johnson, there are students present. I would appreciate we all maintain a certain level of professionalism."

"Gentlemen, gentlemen, please," said Dr. Falcon, the saliva sound on her lips accentuating the plea. "Remain calm."

The pathologist then proceeded to inspect the major organs beginning with the stomach, whose other wall exhibited patchy areas of damage.

"Here," said Falcon. "The duodenum, an obvious duodenal ulcer that ruptured."

"Common things occur commonly," said Riles in a professorial tone, invoking the medical maxim while looking at the medical students present. "Remember that."

"Classic duodenal ulcer," said Falcon as her unsteady hand carved a section out for sample. She then handed the specimen to her chief resident to be labeled.

"When you hear hoof beats, think of horses not zebras," continued Riles to the students. "An old professor of mine always said that."

"What does that exactly mean?" asked a portly medical student, his face ashen and brow perspiring.

"It means don't always predispose yourself to making an exotic or rare diagnosis when analyzing clinical data. Horses are common in these parts, zebras rare. If you hear an animal's hoof beats in all probability it will be that of a horse."

"What a minute," said Falcon with concern, her head peering into the abdomen, nearly inside it. "Shine a light here, just behind the duodenum."

"Looks like a massive hematoma," said Knight.

"From where?" asked Johnson.

"Looks like a definite hematoma," said Falcon. "Whoa, an apparent rupture of the gastroduodenal artery. Wait a minute, actually looks like an erosion of some sort. Similar finding just proximal at the hepatic artery."

"If the hepatic artery cuts loose, death will occur in a matter of minutes," said Johnson. "I cannot recall ever hearing of a spontaneous rupture of the hepatic artery."

"Was the hepatic artery involved?" asked Knight.

"Most definitely," said Falcon while bringing her head upwards to the level position. "It looks like an erosion through the arterial wall, irregular in shape but a definite perforation." A look of confusion came upon her face. "A duodenal ulcer, perforated nearby arteries and diffuse inflammation throughout the entire peritoneal cavity causing damage to the outer bowel walls," said Falcon. "A most peculiar combination of findings."

"What could cause such a lethal combination?" asked Knight.

"I don't know," said Falcon, but I will document the damage and procure a broad series of tissue samples." The pathologist then instructed one of her residents to take of series of photographs prior to removing portions of the involved anatomic areas.

"Make sure all of these sections make it to our lab in Boston," said Riles. "Any patient involved in the LSV study must have their tissue examined there."

"We've been through this a thousand times," said Falcon, her face deep within the corpse. "I do not coordinate that."

"Why Boston?" asked Knight. "Dr. Falcon here is one of the premier pathologists on the east coast. I've trusted her readings for years."

"The protocol," said Riles. "We have an exact protocol in which the same pathology team reads all the slides. It assures continuity."

"But that produces two separate readings on a slide," said Knight. "One from the PGH and one from somewhere in Boston."

"Perhaps," said Riles. "But the reading from Boston is the one that stands. The study began in Boston, Dr. Knight."

"Does someone compare the readings?" asked Johnson. "They should be similar... I mean pathologists must abide by some sort of professional standards."

At that moment Dr. Falcon arose from the depths of the bodily remains with a two-foot section of bowel, dripping with putrid decay. She held up the specimen as if pulling a gifted scarf out of a birthday box, displaying it to the crowd. A sinister sneer was upon her face, brimming with satisfaction.

"Blaaah!" cried out the sound from behind Riles followed by the splash of a copious amount of fluid upon the floor. The crowd turned about to see the pale faced medical student falling backwards to the concrete deck, the forward propulsion of his vomit dictating his direction.

"Oh no!" yelled Riles in unison with the thud of bodily impact. "Oh no!" Looking downward it was obvious that the projectile vomit laid waste to the lower portion of the chairman's legs, soiling his pants and filling his shoes. The fluid created a splash zone involving two other students, both jumping backwards in dismay. However it was Riles who took the direct hit.

"For the love of God!" screamed Riles. "My shoes!"

"Get that kid some attention," barked Johnson, his order prompting Phil and Rick Polk into action. Within two minutes the semiconscious student was aboard a wheelchair and being taken to the emergency room. A fellow medical student also appeared ill and left the room. The chief pathology resident threw a chux pad down upon the puddle of puke.

"They're ruined!" screamed Riles stepping away from the table. He flipped off his shoes in anger to expose socks soaked with spew. "Get me some gloves!" He then tossed both shoes and socks into a nearby garbage can and rolled up his soaked pants to knee level. The dejected chairman then turned about and left the room shaking his head, leaving a trail of greenish footprints upon the floor. He spoke no further.

"He always had a black cloud above him," chuckled Knight in low tone to Johnson. "Ever since our residency days together. Some things never change."

The autopsy continued, revealing diffuse damage to the external layer of all abdominal organs. No additional abnormalities were found. Multiple specimens were sent.

"I want a full copy of your report," said Johnson.

"A copy to me also," added Knight.

"My report will be in the patient's e-chart," said Falcon. "Available for everyone's review. Should be ready in about two to three weeks." She then departed the scene as a pathology tech gathered the bodily remains of Mrs. Biddleton for cremation.

After dumping the medical student off in the E.R., Phil and Rick hustled across the medical center to the gymnasium, grateful for their early departure. It was the long anticipated second half of the season rematch between The Sweepers and The Vital Organs. This time Phil made sure he and the other key players were not on call, and the team had more than five players. The general surgeons were hungry for victory.

"Look what the cat dragged in," yelled Maurice as Phil and Rick entered the gym just minutes before tip off. "Thought you were too scared to show up. A-ha-ha-hah."

"Your goin' down Mo," countered Polk. "Down!"

"V-I-C-T-O-R-Y," said Jackie Rhimes in high school cheerleader fashion.

Shortly afterwards Phil and Maurice lined up against each other at half-court, preparing for the jump ball. The referee was a local high school kid making a few extra bucks that spring. It was his third game in a row that night. Acne pitted his young face.

"Hey Drummer," said Mo. "Gonna be hard to concentrate with your filly in the balcony."

Phil looked up to see Caroline and a nursing friend standing parallel to the baseline with smiles on their faces. Cara looked fantastic in blue jeans and a white tee shirt, and waved directly at Phil.

"She's waving at you honey," said Mo as the ball went up, easily winning the tip off from his distracted friend. The rematch had begun.

The score was tied after the first quarter in what was turning out to be a very physical game. The lone referee had trouble controlling the flow of the game and issued two technical fouls to the Maintenance team after being peppered with profanities. Midway through the second quarter a hard foul from Jack Rhimes almost resulted in a melee, with calmer heads prevailing. The hot hand of Indiana's own Mike Boyce put the Vital Organs up by six at halftime. During the break chatter continued between the teams.

"Hey Mo, tell your boys to turn it down a notch," said Troy Huckabee. "Or we are going to have a donnybrook on our hands."

"A donkey what?" asked Mo.

"A donnybrook," said Troy slowly. "You know a fracas, rhubarb, battle royal, a ruckus."

"What are you talking about?"

"He means a brawl Mo," said Phil. "A fight."

"A brawl? Trust me Drummer, if some sort of a riot breaks out here your boys will need to be hospitalized. I guarantee that," said Mo Rhett.

"There isn't going to be any fight," said Phil. "Come on Mo, it's only a game."

"It's our legacy," said Mo. "Tell Rhimes to keep his meat hook arms off my man in the middle. He should be fouled out by now."

"I will," said Phil with a smile. "I will."

By the end of the third quarter the Vital Organs opened up a ten-point lead, yet tempers continued to flare. Exactly one minute into the fourth quarter a most peculiar event occurred, perhaps a first in the annals of Philadelphia basketball. As the action crossed mid court the sprinting referee made a sharp right hand turn in full stride. His maneuver took him directly out the doorway in an escape from the gym and the fiercely contested game. Sensing physical harm, he was never to be seen again in the gymnasium.

"Stalemate!" yelled Mo.

"Stalemate? This isn't a chess match," barked Rhimes. "We're up by twelve Mo. Our win."

"No way," said Mo. "This game is under protest."

"What do we do now?" asked Phil. "This has got to be a first."

"We can't play without a ref," said Boyce. "There has to be some control."

After discussing multiple options, an exhausted Rick Polk recommended the dispute be continued downstairs over a few cold beers. His proposal carried the referendum and ended the game, leaving the outcome in limbo.

As Phil left the gym he met Cara, who was descending the stairwell.

"What happened?" asked Caroline.

"Ref bolted the gym," said Phil. "I guess he felt threatened."

"Who won?"

"Don't' know, but it doesn't matter. We have their number and can beat them in the championship game," said Phil. "That's one of my final goals before leaving the PGH, to see our team picture with a championship trophy hanging in the department library, for all of eternity. We've lost to them the past three years in a row. Boyce is the X-factor, a real pure shooter."

"Sounds serious. You didn't forget about our dinner date next week, did you?"

"No way. It should be interesting. I'm not sure we technically agreed to go but there is no turning back now."

"I looked up the restaurant he was talking about," said Caroline. "It a pretty upscale venue. I'm going to need to get a new dress."

"What about the limo they're sending? Are we really going to use it?" asked Phil.

"Sure," said Caroline with a smile. "Let's see how the other half lives."

The two then walked down the hallway, parting ways at the end, with Phil reporting to the Torpedo Room. Upon entering the room the post game discussion continued in full swing, with both teams harping on each other.

"Look what the cat dragged in," said Mo.

Phil smiled.

"No, I really mean it. Look what the cat dragged in, " said Mo pointing to the corner of the room where a dead mouse sat.

"My Liberty Bell," said Polk proudly. "My little precious."

Later that night chairman Riles had a long conversation with Vic Fanicci over the phone. He shared the disturbing results of the autopsy together with the looks of satisfaction on his colleagues' faces. The salesman offered reassurance to Riles regarding the overwhelming validity of the study, encouraging him to concentrate on the broader picture. "Nothing else could go wrong," said the Union Park executive, "absolutely nothing." After hanging up the phone a mysterious feeling overtook chairman Riles. Fanicci informed him that Mrs. Biddleton received a placebo and not Lysovage, similar to the other acute abdomen cases. Therefore the blame could not be placed upon their product.

"How could that be?" thought the elder physician. "How could that possibly be?"

Chapter Fifteen
TREKKING

Dr. Thomas Albright was a fit man who enjoyed the mountainous terrain of Nepal. His passion was hiking, commonly referred to as trekking in the Himalayas. Fortunately for him, Pokhara was the central trekking hub of Nepal. Once a year the medical director led a group of UMC volunteers into the nearby mountains for a ten-day journey in April, considered the dry season. Their route was along the Annapurna Circuit, frequently voted the best long distance trek in the world.

"Ready Ranier?" asked the medical director.

"Yes doctor," was her response. Jen was looking forward to the trip for weeks, needing a break from the daily clinical grind.

"Do you know a famous mountain is named after you in the states?" asked Dr. Albright. "A majestic icon of the northwest landscape."

"Would it happen to be called Mount Ranier?" asked Jen. "That's my educated guess."

"Well then you have heard of it."

"Of course," said Jen. "Ever since junior high school. The boys used the name to safely hurl sexual innuendos in my direction."

"Ah puberty," said Albright. "An exciting and confusing time for the teenage male."

"Like let's climb Ranier, let's mount Ranier or I'd love to scale the twin peaks of Ranier," said Jen shaking her head.

"That's nothing," said Albright. "I was raised in Buttzville, New Jersey. The poor girls in my high school had no chance. We were all fixated on rear end comments."

"Oh to turn back the clock of time," said Jennifer. "My dad always said if only I knew then what I know now. I'm starting to realize what he meant."

"True," said Albright. "But there is no turning the clock back. We have to continue looking forward. And by the way, I've had the distinction of making it to the top of Mount Ranier, and it was indeed a glorious climb."

"Well the boys in homeroom were right," said Jen with a smile. "I should have listened to them."

A total of fifteen UMC volunteers signed up for the trek, ten males and five females. Dr. Albright selected a ten-day, moderate intensity loop through the mountains. Only basic gear was required and included a well fitting pair of boots and sleeping bag. No mountain summits were to be approached, which allowed any fit volunteer to participate. Quaint Tibetan teahouses dotted the trail and offered simple meals of local fare. Rustic hotels provided basic lodging in unheated bunk bed style dorm rooms. The deep culture of Nepal and unbridled friendliness of its people permeated the entire route. Albright's selected route offered spectacular mountain views and the occasional Buddhist temple, complete with yoga and meditation classes.

The first day of the adventure involved a rugged two-hour bus ride along a mountainside, followed by a one-hour hike. Day two involved ten miles of hiking up a steady grade, then dinner and an overnight stay in a rustic

Zen monastery. It was the second evening of the trek that found Albright and Ranier outside the monastery teahouse enjoying the view.

"Sore?"

"You bet," said Ranier. "I've lost ten pounds over here without any late night snacks, but I'm still grossly out of shape."

"The trail doesn't get any harder than today," said Albright. "The thin air also plays into the equation. Tomorrow is actually the shortest leg of the trip, a good recovery day."

"I think Sara is really enjoying the trip," said Jenna in reference to her roommate.

"Do you think she will stay longer at the mission?"

"Not a chance," said Jen with a smile. "She needs some alcohol, a cellphone, the internet and her boyfriend. Not necessarily in that order and perhaps all at once."

"Most people enjoy their time here," said the medical director. "It's only a handful that fall in love with the place and people. Like me."

"What brought you here initially?"

"That's simple," said Albright sitting down upon a wooden chair. "I found my wife in bed with my best friend one afternoon. Thought I would surprise her by coming home early, but I got the surprise. I'll never forget that visual."

"Ouch. Sorry," said Jen.

"Not your fault," said Albright. "It was the best thing that ever happened to me. I mean in the beginning it was utter devastation, we were divorced within six months." The director paused to slightly gather his composure, but did not hesitate to continue. "It happened at a good time. We were married just two years, had no children and were poor, so the split was simple."

"How could it be the best thing that ever happened to you?" asked Jen.

"It made me recalibrate, led me to a career in Travel Medicine and Nepal. The past eight or ten years have been wonderful. No regrets."

"Where is she now?

"In Scranton, two kids, a boy and a girl."

"Still with your ex-best friend?"

"No, divorced or separated, I'm not sure."

The devotional bell of the monastery rang, signaling meditation class in fifteen minutes. The couple sat silently for a few minutes, staring at the mountains before them. The sun was setting to their left above a snowcapped peak, the weather cool.

"What about you?" asked Albright. "What brought you here, my inspirational lecture? I do remember you sitting in the second or third row."

"Of course the lecture," said Jen with a smile. "And the fact that I'm in my mid thirties, single and searching for some sort of meaning and direction. The usual stuff of Hollywood movies."

"But this isn't a movie," said Albright. "Right?"

"A horror movie maybe," said Jen. "But not a happily ever after one. At least it doesn't appear to be."

"Oh, Jen, I almost forgot," interrupted Albright. "I received an email from CEO Mitchell just prior to our departure and he wanted me to pass along a message."

"What?"

"He had dinner with chief resident Drummer the other night and Dr. Drummer sends his regards. Wishes you well and safe travels throughout the remainder of your journey."

Jennifer did not respond, the news bringing immediate warmth to her heart. She smiled softly.

"Jen, I know why you are here," said Albright. "Let's face it, you and Drummer were a high profile couple at the PGH. Everyone followed you two. The perfect couple to many."

"Not exactly perfect," said Jen. "Otherwise I wouldn't be here talking to you outside a tearoom, and wondering where the bathroom is."

"Everything works out in the end," said Albright. "Look at me and my life. I couldn't be more content."

"I hope you're right."

"Think of all the good you have done so far," said Albright. "The impact you have had on so many women and their daily lives. How about little Maya? You saved her life Jen.

"I know," said Jen. "I love that girl. But I'm waiting for some sort of spiritual switch to flip. Something needs to click before I leave, at least I hope so."

"Listen," said Albright. "The only advice I have is to listen to the mountains, the mystical power of this part of the world. Look at the women and children along the trail and appreciate the simplicity of their lives, the depth of their smiles. It may sound corny but to me this is heaven. Heaven on earth, free of all those things that trouble you back at home. Once you experience heaven, your perspective on life and relationships can only be different, for the better."

"I did appreciate that on the trail," said Jen. "Everyone was so welcoming."

"Trust me, by the end of your stay here, you will leave a better person. Life will be better for you and everyone around you, including Dr. Drummer."

"I think you may be right Dr. Albright."

"Please, call me Tom," said the medical director. "Now let's get down to the temple for some meditation. I'll have you humming and chanting by the end of the day."

"Thanks Tom, but medically speaking I really have to pee. Where is the bathroom?"

"Over there," laughed the director while pointing towards a shed where two oxen were hitched. "It's an outhouse, but a fancy one at that. Just watch out for spiders."

Jennifer took the medical director's advice. Over the next three days she adapted quite well to the high altitude and felt reinvigorated. On the morning of day number five she was walking at a brisk pace next to her roommate, the morning sun in their faces.

"I'm tuckering out," said Anna Black a bit short of breath. "How much higher can we go?"

"I think we are at max elevation," said Jen. "At least that's what Dr. Albright told me last night."

"What do you think of our spiritual leader?" asked Anna.

"Knowledgeable. Definitely has a love for the area and its beauty."

"I agree," said Anna. "I also think he has some love for a fellow volunteer."

"Who?" asked Jenna, tripping over a rock.

"You."

"No way," said Jenna with a laugh. "What makes you think that?"

"Come on girl," said Anna. "He perks up around you, gets your cup of coffee in the morning and constantly stares at your behind. You must appreciate that."

"Yea, I do."

"Not a bad looking guy," said Anna. "Physically fit, has a great smile and nice butt."

"Yea, I agree. A fantastic smile."

"Only a few years older than us, thirty nine or forty. What's your guess?"

"He married right out of training, was divorced in two years and has been tremendously happy for eight or ten. I'd put him just shy of forty."

"Young for a department chairman," said Anna. "I hear he's dated a lot of nurses back in Philly. Broke a lot of hearts."

"He started the Travel Medicine program," said Jenna. "Landed him the chairmanship at a young age. He loves Nepal, thinks he is in heaven."

"In my condition I'd give him a good roll in the sack right now," said Anna. "God I miss my boyfriend."

"Can't do it," said Jenna.

"Why not?"

"Bad luck. The Sherpa guide told me. These mountains are sacred to them. Trekkers are not allowed to have sex on the mountain."

"No way?"

"I'm not kidding. He told me in broken English that "making sauce" was forbidden on the mountain trail. Would anger the Gods and bring bad luck."

"Making sauce?" said Anna with a hearty laugh. "I'll make sauce whenever I want. In fact I made a little sauce on my own last night."

Jenna burst out laughing as the duo turned a tight corner, the sun now in their eyes. She failed to see a jagged rock on the trail that caused her right ankle to supinate. She let out a yell as her ankle rolled over, the high top boots unable to withstand the force. Two audible pops signified the lateral ligaments of her ankle tearing, sending her on a downward spiral along the steep mountainside.

"Jenna!" yelled her roommate.

Within three terrible seconds her downward tumble was over, placing her body prone on a ledge, unconscious.

"What happened!" yelled Dr. Albright rushing back to the scene.

"She tripped," said Anna. "Tumbled right over the side. It happened so quick."

Looking downward they saw Jenna starting to raise her head and move her extremities, attempting to get up. Her movements were slow.

"Jenna, don't move!" yelled Albright. "Stay still! Do not move!"

Within minutes Albright and the guides skillfully rigged up a series of ropes allowing the director to rappel down to the ledge. Jenna was stunned yet responsive, and moving all extremities. She complained of significant ankle pain and a headache but fortunately her spinal cord appeared uninjured.

"Alright," said Albright after completing a neurological assessment and extremity exam. "Looks like a concussion and bad ankle sprain. Do you remember the fall?"

"No," said Jenna, her voice trembling. "What happened?"

"Sounds like you tripped on a rock and tumbled down the mountainside."

"Oh, my head hurts," said Jen, now holding the back of he skull.

"O.K., just take a few slow deep breaths," responded Albright while wiping some dirt and gravel off Jen's forehead. Her lip was slightly cut but the rest of her face spared. "Let's get you off this ledge. You are one lucky lady."

The director then carefully placed a harness around Jennifer, which was attached to the pulley system above. For several minutes he calmly sat bedside the fall victim, offering reassurance, his firm arm around Jen's shoulder helping to recalibrate her senses. When she was capable of assisting Albright stood Jennifer up while attaching their harnesses together. Upon his command the rescue team above began to slowly hoist the duo up, their bodies intertwined. During the ascent Jennifer constantly apologized while mumbling something about nurse Black making sauce on the mountain. She held on tight to her rescuer during the rise as their frames interlocked to perfection in a peculiar way. The rescue was flawless thanks to the experience of Albright and the Sherpa guides. Jennifer although dazed, was soon atop the trail, supine and receiving medical attention.

"Her pressure is good," said nurse Black while unwrapping a sphygmomanometer from Jen's left arm. "Bilateral breath sounds full. Pulse is eighty-five."

"Good. Just a minor scrape," said Albright while cleaning the laceration on Jen's lower lip. "No stitches necessary."

The medical team then completed a detailed extremity exam on Jennifer, which failed to identify any other injuries outside of her right ankle sprain.

"No bony tenderness," said Albright while holding Jen's ankle. "I don't think it is fractured, let's get a wrap on it."

"Should I call in a helicopter?" asked one of the local guides. "There is a level clearing about one kilometer ahead."

"I don't think so," said Albright in a serious tone. "I think we should be able to get her off the mountain safely. What do you think Jen?"

"No helicopter please," said Jen. "I can get up and walk." She tried to arise from the seated position yet could not, wincing in the process.

"Easy," said Albright while holding her down. "You're in no condition to walk Jen, but I do have a plan."

The team leader decided that he and Anna Black along with two Sherpa guides would head back down the mountain with Jenna. The main group would continue along on the journey, being just four days away from their destination and ride home. Albright had complete confidence in the local Sherpa he entrusted the group to, having traveled with them many times before.

Jennifer rode down the mountain in a crude chair stretcher fastened to the back of a volunteer, protesting the entire way. The Sherpa guides along with Albright set up a rotation to each carry Jenna approximately a half mile, easing the cumulative burden. With Jenna stable the team was in no rush, allowing gravity to assist in their careful descent. They were able to secure lodging and receive food in the local villages, thanks to the guides. Day four of the exodus found them back at the Zen Monastery with Jen free of headaches and able to walk short distances.

"Thanks again," said Jen to her rescue team as they sat around a rustic table eating dinner. Her plate held a small portion of rice, a piece of fruit and an unidentifiable slice of meat. She had learned to trust the local food, her stomach only recently starting to growl.

"Jen, stop thanking us," said Albright with a warm smile. "It's not like we could have just left you there on that ledge."

"I think a lot of the villagers thought you were a goddess descending from the mountain," said Anna. "You know, a blonde with deep blue eyes, sitting in a chair being carried by her servants."

"It is better to travel well than to arrive," said the local priest sitting at the table, considered a bodhisattva by the locals. "What we think, we become."

"Well spoken," said Albright to the priest. "Very well said."

"I'm just glad I can walk," said Jen, now sipping her tea.

"The foot feels the foot when it feels the ground," said the host.

"Wow, I'm approaching Nirvana," said Anna a bit sarcastically.

"Nurse Black remember, better than a thousand hollow words, is one word that brings peace."

"That's beautiful," said Jennifer. "Beautiful."

That night the three guests slept together in a bunkhouse, along with several other trekkers passing through. After coaxing a giant spider out of the room, Dr. Albright dutifully performed a post concussion neurologic check on Jen. She was alert and oriented to person, place and time. He pulled a single blanket up to her shoulders and bid Jen good night. Albright then crossed the room and slid into a bunk beneath nurse Black, a dim candle slowly starting to burn out.

"Good night nurse Black," said Dr. Albright. "Remember the way is not in the sky. The way is in the heart."

"For heaven's sake, enough of the Zen crap," barked Black. "I'm trying to make some sauce up here."

As the UMC director gathered his thoughts he looked to his left where Jennifer rested, her eyes closed, the flickering light shining upon her face. She was truly a goddess he thought, possessing an intoxicating mystique. As the candle extinguished, his mindset approached absolute peace and utter bliss. Like most mortal men before him, he had fallen in love with the deity from Baltimore, who was so far away from home, searching for an answer.

Chapter Sixteen
THE HONEY DO LIST

"I'm not sure," said medical student Kayla Lehigh, her voice cracking.

"You're not sure, well let me ask you again. Was his penis circumcised or uncircumcised?"

"I can't recall," said the third year medical student, wondering why she hadn't taken her mother's advice.

"Perhaps you can answer this next question," said the male inquisitor. "Did he have one testicle or two? A simple question."

"Ah, I'm not sure. Really I have to say I didn't actually, I mean I can't answer that question with one hundred percent certainty," said Kayla, some sweat starting to roll down her right axilla.

"Young lady, these are important questions that need to be answered before we proceed. We can go no further until this information is available."

"I know, I know," said Kayla waving her hands in a somewhat nervous fashion. "It's just that it was late and I'm kind of tired this morning. My memory is a bit vague. I didn't sleep well last night." A bead of perspiration started to roll down her back as she faced the group.

"Oh, I'm sorry to hear that, but a man's future is in our hands. We have to be exact and I'm sure you understand that. Now, did you or did you not get a visual of his genitalia?"

"I did not," said Kayla firmly in a manner that would hopefully put the issue to rest. "I did not."

"How about a rectal, did you perform a digital rectal exam?"

"No," came the sheepish response. "I did not perform a rectal."

"For the love of God what type of physical examination did you perform?" screamed Doc Johnson with a wave of his arms, his arthritic shoulders not allowing them to proceed above the shoulder horizon. "Who supervised this admission history and physical?"

"I did," said Westbrook standing in the middle of the medical group that early morning.

"You did Westbrook?" said Johnson with a smirk. "Oh, well that makes me feel better. So let me ask you Dr. Westbrook, was the patient circumcised and did he have two balls?"

"Yes," said the intern, also starting to sweat.

"Are you sure Westbrook? Because I'm about to go into that room and examine this patient. Would you bet your professional reputation on it?"

"Yes," said the intern. "He is circumcised and has two testicles."

"And why is that important in a middle aged man admitted last night with stomach pains and an apparent abdominal wall defect on ultrasound?"

There was no response from the trembling student or intern. They were on the general surgery floor, just outside the patient's room.

"Does anyone read anymore?" asked Johnson. "I mean when I was a student we admitted the patient overnight, went home and read as much information as humanly possible regarding their disease process, and then regurgitated that information to our attending on rounds the following morning. We physically picked up a book and manually turned the pages in a quest for knowledge."

No one spoke.

"I remember not getting sleep. I remember being tired. But for Christ's sake I knew everything about the disease process that landed that patient, my patient, into the hospital."

Silence.

"I know what the problem is, but there is no cure," continued Johnson. "Drummer, do you know what the problem is with medical students now a days?"

"Cell phones?"

"Exactly," yelled Johnson with a downward drive of his clenched right fist. "Cell phones! A plague upon humanity! Everything is let me check the internet, let me pull up that info, let me Google it! Therefore the brain of a modern medical student is empty, void of any information that can be recalled without the assistance of a cellular device. A real pity, because even in my current state of age appropriate mental decline, I can recall more medical minutia than any graduating student has in their skull. And that's a shame, a real shame."

There was silence among the group. No one dared move.

"Drummer, can you please tell these students, and I use that term loosely, why it's important to know what is going on down in this patient's groin?"

"Because there is a direct correlation between an undescended testicle and an abdominal wall defect," said Drummer. "If a patient has one, you have to be on the lookout for the other."

"Thank you chief resident Drummer. That is the correct answer that I've been looking for. I apologize to everyone else that it took so long to discover. Now let's go inside and examine this patient thoroughly and in the correct fashion, understanding that there is a correlation between an abdominal wall defect and an absent testicle."

The cranky attending along with his residents and three medical students then entered the room. Nurse Hudson accompanied the troop and remained in subtle physical contact with Drummer throughout the visit. Doc Johnson then took a precise history from the patient regarding the onset of his symptoms. He succinctly explored the patient's past medical history and family tree, searching for any hint of previous congenital anomalies. He then examined the patient's abdomen, pointing out the nuances of the exam to the students. Then the moment of truth arrived, as Doc Johnson pulled the bed sheet down below the patient's knees, exposing his genitalia. His gloved, gnarly hands reached downward to inspect the patient's testicles, after which he arose with a smile, staring at his junior resident.

"Lucky guess Westbrook," was his comment. "Lucky guess."

Westbrook just smiled with satisfaction, thankful he had played the odds with his earlier response.

"Get this man prepped for the O.R.," yelled Johnson. "He has an incarcerated bowel due to an abdominal wall defect." The old surgeon then looked at the patient saying, "You need emergency surgery mister ahh...."

"Franklin," said Drummer quickly.

"Franklin, I'm sorry. We need to repair your bowel and my chief resident Dr. Philip Drummer will explain everything to you. Understand? It has to been done today. This is an emergency young man."

"Yes doctor. Thank you doctor."

The attending then turned away and left the room, followed by his medical team, absent Phil and Nurse Hudson. Upon exiting the room they came face to face with Dr. Greyson, who was walking down the aisle.

"Greyson, ever see an undescended testicle in an adult?" asked Johnson to the junior attending.

"Yea," said Greyson. "A guy in our training program only had one testicle. We called him the 'Pete the one-ball wonder', he has about six or seven kids now."

"Thank you for the interesting anecdote," said Johnson dryly. "I'm sure the medical students here appreciate your expertise on the topic."

"How are the students doing?" asked Greyson, his gaze upon Kayla who still looked a bit shook up from her presentation.

"Don't ask," said Johnson while directing the group down the hall to the next room, where it was medical student Kaylee Pitt's turn to present a patient. "Don't ask."

After visually inspecting Kayla Lehigh's curvaceous gait down the hallway Greyson turned the corner towards the elevator. His cell phone purred, alerting him of a text from his wife. Her gynecologist just informed her that the last harvest produced two viable eggs, but the fertilization failed due to a low sperm count. Prior to enrolling in the program Dr. Greyson's sperm count was calculated and considered average, so the gynecologist now recommended the couple refrain from any sexual intercourse until the next egg harvest date in several weeks.

"O.K.?" was the question from his wife in text form. "Can you make it?"

"Sure," responded Greyson while checking a nurse out in the elevator. He had never seen her before in the hospital.

"That also means videos, internet stuff, etc..."

Greyson just paused and smiled, often wondering if his wife was privy to his vices. Apparently she was.

"Please, can you do it for me honey?" was the next text to quickly occupy his screen.

"Sure," responded Greyson as he stepped off the elevator. "For my little Mia, anything." He then continued down the hall several paces behind the young nurse, appreciating her sway and wondering what her name was.

That same evening found Dr. Knight sitting in his bedroom talking to his wife. She was in bed trying to sleep while he sat in a side chair, a computer on his lap. They had just discussed his clinical visit that day with the neurology department chairman at the PGH. An EMG of his right upper extremity identified some progression of his neurologic deficit, when compared to a prior study two years ago. The neurologist now feared a slow steady demise in the function of his right dominant arm.

"It's progressing dear," he said to her for the third time. "Progressing. Do you know what that means to a surgeon?"

"Richard, take it a day at a time. It's in the hands of God. You've had a wonderful surgical career. Think of all the other things you can do in life outside of surgery, like teaching and traveling."

"Funny," said Knight while staring at the computer screen, the other lights off in the room. "I'm only trained to be a cardiothoracic surgeon. If I can't perform surgery it's back to the bottom of the food chain."

"Don't be silly," said his wife pulling the covers upwards to dim the computer's light. "I'll say a prayer for you Richard, that always works. Remember this is a disability, not a terminal diagnosis. We still have each other."

Knight's attention had already diverted to the screen before him, and Dr. Albright's Nepal blog. Albright just posted a slew of photos that day from the Annapurna Circuit trek, which included many of Jenna. His personal medical matters evaporated upon seeing pictures of her being transported down the mountain, with facial abrasions and a bandaged leg. With concern he rapidly read the blog, describing the fall and subsequent rescue. She sustained a concussion and severe ankle sprain per the report, but only after seeing the words "non-life threatening" and "full recovery" did his mind ease. He scrolled back to the top of the blog to carefully inspect each picture involving Jenna. Although fully committed to his wife, he sorely missed the woman he once loved. She was as beautiful as ever, the focal point of most photographs, including one meditating in the lotus position. His mind wandered back to their days together, mostly fantastic, in the center city high rise. It all changed so quickly. Why had he treated her so poorly? Perhaps his physical condition was payback? If so it was fair. He owed her an apology, one sadly never exchanged. She was always faithful to him. He began to recall one hot summer night on the penthouse veranda, when Jenna was wearing a hot pink halter and tight shorts when out of the blue she began....

"Richard what are you doing?" asked the voice from bed. "I can't sleep with the light on."

"Just catching up on some work dear," said Knight gathering his composure. "Be done soon." He then paged back to prior blogs from Albright, scanning Jenna's beautiful body, part of which he paid for in cash. She appeared so happy and full of life, surrounded by Nepali children. A smile came upon his face, realizing the good she was doing, so far away. If only he had the time to do the same.

"Honey, can you do me a favor?" moaned his wife.

"Yes darling, what is it?"

"Please turn off the computer so I can sleep. The light is keeping me up. I have a very busy day tomorrow."

"Yes dear," said Knight who although still a computer novice, cleared his browsing history to keep the peace. "Yes dear, of course."

He gently closed the laptop and slid into bed to the delight of his wife who snuggled her body into the fetal position.

"Good night darling," said Knight.

"Good night."

Mrs. Knight was asleep and snoring within thirty seconds.

Approximately seven blocks away at that very moment Dr. Frederick Riles sat in his study, alone. He had just completed reading the final pathology report on Mrs. Biddleton. The report was littered with medical jargon describing a diffuse inflammatory process causing cell wall disruption and necrosis. Multiple organs were affected including the small and large bowel, pancreas, appendix and spleen. With regards to the hepatic artery the report documented a full thickness erosion that penetrated all three walls of the vessel, leading to an acute bleed and massive hematoma. The primary cause of death was deemed to be an acute exsanguination secondary to a rupture of the hepatic artery. The secondary cause of death was diffuse multi-organ peritonitis. It was obvious to the chairman that Mrs. Biddleton bled to death from a hepatic artery that burst wide open.

Riles was deeply disturbed by the report, realizing that his medical knowledge had no explanation for the findings. An acute rupture of the hepatic artery was a rare event, almost unheard of as a primary diagnosis. Even more peculiar to the medical record was a short addendum below Dr. Falcon's name, which she authored, stating that a "whitish residue was found to be pervasive throughout the peritoneal cavity, and was sent for additional testing." A notation was made that microscopic particles of the residue were sent out to the National Organization of Health, or N.O.H., a last stop for complex pathologic cases, for review and comment. The addendum was brief but implied that additional information would be pending, at a later date.

The chairman had reviewed hundreds of pathology reports during the Lysovage study, none of which contained such wording. Certainly the residue could have been Lysovage derivative, however this patient received a placebo, based on the inside information from Fanicci. A contaminant he thought, or perhaps a foreign body reaction? Whatever the case he had no answer, yet he knew a definitive answer was in the works. His knowledge of the N.O.H. was considerable, and their laboratory coldly efficient. A report from the N.O.H. was never ambiguous and their wording was always the final diagnosis. A "whitish residue" he thought, what could it possibly be?

"Frederick can you please come up here?" howled his wife. "Now!" She was upstairs, readying herself for bed.

Without hesitation he arose from his chair and tossed the report down upon the desk. After decades of marriage the tone in his wife's voice signaled punishment. He slowly trudged up the stairwell to the second floor, wondering what prompted the request. His wife stood just outside their bedroom door, a hand on her hip and a smirk on her face. She was wearing a tee shirt and panties, her normal sleep attire.

"Honey, can you do me a favor?" asked his wife. "Can you please just do me one simple favor?

"Yes dear?"

"Can you please not clog up the toilet every night? I mean the water is up to the top again, ready to flow over."

"What? I didn't clog it."

"Yes you did. I only urinated and then flushed. The water immediately bubbled up to the top. I didn't clog it Frederick."

"How could that be, I haven't been in there in over an hour?"

"Well it's clogged, and I'm not about to unclog it," said his wife. "I'm tired and am going to bed. I've had a long day. You clogged it Frederick, so please unclog the toilet."

The chairman knew he had no chance, the evidence too damning. With a sigh he slid past his wife into the bathroom suite, noticing some sewage on the floor.

"Your problem is your diet. You have to eat more fruit."

He turned right to grab a plunger out of the closet, which wasn't there. Looking to his left he saw the device behind the commode.

"I bought grapes two days ago but nobody eats them. I don't know why I buy them, they just sit there and then I throw them out."

Reaching past the puddle he grabbed the plunger and stared into the bowl, positioning himself upon dry ground.

"You have to drink more juices. What about prunes Frederick? I'll buy some prunes but only if you'll eat them. Otherwise it's a waste."

Upon lowering the rubber cup into the bowl a symmetric wave of bodily excrement breached the rim, soaking his new slippers.

"Maybe you need to see a doctor honey. When was your last colonoscopy? I read you should have one every five years now, or is it ten?"

Forcefully he drove the plunger up and down into the toilet, hoping for only a minor blockage, the resistive dullness of the suck suggesting otherwise.

"Can you please answer me!" yelled his wife over the plunging sounds, becoming more violent with each thrust. "Frederick it is impolite not to answer me. I didn't clog the toilet. Answer me Frederick! Frederick?"

Chapter Seventeen
"V" IS FOR VANESSA

PHIL SAT ON a bench outside the lobby of the Greycliff Apartments, keeping an eye on the street beyond the courtyard. It was an unusually hot spring day in Philadelphia, May a week away. He noticed a bumblebee drifting from one tulip to another, methodically inspecting each bloom in a delicate manner. The insect floated carefree between flowers while emitting a soothing buzz, carrying out its chore. His work ethic was exemplary Phil thought, pollinating plants and flowers without a complaint. He recalled his dad's advise just prior to internship four years ago – "work hard and mind your own business." Did the bee have a plan, or did it just randomly float through the courtyard in search of nectar? Where did it live? Who were its friends? Did it have feelings? Suddenly the bee darted out of a bloom and flew directly before him, hovering in a protective fashion. They made eye contact for several seconds until a soft breeze from the east drifted the drone towards a majestic PJM rhododendron in full display.

He thought of Jenna.

Their time apart was one of her creation, a "test" she tearfully said on their last day together, with only two possible grades – pass or fail. The essential component of the plan was a clause that allowed each member to interact with the opposite sex, guilt free. Up until that point Phil abided by the honor system in regards to this open dating policy, confident the approach would secure a passing grade. However time and distance were starting to erode his moral compass. Caroline Ell seemed so perfect–beautiful, young and intelligent. She was two to three years younger than Phil and despite her attractiveness, somehow unattached. Phil appreciated the fact that Caroline never pushed the envelope on their friendship, sensing that time would be the ultimate judge. Perhaps Mo was correct, maybe she was the pick of the litter.

A long black limousine then pulled up in front of the courtyard, coming to a stop. A chauffeur stepped out of the car in full attire and stood next to the side door, hands behind his back. Phil arose and walked towards his ride. The dinner date was on. Next stop, Caroline Ell's apartment.

At that very moment on the seventh floor of a tony high rise in center city, Vanessa Rose hurried about. Her color scheme that night would be fuchsia or hot pink, depending on the lighting. She wore a tight fitting dress accentuated by a pair of black spiked heel shoes, bringing her height to five feet eleven inches. Three silver bangles adorned her left wrist and rattled as she dropped half a teaspoon of Vaseline into a glass bowl. Her sights that night were directly upon Phil Drummer, whose face and physique stirred something peculiar inside her. After placing the bowl into the microwave she set the timer for one minute and headed towards a mirror. Brown eyes surrounded by smooth dark skin complemented thick jet-black hair, from a genetic stock that was one fourth Asian. A light colored strawberry bra strap slightly exposed itself, subtle yet suggestive. Her push up bra was the latest and greatest, made of some super high tech material that offered her implants up like fresh fruit–ripe on the vine, and ready for harvest. As the microwave timer beeped she pushed both of her breasts to the midline, appreciating the brassiere's conforming character. She then reached into a cabinet and carefully selected the piece de resistance, a packet of strawberry Kool-Aid. Cherry was her second choice but strawberry never failed. The twenty-seven year-old Union Park employee then carefully titrated one half-pack of the sugary concoction into the Vaseline while stirring the mixture. She wasn't sure if it was Drummer's good looks or the fact that he had a gorgeous girlfriend, but she wanted him in a strange way, more so than any recent man in her life. As her cell phone signaled a text she carefully added two teaspoons of water to the brew. The text notified her of a limo waiting outside, double-parked. With a Q-tip she carefully applied the deep red mixture to her lips in a fashion that her older sister taught her. The result was a set of luscious strawberry lips, wet and trashy, ready for some serious action. Turning to the left she picked up a small but horribly expensive bottle of perfume, a souvenir gift from a recent Paris junket. She pump sprayed the cologne twice into the airspace above in a fashion her mother taught her, and then stepped forward beneath the perfume waterfall to coat every nook and cranny of her frame in an enticing fashion. She headed towards the door but almost forgot, diverting back to the mirror. Her right hand reached down and picked up a small stickpin, coated with black opals and shaped in the letter "V". She carefully attached it to her dress at the left breast two o'clock position, thus completing her ensemble. The "V" was for Vanessa.

The venue was Lucca Cibo, an Italian eatery named after an enchanting village in Tuscany. An elderly doorman escorted Phil and Cara from their limo to the maître de, welcoming them with open arms. Phil spotted Vanessa immediately. She was chatting at a side bar with some impeccably dressed gentlemen, then excusing herself upon seeing the couple. The visual of her approach was strangely complemented by the glass of champagne that Phil had on the ride downtown. Her upper and lower body parts moved independently per the laws of gravity, yet her overall package was pure symmetry. While holding both her hands, Vanessa exchanged two air kisses with Cara after complementing her on the sleek black dress she wore. Next she turned her attention to Phil and with a squeeze of his right hand welcomed him to Lucca Cibo, her favorite Italian restaurant. Her body emitted a scent that magically mixed floral and oriental members of the fragrance wheel. She was strikingly beautiful yet despite all the curves, crests and contours that defined Vanessa Rose, it was her lips that attracted Phil, red, moist and pouty, just waiting to be sampled. The attractive hostess then escorted the charming guests to a side bar for some pre-dinner cocktails. After taking a sip of chilled vodka Phil turned to his right and was surprised to see an old friend staring directly at him.

"Phillip? Phillip Drummer? What a small world!"

It was Stacey Ricketts, Jenna's best friend and former roommate, the nidus of the Schuylkill Expressway brouhaha that jettisoned Jenna to Nepal. She was there with her newlywed husband, a tall queer looking attorney with a narrow face and ski-slope nose that resulted in a constant downward and condescending gaze upon humanity. He stood two steps behind his wife, trying to avoid being pulled into the conversation.

"O.M.G!" said Stacey loudly while holding her welcoming arms out. "Look at you Phil Drummer!" was her next line as she surveyed the two attractive women besides him. "Wow!" It was apparent that Stacey already was two glasses of wine into the evening.

"Stacey, good to see you," said Phil tentatively. He then introduced Caroline and Vanessa to her.

"I'd like you to meet my husband," said Stacey, now dragging her spouse's reluctant body into the mix. "Princeton this is Dr. Phillip Drummer, a good friend of mine, with his dinner dates, Caroline and Melissa."

"That's Vanessa with a V," said Vanessa. "Va...nessa."

"This is Attorney Princeton Brown," said Stacey proudly. "A junior partner of the Willard, Weasel and Wang law firm. He specializes in international law with a specific expertise in Asian emerging markets."

"A pleasure," said Princeton followed by an odd inhalation of air up his capacious nostrils. He declined on a handshake.

An awkward conversation ensued between the group, highlighted by a botched comedic reference to the attorney's name and two rival Ivy League schools. Phil prayed for a quick end to the conversation before Stacey could reference Jenna, keenly aware of her poor social tact. His prayer went unanswered.

"Phil, have you been in touch with Jenna?"

"No," said Phil trying to keep his answer short. "She is off the communication grid."

"No she isn't," came the quick retort from Stacey. "About four weeks ago she sent some emails from a nearby city, Peekaboo or something. Doing great."

"Good to hear."

"Going trekking with a group of fellow volunteers into the mountains," said Stacey. "Visiting a few Buddhist temples, the whole thing. Oh that's classic Jenna, she is just so beautiful. Do you miss her?"

"Whose Jenna?" asked Vanessa.

"Phil's girlfriend," interrupted Stacey before Phil could respond. "Have been a couple for the past four years."

"Oh really," said Vanessa with a bemused look. "But I thought Caroline was..."

"No, no," said Caroline with a wave of one hand. "Phil and I are just good friends. We work on the same hospital floor together."

"Stacey, perhaps we can discuss Jenna's trip in private," said Phil. "The whole story may be a bit confusing for..."

"Dear I think we should be going," said Princeton from above.

"Don't be silly," said Stacey. "There's nothing to hide. I'm sure Caroline has heard of Jenna. Haven't you Caroline?"

"Sure I have," said Caroline. "I actually met her once before she left for Nepal."

"You met her once?" asked Phil. "When?"

"She was making rounds in the hospital," said Caroline. "I was in my last year of nursing school. She was so nice to me..."

"Here's a picture of her and Phil," said Stacey with an extension of her smart phone forward. Her cell's screen was massive, and delivered a snapshot of the happy couple, arm in arm, Jenna wearing a bikini.

"I see," said Vanessa with a prolonged stare at the screen. "Wow."

"That's Phil and Jenna at a pool party we were invited to in Bryn Mawr," said Stacey. "Fancy-schmancy place with waiters serving shrimp. Do you remember that Phil? It was only last summer."

"Dear, our table is ready," said Princeton. "The maître de has signaled a second time."

"Sure I remember it," said Phil, now sensing a stare from Vanessa.

"Stacey, really," said Princeton with a tug on his wife's arm. "This reservation has taken months to secure. We don't want to lose it."

"A picture!" said Stacey. "Of chief resident Phillip Drummer and his friends!" She quickly held up her cell phone and targeted Phil, Cara and Vanessa from the waist up. A soft beep signaled focus.

"Stacey please," said Phil, unaware of the gorgeous smiles that reflexively appeared on the faces of each woman at his side. He extended his right hand forward, attempting to disrupt the photo.

"Click."

"Stacey, I must insist," said Princeton firmly. "This dinner has important implications with regards to my career at Willard, Weasel and Wang."

"Oh all right," said Stacey with a smile and step back, her mission of full disclosure accomplished. "Have a nice dinner everyone, it was so nice to meet you Caroline and Melissa."

"I think I need another drink," said Phil while watching Stacey being led away by her husband. She was pounding out text messages in supersonic fashion, a smile on her face, alerting the universe of the chance meeting.

"Me too," said Vanessa. "What an interesting friend."

Within a minute the maître de signaled the group, and led them into the dining room proper, after which Victor Fanicci appeared from a side room.

The meal was scrumptious. Throughout all six courses Vic Fanicci touched upon the benefits of Lysovage. He implored Phil to get on board to reap the benefits of stock options, frequently citing the career of young Dr. Greyson. A bottle of Italian wine accompanied every course of the banquet and by the time dessert arrived the party was inebriated, sans Caroline. The young nurse had an early work shift the following morning and stopped indulging after the first round of spirits.

All was well until Cara went to the ladies room, and Fanicci stepped outside for a cigar, leaving Phil and Vanessa alone. The salesperson told a silly joke and then leaned into Phil's shoulder while laughing, holding the position with a slide of her hand onto Phil's mid thigh. French perfume seduced his senses along with some incidental left breast contact and whiff of Chianti. The temptress then innocently leaned backwards with a smile, yet maintained her hand position precariously close to his man zone. Her homemade lipstick remained lush, the war paint now four hours old. She began to tell Phil how wonderful it would be to work with him on the Lysovage project, and travel the world together. An upcoming trip to Rio and Sao Paulo was mentioned along with an available seat on Union Park's private jet. It was when she leaned back into him to reestablish upper torso contact that all hell broke loose.

"What are you doing!" yelled a visibly drunken Stacey Ricketts from directly behind the couple. She was all liquored up and somehow dissociated from her husband. "Get away from him, you bimbo!" was her crazy cry with a pointed finger.

The entire restaurant immediately looked over to the table, stunned by the outburst. The maître de rapidly began an approach towards the crisis.

"Excuse me?" retorted Vanessa with sass, standing up to face the accuser. "Are you talking to me?"

"Yes I am!" yelled Ricketts. "And you Phil should be ashamed of yourself. Jenna loves you!"

Phil stood up and noticed Caroline approaching the table with a look of concern. He went to speak but was cut off.

"Ladies, ladies, please," said the maître de quietly. "Is there a problem?

"She's the problem," said Stacey, again pointing a finger at Vanessa, the two women face to face.

"Stacey, please," said Phil. "You don't understand what's going on here."

"Are you looking for some drama?" asked Vanessa, her mind flashing back to childhood. "I'll give you some drama."

"Let's take this discussion outside," said the maître de softly. "Where we can discuss it quietly."

"Keep your hands off him," blurted Ricketts. "He's taken." She took one step closer to Vanessa, suggesting physical engagement.

"Don't go there," said Vanessa with a glare and shake of the head.

"Stacey!" yelled the approaching voice of Princeton Brown. "What in God's name…."

"Catfight!" yelled a disturbed guest witnessing the spat.

Stacey, sensing the end of the confrontation, went mental. She abruptly shoved Vanessa backwards, causing her to fall over a chair, her heels upward in V-shape fashion. The crowd went into a boisterous rumble.

The remainder of the scene was surreal to Phil as Vanessa bounced up with a scowl and impressive right hand jab, the maître de saving the day. Her crisp right cross was diverted by the waiter's arm and missed Stacey's face by inches, followed by Fanicci grabbing Vanessa from behind and lifting her away, legs kicking. Princeton Brown together with one of his embarrassed senior partners secured Stacey's arms and dragged her back amid an exchange of profanity. Phil stared at Caroline who was now standing still, aghast by the turn of events. It ended as quickly as it began, the combatants separated and Vanessa adjusting her dress with angry arm movements, her curves still intact.

"Cheap shot," said Vanessa with a smirk. "Cheap shot!"

The limo ride home was subdued, with Caroline being dropped off first. Phil escorted his date to her apartment foyer with a sense of guilt.

"I'm sorry," said Phil. "I don't know how or why that happened. What are the odds of running into Stacey at a restaurant?"

"Everyone warned me that high drama surrounds you," said Cara. "I guess they were right. That was something else."

"Well it certainly wasn't the plan," said Phil somewhat defensively. "But I'm sorry things turned out so bad tonight."

"I know it's not your fault," said Caroline with a turn and grasp of Phil's hand. "But you have a lot going on in your life Phil. Maybe a bit too much."

"I guess you're right," said Phil. "When did things get so complicated?"

"Only you can answer that," said Caroline with a soft smile. "But take your time to figure it out, no rush." She then leaned forward and gently kissed Phil on his left cheek. "Good night Dr. Drummer. Thank you for dinner. I actually had a very nice time."

"You're welcome," said Phil as she walked away, heels clicking on the old marble floor. "Good night Caroline."

Phil returned to the limo where despite the hour, Vanessa convinced him that a late night cordial was in order. She wiped Caroline's lipstick off his cheek. The chauffer drove the couple back downtown to a trendy wine bar, where they unexpectedly ran into Dr. Stuart Greyson, himself running up a tab on the Union Park account. Greyson had a frenzied look in his eyes while taking a small plate of cheese back to a booth, a bleach blonde head of hair in a ponytail waiting for him.

Phil and Vanessa then retreated to a cozy corner table, with a view towards Market Street. They shared a bottle of red wine, she leaning tightly into the conversation throughout. Within thirty minutes she disclosed her personal story, a fatherless childhood with a drug addicted mother who somehow raised a family of four. A high school cheerleader, community college and beauty school dropout and proud recipient of an on line marketing degree. A Phillies fan and Big Sister to a young girl from North Philly named Precious. An available woman who took a punch for the team and sat opposite the doctor she had a crazy crush on. Upon exiting the lounge their limo was absent, her apartment only five blocks away, the toxic mixture of alcohol and hormones in control.

Phil thought it reasonable to walk her home, "for safety reasons." She cited a recent theft in her high rise, prompting him to escort her upstairs. Just outside her apartment door she thanked Phil for the evening with a set of arms around his frame, her curves well in hand. The goodnight kiss was soft and potent, sending Phil's senses back to childhood, a hot summer day with a cool drink, strawberry his favorite flavor. With a backwards kick of a heel she opened the door and pulled Phil into her lair, dimly lit by city lights. He heard a clink of metal as the fuchsia dress hit the floor, the sound of a stickpin, the "V" for Vanessa. She felt an ache in her heart absent for years, which burned throughout the night.

Chapter Eighteen
LEAVE OF ABSCENCE

"Who's the sister in pink?" asked Maurice, staring at the large screen. "That girl is tight."

"That's fuchsia," said Phil. "Fuchsia."

"I put my money on her."

"Here, here it is!" yelled Rick Polk at the screen.

"Ohhhh!," yelled Mo. "She went down like a bowling pin."

"Look at her high heels," said Jackie Rhimes, enjoying the show in the Torpedo Room. "Wait, pause it, can you see her…"

"Pretty in pink up off the canvas," said the color commentator from the maintenance department. "Oh a stiff right hand jab! I think it caught her jaw."

"Nah, it missed," said Phil, having seen the YouTube video for the hundredth time.

"No, it caught her jaw, play it back."

"I was there Mo. Do you see me standing between them?" said Phil. "Trust me, it missed her jaw."

"Who's the tall skinny guy holding back the wild woman?" asked junior resident Mike Boyce, sitting alongside Phil on the couch.

"Princeton," said Phil with a smirk.

"That's not a man's name," said Mo. "Drummer, why didn't your filly get into the mix?"

"Who shot this video?" asked Rhimes.

"Some portly guy in a bow tie at ringside," said Phil. "He yelled 'catfight' during the verbal joust. Give him credit, he was quick to the video."

"A real live catfight episode," said Polk with a shake of his head. "I don't know where to register this in my cranium Phil. One of my top ten *Seinfeld* episodes of all time, meow."

"Does it really have over a million views?" asked Boyce staring at the screen.

"Yep," said Phil. "Only been up on the net for one week."

"You're famous Phil," said Boyce. "Everyone in the hospital is talking about it."

"You are the crown jewel of a catfight video gone viral," said Polk while stroking the Liberty Bell on his lap. "Quite an honor."

"Lucky me," said Phil with a shake of the head. "Lucky me."

Later that morning Polk stood opposite Dr. Knight in the O.R., the only case of the day with a peculiar 11 AM start. The patient was typical for Knight, an entrepreneur from the Main Line rich with capital. Borodin's Symphony #2 got the team off to a good start but trouble set in during the third movement, two of three planned bypass grafts already complete. The tremor that morning in Knight's arm was unique in length, lasting over thirty minutes, during which time Polk stumbled through the third graft.

"Where is your skill set this morning Polk?" prodded Knight, his left hand holding his right forearm still. "Come on, I need your A-game, that's a horrible jump. This guy is a V.I.P." He was looking down upon the surgical field with magnifying loops, unhappy with the resident's work. With a pair of scissors his left hand swooped down into the chest cavity and cut Polk's suture line. "Do it again!"

"Pressure dropping a bit," said the anesthesiologist over the head sheet.

"Give him some pressors Gary," said Knight to the gas passer. "For Christ's sake you're getting paid to help out."

"Maybe we should call in Dr. Hargrove," said the scrub nurse politely. Hargrove was Knight's junior partner, new to the staff.

"Don't be silly Ella," said Knight. "Polk never fails. Westbrook, suck in the wound, he can't see! What are you paralyzed?"

No one spoke, aware of the cruel irony in Knight's comment. Tension caused the shiver in his arm to continue.

Unfortunately the dynamic duo of Polk and Westbrook failed in front of Knight's eyes. Despite their best effort, they were unable to complete the final arterial bypass graft.

"Poor protoplasm," said Polk with sweat soaking his surgical cap. "The vein is just falling apart. I'm sorry Dr. Knight. I can't do it. I'm sorry."

"Eating up the pressors," said the anesthesiologist. "Let's get a move on people."

Time stood still as Knight stared into the wound, physically helpless. Suddenly the circulating nurse silenced Borodin's symphonic masterpiece and piped in *God Bless America*, a high noon tradition in room four. Knight froze, fully realizing his structured world was unraveling. He looked at Ella Frey, his trusted scrub for decades, who gently shook her head with moist eyes. The defeated surgeon let the anthem play out to completion.

"Stop the music," said Knight sharply. "Get me Dr. Drummer. Stat!" While waiting he wondered what the great Alexander Borodin would do in his situation. The answer was clear.

Within ten minutes Phil burst into the room, a trailing catcall from the hallway behind him. He was informed of the situation at hand and quickly went to work beside Polk, under the watchful eye of their mentor. Knight's gross motor skills allowed him to harvest another vein graft from the patient's leg, which permitted the two chief residents to complete the case, a necessary role reversal. Their combined skill saved the day. The patient's vital signs stabilized and within forty minutes the crisis was over. Phil and Rick helped take the patient off bypass and began to close the sternum with wire sutures. It was then that Knight stepped back from the table.

"Ladies and gentlemen, it is with deep regret that I must inform you," said Knight. "You have witnessed my last surgical case."

Silence.

"As you can plainly see I have been dealt a cruel blow. A curse that cannot be overcome, no matter how hard I try. An affliction that will not leave me, one that perhaps I deserve."

Phil noticed tears now streaming down Ella's face.

"But it is time," said Knight, a pensive look down upon the surgical field. "It is clearly time. There is no doubt."

He then looked up at Phil and Rick and extended his quivering arm across the table, bloody handshakes exchanged.

"I envy you two," said Knight. "Good health, excellent skills and a full surgical career ahead. Out of all the residents I've seen, you two are the best. Make the most of every day men and remember where you trained. There is no place better than the Philadelphia General Hospital. Godspeed my friends."

"Thank you," replied the residents in unison, at a loss for further words.

He then sadly turned to Nurse Frey, gathering his composure.

"Ella, you have been at my side for over twenty years and I am forever grateful."

"Thank you Dr. Knight," came the tearful response. "Thank you."

"Without you I am nothing," said Knight blinking his eyes. "Words cannot express my gratitude and thanks. It is you that I will miss the most, always to my right, always ready, always prepared."

Nurse Frey began to openly sob, unable to speak.

"You are everything good in life," said Knight. "God fearing, family first, and full of joy. I shall always be grateful for your professionalism, as shall all the patients we cared for together. God bless you Ella Frey. You shall always be my dearest friend," concluded Knight with both hands extended towards her in appreciation.

"Thank you doctor," came the emotional reply from the nurse, their hands clasped together. "God bless you."

Knight then stepped back and peeled off his gown and gloves, recalling the first time he scrubbed in as a student, some thirty-five years ago. He looked towards the end of the table at a dumbfounded medical student staring in his direction, wishing they could magically change positions. Then, with conviction, the great Dr. Knight exited his beloved operative room, where Borodin would never be heard again. That afternoon he informed Dr. Riles of his need for an indefinite medical leave of absence, which the chairman granted.

Phil spent the evening alone in his Greycliff apartment, trying to recalibrate his bearings. Too much was on his plate including the Knight episode, a viral video, an employment contract, Vanessa, Caroline and of course

Jennifer. He was also trying to prepare for what would certainly be a contentious Morbidity and Mortality conference, in which Julia Rudenko was the patient. He was scheduled to present her case, which involved the use of Lysovage, at the surgical meeting. Earlier in the week he physically examined Ms. Rudenko, having discussed her current symptoms, treatment and future treatment options.

He began to analyze Rudenko's medical records, now scattered across his desk, in need of organization. To ease the burden Phil removed himself from the grid that night, shutting down all cell phone and communication devices. The freedom from social chatter–although unnerving–felt great, making him wonder how liberated Jennifer must feel.

Peculiar to the case were Rudenko's pathology reports, specifically the multiple biopsies obtained by Dr. Johnson. Immediately after the surgery Phil secured a printed report from clerk Wilma Williams, in preparation for an anticipated complication conference. The report described a diffuse inflammatory process throughout the patient's abdominal cavity, causing widespread cell wall destruction throughout the small and large intestines. He had the printed report, yet the computer system was unable to retrieve his copy. The electronic medical record rather contained a pathology report from the exact same operative date containing similar but non-identical wording. The electronic report described a diffuse inflammatory process or peritonitis, but no cell wall destruction or breakdown. The pathologist name at the bottom of the report was the same. It was a slight difference thought Phil, perhaps an addendum dictated at a later time by the pathologist.

He heard a knock on the apartment door, an unanticipated intrusion upon his solitude. Opening the door, he met neighbor Troy Huckabee, who just needed to talk.

"You're like the epicenter of everything going on," said Troy. "A true lightning rod."

"Maybe," said Phil. "I call it bad luck."

"What happened in the O.R.? The hospital is a buzz about Knight stepping down."

"I'm not sure he is stepping down," said Phil. "A temporary medical leave of absence, is my understanding."

"People are saying he had a grand mal seizure," said Huckabee. "What happened?"

Phil described the event in a somber tone, downplaying the neurologic aspect. He respected Knight too much to make light of his physical demise. Huckabee sensed his reluctance and did not push the discussion further.

"Hey, two weeks to the big game," continued Troy, quickly changing gears. "How about a few practices?"

"No way Troy," said the senior resident. "I'm swamped for time. My worlds are colliding. Plus, in a blink of an eye, I may be gone."

"Funny how time flies," said Troy. "I can remember meeting you and Jen in this very hallway three years ago. I wanted to marry her."

"She has that effect on men," said Phil with a shake of his head.

"Hope she is doing well," said Troy.

"Last I heard she is still trekking the Himalayas, must be nice."

"Hopefully she doesn't have the internet," said Troy with a smile.

"Agree," said Phil curtly, signaling an end to the conversation. "Good night Troy."

Phil returned to the Rudenko presentation for another hour. He strangely recalled the Morbidity and Mortality presentation of Willie Brown four years ago. An odd case that helped convict Jim Turner of first degree murder, the former resident of Troy's apartment. He wondered how

Jim was doing in prison, somewhere in upstate New York. He often thought of sending him a letter, but never did. Looking to the right he viewed a corkboard picture of his parents, each in their late thirties with two small boys in their arms. Mom beamed with a fantastic smile and dad his trademark grin, never showing any teeth. His father's eyes seemed to be looking past the photographer into the future, as if understanding the cruelness of time. Everything was happening so fast thought Phil, now on the doorstep of thirty and still reaching for some goal. Time to slow it down and enjoy the journey. He took a few slow deep breaths while closing his eyes, appreciating the silence.

Another rap on the door startled him. Huckabee again, he thought.

Upon opening the door however he was shocked to see Stacey Ricketts standing before him, tears in her eyes. She looked horrible, and he immediately thought of Princeton and the retribution that surely rained down upon her. Serves her right thought Phil, crazy woman. She held a tissue in her right hand.

"Oh it's you," said Phil flatly, the catfight video reloading in his mind. "How can I help you?"

"It's Jenna," said Stacey bursting into a sob. "She's sick Phil, really sick. Being rushed home."

"What?" said Phil, still a bit leery of Stacey Ricketts. "What do you mean, sick?"

"Some sort of a virus, she's flying to Germany now," said Stacey holding up a piece of paper with her left hand. "The medical director in Nepal sent me this email."

Phil slowly reached out for the paper, cautious of a layperson's interpretation of an illness. "Why you?" he asked. "Why an email to you?"

"She put me down as an emergency contact," said Stacey. "Said I was the only one that cared about her."

Phil ignored the comment and reached for the paper. It was indeed an email from Dr. Albright addressed to Ms. Stacey Ricketts-Brown, stating that Jennifer had contracted a serious gastrointestinal illness. It went on to report that she did not respond to traditional treatments available in Nepal, therefore triggering a medical evacuation to Germany, where she would be stabilized before returning stateside. The wording of the transmission was vague, intended for a non-medical recipient. Albright ended the communication by stating Jennifer was medically stable and in good spirits. The email was dated three days earlier.

"Stacey this email is over three days old. What took you so long to get here?"

"Don't yell at me Phil, I can't even think straight. My life has been hell this week."

"I'm not yelling Stacey," said Phil, aware of her emotional state. "I'm sorry."

"She's sick Phil. She needs our help."

"Stacey, were there any other emails? Phone calls? Text messages? Anything?"

"No."

"Are you sure?"

"Yes I'm sure, I've checked everything. Nothing from Jenna, which is strange. She knows how much I worry."

Phil just stared back down upon the email, searching for answers. A gastrointestinal illness, which one? Why no response to treatment? Where in Germany? Was she really stable? Why hadn't she notified him?

"Phil, Jenna needs us," said Ricketts. "Our girl needs us, right now."

"I know," said Phil, now with a look of concern. "I know."

Chapter Nineteen
HOMECOMING

Jennifer first felt the growl in her stomach at the Zen monastery, during her mountain descent. The team's unplanned exodus relied upon the food supply of local villages, awash with bacterial load. In her case it was a juicy fig, rinsed with water flowing downstream from another village with no concept of sewage management. While enjoying the local fare Jen was unaware of the chance introduction between a parasitic cyst endemic to the area and her digestive tract. Without warning, the trophozoite stage of a particularly virulent *Entamoeba histolytica* was released by the cyst, leading to a colonization of her large bowel by the parasite. Since the scientific term "histolytic" meant "tissue destroyer," she was in serious trouble. Initially she thought the symptoms were just a slight escalation of gastrointestinal distress that afflicted most volunteers in Nepal, yet her condition worsened. She suddenly thirsted for water and became quite adept at spotting rustic outhouses on the trail. As replicating amoeba bore into her intestinal wall, an unpleasant constellation of symptoms developed including weight loss, fatigue, abdominal pain and fulminating dysentery. By the time she reached the UMC mission, Jennifer was in serious need of intravenous hydration and medical management. A stool specimen confirmed the diagnosis of amebiasis, commonly referred to as amoebic dysentery.

Dr. Albright personally directed her medical care, having frequently treated amebiasis in the past. He appropriately started Jennifer on an antibiotic called metronidazole three times daily, along with an intense rehydration regimen. Initially she felt better but her improvement plateaued within a week. Concerning to Albright was a persistent electrolyte imbalance, the result of delayed fluid replacement due to the slow journey back home. One week after returning to the mission, her clinical status was beginning to deteriorate.

"Jen, I'm going to send you home," said Albright as he sat beside her on a cot.

"No, I'm O.K," said Jen, pale and thin. "Feeling better."

"Not your decision" said Albright. "I've done all I can here at the clinic. Your sodium level is dangerously abnormal."

"Just need some salty pretzels," said Jen. "Can I have more water?"

Albright was also concerned about her mental status and situational awareness, signs of sodium imbalance. Brief episodes of disorientation over the past twelve hours triggered the evacuation plan, currently in progress.

"Jennifer better?" asked little Maya in broken English. She had been at the bedside along with Albright throughout the past week. With a damp cloth she wiped Jenna's forehead, easing the persistent low-grade temperature.

"I'm all better," said Jennifer attempting to get up. The room immediately began to spin for her, prompting Albright to ease her back down upon the cot.

"In one hour a helicopter will be taking you down to Kathmandu," said Albright. "A Red Cross transport will then fly you to Munich, for further stabilization prior to heading home."

"Philadelphia?" asked Jen. "The PGH?"

"Of course," said Albright with a smile. "I've already notified your emergency contact and made the infectious disease team aware of your flight plans. Everyone is aware of the situation."

"O.K.," said Jen tentatively, unable to recall her emergency contact. "Maya, thank you for taking care of me." She reached out a weak arm to gently stroke the girl's hair, which felt soft. "I'm so glad we met."

The orphan girl grinned and stepped forward to hug Jennifer, who over the past few weeks meant everything to her. Maya then reached beneath the cot and pulled out a long colorful flag, nine feet long and eighteen inches wide. The cotton fabric of the banner almost buried the little girl who held it towards Jennifer so proudly.

"What? Maya, what is this?" said Jen in surprise.

"It's a Tibetan prayer flag," said Albright. "Some elderly woman in the village made it for you. They heard you were sick and leaving soon."

"Oh my goodness, it's beautiful," said Jen. "Thank you Maya."

"Welcome," said the girl so proudly.

"The five colors represent the elements," added Albright. "The blue with red border is specific for health and longevity, while the written text has many prayers and mantras for good health."

"It's beautiful," said Jen while stroking the fabric in her hands. "Please tell all the women who made it thank you." She pulled Maya close to hug her again. "Thank you."

"And thank you Tom," said Jen weakly. "Sorry about all the trouble, you know falling off a mountain, getting dysentery, soiling up all your linen."

"Everyone told me excitement follows you Jen. I guess they were right," said the director as he leaned down and kissed her on the forehead. "You'll be fine. Say hello to everyone at the General. I'll be back in August."

"Thank you again," said Jen, appreciative of his expert care and soothing contact.

Within two hours she was in Kathmandu, and a bit more confused. She recalled the jet taking off from the capital city and banking to the right, providing a majestic view of the Himalayas. Looking down upon Nepal she said a prayer for those in need, thankful of her time there. A metabolic coma then deposited her mind into an amnesic state for the next ten days. During this time she experienced a recurring dream:

It was her wedding day. A beautiful morning in West Philadelphia, just outside a church made of stone. The shrill of the pipe organ prompted a glance to the man beside her, tears in his eyes, asking if she was ready. She told her father yes. Two rear church doors suddenly opened prompting a capacity crowd to look backwards in anticipation, Mendelssohn's *Wedding March* echoing throughout the hall. She became a bit short of breath after taking a step toward the altar, down a long aisle, where the groom waited. Looking ahead little Maya led the way, a bed of rose petals behind. The church walls were adorned with vertical Tibetan flags, somehow flapping in the breeze, offering prayers of victory over obstacle. She spotted her childhood girlfriends in the back row, now women, a few with spouses. Her Aunt Estelle smiled as she passed by, wearing the same dress and hat outfit from the last two family weddings, her husband Chester beside her, white socks and all. Uncle Frank was there with Aunt Mike, who wore a seersucker suit with bowtie, always in style. Even Uncle George made it in from Chicago, her favorite who always seemed to be away on a business trip.

Next to him was Aunt Betty, a spinster who never forgot to send a birthday card every year with five dollars inside. It was her day and they were family, cut from the same cloth, gathering in her honor. Halfway down the aisle her father's hand calmed some nerves, the groom now coming into focus. She loved him so much. It was all happening so fast. Why so lucky? To her right she spotted Dr. Knight standing erect, Mrs. Knight at his side. He wore the same fashionable tuxedo he had on the night of their fateful car accident. On his face was a smile that conveyed acceptance and peace, their relationship now full circle. To her left stood Mr. and Mrs. Drummer, how so since they were deceased? Hundreds of candles lit the altar behind the priest, doctrine in hand and altar wine on his breath. Suddenly the moment came, when he stepped forward to accept her hand, held out by her father. So surreal she thought, maybe a dream, he being too good for her. Their hands met and she looked upwards into his brown eyes. Dr. Philip Drummer!

"Dearly beloved, we are gathered her today to join together this man and women in the holy sacrament of matrimony...."

Looking to her right she saw the groomsmen standing tall, Phil's cronies, the usual suspects. The best man, brother Joe stood calm and relaxed. To the left stood maid of honor Stacey Ricketts. There were no other females besides Stacey, strange thought Jen. She nervously glanced at Phil, sweat on his brow. Did she pressure him into the ceremony? He looked a bit pale and uneasy. Something old, something new, something borrowed and something blue. Was the lucky acorn old or borrowed? The lucky acorn, she forgot the lucky acorn! Frantically she looked at Stacey.

"The acorn," she whispered to her maid of honor. "The acorn!"

"What?" asked Stacey.

"The acorn! My lucky acorn, I don't have it."

Phil then squeezed her hand and she felt the acorn. He had it all the time, ever since their first date long ago. Go on, she thought to the preacher man. Make it quick, so I can forever be Mrs. Phillip Drummer.

"Who gives this man to be wed?"

"We do," said Phil's parents proudly.

"Who gives this woman to be wed?"

"I do," said her father and Dr. Knight in unison, causing a rumble through the crowd.

"If any person can show just cause why they may not be joined together, let them speak now or forever hold their peace." The words "forever hold their peace," rattled around the church for what seemed an eternity to Jen. The church was silent as the Reverend looked over Phil and Jen's shoulders with a smile, no objections. He then inhaled to speak.

"Stop!" yelled a female voice from the rear of the church. "Stop the ceremony!"

Everyone looked backwards to see the shapely silhouette of a female in the rear vestibule, the blazing sun behind her. She wore high heels and had shoulder length hair with thin, toned arms, standing with one foot slightly in front of the other.

Silence.

"He doesn't love her," said the woman, her voice carrying well. "He loves me!"

Jen looked at Phil for response, but his bemused face suggested otherwise.

"Tell her Phil," said the woman, taking a step forward. "Tell her who you really love."

"Phil," whispered Jen. "Who is she?"

"I was wondering where you were, wench!" shouted Stacey Ricketts with a scowl on her face. She tossed her bouquet of flowers to the ground while rolling up her sleeves.

"Phil?"

"We love each other," continued the siren. "While you were away climbing some mountain we fell in love Jen. Isn't that right Phillip?" She continued her approach towards the altar, a beautiful face coming into view. "Madly in love with each other."

"When the cat's away, the mice will play," said groom's man Jackie Rhimes. "Meow."

"Whore!" screamed Stacey as she took a step towards the aisle. "Get out of here!"

"Phil, who is she?" pleaded Jennifer, but there was no response. "Do you know her?"

"Tell her Phil, before it's too late, for everyone's sake. Tell her you love me."

"Phil?" asked Jenna with tears running down her face. "Who is she? Do you really love her?"

"Phil, Phil, Phil!" began a chant from the row of groomsmen as if they knew the harlot.

Jenna suddenly became faint and dropped the acorn, allowing it to roll towards the pews. Maya stepped forward to pick it up and put it in her pocket.

"Tell her Phil," said the wedding crasher with lips so full. "Tell her the big news."

"Get out of here bitch," yelled Stacey now beginning a sprint down the long aisle. "It's not your day!"

"Phil, what news?" asked Jenna, short of breath. "Phil, honey?"

"Catfight!" yelled a crazed guest as Stacey sped by.

"I'm pregnant everyone," said the gorgeous woman with a smile and raise of her arms in exaltation. "Pregnant! It's a boy and we decided to name him Phillip, after his father." She kissed her fingertips and brought them to her belly bump, rubbing it tenderly.

Suddenly the entire church started to spin counterclockwise as Jen staggered. Oh no, she thought as a horrific growl took hold of her stomach. Not today, please. Not on my wedding day. She looked to the right for an exit but was unable to move, her legs too weak. Stacey's impact upon the unwelcomed guest was ferocious, causing her legs to fly up into the air. A stomach pang of historic proportion then struck the bride, unleashing a horrific discharge of dysenteric debris onto her shoes and red carpet. My white dress thought Jenna as she blacked out. My beautiful white dress.

She heard Dr. Knight's voice first, asking to put the floral bouquet upon the night table. He politely requested the flowers be watered twice a day. He spoke words of apology but the context was unclear. Polk's voice then drifted in and out or her sensorium along with the youthful voice of someone named Kayla, who probed her bodily orifices. However it was a soft caring voice that brought her back to life, asking her to wake up.

"Hey girl, can you hear me?" asked Nurse Hudson. "Jenna, wake up!"

Upon opening her eyes she squinted from the bright overhead lights. Looking to her left she saw a beautiful display of sunflowers, her favorite. Get well soon balloons littered the ceiling.

"Good morning Jennifer, rise and shine," said Hudson.

"Where am I?" asked Jen, rubbing her eyes.

"The PGH," said Hudson as she fluffed the pillow behind her head. "General Surgery floor, you got here about six hours ago."

"What?" asked Jen, "How can that be? But my wedding, my wedding, it was ruined, who was that woman? Oh what a disaster!"

"I think you've been dreaming," said Hudson. "But then again I've had two weddings that truly were disasters."

"My dress, it was ruined and the acorn… the acorn," said Jen sitting up in bed. "Where is little Maya?"

"An acorn? Maya?"

"Yes, oh it was a beautiful day for a wedding, but then suddenly she appeared, you know when the priest asks for anyone to speak now or forever hold their peace."

"Who did you marry?"

"Phil. Who else would I marry?" said Jennifer sharply. "Philip Drummer. Where is Phil?"

"Of course, Phil Drummer. Who else does anyone around here dream about? Now you are coming to your senses," said the nurse remembering how good Drummer felt in her arms. "Alert and oriented, fully recovered."

"Lucy is that you?"

"Yes Jen, Juicy Lucy. Remember all our crazy nights out together."

"Oh Lucy, its so good to see you. Where am I?"

"The Philadelphia General, and we need to get you cleaned up woman. Some man company is coming soon."

Over the next fifteen minutes Nurse Hudson unleashed an emergency primp job upon her girlfriend. She sponged her body down and combed her straggly hair. Mascara followed with a touch of eyeliner and rouge. Then came the lipstick.

"Pink?" asked Jen.

"Yes," said Nurse Hudson. "It goes with the sunflowers and morning sunlight, trust me."

"But it doesn't match the gown," said Jen.

"I'm getting you a new one," said Hudson as she carefully placed the lipstick on her friend. "Pucker up sister." A quick gown change pulled some baby blue with floral into the mix, the ensemble complete.

"You still have it Jen," said Hudson proudly. "But then again you've always had it."

"Thanks Lucy, I haven't been pampered like that in a while."

The two women then heard the elderly voice of Dr. Johnson approaching, pontificating to a crowd.

"Oh, wait, one more thing," said Hudson as she fumbled in her pocket. The head nurse then pulled out a small bottle of perfume and carefully spritzed two pumps of the potion into Jen's overhead airspace. She pulled the bed cover up to her waist, elevated the back of the bed to forty-five degrees and faced the doorway, standing erect for inspection.

"Ah Nurse Hudson tending to our new admission," said Johnson with a plodding gait into the room, a group of understudies in tow. "What a wonderful sight."

"Good morning Dr. Johnson," said Hudson with professional attitude. "Just taking some vital signs doctor. The patient is stable."

"Thank you Nurse Hudson," said Johnson as he positioned himself at the head of the bed. "Good morning Jennifer."

"Good morning," said Jen, quickly scanning the crowd.

"Now, Dr. Polk, which medical student admitted our patient last night?"

"Medical student Lehigh," said Polk, some donut powder on his scrub top. "Kayla, would you please present the patient to Dr. Johnson."

"Yes," said Kayla stepping forward with a clipboard in her hands. Looking down she began to recite her history and physical exam.

"Stop," said Johnson. "Put the clipboard away young lady. Use your memory."

"Yes… of course," stammered Kayla. She then tucked the clipboard under her arm and began to speak. "This is a thirty-six year old female who approximately three weeks ago while in Nepal developed the insidious onset of diarrhea."

Jenna rapidly scanned the crowd, shifting a bit upright to view the entire team. No Dr. Drummer. She was short of breath.

"A stool specimen confirmed the diagnosis of amebic dysentery and she was appropriately started on Flagyl."

"What do you mean by "appropriate" medical student Lehigh?" asked Johnson. "What is the standard treatment for amebiasis?"

It was then that Phil drifted into the room in response to a text from Nurse Hudson. Prior to that he was unaware of Jen's midnight arrival. They immediately made eye contact. He was caught off guard by her sick, gaunt frame.

"Oh a guest appearance," said Johnson with a cocked eyebrow towards Phil. "How lovely. Dr. Drummer, we have a case of amoebic dysentery here, can you enlighten us on the causative agent of such a malady?"

"Ah," said Phil, his memory banks racing. "Entamoeba?"

"Is that an answer or a question?" asked Johnson smartly.

"An answer."

"Entamoeba what?" asked Johnson, not afraid to make the golden boy squirm for the sake of education.

Phil slowly shook his head, waiting for a neural synapse in his head to fire, which it did. "Entamoeba histolytica."

"Correct," said Johnson. "Medical student Lehigh, can you please enlighten us with regards to the life cycle of Entamoeba histolytica?"

Jen wanted to get out of bed and race towards Phil, but she physically could not. Her heart started to beat rapidly, causing a cardiac monitor to beep. Nurse Hudson reached overhead to silence the tone with a smile. She noted Phil's hair to be cut much shorter, giving him an intelligent, mature appearance. Otherwise he looked the same.

"Doesn't anyone read anymore?" asked Johnson incredulously. "I mean when I was a student we admitted the patient, went home and read as much information as humanly…."

Phil simply smiled at Jen across the crowded room. He estimated she had lost at least twenty pounds, maybe more. She would get better, he was confident of that. Her blue eyes still shined bright. He noticed the pink lipstick.

"Drummer, do you know what the problem is with medical students now a days?"

"Cell phones."

"Exactly," yelled Johnson with a downward drive of his clenched right fist. "Cell phones! A plague upon humanity! Everything is let me check the internet, let me pull up…."

It felt so good to see her, thought Phil. Jennifer Ranier. He had trouble believing she was back in Philadelphia. Oh it was so good just to see her beautiful face again. He wondered who sent the massive bouquet of sunflowers.

"That's it!" yelled Johnson as he began an approach towards the door, hands waving in disgust. "I've had enough incompetence for one morning! I'm going to walk back in this room at exactly fifteen hundred hours today and everyone will be present. Only then shall we discuss amoebic dysentery in fashion befitting this institution. For Christ's sake people, this is the Philadelphia General Hospital, I expect much more from you all."

The crowd parted rapidly to vent the crotchety attending into the hallway, his red face flushed with anger. One by one the group followed their shepherd, like sheep lost in the field. Phil stayed behind and approached the bed slowly, as Nurse Hudson adjusted an oxygen monitor on Jen's index finger.

"Welcome back," said Phil awkwardly, not knowing whether or not to kiss her. He held out his hand. Jennifer immediately burst into tears and grabbed his hand, pulling him towards her. She leaned her body forward and hugged him, weeping bitterly. She felt so slight in his arms, weak and febrile. Leaning forward he rubbed her back as Nurse Hudson compassionately stroked her hair.

"You wanted me?" said a voice suddenly from behind. "I'm sorry I'm late."

They turned back to see Nurse Caroline Ell standing in the room, reporting for duty. She wore a serious face, standing erect.

"Ah yes Nurse Ell," said Hudson, about to go off shift and gathering her composure. "I texted you a while ago for a sign out on Ms. Ranier."

"I'm sorry, there was a bad accident a few blocks away, traffic was backed up for miles. I got here as soon as I could."

"That's O.K. Caroline," said Lucy. "I'm glad you got her safely."

Phil cleared his voice and stood erect between the two women, a bit uneasy, not knowing what to say. Jennifer used both hands to clear mascara stained tears of joy from her face, still short of breath. She inhaled deeply and looked towards Caroline. An awkward silence ensued.

"This is a young healthy female admitted last night with a diagnosis of amoebic dysentery," said Hudson in a professional manner. "Several weeks ago while in Nepal she developed a fever with acute abdominal pain followed by gastrointestinal distress. Initially she was treated with metronidazole but her sodium level failed to correct, prompting an evacuation to Germany where...."

Chapter Twenty
THE PATHOLOGY REPORT

"Borax? What the hell is borax?" said Dr. Riles to the pathologist over the phone.

"How do I know," said Dr. Falcon. "Some kind of element. I'm only telling you what the report says." In her hand was the final pathology release on Mrs. Biddleton from the National Organization of Health.

"You're talking about the N.O.H report?" asked Riles. "Mrs. Biddleton's pathology report, my Mrs. Biddleton?"

"Of course the N.O.H. report," said Falcon. "And yes, your patient, the former Mrs. Biddleton, medical record number 8253520."

"Must have been a contaminant from the factory," said Riles. "I mean in all my years of medicine I've never come across Borax in a hospital or surgical setting."

"Maybe," said Falcon. "I think it's a common cleaning agent. I'll email you the report."

"Borax? Strange," thought Riles.

"I'm sure you are aware that I have to report this finding to the hospital board and Department of Health," said Falcon. "Standard operational protocol in an intraoperative death."

"She was a D.N.R.," said Riles sharply. "We could have saved her if she wanted to live." His ego did not permit a recall of the Tulipes with Raspberry Sorbet.

"Regardless, I'm also going to copy the email to the board and health department," said Falcon. She then dragged the report on her computer to a mail system and hit the "send" button. "There, you have it. Any other questions?"

"Yea, what the hell is borax, and how did it get inside my patient?"

"No idea," said Falcon. "Call with any further questions." Click.

Riles immediately opened the email, noticing the report was carbon copied to the hospital board of trustees and the Pennsylvania Department of Health. The official logo of the N.O.H. was emblazoned across the top. The N.O.H. he thought, big shots from Washington who never treated a patient, pathologists who know everything about everything, but only when it's too late. Who made them the authority? The report's gross description section described a white, powdery substance submitted in multiple samples. The main text of the report unleashed a landslide of technical jargon, a narrative of multiple biochemical assays, all with similar results. The final conclusion section simple said in bold print: Final Diagnosis – BORAX.

The chairman read the report several times, the result always the same. He then picked up his cell phone and made a call.

Vic Fanicci's phone woke him from a late afternoon nap, induced by an alcohol haze from the prior night. He was alone in his apartment, sprawled out on the couch. Vanessa was gone, needing time to "sort things out," ever since her restaurant wrangle. He missed her company in a manly way, but otherwise her absence meant nothing, typical of a mid-life affair. He spent the prior evening at

Lucca Cibo, bellied up to the bar, in search for some new female companionship. After the third drink he befriended a divorced mother of three with a love for tequila, who bought into his state of sorrow. Her body parts sagged and protruded in a disproportionate fashion from a tight blue dress, yet she paid attention to his lines. Within two hours he was drunk and she still steady, despite running up a stiff bill on the Union Park account. It was only when she leaned forward to get off the bar stool and visit the ladies room did Fanicci smell success, her cleavage passing close to his grin. Reaching into his pocket he popped a pill marketed to erase the calamity of erectile dysfunction from the face of the earth, complements of a fellow drug salesman. He looked past the bartender into a mirror with a smile, knowing the pill was potent, and not a placebo. It would be his last drink he thought, alcohol the only variable that could possible spoil his sordid plans. Unfortunately the divorcee in blue never returned, having gotten her belly full of top shelf liquor, complements of the lonely man at the bar. His memory from that point forward was vague. More alcohol and a staggering walk home where he had to take expected pharmaceutical matters into his own hands, passing out with a pornographic DVD on the tube. The call from Riles startled him, some saliva down his cheek onto the pillow.

"Tony, it's me, Fred Riles. Are you busy?"

"No, no," said Fanicci sitting up, his head pounding. "What's up?"

"Got the final report back on the Biddleton case," said the chairman. "They found borax in her gut."

"Borax? What the hell is borax? Isn't that an insecticide?" He held his hand up to block the bright afternoon light.

"I'm not exactly sure what it is," said Riles. "The pathology department called it an element. Regardless we need to carry out due diligence on our part. This report is going to our hospital board and Department of Health."

"Borax? Isn't that in toothpaste?"

"Listen Vic, it was probably a contaminant from the factory," said Riles. "I need you to get working on your end and see if borax exists anywhere in the lab."

"I doubt it came from the lab," said Fanicci. "But then again I'm not a scientist."

"Well neither am I, but you and I are the only one who seem to care about his project, so let's act fast, very fast!"

"Alright, alright, take it easy Fred," said Fanicci, now getting up to walk into the kitchen, his underwear sagging and knee high black socks still on. "I'm sure there is a reasonable explanation."

"There better be," retorted Riles. "I'll check with the O.R. staff and see how they clean the laparoscopic equipment. What type of cleaning agent they use. Maybe there is some borax in the mixture. Who the hell knows?"

"Hey Fred good news," said Fanicci as he stared into an empty refrigerator. "I spoke to our company V.P. and he decided to move up the Lysovage announcement. They want to get the product to market ASAP."

"How soon?" asked Riles. "I mean we may have a major wrench in the works Vic, a death, a probable contaminant. Serious stuff."

"It won't be a problem once the product is released," said Fanicci, suddenly remembering the woman in blue from the night before. "Just more info coming in too late to matter Fred. I support the early launch."

"How soon Vic? How soon?"

"Three to four weeks. Enough time for you?"

"I may need more," said Riles. "I can't commit to such a tight schedule."

"Fred, Fred," said Fanicci. "Keep an eye on the bigger picture, not just this one case. You and I have been working on this project for a decade now. The end is near, for both of us. Don't tell me you can't put a ten minute speech together on Lysovage."

"The venue?" asked Riles. "On such short notice where are you going to hold the event?"

"Dah, hello?" said Fanicci heading to the bathroom. "The convention center directly across the street from the PGH. You know the one with the Union Park Biotech sign in two story high letters across the top."

"What the hell is Borax?" yelled Riles. "And why now?"

"Listen Fred," said Fanicci as he positioned himself on the commode. "Take a day or two off, celebrate what you've done over the past decade. This is major medical news. It's your life's work. Be proud and believe me, Union Park is going to make the announcement a world class event."

No response.

"I'll have the boys in the lab get to the bottom of this borax stuff," said Fanicci, now under duress, and remembering to never order oysters Rockefeller again. "Will have their answer in no time."

No response.

'Fred, you worry too much. Let me do the worrying, that's my job. You save patients and I do the worrying. Deal?"

"I guess so," said Riles. "There is no other deal in town. Thanks for your time Vic, keep in touch."

Fanicci hung up the phone with a shake of his head. The maître de had to know who the divorced lush was with the saggy chest. If she needed tequila that badly, she definitely needed a sugar daddy.

Exactly twenty-four hours later Dr. Riles sat in the dingy office of Professor Oliver Shoebottom, a long time member of the University of Pennsylvania's chemistry department. Riles had set up the meeting with Shoebottom, who by chance was a leading authority on borax, a field of expertise that could only exist in academia. Shoebottom was a quirky eccentric, brilliant, absent-minded and habitually late. He was set to retire at year's end and his office was a mess, with stacks of dusty papers, books and journal articles scattered throughout. He was forty-five minutes late, having finished a lecture across campus over two hours ago. An heirloom clock clicked away the minutes as Riles impatiently looked out the solitary window, a red brick wall the only view. His search for borax in the PGH operating room turned up negative, contributing to his angst.

Suddenly the door opened with Shoebottom backing into the room, a stack of papers in his arms. Short and a bit overweight, with thick gray hair and matching mustache, he sported fresh chalk over the back of a wrinkled blue shirt. A bowtie failed to match the shirt beneath a pair of suspenders.

"Apologies doctor, apologies on my late arrival," said the professor hurriedly in a high-pitched voice. "Oliver Shoebottom here."

Riles extended his hand, prompting the professor to nervously find a spot for the papers. He then shuffled around to face the surgeon while taking a faded handkerchief out his right front pocket to wipe his nose, before returning the handshake.

"How can I help you doctor?" asked Shoebottom as he looked over his thick glasses.

"Yes, well actually just trying to learn a bit about borax," said Riles, who then proceeded to ask a few open ended questions.

"A borax problem? You've come to the right man. Shoebottom is my name, and borax is my game." He held his index finger up for dramatic flare.

"Yes, well then good," said Riles. "What can you tell me about it?"

"Ah borax! It goes by many names including sodium borate and disodium tetraborate," continued the professor, with a whimsical wave of his hand. "But the exact name for the natural mineral commonly referred to as borax is sodium tetraborate decahydrate." He pronounced the chemical name very slowly and precisely, with apparent reverence.

"I see. Where does it come?"

"The ground, out of mines!" said Shoebottom in a low shout. "Been around forever. Was first used in 10th century China for ceramic glazes. Most of it comes from California now. Big industry. Big, big industry."

"How can someone obtain borax and what does it look like?"

"Commercially it's a plain white powder and you can get it anywhere," said the professor with a wave of his right hand. "Any big box store in the country carries it. I can pick it up on the way home if I wanted to."

"Is it a controlled substance?" asked Riles. "You know, by any government agencies?"

"No, no," laughed the expert. "Borax is everywhere, you name it, and borax may be in it.

"Like what? What common everyday items contain borax?"

"Insecticides, toothpaste, skin balms, hand soaps, detergents, diaper rash creams, fertilizers, stain removers and air fresheners," said Shoebottom. "I can go on forever. The point being borax is ubiquitous in today's world. The stuff is even used to stop radiator leaks."

"What happens if it gets into the human body, say the digestive tract or stomach?" asked Riles.

"Not much," said the professor. "It's an innocuous element." He paused for several seconds, blinking his eyes as if his brain stalled. "Believe it or not some crackpots take it as a natural remedy, a so-called daily supplement. Claims it cures gout, cancer, obesity, infections and even osteoporosis."

"Does it work in that regard? A home remedy?"

"No. Never proven in the scientific community," said Shoebottom. "Now I should point out that borax is safe in small amounts. Larger amounts can tilt the table, especially if hydrochloric acid is nearby."

"How so?"

"In the right setting, the combination of borax and hydrochloric acid will make boric acid, which will destroy any human tissue on contact. Absolute destruction I may add. Boric acid is nasty. Look here," said the professor rolling his sleeve up to expose a scar on his forearm. "A careless freshman back in 1967 spilled some on my arm. His name was Mike something or other. Gave him a D minus. I wonder where he is now?"

A chill went up Riles' spine as he stared at the teacher's scar, recalling the autopsy on Mrs. Biddleton. An ulcer had ruptured her duodenum where hydrochloric acid was naturally stored by the body to digest food, causing the acid to spill into her peritoneal cavity–the same cavity where the N.O.H. reported borax to be found.

"What's the big deal with borax over there?" asked Shoebottom. "What's all the fuss?"

"Over where?" asked Riles.

"The Philadelphia General. I mean, I've been at this university for fifty years working on borax and no one from the hospital ever contacted me. Now, all of a sudden twice over the past six months you've called with questions."

"Twice?"

"Yes twice, doctor. Remember our conversation over the phone sometime back? You asked a lot of the same questions."

"I've never spoken to you in the past," said Riles, now alarmed. "Never. Today is the first time we met."

"Well someone did," said Professor Shoebottom. "Asked all the same questions, you know what happens when borax gets inside a human? Can it harm a person? Where to get it? I just assumed it was you."

"Do you remember the name of the caller?"

"No. Memory is going doctor. That's why I'm retiring in a few months. They say early Alzheimer's but I disagree. Can still do the daily crossword puzzle in under forty-five minutes, with one eye closed." He then let out a giggle. "A ha, a ha-ha."

"Think hard professor," said Riles as he leaned forward towards the educator, trying to trigger his memory banks. "It's very important. Is there any way you can recall the name of the caller in the past? Even the first name?"

"No, absolutely not," said Shoebottom. "I have to write everything down nowadays. I can say it was a male calling, seemed intelligent, beyond that, no other recollection. For heaven's sake, I can't even recall the name of my cats at home."

"Any recall of his voice?" asked Riles, continuing to grasp for more information. "A dialect, words used, references to any department at the PGH?"

"Nope, the vault is empty. Hello is anybody home?"

"Was the caller a doctor?" asked Riles. "Can you even recall that?"

"Not sure," said Shoebottom. "You know I've traveled all around the world lecturing on borax. Could have made a fortune on it but I stuck with my academic mission."

"A fortune? How so?"

"As I said, big industry. They wanted me to be their "yes man" over time, saying how safe borax products were to goose the marketing machine. Wanted me to get in front of the FDA to stretch the truth. But I would not, and to this very day, have no regrets."

"Why?"

"A man needs a moral compass doctor, something to anchor his lifeline onto. I may not be the richest man on campus, but I'm the happiest. Can look myself in the mirror at night and smile, knowing I've always spoken the truth."

"One last question professor before I leave."

"Yes, what is it?"

"Was the caller's voice old or young?" asked Riles slowly. "The caller from several months ago, is there anyway you can estimate their age? Take your time professor, try and recall. Please, try and recall."

"Goodness gracious man, I can't even recall the names of my own children! The memory, it's going! Maybe I should start taking borax? Perhaps it can treat Alzheimer's? Hey, a cure for Alzheimer's with me as the patient. It could be my last great contribution to mankind. I smell a Nobel Prize! They say I have Alzheimer's but I don't believe it. Can still do the daily crossword in less than ten minutes, with both eyes closed. A ha, a ha-ha."

Chapter Twenty One
LOOSE CANNON ON DECK

"The decision is final Frederick," said Joseph Carter, Vice President of Union Park Biotech. "It's the board's decision, not mine."

"I may need more time," said Dr. Riles, seated across the table from the executive. "I mean I have to check my surgical schedule. My patients come first." He had not yet discussed with anyone his conversation with Professor Shoebottom, still searching for some explanation.

"What's the budget cap?" asked Fanicci.

"No cap," said Joe Carter with a smile. "You have the green light to make the Lysovage announcement a historic event Vic. Make me proud."

Fanicci just smiled as he looked around the table. Finally he thought, in one week it would be over. Once Lysovage was released to the masses his job would be done, except for placing his signature on the back of a big fat bonus check.

"Does the convention center have their own security teams?" interjected hospital CEO John Mitchell. "I mean my son-in-law runs a private security firm, perhaps the convention center can use some help that evening. A very professional firm, I may add."

"I'm sure they can," said Carter. "Vic, make sure John's security team gets on board that day. It's a Friday night so pay them time and a half for their services."

"Right," said Fanicci.

"Gentlemen, I would like to thank each of you for your hard work and dedication to the Lysovage Project over the past ten years," continued Carter in appreciation. "What we have accomplished is epic in nature, and the product coming to market will benefit people globally. From a professional standpoint I'm proud to have been a part of it, and from all of us at Union Park, we thank you. " The vice president then stood up and said with a smile, "Now everyone, enjoy the evening. This meeting is adjourned."

The attendees began to disperse until Dr. Riles spoke. "Wait! We haven't covered all the items on the agenda. What about the factory? Were there any signs of borax in the factory?"

"Excuse me?" asked Carter, turning back to face Riles. "Borax?"

"Ah yes," said Fanicci. "The topic slipped my mind."

"What topic?" asked Carter. "What the hell is borax?"

"Some traces of borax were found in a patient..."

"A possible contaminant in one placebo," said Fanicci while cutting off Dr. Riles. "No big deal, an isolated event."

"Great," said Carter. "Sounds like a housekeeping event on your end. I'll pretend I never heard about it." The vice president then headed towards a spiral stairwell that led upstairs. "Got to get on deck, the captain is going to let my granddaughter blow the ship's horn. Enjoy the cruise gentlemen. Anchors Aweigh!"

"How can you forget about that?" asked Riles, pinning Fanicci into the corner of the room. "I thought that's what this meeting was going to be about?"

"Fred, Fred, keep your eye on the prize here. The big picture."

"Don't tell me what to do," said Riles. "Something is amiss."

"Listen," said Fanicci, now growing impatient. "A complete sweep of the factory failed to turn up any signs of borax. Not a trace. It doesn't exist in the factory. It's that simple."

"Are you sure Vic? Absolutely sure?"

"Yes," said Fanicci. "I spent two full days in the factory with the Q.A. team. It's a sterile environment Fred. We're a global pharmaceutical firm, not a mom and pop outfit. For Christ's sake, you've been out to the factory numerous times. There isn't a strand of hair unaccounted for in that place."

"What about the vials before they are shipped? Are they checked? Can they be tampered with?"

"Tampered with? What are you talking about Fred? Are you suggesting there has been some sort of foul play here? A crime?"

"This is where I leave gentlemen," said CEO Mitchell with a nervous wave of both hands. "The less I know the better. See you on deck."

"Fred, each vial of Lysovage is sterilized, sealed and then passed through an assay machine at the factory. The machine confirms an absolute pure product, free of any contaminant before it leaves the factory. Each vial then carries a barcode allowing us to track the product with absolute precision. There was no contaminant from the factory Fred. None. Case closed. Let it go."

"Well, then where did the borax come from?"

"Who knows, maybe the lady was taking it orally. Some people take it in pill form to ward off evil."

Both men paused, staring at each other.

"The only samples I haven't checked are the ones at the hospital," said Fanicci. "You'll have to get those vials back to me."

"Woooooo," sounded the horn from above deck. "Wooooo, woooooo!" The blasts echoed through the harbor.

"What samples?"

"The ones waiting to be used, before we shut down the trials," said Fanicci. "There are thirteen vials left in the O.R. somewhere."

"Right, right," said Riles. "I never thought of that Vic. I'll get them to you as soon as possible, you know, maybe recheck them in that assay machine."

"Great," said Fanicci with a smile. "That's thirteen vials, lucky number thirteen, easy to remember. Just like I'm going to get lucky tonight. Enjoy the cruise gentlemen, and remember what happens at sea, stays at sea." He then vanished up the stairwell.

Riles then turned and looked at the only remaining person in the room, the ship now in motion.

"Why so quiet Stuart?" asked Riles. "You haven't said a word. That's unlike you."

"Just thinking of the wife back in Philly, you know the whole pregnancy thing."

"Why isn't she here Stuart? This would have been the perfect occasion to bring her. Personally, you have an uncanny way of making Mrs. Greyson disappear when tight skirts are around."

"She's a bit under the weather," said Stuart. "We are hoping maybe morning sickness. I can only hope. It's been a long stressful process for us all. I'm sure you can understand that."

"Listen up young man," said Riles with a stare. "Do not repeat your mistakes from last year's cruise, understand?"

"Yes sir."

"I'm frankly appalled that you tried to invite two female medical students on board. What were you thinking? Do you want to get us all arrested?"

"No sir."

"Keep you nose clean, Stuart. You're a married man and I hope that means something to your generation."

"Understood."

"And stay away from Vanessa," said the chairman now pointing his finger directly at Greyson. "Do not embarrass yourself. She works for Union Park. Is that clear?"

"Perfectly clear."

"Great. Now let's get on deck to see the Boston skyline at night. God I miss Boston."

"Aye aye captain. Aye aye."

"Woooooo," sounded the horn one last time. The annual Union Park "Booze Cruise to Nowhere" was underway. The ship, a super yacht co-owned by Union Park and another wealthy pharmaceutical giant, sailed out of Boston. The vessel was the best money could buy, with a length of 530 feet and speeds capable of twenty-five knots. Twenty posh private cabins were available for select dignitaries, and several large common areas provided space for group meetings.

"Pop!" went the cork flying off the champagne bottle in Polk's hands, flying into the sea. At the very tip of the bow stood Rick Polk and Phil, the wind in their face and the lights of Boston in their eyes. In between them snuggled Nurse Hudson, a last second fill in for Caroline Ell. "To residency," yelled Polk over the wind, the froth from the bottle soaking Phil. "Hail to the chief resident! Philip Michael Drummer! The greatest chief of them all."

"Hail to the chief!" echoed Hudson with a squeeze of Phil's torso, her arm around it. She never tired of having him at her side. She wore a snappy black dress that got the attention of the ship's captain as he welcomed her aboard.

Polk took a hearty swig of champagne from the expensive bottle and then passed it to his friends, the first of many toasts that evening. Rick waved to boats passing by, their passengers gawking in awe at the yacht. The inner harbor quickly faded in the distance.

"Thanks for the invite," said Polk. "I feel so special to be part of your world, the rich and famous."

"I'm sorry to say but you were on the B-list," said Phil, the wind blowing his hair in all directions. "Caroline was on the A-list, since she somehow got involved with Union Park. They even sent her a formal invitation with a gift card to a dress shop downtown."

"Why isn't she here?"

"Let's see… the catfight video, Vanessa on board, Jenna descending from the mountain, take your pick."

"You should have your own reality show Phil. I certainly would watch it," said Polk followed by another slug of champagne. "It would be a smash."

"I actually think she volunteered for this weekend's hospital shift," said Phil. "Who can blame her?"

"She did," confirmed Hudson. "Asked to work the entire weekend. She is a great nurse, her patients love her."

A waiter then approached the threesome with a tray of hors d'oeuvres. She smiled at the guests prior to seeing the fare engulfed by Polk.

Lucy Hudson then stepped backwards and pulled out her cell phone. "A picture, of my two favorite residents of all time. Even better than the two bums I married. Line up boys."

Rick and Phil obliged as if listening to their mother. They turned towards the nurse and gathered close for the photo, a smile on their faces, champagne glasses in their hands.

"Click."

"Do you think we look gay?" asked Polk. "Not that there's anything wrong with that."

"The Outing Episode," said Phil, "One of the most popular *Seinfeld* catchphrases of all time. Don't insult me."

"My boy, I'm proud of you. Episode 57."

"Let's get inside," said Phil as the yacht gained speed in the open sea. "It's getting cold up here." As the final crescent of sunlight dropped below the horizon, Phil, Rick and their nurse mom vanished into a deck below, already loud with celebration.

The next four hours were a blur to Phil, loud music, fantastic food and waiters constantly replenishing his wine glass. He briefly spoke to vice president Joe Carter and his arm candy, a woman just a bit older than Phil who had the body composition of a cartoon vixen. Carter again urged Phil to get on board with Lysovage before it was too late, the consummate businessman. Throughout the pitch the vice president's trophy wife jiggled and giggled, yet did not speak. Two of his grandchildren played behind him, tended to by a blue-eyed au pair from Holland. The executive's first wife lived in Charleston, and his second in Naples, both set well for life.

He engaged in strange conversation with Vic Fanicci, who had his arm around a middle-aged woman with Tequila breath, wearing a new dress and silver earrings. She flaunted an old-fashioned beehive hairdo with a dark root base and hydrogen peroxide top. When conversing the woman kept her eye upon the wine porter with a look of concern, watching his bottle run low. Fanicci's vocal cadence was rapid–almost manic, as he patiently kept his eye on the prize.

A discussion with John Mitchell also ensued, the CEO asking if Phil had reviewed the employment agreement, and whether his lawyer friend could help out. Mitchell rambled on about the stability of the PGH, stating it would be financially imprudent for a young surgeon to strike out on his own. He held a glass of scotch in his hand, a trademark of his generation. His wife of forty years smiled politely bedside him, holding onto a Manhattan, paying no attention to his speech.

Stuart Greyson commanded a crowd of women around him, young to middle-aged girls who seemed quite at ease. He was consuming alcohol at a striking rate despite his chairman's wary eye. At one point Phil noticed his right hand drift down onto the firm buttocks of a fine looking lass beside him, gently squeezing as if checking the ripeness of a peach at the market. Oddly, the woman didn't even flinch, allowing the sampling of forbidden fruit to proceed.

Behind Greyson stood the ship's captain, a tall handsome man who by the looks of it wasn't married to the sea. He gawked directly down upon Nurse Hudson, who stared up in a manner friendly to any seaman, her lips so full. She politely laughed at his nautical jokes, wondering what criteria could have possibly made him captain of such a gorgeous vessel. At their side was Rick Polk, trying to rid the ocean of jumbo shrimp, an oxymoron that always befuddled Phil.

The Love Boat thought Phil, and here he was alone, wondering if Jen's guilt free clause was affected by Maritime law.

Just then a soft tap on his shoulder interrupted his musings. Turning, he saw Vanessa in a blazing electric crimson dress, aflame with sensuality. Thick black hair hung perfectly across her right shoulder, full and wavy, some manicured fingernails running through it. Cherry lipstick screamed out to be sampled, and a glass of red wine and exceptionally high-heeled shoes brought her whole package together. She didn't speak but kept her lips slightly a gap in subtle pout mode.

"I was wondering where you were," said Phil, staring at the titillating woman before him. He smelled the same exotic perfume from their Lucca Cibo dinner date.

"Sorry, always working," said Vanessa. "Had to schmooze some bigwigs from Washington on another deck. Done and over."

"Are you still on company time?"

"No Doctor. I'm on *Vanessa* time," smiled the hostess. "The best time of all."

"Vanessa!" came the scream from over Phil's shoulder. "My girl, where have you been!"

Phil turned to see Stuart Greyson brush past him with arms wide open, his female posse trailing. Without hesitation he aggressively embraced the Union Park employee, nearly causing her wine glass to spill over, his hands just below her waistline.

"I thought you fell overboard," said Greyson while pulling back just slightly from his grip, his face within inches or her.

"Ah no, I didn't," said Vanessa using her free hand to push his chest away. "Been on board all the time Dr. Greyson."

"I met all your friends," said Greyson with a hand wave back towards the girls who were now starting to swirl around Phil. "But I missed you," said the doctor with a pucker of his lips. "My little Nessa."

"Ah excuse me," said Vanessa. "I have to tend to some matters upstairs." She then turned to distance herself from Greyson but his right hand grasped her forearm, pulling her back.

"Where are you going Vanessa?" said Greyson. "The young doctor needs some attention."

She tried to pull away but Greyson wouldn't allow it, an evil smirk on his face. Phil went to step in, but was suddenly cut off by a circling Dr. Riles, who burst into the scene, positioning himself between the two.

"Dr. Greyson may I have a word with you," said Riles sharply. "In private, that is."

Greyson's smirk turned into a scowl while looking directly at the chairman. He slowly turned his gaze back upon Vanessa, holding it for a second before releasing her forearm. The rebuked physician then turned slowly back into the troop of females behind him, disappearing into their midst.

"I'm sorry," said Dr. Riles to Vanessa. "I'm afraid he has had a bit too much to drink. I apologize for his behavior."

"No problem," said Vanessa, running her hands down upon her waist and adjusting her dress. "Thank you doctor. Apology accepted."

Exactly two hours later Phil found himself in a cozy circular red booth on the sky deck, with Vanessa. They were alone in the room, which had a glass ceiling, allowing a gaze upward into the heavens. Their bodies were pressed together by the dangerous combination of alcohol and hormones. While staring at the moon Phil thought it winked back, his sensorium completely off keel.

"Wow, what a night," he said. "I've never seen the moon so bright. It's almost smiling at us."

"A blue moon tonight," said Vanessa. "Once in a blue moon."

"Look, a shooting star!" said Phil.

Vanessa gently tucked her head into his, rolling her hair back and forth. She had fallen in love with her client, a handsome young doctor coming into his own. A deep sigh pressed her chest against his. It was then Phil noticed the captain just outside the room pointing upwards into the night sky. His right arm was firmly around Nurse Hudson's frame, she with a hand in his back pant's pocket, an old trick from high school days.

Phil then felt Vanessa's lips upon his left neck, her body pushing further into his. His gaze however remained fixed upon the skipper, who was suddenly getting his own sextant on with Hudson, the old seadog with a handful of booty. Vanessa's right hand then joined in on the assault, her left around Phil's neck, pulling him closer, into a haze of passion. Yet despite the moment, Phil somehow could not keep his mind off the outer deck action, remembering the taste of Hudson's lips. It was when the skipper appeared to be focusing the head nurse's attention on the big dipper, that a polite tap on Phil's shoulder startled him. He looked up to his left, the show over for now.

"Ah excuse me sir," said the officer in uniform. "Mr. Carter would like to see you immediately."

"Me?" asked Phil, with Vanessa still in tight.

"You are Dr. Drummer sir? Yes?"

"Yes."

"Then yes, you sir. It shall only take a moment," said the mate with a British accent. "He needs to speak to you. Please pardon my interruption ma'am." The sailor tipped his cap at Vanessa.

Phil excused himself from Vanessa who ran both hands through a head of messy hair, needing time to cool her fervor. He then extracted himself from the leather booth, taking some time to gather his sea legs. He followed the messenger towards the cabin of Mr. Carter, Vice President of Union Park and employer of Vanessa Rose.

His cabin was the best on the boat, massive, opulent and over the top. Two attendants stood in the corner of the room, one male and the other female. The V.P. was blunt, perhaps due to the lateness of the hour.

"Dr. Drummer, I just wanted to let you know how delighted I am that you've joined the team as one of our Lysovage breakthrough consultants," said Carter.

"A consultant?"

"Yes. Someone involved with a Union Park product that can communicate the good news throughout the medical community," continued Carter. The V.P. then mentioned a conversation that evening with CEO Mitchell regarding

Phil's financial status and need for an attorney. He offered Phil the use of Union Park's legal team, who excelled in contract negotiations.

"Thank you sir."

Carter then snapped his fingers at the male attendant, who stepped forward with a manila envelope, offering it to Phil.

"What's this?"

"A consultant's fee doctor, ten thousand dollars in cash, reimbursement for your time and effort in advance," said Carter.

Phil declined to accept the payment but was ignored, the attendant mashing the envelope into his arms and escorted him out. The bizarre transaction was over in five minutes, prompting Phil to find his way back to the sky deck in search of Vanessa. When he entered the lounge she was gone, the captain running through the room with his radio blaring.

"Trouble below," he yelled. "Your girlfriend perhaps?"

Phil followed in pursuit, his head spinning with a handful of cash.

The duo approached a cabin door where an unconscious sailor lay prone on deck, his mouth bleeding. The door to the room was open and the voice of Stuart Greyson could be heard inside.

"You whore!" he yelled. "Too good for me now?"

Phil turned the corner to see Vanessa in a defensive stance across the room, a hot pink bra partially exposed by a torn dress strap. She had terror in her eyes and a bruise welling up on her check. Between them stood Greyson, in a drunken testosterone rage.

"I'm the one you should be spending time with," yelled Greyson in his underwear. "Not Drummer." He was unaware of the captain and Phil behind him.

"He's gone crazy," yelled Vanessa from across the room. "I came down to check on one of my girls and he dragged me into the room!"

Greyson spun around to face the captain and Phil.

"Stand down!" said the captain firmly. "As captain of this ship I order you to stand down now young man."

"Don't tell me what to do Captain Crunch," howled Greyson. "You and her are both being paid to service me! So shove off."

"Stuart take it easy," said Phil. "You've had a bit too much to drink."

"Screw you Drummer–and your pretty boy act. You're the biggest fake of them all. I'll kick your candy ass!"

The captain then called for assistance over his radio as Phil took a deeper step into the room, attempting to reach Vanessa. The maneuver provoked Greyson who bull rushed Phil, fists flying. His bodily contact drove Phil into the wall, spewing one hundred dollar bills into the air. The jolt knocked Phil's memory back to grade school, the last time he was involved in fisticuffs, when he squared off with an eight grader named Butch. Greyson followed with a wild round house that caught Phil's right jaw, tossing him backwards again, Vanessa screaming. Phil suddenly saw two security guards fill the doorjamb, the captain behind them. As Greyson went to toss another punch, Phil instinctively ducked, and countered with a quick right jab directly into Greyson's face, the impact breaking his right hand. As Greyson dropped to the floor his left front incisor tooth sailed across the room with a wad of blood, hitting the wall, and falling next to his limp body. The fight was over, as was Greyson's career as a pugilist. Vanessa ran into the safety of Phil's arms, sobbing wildly.

She spent the remainder of the night in the security of Mr. Carter's suite, recovering from the assault. Phil refused to pick up any of the money and retreated to a separate cabin, trying to sleep with a bag of ice on his swollen hand. He blankly stared into the dark sky at the blue moon, thinking only of Jenna, wondering if she was looking at it too?

At that very moment, approximately 264 nautical miles to the south, Jennifer was looking out the window, but the sky was cloudy. She had not been feeling well over the past forty-eight hours, the weekend hospitalist not thinking much of it. Shortness of breath was her main complaint, together with a pounding headache. Her appetite remained poor.

"Thanks," said Jennifer to the nurse caring for her. "I hope it helps. I'm not feeling too well."

"I'm sure it will help," said Nurse Caroline Ell as she drove her thumb down upon the syringe of medicine, releasing it into Jenna's vein. "I'm sure it will help. Trust me."

Chapter Twenty Two

A DAY WITH RICHARD

"A broken hand! It's over Drummer," said Maurice. "Ha, ha, ha!"

"It had to be your shooting hand," said Rhimes.

"Why didn't you knock him out with your left hand?" chimed in Polk.

"Listen everyone," said Phil, wearing a soft splint on his right hand. "It's only a hairline fracture, the orthopod told me three to four weeks." He was the only one standing in the Torpedo Room, the others scattered about on chairs and Polk's couch.

"The game is in one week Phil," said Mike Boyce. "The championship game, one week."

"Ain't enough time boys," said Mo. "Gonna have to start Polk in Phil's place. I smell a victory."

"I can handle the rock," said Polk.

"You couldn't handle my baby sister," said Mo, "Yet alone the basketball."

"I've got a bigger problem," said Phil. "Dr. Riles has asked me to give a ten minute speech at the Lysovage launch party, which is the same night as the big game."

"What! No way!" yelled his teammates. "No, no!"

"An honor," he said. "A chance to make a name for myself on the national stage. I couldn't turn him down."

"What time is the event?"

"Seven o'clock in the evening, in the convention center."

"Phil, the games at six," said Rhimes. "Please, tell him no."

"I can't," said Phil. "Especially after what happened on the cruise. The guy was so embarrassed."

"Listen everybody," said Stan the Beer Truck Man who now spent about as much time in the Torpedo Room as Polk. "I've been saving the last remaining keg of Schmidt's beer in the world for a special occasion, and I think a post championship game party would be that occasion. We can host it here, in the Torpedo Room."

Suddenly there was a knock on the door.

"Who the hell knocks?" asked Rhimes.

Polk opened the door to his apartment and stepped backwards in silent awe. Standing directly before him was Dr. Knight, wearing a shirt and tie, beneath his starched white coat. It was nine o'clock in the morning.

"May I come in, Dr. Polk?" asked Knight.

"Yes, yes sir," said Polk. "Welcome to my humble abode."

"Thank you," said Knight. "Not easy to find this apartment Dr. Polk, but very nice," he said while stepping into the room and scanning the guest list. "I like what you've done with the place."

"Thank you Dr. Knight," said Polk while quickly picking up some of his laundry. He then shoved Mo's feet off a make shift coffee table.

"Reminds me of an old room we took over back in my time," said Knight, his eyes looking up with nostalgia. "Third floor of the old Hoban building. Knocked down about twenty years ago."

"Did it have a name?" asked Boyce.

"Yes it did Dr. Boyce," said Knight. "We called it "The Grinder". This place reminds me a bit of it."

"Nice."

"Yes," said Knight. "However the reason I am here gentlemen is not to walk down memory lane. Rather, I'm looking for some volunteers for a new project I'm leading."

Polk cleared off some newspapers from a chair, and slid it towards Knight, who sat down. A meow was heard from behind the wall.

"I'm in the process of setting up a small clinic in West Philadelphia," said Knight. "A free clinic specifically designed to curb cardiovascular disease."

The group stared back at Knight.

"You know, monitoring blood pressure, controlling blood sugar, smoking cessation programs. Educate the population. It's more of a grass roots and taking it to the streets approach. Believe it or not, it's something I've always wanted to do, and now is the time."

"Sounds great," said Polk. "Count me in!"

"It will be staffed by volunteers and that's where you men come in," said Knight. "I would appreciate any time you can offer once the clinic is up and running."

"Sure, definitely," said the crowd, including Phil. "No problem."

"Fantastic. Of course it's purely voluntary," said Knight. "No obligations."

"It would be an honor," said Polk to his mentor. "Sounds like a great idea."

"Thank you gentlemen," said the surgeon, now standing up. "The whole project is in its infancy, just looking at some space up on 56th street. I'll keep you posted on progress."

Before leaving he looked at Phil saying, "Dr. Drummer a moment of your time please, in private."

"Sure," said Phil heading out into the hallway with Knight.

"Listen Drummer, Jennifer isn't doing too well up on the floor," said Knight, the two in a tight corridor.

"I know. She looks weak, short of breath."

"Exactly," said Knight. "We need to keep a close eye on her. You and I, we owe it to her. Quite frankly she has no one else."

"Agreed," said Phil.

"It's these hospitalists," barked Knight. "Shift workers who drift in and out every eight hours, just passing the buck." Knight trusted no one outside of the surgical field, especially medical physicians employed by the PGH. The role of a hospitalist represented a nationwide trend of placing the burden of inpatient medical care on their shoulders, excusing community physicians from having to round on their patients. Knight felt it was just another step towards a disaster he liked to call national health care.

"I already found one of her medications somehow cancelled," said Phil. "Had to reorder it."

"Exactly," said Knight in a low tone as maintenance workers passed by. "I don't even know who these hospitalists are half of the time, there are so many."

Phil paused, allowing Knight to vent.

"Listen, we need to check her carefully on a daily basis. You in the morning and me at night," continued the elder physician, now starting to walk down the dimly lit hall. "I've been visiting her every night around ten o'clock, checking her labs, vitals, etcetera."

"Sounds like a plan," said Phil.

"I've got a strange feeling," said Knight. "Something isn't adding up. Her numbers look good but she doesn't. So let's take care of her – together."

"Got it," said Phil sidestepping a dolly passing by filled with medical supplies. "Right."

They shook hands and Knight found his way above ground, heading to Dr. Riles' office. He was late for another one of CEO Mitchell's bimonthly "take the pulse" meetings with the department of surgery.

"Sorry I'm late," said Knight. "Miss anything?"

"No," said Riles. "John was just updating us on some construction plans for the new east wing."

At the table were Knight, Riles and Johnson, the latter again exercising his right to remain silent. Dr. Stone was away on vacation. Over the next twenty minutes they discussed nothing of importance, a prelude to the main topic, which was Dr. Greyson and his recent misconduct. Riles introduced the topic, summarizing the Boston cruise events succinctly to the group.

"A disturbing story to say the least," said Knight. "Did this girl, or rather woman named Ms. Rose file charges?"

"No, not as yet," said Riles.

"She was a Union Park employee?" asked Knight, recalling a view of her in the now infamous catfight video.

"Yes," said Riles. "Actually a very intelligent woman, committed to the company and Lysovage's success. A valued employee, according to their V.P. Joe Carter, who was also on board."

"Isn't this the second time Greyson had a problem with her?" asked Knight. "Wasn't it last year on that very same cruise that he almost ended up overboard?"

"Unfortunately yes," said Riles, his eyes looking down. "Yes it was."

"And didn't we officially reprimand him that any further misconduct would not be tolerated?"

"Yes, again," said Riles.

"John, what is the hospital's position on this?" asked Knight to CEO Mitchell. "I mean Greyson represents the

PGH health care system. If this story gets into the press it could be a real black eye to the hospital."

"We certainly do not condone the behavior," said Mitchell straightening in his seat and clearing his throat. "But, until any official charges are brought forward, we have no mechanism in place to respond to what up until this point has been a "domestic dispute" between two adults." He nervously tapped his fingers on the desk while responding.

"A domestic dispute my ass!" yelled Johnson, breaking his self-imposed silence. "The coward hit the girl, probably would have raped her if help didn't arrive in time."

"Speculation," said Riles. "There is no indication that a sexual assault was imminent, Dr. Johnson. Please, the last thing we need here is sensationalism."

"You're just trying to protect him," said Johnson, leaning back with a wave of his hand in the air. "You hired him, now it's time to fire him. The guy is a time bomb. Wake up, Fred."

"At a minimum I believe he should be put immediately on probation," added Knight. "We need to respond swiftly. I also recommend mandatory anger control management along with alcohol and sex counseling. He needs help."

"What! Richard, a bit harsh, don't you think?" said Riles. "I mean look around this table, we all have skeletons in our closets."

"Don't pull that crap on me," said Knight. "He is a repeat offender, a womanizer who preys upon vulnerable medical students, and now has some sort of a fascination with a young woman from a pharmaceutical company. Stop protecting him Fred. He's our problem now, so lets address it together."

"I'll bring it up to the board of trustees," said Mitchell calmly. "Will be meeting with them tomorrow. I'll relay all of your concerns to the board. Trust me, I fully understand the magnitude of this recurring problem. The situation will be addressed–directly."

Silence ensued for the next twenty seconds before Johnson spoke out again.

"Fred, what about the borax found in your patient? What's going on with that?" asked the elder surgeon. "I'm sure it was in all the other experimental rats."

"A stray contaminant," said Riles. "At least that's what it appears to be. No signs of borax in the O.R. or the factory."

"Well, what happened then?" asked Johnson. "Did it just drop out of the sky? It had to come from somewhere."

"Fred, you need to notify the police immediately," said Knight. "Or I will."

"Oh there you go again Richard, overreacting," said Riles. "The police? Why would we need the police involved?"

"Why?" cried Knight. "This department has a history of strange events, as you and I well know. As chair, you can't assume anything. I learned that lesson the hard way when your two predecessors dragged their feet." He pointed to Riles. "Notify the police at once."

"Richard we are investigating this very seriously," said Mitchell. "Again it is on tomorrow's agenda with the board. The Department of Health is also looking into the whole matter. I believe due diligence is being carried out. I agree with Fred. Triggering police activity is unwarranted at this point."

"You were on the cruise also," said Johnson, now pointing his own finger at CEO Mitchell. "You're part of this whole craze. So how can you remain impartial?"

"Listen, listen, please," said Riles with a raise of his hands. "Everyone please calm down. For the sake of transparency there were a few vials of Lysovage remaining in the operating room that are in the process of being forwarded to the Union Park lab. So the situation is still unfolding. Perhaps an answer will be found once the samples are tested.

"Are you nuts?" asked Johnson. "Send them to an independent lab. Of course Union Park is going to say they are clean. Sending them to their maker is ludicrous."

"I agree," said Knight. "A neutral party needs to be involved."

"The Lysovage clinical trials are complete. The study is over," said Riles emphatically. "Once this borax matter is cleared up everything will return back to normal. Quite frankly Drs. Knight and Johnson, I've been amazed as to your demeanor towards this product. I consider your behavior an insult to my professional endeavors."

"I'm leaving," said Johnson while standing up. "I hope your malpractice insurance is up to date. Because once that product goes to market, the plaintiff attorneys will be feasting on your carcass. You won't even know what hit you." The cranky surgeon then walked out of the room as quickly as his decrepit body allowed.

The meeting awkwardly adjourned with all parties a bit shaken. Knight headed down to the operating room proper to talk to the supervisor, a woman he knew quite well. They discussed the receiving and handling of the Lysovage vials throughout the trials, she stating only those physicians involved in the project had access to the storage unit, with samples randomly being taken out prior to each case. She reported to Knight the left over vials were recently sequestered by Dr. Riles, the operating room now void of any samples. Lastly they discussed her involvement in the search for borax in the laparoscope cleansing process, an endeavor that came up empty. Simply put, there was no borax in any of the cleaning agents involved.

At one o'clock in the afternoon Knight had lunch with his financial advisor, a man in his mid-sixties, who knew his client well. They discussed Knight's future earning capabilities in light of his recent physical limitations. Thankfully the surgeon had a disability insurance policy that no longer existed, one commonplace to the 1980s. The policy paid him money for loss of capacity at nearly 100% of his current wage. Fortunately for Knight the company that underwrote the plan still existed.

"Remember when I put that contract before you?" asked the advisor. "So long ago?"

"Sure," said Knight. "I just completed residency and my father sent you down to meet me. Told me it was important to get disability insurance. You took me out for a Philly cheesesteak down on South Street. You must have made a bundle over time on this one."

"You were young, healthy and a bit cocky," said the insurance salesman. "Never thought you would need the insurance. Well here we are."

"Yes, here we are, unfortunately. Where did the time go?" asked Knight. "I went to bed at age twenty six and woke up at fifty-nine. What the hell happened?"

"Time can be a thief Richard. But trust me, you still have plenty of time. Make the most of it, especially now since money will not be a concern, thanks to your wonderful financial advisor."

"You too were cocky back then," said Knight. "How's your wife? Still have the same one, the tall brunette?

"Don't be silly," said the advisor. "Been through two of them since. Take my advice Richard, don't get divorced at this stage in your life, too costly."

"Not a problem," said Knight. "The marriage has never been better."

"That's good news."

"Yes," said Knight. "But this crazy neurologic condition has recalibrated my thought process. I'm not invincible, just a mere mortal. Humbling experience."

"Good for you Richard," said the advisor. "Now lets discuss this clinic. Free clinics cost money Richard, lots of money."

Mid afternoon found Knight teaching an anatomy class at the medical school, followed by a curriculum meeting at Penn, where he sat on the pre-med advisory board. He thrived on the young energy pulsating from both a medical center and university campus. At four o'clock he was sitting in the musty office of Professor Shoebottom, a meeting arranged by Knight to discuss recent borax concerns. Unfortunately the absent minded professor lived up to his moniker and arrived at six o'clock, wondering where Dr. Riles was, and why he wanted to meet again? Knight left an hour earlier.

Dinner was back home at six, during which time Mrs. Knight pointed out a two-page article in the *Philadelphia Chronicle* on Lysovage. Knight carefully read the piece, which described a ten-year research project under the direction of Dr. Frederick Riles, the esteemed Professor of General Surgery at the Philadelphia General. The article described the product both on a molecular and clinical level, explaining its magical action. The writer trumpeted the drug, citing excellent clinical results and minimal complications in a massive double-blinded study, carried out in Boston and Philadelphia. An initial public offering was set for Union Park's wonder drug that Friday morning along with an announcement ceremony in the evening, at the convention center. In the middle of the article was a picture of Riles, holding up a vial of the white powder in awe, with Greyson at his side.

The visual of the two roiled Knight.

The caption beneath the photo read, "Drs. Frederick Riles and Stuart Greyson, research pioneers in the development of a breakthrough drug called Lysovage."

"What a handsome young doctor," said Mrs. Knight in reference to Greyson. "He reminds me of you a long time ago."

Knight held his lip.

"What do you think of the article dear? Were you involved in this research project?"

"The article is littered with inaccuracies," said Knight. "Yellow journalism. Borderline fiction. And no, I was not involved in the project." He skipped on dessert that evening, his appetite ruined by the fourth estate.

A postprandial nap was followed by a few painful innings of a Phillies baseball game on television. At nine o'clock Knight went out for a walk, to the Philadelphia General and Jennifer's room.

"Our girl is doing a bit better," said Nurse Hudson standing next to Jennifer's bed. "Had to go out for a little makeup run this evening, her request."

"A sure sign of improvement," said Knight as he stared at a computer screen in the room, her labs rock solid.

"I walked up and down the hallway today," said Jenna. "Feeling stronger."

"Must be the antibiotic change that I recommended," said Knight. "There's a chance you may have had a resistant strain of bacteria. I can't believe the infectious disease team didn't consider that."

Jenna just smiled at Knight. Some things never change she thought. If anything he was consistent. She deeply appreciated his personal concern.

"We had a little confusion here the other night," said Hudson, trying to play down the magnitude of the news while fluffing Jen's pillow. "A slight medicinal error, nothing major."

"Lucy, I told you not to say anything," said Jennifer. "You promised."

"What are you talking about?" asked Knight. "Any error in a hospital is major, as far as I'm concerned."

"Jen had a headache last night and the hospitalist ordered a medication with some aspirin in it."

"She can't have aspirin, she's on a subcutaneous blood thinner, prophylactic dose." Knight was referring to a daily injection of a blood thinner given to Jenna, hospital protocol for anyone bedridden for a significant amount of time to prevent blood clots.

"I know," said Nurse Hudson. "It should not have been ordered."

"Don't tell me she got the aspirin," said Knight. "I mean the computer system should warn any nurse trying to give that combination. The computers shouldn't allow it."

"Well somehow she did," said Hudson followed by a pause. "Get the medication that is, but nothing happened."

"I'm fine," said Jenna. "The medication worked, my headache was gone in about fifteen minutes."

"I want that hospitalist on the line right now," said Knight in disgust. "This is how it happens, they get a call, give an order and vanish at 5 PM! Get him on the line now, not the night shift stooge, I want the guy or gal who gave that order."

"But I'm not sure we can get the doctor at home," said Hudson.

"I want her stool checked for occult blood and a stat hemoglobin and hematocrit," said Knight, starting to warm up. "Idiots!"

"I told you not to tell him Lucy."

"What about the nurse involved? Didn't the computer warn her of such an interaction? Aspirin potentiates a blood thinner, a second year medical student knows that. She could have bled to death!"

"Well there was a warning on the screen, but the nurse who administered the medication was new, very new. I did discuss the matter with her and...."

"Who is she?" asked Knight. "Get her on the phone now."

"Oh no Richard, please don't. It's Caroline," said Jenna. "She is so nice to me."

"Caroline who?"

"Caroline Ell," said Nurse Hudson hoping the name didn't trigger anything in Knight's memory banks.

"The girl in the YouTube video with Drummer?" asked Knight. "Are you kidding me?"

"What YouTube video?" asked Jennifer. "Phil was in a video with Nurse Ell?"

Nurse Hudson acted quickly and grabbed Knight by the forearm, escorting him into the hall. She was one of the few nurses who knew how to handle Knight, based on past experience. She scolded him for his actions in regards to Ell, stating she was an excellent nurse. She would get the hospitalist on the line that evening, but not Nurse Ell. She told Knight he was overreacting to a possible side effect that never occurred.

After reaming out the unsuspecting hospitalist over the phone, Knight left the hospital.

He stopped at a local tavern situated between the hospital and home, an upscale bar he knew well. Without asking the bartender poured him exactly two jiggers of top shelf vodka, a vice he refused to surrender. He arrived home at eleven o'clock, his wife already in bed. After turning off the nightlight the doctor stared at the ceiling, wondering if the series of events he was about to trigger were justified. The answer was yes.

Chapter Twenty Three
THE CONFESSION

"How exactly did you come about this information?" asked Dr. Riles. "I mean if you look into the computer now, no such report exists."

"I printed it out on the floor," said Phil. "Two days after Mrs. Rudenko's surgery. It came up in her electronic medical record then. I like to start gathering information on patients early, in preparation for future conference presentations." He was in Riles' office, standing in front of a massive oak desk.

Riles was staring at two separate pathology reports on Mrs. Rudenko, each similar yet not identical. The original report was no longer in the patient's electronic chart, only the second report technically existed. His trained eye immediately noticed the second report was more vague in regards to the findings in Rudenko's abdomen, and certainly more beneficial to the Lysovage issue.

"Interesting," said the chairman. "Have you shared this information with anyone else?"

"No sir."

"I can't explain the discrepancy, but I will look into it Dr. Drummer. Thank you for bringing it to my attention."

"You're welcome Dr. Riles."

Dr. Riles leaned back into his leather chair and looked up at Phil while taking off a set of reading glasses. He gave a pensive pause, as if scripted, thought Phil. His overly bright dental caps caused Phil to recall their first meeting, five years ago at med school graduation. So much had happened since then.

"Any final decision with regards to our offer?" asked Riles. "Several other physicians have applied for the position. Excellent candidates I may add… but we are holding the spot until you decide. Associate Professor of Surgery at the Philadelphia General Hospital is quite a title young man."

"I know. I know. Thank you sir," said Phil. "I appreciate that but I'm still trying to get through the legal terminology. I'm sending the contract back home to a lawyer my dad used to know."

"No rush, no rush, take your time young man."

"I appreciate that Dr. Riles. A lot has been going on lately."

"How about the Lysovage issue? You have until this Friday morning to decide. After that, the stock options are off the table."

"Still undecided," said Phil. "Especially after what happened on the cruise. Maybe I'm not ready for such a commitment."

"The cruise issue is over! An isolated event," retorted Riles, now breaking from his calm demeanor with Phil. "Dr. Greyson realized the mistake he made and apologized to all parties involved. Case closed. As for the project, everyone involved couldn't be more excited, the end so near. We are coming down the home stretch Dr. Drummer. Nothing can go wrong at this point in time. So take some advice from your department chairman and get involved. It's the definition of a win-win situation. A once in a lifetime opportunity awaits you. I suggest you take it."

"Thank you Dr. Riles", said Phil. "And thank you for the opportunity to speak at the Lysovage event this Friday. A real honor."

"You're welcome Phillip. It's my pleasure. Now about these reports, you let me handle it. Understood?"

"Yes sir," said Phil. "But the conference on Mrs. Rudenko is set for tomorrow morning. I have to present her case to the department. What report should I use?"

"I'm going to cancel the conference," said Riles. "We all have too much on our plates this week. I'll discuss the reports with the pathology department and get to the bottom of this issue. Understood?"

"Yes sir."

"I would ask of you not to discuss the matter with anyone else. O.K.?"

"Yes Dr. Riles."

"Let's keep it between you and I, hopefully future colleagues at the PGH. It would be a good start to our professional working relationship together. Yes?"

"Yes, understood," said Phil.

"Marvelous," said Riles. "Have a nice day Dr. Drummer and thank you for bringing this matter to my attention.

When Phil arrived back at the Greycliff, Vanessa was waiting outside his apartment door, unannounced. She was talking to Troy Huckabee in the hallway, both casually leaning with their backs against the wall.

"You are just too beautiful Miss Vanessa," said Huckabee, dialing up his southern drawl a notch. "Please tell me you are going to be my neighbor."

"Break it up Troy," said Phil. "And please don't listen to him Vanessa, his parents grew up in Manhattan. It's the southern man shtick."

"Why Philip Drummer," said Huckabee. "Do you know this beautiful southern belle?"

Phil politely broke up the discussion and escorted Vanessa into his apartment. He was unaccustomed to seeing her in civilian clothes, a pair of shorts, tee shirt and sneakers, yet she still looked great. Her lips were a natural dark red.

"What's up?" asked Phil. "Why the visit?"

"I handed in my resignation to Union Park this morning," said Vanessa sharply. "The whole charade is over... at least for me."

"Charade, what charade?" asked Phil. "The Union Park super bowl is in exactly four days. Dr. Riles is going to spike the ball in the end zone. I'm one of the guest speakers. You can't leave me now. You're one of the main reasons I got involved, remember?"

"Phil, listen. Everything I've told you about me is true. The absolute truth," said Vanessa, her eyes fixated directly into his. "I've never lied to you. Remember that. However I've had it with Union Park, nothing is real there. The cruise was the final straw, I've had it."

"What are you talking about?"

"They turned me into something I didn't want to be," said Vanessa. "Someone I don't want to be. Too much money is harmful, I'm convinced of that."

"What are you like a corporate operative or something?" asked Phil. "A government agent? What's up? You're starting to worry me Vanessa."

"Phil, what I'm about to tell you is embarrassing... but the truth. I've got to come clean with everyone, especially you, in order to move on."

"Alright," said Phil with trepidation. "I want to hear it – for both our sakes."

"Phil I run a high price escort service, for businessmen, specifically those involved with Union Park," said Vanessa bluntly. "It's my job, or was my job until a few hours ago."

She stared at Phil, a tense smile on her face. "There, that was the hard part. It's over."

"O.K.," said Phil slowly, things now starting to make sense. "Didn't see that one coming."

"And I'm sorry to say I used to be an escort myself, in my teenage years... for just a brief period of time. That's how I met Vic's prior boss, before he died."

"O.K., you may want to stop there," said Phil.

"We fell in love, at least I think we did. I was so darn young and naïve. He hired me, they still needed girls, I knew a few, and voila, I was the grand dame of a group of prostitutes. Happened kind of fast." She looked down and shook her head. After a moment she drew in a deep breath and looked up at Phil, somewhat apologetic, and turned both palms of her hand towards the ceiling.

"And here I am," she said. "Confessing to a man I barely know that I'm a former hooker, a recent panderer, and currently unemployed." Tears begin to roll down her face.

"Why? Why now, why tell me?"

"You," said Vanessa her voice cracking, and wiping tears away. "You, it's all because of you Phil."

"Me?"

"Yes you."

"I don't understand?"

"You came into my life and made me realize that I'm better than that. Much better. You brought my heart back to life, made me feel like a young woman should." Tears were now pouring down her face. "You saved me."

"Vanessa it's O.K., please don't cry."

"Thank you." Her sobs now out of control. "Thank you so much."

"Don't cry Vanessa."

"I love you Phil," she cried. "I know it's not what you want to hear, but I love you. I can't help it."

She dove her body into his, Phil holding on tight, not knowing what to say.

"I'm sorry, I'm sorry Phil. I know you have Jenna. I can't help it."

"It's O.K," said Phil. "It's alright."

"Oh gosh, look at me," said Vanessa pulling back a bit. "Crying like a little girl." Mascara ran down both her cheeks. "I'm sorry Phil, so sorry."

"It's O.K. Vanessa," said Phil, now wiping away some of her tears. "I understand. I'm glad you told me, things are making a bit more sense."

"I must look a mess."

"No, you look great," said Phil now wiping a tear near her lips. "Absolutely beautiful as far as I'm concerned. Really. Quite beautiful."

She kissed him–a passionate kiss of gratitude with a touch of intimacy, setting her repentance to rest. She was at his mercy, her confession complete, with nowhere else to go. Phil realized the true feelings he had for her, undeniable emotions ready to run amok. His mettle was tested but he held firm, kissing her on the forehead. Softly he brushed back a few strands of hair from her face with a smile. She felt so good in his arms.

"Let's get you something to eat," he said. "And talk some more, alright? That will help."

"I'd like that," said Vanessa, gathering her composure. "Thank you."

Over the next hour the two had lunch together, discussing in more detail Vanessa's Union Park days. She described her job as one long vacation, an around the world junket funded by profits reaped by Union Park and the powerful men surrounding her. She was reimbursed handsomely, put away some money, but had no future plans. She deeply cared for the girls on her team, which brought her up to the topic of Stuart Greyson.

"He's scum," she said. "A deeply disturbed, immoral man."

"Different from his outward appearance," said Phil. "Women swoon in his presence."

"Those are the ones you have to look out for," she replied. "Let me make it clear. I never slept with him. O.K.? That's the truth."

"Yes, best news of the day so far. Thank you."

"Every girl selected by him has complained bitterly, and doesn't want to be around him anymore. Would sooner quit then be assigned to his presence. He is a perverse individual."

"Enough said, please don't go into any more detail. I may be working with the guy for years to come," said Phil.

"A sexual deviant, let me just wrap it up with that remark. The man is a sexual deviant, and needs help."

"Understood," said Phil.

Then, as if trying to decide, Vanessa leaned forward and took a deep breath. Phil sensed something of importance about to be said, wondering what could possibly remain. She reached out and held his hand, causing his heart to beat rapidly.

"Phil," said Vanessa. "They're fudging the data."

"What?" asked Phil. "What are you talking about? What data?"

"The Lysovage data, they're messing with the pathology results. I know it. They're altering the reports."

"I'm sorry, can you repeat that Vanessa? I thought I heard you say that pathology reports are being altered.

"That's exactly what I said Phil."

"Are you sure Vanessa? How can you be sure?" asked Phil, now getting up and pacing throughout the apartment. "That's a monumental accusation. Do you realize the implications of such a statement? I mean Dr. Riles has been working on that project for over ten years. It's his life's work, Vanessa."

"Phil, I lived with Fanicci for three years, he is a nice man but also a borderline alcoholic who talks too much. Over time I've picked up snippets of cell phone discussions and references to a pathology lab in Boston."

"You're blowing my mind with this one Vanessa. I don't know what to say..."

"I know, I know," said Vanessa. "It's just that I don't know where to go from here, what to do."

"Well neither do I," said Phil. "What about me? Now I'm privy to this information. I'm compromised Vanessa. Remember, I'm an integral part of the drug's coming out party this Friday night."

"I'm sorry, I shouldn't have told you."

"Are you sure Vanessa? Sure about this? Be more specific. You have to be sure. A man's professional reputation is on the line."

"Over time," she said. "I put together information over time. For example, talk about PGH results versus Boston results. The Boston results mattering and the PGH results being voided out. Over the past six months the chatter has become more frequent, more animated. I even heard him ask for assurance that electronic records can be changed without a trace, without leaving an electronic trail."

"Oh my god," said Phil. "I can't believe it." The two Rudenko pathology reports now making sense.

"It's true Phil. Why would I make such a thing up?"

"Who was he talking to?" asked Phil.

"I don't know. I admit he never called anyone by their name over the phone with me around. I'll give him credit for that."

"Wow," said Phil. "Wow. What now?"

"I don't know," said the young woman sitting in his apartment. "But I've come clean. I'm done with Union

Park. I'm sorry I got you into this mess but I thought you should know, before you get in any deeper. I told you for your own good Phil, really. I hope you understand."

Later that evening Phil called Dr. Riles, politely declining on his recommendation to buy stock in Union Park, and thanking the chairman for the offer. He agreed to speak on Friday night at the conference, however made it perfectly clear that he wanted no further involvement with the Lysovage product. He had not decided about the academic staff position on the table, asking Riles for some additional time to decide. The chairman reluctantly accepted his decision regarding Lysovage, wondering what had occurred since their discussion earlier in the day.

Approximately one hour later Dr. Riles received a second phone call, from CEO Mitchell.

"Fred, Phil Drummer visited me earlier today," said Mitchell. "Requested an emergency meeting with me."

"And..." said Riles. "What was discussed?"

"The young man brought me two pathology reports on a patient, let's see," said Mitchell shuffling some papers. "Named Rudenko, Julia Rudenko."

"Yes," said Riles. "Ms. Rudenko is my patient. She is enrolled in the project."

"Yes, well apparently two separate pathology reports exist regarding her surgery under the direction of Dr. Johnson," said Mitchell. "You are aware of this, yes?'

"Well, I know she is my patient," mumbled Riles. "I was away when..."

"Fred, Drummer told me he visited you earlier today and gave you a copy of the reports."

"Oh yes, of course I know about the reports. I was, ah, we just miscommunicated there a bit, sorry. Of course I know about the reports."

"We have a problem here Fred, that I can't explain. How can two separate reports exist on the same pathologic specimen? Is this the norm?"

"I have no explanation for it," said Riles firmly. "None whatsoever."

"Do all patient's in the study get two reports?"

"Again, John, this has caught me off guard. I just found out about it today. Give me some time to look into it. I'm sure there is an explanation."

"There's more Fred. Victor just called to let me know that Vanessa Rose quit today. Just walked out the door."

Riles didn't respond.

"Fred, do you hear me? Do you realize how much information that girl has about Union Park and this whole project?"

"Why did she leave? Did Victor say why?"

"Nope. But I'm sure Stuart's behavior played into her decision, which by the way reminds me, the board of trustees put him on probation for one year. They also want him enrolled into an anger management program."

"What about alcohol or sex counseling?"

"No. I went to bat for him on that. But the board was firm in their decision. A certified letter will be arriving at Greyson's office tomorrow. I'll follow up with a phone call."

A long pause was interrupted by Riles.

"John, what the hell is going on? In less than four days the culmination of my entire professional life is about to be broadcast worldwide, and now all this. The wheels are coming off the goddamn wagon."

"Greyson is Greyson," said Mitchell. "You unfortunately know that better than anyone else. Vanessa Rose is a Union Park problem, not ours, she will drift away sooner or later. But these pathology reports are problematic, especially if they end up in the wrong hands."

"I know, I know."

"By the wrong hands I mean Knight or Johnson, they are just waiting for a reason to sink your product."

"Yes. A disaster for them to catch wind of it."

"Listen Fred, Drummer is the key. You need to keep him quiet for a few days. Have him lay low. Once the product is out to market, it will all blow over."

"Got it. John, what the hell is going on? Am I the only person out of some loop?"

"Fred, I'll ask you one more time. Are you sure you have no knowledge whatsoever as to how two separate path reports exist, one on paper, and the other on electronic record?"

"Absolutely not!" retorted Riles. "I'm a man of integrity! Never in a million years would I manipulate research data. Never!"

"Yes, yes. I'm sorry Fred but I had to ask. Listen old friend, we've been in this together for some time. Let's stay the course, stay firm and finish strong. All the great ones finish strong. Right?"

"Right, right," said Riles, his voice lowering. "Finish strong. I'll look into it and call you tomorrow. Good night." He hung up the phone.

Riles decided not to discuss the matter with the pathology department, until after Friday's presentation. Mitchell was right. Drummer was the key and the less people involved, the better. He went home to a surprise party thrown by his wife, in anticipation of Friday's big announcement. It took great personal effort for him to keep smiling, as adulations rained down upon him. The surgical chairman did not sleep well that evening. He was upset about a chief resident going over his head with a concern, after agreeing not to. He had broken a surgeon's code of camaraderie.

The next morning he woke early and headed downstairs to breakfast. Into a bowl he poured some cereal, the same brand for the past quarter century, and added a banana. A cup of coffee accompanied a single glass of orange juice, along with a multi-vitamin for men. He flipped on the radio, the dial set to his favorite station. Next he turned towards the garage door in anticipation of the daily newspaper in the driveway. It was at that moment he spotted a yellow sticky note attached to the refrigerator door with his wife's handwriting on it. He reached out and grabbed it.

The note simply read: "Fred – Professor Shoebottom called, sorry he missed the meeting. His memory is starting to come back to him. Please call. – Carol."

Chapter Twenty Four
A MED CENTER VIBE

A TERTIARY CARE medical center is a hotbed of activity where thousands of workers and patients converge daily. An indescribable energy is emitted from such an atmosphere, overflowing with technology, pathology and human emotion. Hallways are jammed as those inside hustle to their next appointment, diagnostic exam or surgical procedure. People of all race, color and creed flow through a maze of corridors in search of good health. Somehow all of this perceived chaos works, from the valet attendant outside to the complex neurosurgical procedure inside, on a daily basis. Such a med center vibe existed within the PGH, just forty-eight hours prior to the big announcement.

Early morning found Stuart Greyson standing in front of several key members of the board of trustees. They notified him of a one-year probation and need to enroll in an anger management program. His excuses of workplace stress and a wife's emotional battle with infertility fell upon deaf ears. The board would hear nothing of it, and within twenty minutes, the sentencing was over. The young surgeon was warned that any further misconduct would result in his immediate expulsion from the medical center and surgical staff. A dejected Greyson stepped out of the boardroom into a busy corridor to the left, his body pushed forward by the momentum of the throng of individuals passing by. He ran directly into Nurse Hudson, who was heading in for a day shift.

"Good morning doctor," said Hudson in a hurry.

"I guess you can say that," said Greyson with a smirk. Greyson had kept Nurse Hudson in the know regarding the fallout from the cruise.

"Judgement day?" asked Hudson.

"Yea, but I'd call it an overreaction from a bunch of businessmen who don't understand the stress of being a surgeon."

"You're still with us though, right?"

"Yea, just a slap on the hand," said the surgeon. "Can't stop my mojo. I'll show them."

"There you go," said Hudson, now turning into an elevator. "Have a great day. See you on Friday."

Hudson rode the jammed elevator to the tenth floor of the Kirby pavilion, her body mashed into that of a red faced second year medical student. She exited onto the general surgery floor, meeting up with Nurse Ell.

"Morning Cara," said Hudson. "How are you today?"

"O.K.," said Ell unenthusiastically. The prior evening she had asked Phil out for a drink to "catch up" on things since the Lucca Cibo debacle. He declined, stating too much was on his plate that week, yet they talked for some time. He again apologized for the vortex of drama surrounding him which had sucked her inside. She accepted his apology. The conversation ended well but with no reconnect in sight.

"I'm assigning you to Jenna today," said Hudson. "No mistakes, understand?"

"Yes. It won't happen again."

"Everyone is keeping a close eye on her," said Hudson. "I mean everyone."

"Understood," said Ell. "I'll take good care of her."

Rick Polk then rushed by the two with a coffee in one hand and doughnut in the other. Closely behind him was intern Westbrook with a concerned look on his face.

"Morning ladies," said Polk passing by.

"Where's the fire?" asked Hudson.

"Late for Doc Johnson in the O.R.," said Polk. "I let Westbrook put in a central line this morning and I think he gave the lady a pneumothorax." He was describing a special intravenous catheter placed directly beneath the collarbone that when misplaced, can puncture the nearby lung.

"On who?"

"The old gal short of breath in 1034," yelled Polk. "Please check the stat chest x-ray I just ordered, and put some oxygen on her."

"Right," said Hudson.

Polk and Westbrook then disappeared down a stairwell past a group of medical interns heading upstairs.

"There he is!" yelled one of the senior medical residents to the group. "The man who lives in the hospital!"

"That's him, that's him." One student quickly took a picture of him on her cell phone.

Polk raised his right arm overhead and rolled his hand, as if blessing the congregation, everyone staring in awe. "God bless you all," he said while continuing his descent. "God bless you all."

The duo exited on the O.R. floor and turned right into fellow surgical residents Boyce and Rhimes.

"What, what?' said Polk. "My brothers from another mother."

"Doc Johnson's flipping out. You're late!" said chief resident Jackie Rhimes without stopping.

"Westbrook dropped a lung upstairs," said Polk. "Where you boys headed?"

"To the E.R.," continued Rhimes. "Gunshot to the gut. Better get in their quick, the old man is hot."

"Roger," said Polk. "What room is he in?"

"O.R. six!"

Rhimes and Boyce then ran down a crowded stairwell towards the E.R. where a forty one year old man awaited. He was caught in bed with his friend's wife and took two rounds from a nine-millimeter pistol to the abdomen. Upon entering the trauma bay they stepped into a blood bath as hospital personnel attempted to stem the tide. The bullets tumbled through the victim's bowels and unfortunately hit his right renal artery. Chaos transpired as the two residents along with a vascular fellow decided to immediately open his abdomen in an attempt to save his life. Nurses poured in I.V. fluids and banked blood as the trauma bay was converted into a surgical theatre. Within minutes the unsupervised surgical endeavor made its way down to the bleeding vessel, which was quickly cross-clamped by a sweating fellow.

"Now what?" asked the vascular trainee to Rhimes. His hand shaking on the clamp, the bloodletting somewhat eased.

"How should I know, you're the vascular man," said Rhimes. "I got you down to the spot. Can't you sew it?"

Suddenly another burst of donated blood sprayed out of the patient's abdomen in all directions.

"I thought you had it clamped!" yelled Rhimes. "What the..."

"I did, I did..." said the vascular fellow. "It's his aorta above! It cut loose!"

Up until that point the young surgeons were unaware of the more proximal aortic wall injury that occurred during the patient's moment of reckoning, which suddenly burst open. An immediate and uncontrollable blood letting ensued. Within ten minutes the gunshot victim was pronounced dead. He was the 56th murder so far that year in the City of Brotherly Love.

Upon exiting the trauma bay Rhimes looked up to see Phil running towards him.

"Too late?" asked Phil.

"Yea, he boxed. Aorta cut loose, should have seen it." The outfit that Rhimes wore was covered with bright red blood. "Got to change my scrubs. My socks are soaked."

"Sorry, I heard the code and got down here as soon as possible. I was stuck up in Riles' office."

"Hey, can one of you guys help me?" asked an E.R. attending, a tall lanky middle-aged man with oversized ears. "Got an alcoholic with an esophageal bleed, need to ice lavage her and having trouble with the N.G. tube." His request was urgent.

"No problem," said Phil, who then followed the physician down to room six to assist.

Sitting up on the gurney was a fifty-six year old female with a fatal attraction to vodka, dying from liver cirrhosis. She was vomiting up blood and alcohol, her eyes bright yellow, abdomen obtunded and legs swollen. Phil helped the E.R. attending pass a tube down into her stomach by using an old trick Doc Johnson taught him.

"Sip from the straw," said Phil as he snaked the long plastic tube down the patient's nose, hoping it dove into his esophagus below. "Sip, come on now, sip the water." A nurse was holding up a cup of water to the patient's mouth with a straw in it. The gimmick worked and the nasogastric tube found its way into the patient's bleeding gastrointestinal tract. The attending then flushed the patient's stomach with ice water, hoping to ease the bleeding and prolong the inevitable.

"Thanks Drummer," said the attending. "Thanks a lot."

"No problem," said Phil. "Glad it worked." He then headed towards the exit.

"Hey Drummer," said the E.R. attending. "Thanks for all your help over the past four years. It was a pleasure. You never lost your cool down here. And that's rare. Good luck wherever you end up."

"My pleasure working with you Tony," said Drummer. "Keep the faith."

Phil left the E.R. and headed up to the main floor, where he ran into CEO Mitchell. Mitchell was on his way to yet another "take the pulse" meeting with the pathology department with a few questions in mind.

"Dr. Drummer, I spoke to Dr. Riles last night and he was appreciative of your concern regarding the pathology reports," said Mitchell. "Thank you for bringing the matter to my attention."

"Really?" asked Phil. Earlier that morning Dr. Riles paged him to his office and reamed him out, distraught over Phil's decision to go above his head with the pathology information. The chairman was also upset over Mrs. Rudenko seeing another surgeon for her abdominal pain, especially since the surgeon was Dr. Johnson. He felt Phil played a roll in her decision process, after he talked to and examined the patient just several days earlier. Throughout their discussion Phil noticed a peculiar look in the chairman's eyes, a bizarre combination of fear and anger, during which time he threatened not to graduate Phil and his cronies. He paid particular note to Rick Polk and his "den of iniquity" somewhere in the hospital basement. Phil was concerned over an odd disconnect in his chairman's thought process, as if greater matters occupied his mind.

"Sounds like some transcription oversight," said Mitchell. "I'm meeting with the pathology department now to discuss the matter."

"I'm sure it was," said Phil. "I'm sure it was."

Phil then continued down the hallway towards the operating room where Mrs. Rudenko was under the knife of Doc Johnson. He ran into Mo Rhett on the way, pushing a dry mop in front of him.

"Yo, yo, Drummer. How's that hand doing?" asked Mo.

"Still there," said Phil, now walking besides the maintenance man. "Where you headed?"

"The gym," said Mo. "Gonna work on my jumper for the big game tomorrow night. Sorry you won't be playing."

"Don't count me out Mo and by the way, shouldn't you be working?"

"Got my thirty minute lunch break," said Mo. "10 A.M. to noon. Union rules."

"I need a union," said Phil, still stinging from his meeting with Riles.

"Hey, almost forgot," said Mo. "Some big shot with shiny teeth was down in the sub-basement real early this morning. Looking for the Torpedo Room, had two security guards with him."

"Oh no," said Phil. "Polk's streak."

"I played dumb and sent him up two levels to the laundry floor, but he looked intense. Later Drummer."

"Later Mo, thanks for the info."

Phil then entered operating room number six, where Mrs. Rudenko was on the table. Polk and Westbrook were scrubbed in, the case nearly complete.

"Chalk another one up for lyso-bomb," said Johnson. "Look at this poor girl's innards. Firecracker red!"

"Like all the others," said Polk.

Phil peered into the abdominal cavity of Mrs. Rudenko. She had in fact pleaded with him to take over her care, not wanting to return to Dr. Riles. He tactfully suggested a second opinion with Dr. Johnson for her abdominal pain, hoping it would fly under the radar. Her intestinal walls and vital organs were visibly ulcerated.

"Again, no visceral perforation, just a goddamn burn affect on every organ," said Johnson in disgust. "I'm sorry to say but I'm getting used to it."

"Maybe they'll discuss it at the Lysovage coming out party tomorrow night," said Polk. "Are you going Dr. Johnson?"

"Not in a million years," said Johnson. "I'd sooner go to a funeral. And trust me, this complication will never be discussed at that spectacle. The pharmaceutical machine running the show will not allow it. They're pulling the strings, and all those involved are just puppets, dancing their lucrative dance."

"A lot of hoopla surrounding the event," said Polk. "I even saw a few billboards in town announcing it."

"Drummer, I see you're a guest speaker, what are you going to talk about?" asked Johnson as he sutured the patient's abdominal muscles together. "The truth, I hope."

"Just a short five minute blip after Dr. Riles and Greyson," said Phil trying to downplay the event. He was shaking his head at Polk, the instigator. "Gonna briefly touch upon future directions for the product and its role for the next generation of surgeons."

"You know there are laws that protect whistle blowers," said Johnson. "If I had the microphone I'd spill my guts, just like Mrs. Rudenko did in honor of the great project. Look at this poor hard working mother on the table. She didn't sign up for this."

"Whistle blowers make a ton of money," added Polk. "So sing my friend, sing like a canary."

Phil ignored Rick's banter.

"Nurse Cross," said Johnson while stepping away from the table.

"Yes doctor?"

"How many specimens have we taken here today?"

"Let's see, about twelve," said the nurse. "Exactly twelve."

"Please be sure to specifically ask the pathologist to test each specimen for borax," said Johnson as he peeled his gloves off.

"Borax?" asked the nurse.

"Yes, borax," said Johnson with an emphasis on the letter "B." "That's B-O-R-A-X."

"What's borax?"

"Who knows but don't bother going to the big broadcast tomorrow night," said Johnson heading towards the door. "It certainly won't be mentioned there."

After the case Phil and Rick headed to lunch and then back to the Torpedo Room. Phil failed to mention his conversation with Mo earlier in the day, hoping it wasn't Dr. Riles searching for his lair.

"Phil, what the hell is borax?" asked Rick, the two approaching the Torpedo Room door. "And what the hell is Stan doing outside the room? Is that a keg of beer?"

Outside the door was Stan the Beer Truck Man waiting patiently next to the last remaining half-barrel keg of Schmidt's in the world. The ex-brew master had a concerned look upon his face, standing watch over his prized possession.

"What's this?" asked Stan while pointing at the door.

A bright orange rectangular sign was stuck to the door with the word "EVICTION NOTICE" stamped across it, followed by lesser legal print below. A padlock had been drilled into the door, rendering the room inaccessible. The faint meow of the Liberty Bell could be heard on the other side.

"What?" said a shocked Rick Polk. "What? I mean who? What's going on?"

Stan had no idea, stating he had arrived thirty minutes earlier with the adult beverage, the door already sealed. Mo Rhett then turned the corner with a shake of his head.

"It was him again," said Mo. "The old guy with Chicklet teeth. His badge said Dr. Riled or something like that, Chairman Department of Surgery."

"I knew it," said Phil.

"The streak," said Polk, "He's trying to break my streak."

Over the next several minutes Phil informed his colleague of the earlier discussion he had with Riles, including his bizarre demeanor and backlash against the chief residents. It was Mo Rhett who brought calm to the discussion.

"Rick, the streak can't be broken," said Mo. "You've come too far."

"I agree," added Stan.

"Listen," said Mo. "If I take you guys to a place–a very special place, can you promise never to tell anyone it exists?"

"Sure, sure."

"I mean it's my happy spot, our spot, the Department of Maintenance's spot, of which I am a senior employee."

"Yea, yea."

"Promise? I'm doing this because I love you guys."

"We promise Mo, come on, you practically raised us," said Polk.

"Then follow me," said Mo with a look over his shoulder.

They found a dolly to place the beer keg on and began an exodus to the Promised Land. Half way down the hallway the Liberty Bell darted out into Polk's arms, having jimmied her way from beneath a wall. For the next ten minutes the faithful followed their leader, down a series of dim hallways to an outdated freight elevator with an old fashioned metal gate across the door. Once inside Mo took out a round red key from his pocket and placed it into an inner panel, bringing the beast to life. With a smile he looked at the team and turned the key causing the hoist to jerk downwards, deeper into the bowels of the hospital. The open air cart passed several abandoned floors, remnants of clinical wards gone by, some still littered with medical paraphernalia. Suddenly it hit bottom and the power cut to the machine. All was quiet. Mo reached forward and opened the metallic gates with an extended hand, welcoming his guests.

"Gentlemen, welcome to the Congo."

The Congo was the sub-basement of the old Fox Pavilion, one of the first ever medical wards built in West Philadelphia over two hundreds years ago. Over the centuries a massive medical center grew up around it, yet somehow it remained, thanks to a never-ending series of power lines running through it. The Congo was strategically located near the main power grid from the street and represented a direct route for electric flow into the center. It was three stories below ground level, dimly lit by blue lights mandated by city code and cool, maintaining a year round temperature of 55 degrees. Scattered everywhere were power lines, running haphazardly through the space, traversing concrete walls.

They heard a noise down a narrow hall to the right.

"What was that?" asked Polk. "Is this place haunted?"

"Where in God's name are we?" asked Phil.

"Why is it called the Congo?" asked Stan.

"It's the Congo because no white man has been down here in I'd say over a century," said Mo. "At least not to my knowledge."

"What's that noise?"

"Don't worry Rick. It's just one of the boys," said Mo. "We have a few cots set up down the hall, you know for emergency purposes."

"Emergencies? What are you talking about?"

"Personal emergencies, you know, like when the old lady flips out and you have to lay low somewhere for a few days," said Mo. "Or when there's some trouble in the hood and you have to vanish for a week or two. Stuff like that."

"Oh."

"The smart rabbit always has more than one hole," said Mo. "Always remember that. Now follow me."

He lead the expedition down a cement floor hallway that opened up into a cavernous room, littered with some hospital furniture, a few mattresses and a small refrigerator, with a radio on top. Jazz music played softly from a university radio station across town. There were two other workers lounging in the area clad in mandatory grey maintenance department uniforms. They both tentatively stood up when the guests arrived, a look of concern on their faces.

"Probably presume you are Doctor Doolittle," said Mo as he walked towards the fellow workers to explain the situation.

"I believe that's Dr. Livingstone," said Phil.

"Yea, yea, whatever," said Mo. "Hey guys, I've got a brother here in need of some shelter for a few weeks, gonna set him up down here for a while. Alright?"

Within thirty minutes Rick Polk tucked into his new quarters, reassured that the space was technically still within the hospital proper. The streak was alive. Stan felt the ambient temperature was perfect for his keg, despite the fact it spent the last twenty-five years in his attic. Phil helped his friend settle in by finding some sheets for a cot and running down supplies for the Liberty Bell.

At approximately six o'clock in the evening Phil exited the medical complex onto 34th street. As he crossed University Ave., he looked to the left at a stationary car waiting for the light to turn green. His eyes met that of the driver, whose face was strangely familiar. Inside the vehicle was Detective James of the Philadelphia Police Department. James headed the investigation four years ago surrounding the deaths of Dr. Knight's patients. He hadn't seen Phil in years, yet recognized his face, nodding slightly. It took Phil one more city block to recall his name, causing a chill to run down his spine.

Detective James drove his vehicle down South Street across the Schuylkill River, into center city. Thick rush hour traffic hampered his progress. He turned left on Seventh Street towards the tony Washington Square neighborhood, occasionally peering down at an address written on a scrap of paper. He pulled the city vehicle up to a magnificent brick Federalist house, surrounded by a low wall and wrought iron fence. The grounds on each side of the walkway were meticulously groomed with a fresh layer of mulch and perennials. A crowded finch feeder hung from a Japanese maple, steps from the front door. The detective checked the address again before reaching upwards and tapping a lion head doorknocker. The light tap, tap, tap echoed through the center city mansion. He waited for several seconds before the door swung open.

"Yes, may I help you?" asked a woman in a blue skirt and blouse, buttoned to the top with a collar pin in place.

"Mrs. Knight?"

"Yes."

"Mrs. Knight, I'm Detective James of the Philadelphia Police Department," said the lawman while holding up his I.D. badge. "Is your husband home?"

"Why uh, yes," said Mrs. Knight holding her hand to her chest. "I'll have to check."

"Nothing is wrong ma'am, there is no emergency," said Detective James. "I just need to have a few words with your husband if possible."

Then, down the long corridor behind Mrs. Knight the frame of Dr. Knight appeared, causing his wife to turn backwards, speechless.

The sleuth made immediate eye contact with Knight, who then looked at his wife.

"It's O.K. Margaret," said Knight. "Everything is alright. Please, let the detective in."

Chapter Twenty Five
TIES THAT BIND

Dr. Frederick Riles hated Philadelphia and everything about it. An angry driver just passed him on the Schuylkill and flipped him the bird with a complementary blow of the horn, irate over his driving skills. Having just suffered through a forty-five minute delay on the expressway because of a "roving PennDot crew," the beleaguered chairman was apparently going too slow for the native Philadelphian, whose bumper sticker screamed "Boston Sucks!" He hated everything about the city obsessed with a boxing movie from 1976, including greasy cheesesteaks, soft pretzels, scrapple and a subpar football team. It's not like he didn't try. He once attended an Eagles game, only to be hit in the head with a snowball aimed at Santa Claus. He woke up early one New Year's Day to attend the Mummer's Parade in arctic conditions, only to have an intoxicated high school student reeking of marijuana vomit on his right shoulder. He was mugged in Fairmount Park, spit on at Suburban Station by a homeless man, and had his car stolen in West Philadelphia. A bad batch of barbecued pig from the local Italian Market kept him out of work for three days to allow an inflamed gallbladder to simmer down. Even his wife refused to fly out of the local airport, thanks to a rude baggage handler making fun of her New England accent. Simply put, the gritty, beer-guzzling City of Brotherly Love made him yearn for the culture of Boston, where the Riles names meant so much, for so long.

Flashing red lights suddenly appeared in his rear view mirror. "Rrrrrrr" went the siren. "Rrrrrrr." A city policeman was in pursuit with headlights blinking, prompting the surgeon to pull over to the cramped roadside. He even hated the puke powder blue and white color scheme of city police cars. A middle-aged officer with a scowl on his face then approached the driver's side of his car.

"Yes officer?" asked Riles.

"Vehicle registration and driver's license," said the officer.

"Is there a problem?" Some cars passing by at 65 miles per hour were blowing their horn.

"I said vehicle registration and driver's license," said the officer. "Now please."

He handed the officer his cards, noticing the policeman's right index finger was missing. The officer returned to his vehicle for several minutes, during which time Riles wondered how he could "protect and serve" without a trigger finger. The sign before him said "Gladwyne Exit 337." He almost made it.

"Do you know how fast you were traveling sir?" asked the officer returning the cards back to Riles.

"No. I do not."

"Seventy-nine in a fifty-five mile per hour zone sir. Were you aware of that?"

"Officer someone just a few seconds ago blew a horn at me and flashed an obscene gesture," said Riles. "I was a bit shaken."

"This is a high fatality area," said the officer. "We've been trying to cut down on speeders for the safety of everyone."

"I didn't know that officer."

"Fifty-five miles per hour is the speed limit on all two lanes throughout the Commonwealth of Pennsylvania," said the policeman. "Excessive speed is the primary cause of fatal accidents, I'm sure you can appreciate that?"

Riles knew he was on the fence, the officer deciding upon a warning or stiff ticket. He wondered if the policeman was under pressure to meet a monthly ticket quota. "Yes sir, I fully understand and appreciate that. I am truly sorry."

"Just last week there were two fatalities on this very stretch, young kids, separate accidents."

"I'm a surgeon at the PGH," said Riles. "We are up all night taking care of unfortunate accident victims. I mean just last week we put back together a city policeman involved in a serious collision." A white lie never hurt.

The officer just stared down at Riles, having already written out the $180 fine. He didn't like his personal appearance but the wounded officer comment struck a chord. Maybe someday he would be on the surgical table, looking up at the surgeon's aristocratic face. A decision had to be made.

"You from around these parts?" asked the officer.

"No. No," said Riles with a smile and shake of his head. "From up north."

"I see," said the officer. "Where up north?"

"New England area," said Riles. "But I love Philadelphia. Moved here three years ago. Absolutely love it."

"Oh yea?" asked the officer starting to soften up. "What do you like best about our city Dr. Riles?"

Riles froze, his mind absolutely blank, a truck blowing its horn. "Ah, well, there are so many things to love," stammered the surgeon. "Ah, that's why they call it the City of Love."

"Just give me one thing," said the officer. "It's my hometown."

Riles could not tell a lie. He could not think of one admirable thing in the whole wretched city.

"Just one thing doctor, and we can call it an evening."

Then like a bolt of lightening the answer popped into his head. "Schmidt's beer. I love Schmidt's beer," said Riles with a proud smile.

"What did you say?"

"I said Schmidt's beer. Philadelphia's own home brew. One beautiful beer."

"Are you some sort of a smart ass?" asked the officer. "That brewery shut down thirty years ago."

"Ah, well, actually out at the casino...."

"My father worked his butt off in that stinking brewery for twenty years until they ran it into the ground and fired him," growled the policeman.

"Well it's my understanding that a comeback...."

"I can remember the night he came home and told the family, my poor mother cried all night. I was just a little kid hiding in the corner, but now I feel his pain."

"Ah, perhaps a microbrewery with a similar...."

"Dad never recovered," said the officer with an angry, nostalgic gaze. "Was on unemployment for years and then all of a sudden left us, all thanks to Schmidt's beer."

"Officer, maybe there has just been a misunderstanding...."

"I don't think so," said the officer while detaching the ticket from his pad and handing it to Riles. "Not on my part. Enjoy the ticket with your next Schmidt's buddy, and slow down!"

The surgeon took the ticket and waited for the policeman to pull away from the scene, it was now eight o'clock in the evening. He carefully drove two hundred yards down an exit ramp into the stately suburb of Gladwyne. A mile later a massive black metal gate with the letter "G" marked his destination, opening up to a long, tree lined driveway. Halfway up the approach a golden retriever named Stuffy ran along side the car, his tongue flapping in the breeze. The mansion sat atop a knoll, looking out over the Main Line, with a red Porsche parked in picturesque fashion outside. Wondering if anyone was home, he approached the double front door flanked by white columns and an overhead portico. He reached forward and pressed the doorbell, which triggered the regal Westminster Quarters chime.

Stuart Greyson answered the door, not surprised by the chairman's arrival. He let the visitor inside along with Stuffy, wagging his tail.

"Good evening Stuart," said Riles. "I hope I didn't startle you."

"No problem," said Stuart. "I was upstairs in the bathroom, barely heard the doorbell. We just installed a flat screen T.V in the master bath, heaven on earth."

"Ah yes, I see," said Riles, admiring the majestic chandelier hanging above. The most god awful lavish designers in the Delaware Valley had tastefully furbished the entrance foyer, no expense spared. "Who could ask for anything more?"

"The combination of ESPN and a good bowel movement is a carnal experience," said Stuart. "Beyond my expectations."

"I can only imagine," said the chairman.

Greyson escorted Riles into an oak paneled study adjacent to the foyer. Oil paintings crowded the walls, and a large world globe sat in the corner, covered with dust. A once priceless collection of bounded surgical journals dating back to 1922 filled the bookshelves, now worthless due to the internet. Two oversized leather chairs sat to the right of a massive desk, with an ornate chess set adjacent on a small table. The two men sat down opposite each other.

"Ready for tomorrow?" asked Riles. "The big day has finally arrived."

"A chip shot," said Greyson already getting up to walk across the room. "Glass of brandy?"

"No thank you Stuart," said Riles, waiting for the host to return. He scanned the room, a portrait of Stuart and his wife Mia, arm in arm behind the desk. Stuffy was curled up on a rug sitting in front of a fireplace.

"Why the surprise visit?" asked Greyson, powering himself with a slug of brandy. "Is it to tell me my stock percentage is back up to fifteen percent, what I deserve? If so, great news, and thanks."

"Now Stuart, allow me to remind you again that the stock decision was made by the scientific board and founding fathers of the study. It was not my call. And remember, you came late to the table."

"You had a play in the process," said Stuart. "I guess I just expected more from you. That's a lot of money."

"Yes, well I believe I've given you more than money can buy young man," said Riles with a nervous shift in his seat. "I hope you fully understand that."

"It doesn't matter," said Stuart. "Nothing you do from this point forward will surprise me." He took an angry gulp from the glass. "In a year or two, nothing will matter. This whole place will probably be gone."

"Don't talk such nonsense," said Riles. "You and Mia have your whole lives together. Count your blessings…"

"Stop right there," said Greyson. "I've heard that speech way too many times. Save your breath."

"Stuart a lot of what is going on is your fault," said Riles sharply. "Marriage is a commitment predicated upon mutual respect and fidelity."

"I said stop," said Greyson while standing up and walking towards a bay window with a commanding view of the yard. "We've been through this before, what goes on between Mia and I is none of your business."

"I disagree," said Riles. "It is my business."

"Then why didn't you stick up for me on the cruise ship?" asked Greyson. "Why did you let Union Park decrease my take to five percent? Why didn't you talk to the hospital's board of trustees?"

"Stuart, I've already bent over backwards for you. I hope you understand that. Everything I do is for your best interest."

"That's not the way I see it," said Greyson with a shake of his head. He returned to the cart for another glass of brandy.

"I suggest you ease up on the drinking too," said Riles. "That may be one root of the problem."

The young surgeon didn't respond.

"Stuart, do you have any idea as to how borax got into one of our study patients?"

"No. A contaminant I guess."

"I'm concerned that borax may have gotten into a few of our Lysovage and placebo samples towards the end of the study," said Riles. "In fact Dr. Johnson just operated on a patient today and sent the pathology specifically for borax testing."

Greyson did not respond while sipping on the brandy and pursing his lips.

"That deeply concerns me."

"Why?" asked Stuart. "The study is over."

"Do you have any idea where it came from Stuart?"

"No. It doesn't matter, after tomorrow all we have to do is start signing the royalty checks."

"I strongly disagree. It does matter since a patient died with borax in their gut," said Riles. "The Department of Health is still investigating the whole matter."

"Let them investigate," said the surgeon. "I've got nothing to hide."

"I didn't suggest that," said Riles. "Why would you think there is something to hide?"

Greyson did not answer while finishing the second glass of brandy, his cheeks turning a rosy hue. He slowly ran a hand through his hair, restoring the wave in front. He then looked down to the floor.

"Talk to me Stuart. I'm here to help."

"There's nothing to say."

"I hope not, but I'm here to help," said Riles allowing some time to pass. "Do you have anything to tell me Stuart?"

"Mia will be home any minute now," said Stuart while turning away. He started to walk out of the room. "She'll be glad to see you. I'll be upstairs." Stuffy raised his head as his master began to exit.

"Stuart."

"Good night," said the surgeon continuing to exit.

"I spoke to Professor Shoebottom this morning," said Riles loudly. "He mentioned your name. Wanted me to say hello."

The news caused Greyson to stop in his tracks, his back to the chairman.

Silence.

"Funny what an old man can remember," said Riles in amazement. "He had an old headmaster back in boarding school named Greyson, a real S.O.B. Somehow the name stuck in his head."

A grandfather clock ticking in the corner provided the only semblance of time. Old Stuffy was already asleep and let out a faint yelp, dreaming of days gone by.

"Why Stuart? Why did you do it?"

"Shoebottom is a demented old man," said Greyson. "Can't even remember his kid's names."

"After all the hard work and years of sacrifice, why now?"

"He has dementia, still thinks F.D.R. is president."

"What good could have come from it?" asked Riles. "What in God's name were you thinking?"

"No one will believe him," said Greyson. "He's a crazy old man."

"Stuart for Christ's sake, we have a fatality on our hands! You and I were the only ones with access to the Lysovage samples. And it wasn't me!"

"I don't know what you are talking about?" said Greyson defiantly. "I'll be upstairs."

"Stuart you killed someone!" screamed Riles, his voice echoing through the mansion. "Mrs. Biddleton is dead. Do you understand the consequences of your action? Dead!"

"She perforated an ulcer," said Greyson, now turning back into the room to face his accuser. "You were at the autopsy. How did I cause that?"

"The hydrochloric acid from her stomach turned the borax into boric acid!" screamed Riles while pointing his finger at Greyson. "The goddamned acid ate right into her hepatic artery. She bled to death!"

"Not my fault," said Greyson.

"It is your fault," said Riles. "Professor Shoebottom specifically remembered talking to a Dr. Greyson several months earlier, from the Department of Surgery. He recalled being asked multiple questions about borax and its effects upon the human body."

"The man is senile. No one will believe him."

"Stuart, tomorrow morning I am going to report you to the Philadelphia police department. A terrible act has been committed. Why, I do not know. I've given you everything."

Stuffy continued to bark in her sleep, all four legs now running through green pastures, her rear claws clicking upon the hardwood floor. Riles stared directly at the young surgeon, in demand of a response.

"Why, just tell me why?" pleaded Riles. "I need a reason why I shouldn't go to the police."

No response.

"Stuart, answer me now," demanded Riles. "Or you will be answering to the police tomorrow. It's your choice."

"He told me it was harmless," said Greyson. "May cause some inflammation but otherwise harmless. For god's sake, he told me some people take it as their daily vitamin."

"Why Stuart? Why would you want to sabotage the project?"

"I didn't want to kill anyone," said Greyson, the brandy now acting as truth serum. "I just wanted to upset the applecart. Mess up the results a bit. Maybe I'd look better when the dust settled."

"Why Stuart? Why?"

"You," said Greyson with a frown and nod of his head. "Mostly you, a lot of it Vanessa, some of it Fanicci and the whole fifteen percent stock deal. I'm getting screwed out of millions of dollars."

"Why me? What did I ever do wrong?"

"You never liked me, from the moment we first met," said Greyson with a grimace. "Never."

"That's not true," barked Riles. "I gave you every opportunity to redeem yourself, time after time, but that stupid libido of yours always got in the way. And Vanessa, I don't understand. You mean nothing to her."

"There's something about her that makes me crazy," said Greyson. "The more I can't have her, the more I want her."

"Listen to yourself!" yelled Riles. "You sound like a teenager in high school. For Christ's sake, grow up already."

"I think I love her."

"Are you insane?"

"She's paying the price for it now," said Greyson with a smile. "Unemployed. No more European flings with her beau."

"You were jealous of her?" asked Riles. "A high priced call girl got into your head? Stuart, she was just a toy for Fanicci. Look around! Look at what you have!"

Greyson just stared at the bottom of the empty glass, wondering if another drink would help. He then slowly looked up at Riles, their eyes meeting, the elder surgeon shaking his head.

"No one will ever know," said Greyson. "Why should they? Let's keep it between you and I."

"I'm reporting it to the authorities Stuart."

"We'll say it was a random event, a contaminant that somehow always ended up in a placebo vial," said Greyson with a frenzied look. "Talk about dumb luck. We can still walk away smelling like roses." His speech was becoming rapid. "I'll take two percent if that helps."

"No Stuart," said Riles sadly. "What you did was wrong. Very wrong."

"But your life's work, it will all go down the drain," said Greyson with a convincing step towards Riles. "You will be disgraced worldwide. Do you really want that?"

"No, but I have my morals," said the chairman firmly. "Perhaps that's the difference between you and I, moral fiber. I will be notifying the police in the morning."

"Mia told me about the estate plans," said Greyson with a glare. "She told me you wrote me out of the will, completely. Why would you do such a thing?"

"That's none of your business," said Riles.

Suddenly Stuffy jumped up and headed towards the door, his tail wagging. A car door closing was heard just outside. Both men stopped speaking as the front door opened.

"Hey Stuffy baby," said Mia Greyson over the audible sound of rustling shopping bags. "How's my good boy? Hello Stuart, do we have company?"

"In her love," said Greyson.

Mia Greyson stepped into the study.

"Daddy!" was her cry while putting down the shopping bags and heading across the room, her arms wide open. "What brings you here tonight?"

"Just came out to say hello," said Riles while hugging his daughter. "How's my little girl?"

"Great daddy, mom and I just went on a King of Prussia mall shopping spree. Wait till you see the dresses we bought for tomorrow night."

"Your mother bought a new dress?"

"Oh daddy, she looks so beautiful in it. I can't wait."

"Hi honey," said Stuart.

"Wow, what a surprise," said Mia. "What are you two men talking about in here? Man stuff?

"Yea," said Stuart. "You know football, car engines, politics."

"Where is Frederick junior?" asked Riles.

"Oh he is getting into town a bit later than expected," said Mia. "He plans to stay in center city with you."

"Wonderful," said Riles. "Simply wonderful."

"Oh daddy, I'm so excited about tomorrow night," continued Mia with a delighted look into her father's eyes. "I'm so proud of you."

"Thank you," said Riles. "And I'm so very proud of you."

"Love you," said Mia while kissing her father on the cheek. "I'll leave you two boys alone now. Got to call mom, you know, girl stuff." She then left the room with Stuffy following behind.

"We're almost done," said Stuart. "I'll be out in a bit dear."

"Good night Mia," said Riles. "I love you."

"Great girl," said Greyson. "I love her so much."

"Don't bullshit me Stuart," said Riles. "You are going to be arrested tomorrow morning and yes, you are out of the family will."

"That's too bad," said Greyson. "I mean with all the good news and everything." He had an evil smirk on his face. "I'd hate to ruin it."

"What are you talking about? The whole project is over, destroyed thanks to you."

"Don't you think Mia looked great tonight?" asked Greyson. "Alive and full of energy?"

"What are you talking about?"

"Didn't she look so full of life?"

"No, please no."

"She's pregnant daddy. Your little girl is with child. The good lord has finally blessed us with a child. Praise the lord. Hallelujah!"

Riles stood speechless.

"You're going to be a grandfather," said Greyson. "Imagine that. Congratulations grandpa."

Riles stepped backwards and sat down into the leather chair, both hands supporting his head, looking downward.

"If it's a boy she wants to call him Frederick, after her father," said Greyson. "Little Frederick. I love it."

The chairman couldn't speak, finally he thought, a grandchild. His wife will be so happy. Finally, their prayers answered.

"Pop-pop. Do you mind if I call you that? Pop-pop?"

He then looked up at the conniving, two timing murderer known as his son-in-law, standing before him with a smile. Greyson was trouble from the moment he laid eyes on him, so long ago. It was amazing how one person could cause so much carnage in a family.

"I swore secrecy to Mia," said Greyson heading for another glass of brandy. "She thinks it's bad luck to tell anyone, so please keep it a secret. What happens in the man cave stays in the man cave."

"You bastard," said Riles.

"We don't want to get her too excited," said Greyson. "The doctor said to avoid stress at all costs."

"You dirty, no good bastard."

"It would be a pity for our little boy to grow up without a father," said Greyson. "Maybe that was my problem, dad was never home. See what happens when a child grows up fatherless?"

"May the lord have mercy on your pathetic soul," said Riles with an angry step towards the exit. He left without saying another word, speeding home, daring any policeman to pull him over.

The following morning Dr. Frederick Riles woke up early to begin his routine. He ate breakfast outside on a back terrace listening to the early city sounds, the sun just starting to peak over the rooftops. It was going to be a glorious Friday he thought, knowing his decision was final.

At exactly eight o'clock he picked up the phone and carefully dialed a number, bringing the phone to his ears. After the sixth ring a voice said hello.

"Victor," it's Fred. "Good morning."

"Fred, what's up?" asked Fanicci. "Is there a problem?" Fanicci had a terrible headache thanks again to a night of celebration with the Union Park bigwigs. Next to him was the unconscious body of a woman reeking of Tequila.

"No, no problem," said Riles with a chuckle. "Just wanted to tell you that the remaining vials from the hospital won't be coming back to the factory."

"Why?" asked Fanicci flinching from a direct look into the wrinkled face of the woman beside him, some drool on her cheek.

"Well after the study ended someone on staff took the liberty of destroying the samples," said Riles. "Some independent thought, imagine that?"

"No problem," said Fanicci. "It's a moot point."

"I agree," said Riles. "The project is over and that's that."

"Hey, glad to hear you are finally loosening up," said Fanicci with a wince, his bed partner now letting off some gas. "Thanks for the info, anything else?"

"No that's it," said Riles looking down at the empty glass vials before him, the contents deep into the city sewer system. "See you tonight."

The chairman opted to walk to work that morning. Ten blocks away he discreetly deposited twelve glass vials into a dumpster just outside a Chinese restaurant. He waited to watch a city worker toss the trash into the back of a garbage truck, which mechanically pulverized the evidence into a thousand pieces.

Chapter Twenty Six

THE BIG GAME

It was a typical Sunday afternoon back at his childhood home, dad off early from work at two o'clock. Like any good father he played some baseball across the street in the sandlot, despite a crooked knee and partially torn rotator cuff. He pitched with the best of them when softball was king, and was still able to command some attention with an underarm fastball. Uncle Barney sat on the patio having just finished a second bottle of beer from the local brewery, the inside brim of his tan fedora hat lined with lottery tickets. The Phillies were on the radio and old Ralph the dog was out cold under the shady umbrella. Inside the kitchen, mom sweated over a tray of lasagna with the radio playing polkas.

Phil and brother Joe came up the brick driveway with dad in tow, sneezing from the roses in bloom.

"Are you ready?" asked Uncle Barney with a raise of his hand.

"Yea," said brother Joe.

"A runner on first, no outs," said Barney. "The batter hits a line drive at the first baseman who dives, but can only trap the ball. The runner on first thinks he caught the ball before it hit the ground and returns to first."

"Wait," said Joe. "The ball hit the ground first, before the first basemen caught it?"

"Yea," said Barney.

"Alright, go ahead."

"The first baseman then touches first base and then the runner, who has his foot on the bag. What's the ruling?" Barney was "drinking buddies" with a major league umpire and constantly tried to stump his nephews. Every visit involved a question involving the rules of baseball, many arcane in nature.

"Wait a minute," said brother Joe, who umpired local games all summer long. "He touched the bag first?"

"Correct."

"That's an easy one," said dad as he went into the kitchen. "Even Ralph knows that."

"What's the ruling Joe D?" asked Barney with a grin.

"The batter is out," said brother Joe with a raised fist," and the runner on first is safe." He motioned his hands in the safe position.

"Is that your final answer?" asked Barney with both hands raised. "Your final answer?" He always tried to make you think twice about the answer.

"Final answer," said Joe D.

"That is correct," said Barney.

"Good one," said Joe.

"What if he touched the runner first?" asked Uncle Barney. "Then what?"

"Double play," said Joe B. "Double play."

"That is correct."

During dinner dad discussed college majors with his two sons, brother Joe leaning towards computer science. His simple message that evening was to "make a difference." No matter what path in life they took, he asked his boys to "make a difference" in their respective field. Only then would they be successful...."

The chirp-chirp-chirp sound of the alarm signaled the abrupt end to the dream even though Phil could still smell mom's lasagna. It was the big day he thought while staring at the cracked ceiling above. A big game followed by an even bigger speech. While brushing his teeth he thought of dad and his quips. "Work hard, mind your own business, listen to your heart and make a difference." They were simple lines with powerful messages, now signposts for a meaningful life. Dad was always right thought Phil with a smile and spit. Always. While looking up at the mirror he realized he was starting to look like his father.

Chairman Riles begrudgingly gave Phil the day off, to prepare for his brief speech. His statements however were already completely scripted by the Union Park marketing and legal departments. He had no wiggle room and was forbidden to ad lib at the podium. The presentation included four slides that would project overhead, again fashioned by the pharmaceutical giant sponsoring the event. Phil practiced the speech to Riles and Fanicci two days earlier. "Get in and get out," said Fanicci during the dress rehearsal. "Just get in and get out." It all seemed too easy.

Later that morning Phil visited Jenna, after meeting privately with the Infectious Disease specialist just outside her room. Her progress was sluggish and the specialist was a bit perplexed, wondering aloud if some other exotic parasite endemic to Nepal could be in the mix. She ordered a new battery of tests that morning, hoping to rectify the situation. Phil thanked her for the consultation, before stepping into Jen's room.

He discussed the infectious disease doctor's concerns with Jennifer who appeared weak and pale. He reviewed with her the ongoing workup, including the need for additional blood work. The visit went well until he went to leave the room.

"Is Vanessa going to be there tonight?" asked Jennifer.

"Vanessa? From the drug company?" asked Phil, caught off guard by the question. He was unsure if Jennifer knew of her.

"Yea, the girl in the catfight video," said Jen. "Dr. Knight told me about her, or I should say about the video."

"Dr. Knight told you about the video?" asked Phil. "How the heck did Dr. Knight find out about that?"

"The video has over a million views Phil," said Jennifer. "You are famous."

"Yea, I'm sorry I didn't tell you about it Jen, the whole night was surreal. Stacey went berserk."

"I'm disappointed Stacey didn't tell me about it," said Jen. "We were so tight, but now she has her Princeton. Everything is Princeton this and Princeton that."

"She was probably too embarrassed to discuss it."

"She's beautiful Phil, Vanessa that is," said Jennifer. "Is she going to be there tonight?"

"Yes, yes she is Jen," said Phil trying to maintain a look of innocence. "Up until a few days ago she worked for Union Park Biotech."

"What happened? Why did she quit?"

"That may take some time to answer," said Phil while shaking his head. "Quite some time."

"Tell me, I have time," said Jen trying to prolong the visit. "I'm not going anywhere."

"Listen Jen," said Phil with a step back towards her. "It's all too complex, everything in my life is crashing together." He then sat on the bedside. "Too much pressure, my speech, a job offer, Union Park, graduation, a big basketball game and..."

"I wish I could come," said Jen.

"And you Jen, I worry about you the most."

"I still wish I could come."

"It's going to be a boring speech."

"I mean to the game. I know how much winning that championship means to you." She smiled and put her hand on his. "It's that team photo you want hanging in the general surgery library, right?"

"Right. I'll have somebody videotape the game," said Phil. "Then we can watch it together, when you are stronger." He kissed her on the forehead. "Keep getting better Jen, love you."

"Good luck," said Jen.

Phil then walked down to the outpatient orthopedic department and met with his surgeon. After signing a legal document releasing the bone doctor from liability and possible future income loss, his cast was removed and his hand tightly wrapped with a bandage. Phil would play that night despite some pain and a broken metacarpal bone.

The young surgeon left the hospital and walked downtown to the apartment of Vanessa Rose, where over the next two hours they discussed their immediate options together, acutely aware of the turbulence ahead.

In an apparent show of good sportsmanship the championship game was moved up to five o'clock by Sweeper captain Mo Rhett, allowing Phil to play the whole game. Thirty minutes before the big game Rick Polk attempted to rally the team in the locker room.

"This is it men," said Polk inside the old locker facility adjacent to the gym. "The big game." Polk paced like a caged tiger in the room. Surrounding him were the Vital Organs, losers of the championship game for the past three years. It was the team's last chance to bring home the trophy with senior residents Polk, Rhimes and Drummer onboard.

"Everyone has enjoyed a great athletic career in this room except me," continued Polk, slugging down a sugar bomb energy drink. He wore a red, white and blue headband with matching wristbands made of cotton. "Phil a star in college, Boyce on the state championship team, and Jackie the Police Athletic league champ."

"I think your shoe has some dog crap on it," said Rhimes while pointing to Rick's sneakers. "You may want to wipe it off."

"But me, nothing. This is my last chance," said Polk. "I never want to feel the horrible pang of a loss like last year."

"Rick, you missed last year's championship game," said Phil. "Remember, the Star Trek convention was in town that day?"

"All I ask it that everyone play their best game," said Polk, ignoring Phil's comment and swinging his fist. "Hustle, make the extra pass and get that loose ball." Sweat already soaked his armpits.

"Hey the toilet in here is overflowing," yelled Westbrook from the single toilet stall. "Dang it, my socks just got wet."

"This is our day!" yelled Polk. "Our game, our championship! Now let's get our hands together." He held out his right hand and for the last time the team gathered together as one. "On three – Vital Organs. One, two, three – Vital Organs!"

It was then they all heard it.

"*S-U-C-C-E-S-S, that's the way we spell success.*"

"What the hell is that?" asked team captain Polk.

"*S-U-C-C-E-S-S – Success!*"

"I love that cheer," said Jackie Rhimes.

The team exited the locker room to see a cheerleading squad waiting for them in formation. They held up a sign for the team to run through saying "We Love the Vital Organs." Nurse Hudson wore her old high school uniform with the distorted letter "C" across the chest, signifying her as the captain. A few other nurses just wore a set of surgical scrubs including Caroline Ell. They all held pom-poms in their hands waving them overhead.

"Let's do it!" yelled Polk as he led the team, crashing through the paper sign. It was the highlight of his athletic career.

"Now I've seen everything," said Mo Rhett, who already had his team on the court for warm ups. "Hey Drummer, where's the cast?"

"It's a miracle Mo," said Phil, raising his arm in pain. "A miracle of modern medicine. Thanks for moving up the game time, I really appreciate it."

"No problem," said Mo. "It was the honorable thing for me to do."

"Hey, who are those two guys?" asked Mike Boyce while pointing at the maintenance squad.

Phil turned around to check out the maintenance squad running through lay-up drills. He knew all of them except two who appeared to be six foot seven inch twins, both dunking the ball with ease. They were wearing long pants and sneakers with matching uniform tops.

"Hey Mo, who are they? I've never seen them before."

"Who?"

"The two big guys. Where did they come from?"

"Oh, the Johnson brothers?" replied Mo innocently. "They've been with us all along, just missed the first half of the season. Ike and Marcus."

"Are they twins?"

"No, well maybe," said Mo. "Irish twins I think. Real close in age."

"They don't work here!" objected Polk. "I live in this building, and I've never seen them before!"

"Sure they do," said Rhett. "Night shift, two of my best workers. Very meticulous to detail, I might add."

"No they don't," said Polk. "They're ringers you brought in for the big game Mo. Hired guns. This game is under protest. I'm reporting it to the commissioner."

"Commissioner? What commissioner?" asked Mo. "I run the league."

"Mo, they're wearing Chick-fil-A shirts with their names embroidered on the front," said Phil incredulously. "It looks like they are on their lunch break. They're even wearing uniform pants."

"Maybe they have two jobs," said Mo. "Can you blame someone from trying to get ahead? Now come on, let's play some ball."

Phil and Rick just stared and smiled at the maintenance team leader, a wily one. They knew the game would go on despite the two blue chip recruits. It was now or never. Phil then felt Nurse Hudson bump into him, leading with the letter "C."

"Do you like squad I put together?" asked Hudson with a proud smile.

"Love it," said Phil. "Especially the captain with her pom-poms."

The first half was a massacre. Maurice neglected to inform anyone that the Johnson brothers were former members of the city's public league all-star team. The dynamic duo treated everyone present to one jaw-dropping move after another. The halftime deficit was eighteen points, in favor of the Sweepers.

"An old coach used to tell me that it's not the X's and O's, but rather the Jim's and Joe's," said Mo with a cackle. "And I got the Jim's and Joe's."

Phil was in pain and could barely respond, his right hand now swollen. His jump shot was way off and he was a nonfactor in the first half. Nurse Hudson kept a bag of ice on his hand as he sat on the floor, leaning against the wall.

"Thanks for coming," said Phil sadly to the nurse. "Sorry it's not going to turn out like we planned."

"Don't be silly," said Hudson. "The girls and I are having a blast. I remember all the cheers like it was yesterday."

Phil laughed, noticing that Caroline was across the floor talking to Dr. Boyce, offering her own one on one support.

"Looks like we've got a little love in the air," said Hudson while looking across the gym. "Who would have thought the Indiana boy?"

"Since when?" asked Phil somewhat perturbed.

"A few weeks," said Hudson. "You can tell on the floor when chemistry is present, they just gravitate to each other." She then moved the ice to the other side of Phil's hand. "They make a great couple."

"Hey Drummer, where's your captain?" asked Mo. "In the ICU?"

"He went down the hall to the canteen," said Phil. "Mentioned something about an energy drink."

Just then the Johnson brothers came up to Maurice to exchange a few handshakes and man hugs. Phil heard a series of ah-rights between the teammates and Mo thanking them for their time. The brothers then turned around and began to walk towards the exit. Halfway across the floor Ike Johnson turned around to speak.

"Yo Mo, thanks for moving up the time man," said Ike. "Otherwise we couldn't have made it."

"Yea, yea. No problem," said Mo quietly. "Later boys." He glanced at Phil with a guilty look.

"So they were on their lunch break," said Phil with a shake of his head. "Now I've seen it all Mo. Unbelievable."

"Hey Drummer, you best stop talking and start scoring," said Maurice while walking back to his team. "You got two quarters to close an eighteen point gap brother. If not the trophy stays in the Congo, where it belongs."

"*T-E-A-M, T-E-A-M! We've got the team that's going to do it to them! Power and might, ready to fight, go Vital Organs!*"

A rejuvenated Vital Organs squad came out firing in the third quarter, thanks to the hot shooting of Mike Boyce and the absence of the Johnson brothers. The Sweepers were in disarray, their lead cut to seven points heading into the final eight minutes.

As both teams took the court to start the fourth quarter Phil looked around and tried to take it all in. He loved playing in the old gym and this was his final game. He glanced overhead at the fans lining the balcony rail, hospital personnel and locals, all enjoying a great event. What an atmosphere he thought. They had to win. They just had to win.

Maurice Rhett found his old Big Five League form in the fourth quarter, hitting a few shots that brought back memories of days gone by. But the x-factor was Mike Boyce, who was playing with a passion never before seen. The high school phenom was hitting jump shots from all over the court, causing Caroline to cheer wildly. With fifteen seconds to go the Vital Organs were only down by two and had the ball, bringing it up court.

"Time out," yelled Phil. "Time out."

The team huddle was chaotic until Phil took control, diagramming a play to have Jackie inbound the ball to him while Boyce ran off a pick set down low by Polk. Phil would flip the ball back to Jackie to hopefully find Boyce open in the corner. Boyce would take the final shot. If he was covered Jackie would take the jumper and everyone would crash the boards for the rebound.

"I wanna take the final shot," said Polk as the team broke huddle.

"You're nuts," said Phil. "Set the pick."

Mo Rhett however was indeed a wily captain, and came out with his team playing a zone defense, which completely confused the doctors. Jackie easily inbounded the ball to Phil who turned uncontested towards the defense, which was packed into the paint and along the baseline. Polk and Boyce were bottled up in the zone, yet Phil flipped the ball back to Jackie, who wasn't looking. The ball hit off his knee and squirted into the midst of the zone, directly into the hands of Rick Polk. He thought of shooting but was swarmed upon by the taller defenders. Out of the corner of his eye he spotted Boyce somehow alone in the corner, and tossed him the ball just as he was hammered to the ground.

The referee blew his whistle to call a foul on Maurice but the noise level was too high. Boyce launched a three-point jump shot from the corner with time running out which swished through the net, setting off a wild celebration.

"Foul, foul!" screamed Maurice. "I intentionally fouled the man!"

The foul was indeed called before the shot, which put Rick Polk on the line shooting two. It took several minutes to clear the floor before the fifth year resident stepped to the line.

"Intentional foul," said Mo with a smile, as Rick bounced the ball several times. "The oldest trick in the playbook." Phil was lined up next to him just shaking his head. So close he thought, so darn close. "I've seen this boy shoot a foul shot," said Mo. "It's over Drummer."

The first foul shot was a line drive that hit the back of the rim and ricocheted several feet straight into the air, coming down directly through the hoop. The crowd roared. The deficit now only one point.

"Overtime Mo, I smell overtime," said Phil.

"*Shoot it Rick, shoot it Rick, shoot it Rick, shoooot,*" went the cheer.

As Polk dribbled the ball in preparation for the second shot sweat poured down his face, his headband soaked. He brought the ball up to his chest and stared at the rim, finally his big moment. He felt good until Mo spoke.

"You're shoelace is untied."

The well-timed comment distracted the captain, causing him to look at Maurice. Then, inexplicably, Polk felt it appropriate to wink at Maurice and blow him an air kiss.

"This one is for you Mo," said Polk who heaved the ball up towards the rim.

From the moment the ball left Polk's hand it never had a chance. In fact the ball approached the rim with no spin on it, in knuckleball like fashion. It reminded Mo of an old Globetrotter trick when a string was attached to the foul shot. The orb barely nick the front left rim and dropped straight down to Phil, who had just treated Maurice to an old spin move his college coach taught him. Phil's healthy left hand softly tapped the rebound back upwards as the buzzer sounded, and into the basket. The tip in counted and there would be no overtime!

"The Vital Organs win! The Vital Organs win!" screamed the crowd.

Fans flooded the floor from every corner of the small gym, shouting with joy. Neighborhood children jumped up and down alongside the victors and their cheer squad. Stan the Beer Truck Man ran wildly through the crowd waving his hat overhead. It was one of the highlights of Phil's athletic career, a moment he had dreamed of for years. Finally they had broken through the maintenance department juggernaut and won the coveted championship.

"Hey Drummer," said Mo while being jostled around by the crowd. "Good game man," he said with a broad smile. "You deserved to win." "Thanks Mo," said Phil while shaking his hand. "It was a pleasure playing against you all these years. I'm going to miss it."

"Me too," said Mo. "Me too."

In the post game ceremony the commissioner named Mike Boyce the tournament's most valuable player. Maurice presented the championship trophy to the Vital Organs who hoisted it high above their heads in celebration. A photograph capturing the event was later framed and placed upon the library wall of the department of surgery. Hollywood couldn't have written a better ending.

"I wish this moment would never end," said Nurse Hudson as she slowly walked out of the gym with Phil, her arm tight around his waist. "It's magic."

"Me too," said Phil. "Me too."

Chapter Twenty Seven
A SLIGHT MISCONCEPTION

After a quick shower Phil dressed and ran across the street to the Union Park convention center. Was his dream last night truly a message from his dad he wondered, to "make a difference?" He was just an innocent bystander during the bizarre events of his first and second year, but now it was different. He was an active player in something strange, about to explode. Stretch limousines were double-parked outside the convention center framed by crisscrossing spotlights in the sky. A palpable sense of excitement overtook Phil as he approached the front entrance.

Hundreds of guests were packed outside the main hall in an ornate lobby. Chandeliers hung from the ceiling as a balcony string quartet played Mozart from above. After passing through a SWAT like security team Phil ran directly into Vice President Joe Carter and his scrumptious figurine who, actually said hello, her voice barely audible. The Vice President spoke nothing of the cruise debacle, rather choosing to pontificate upon the greatness at hand. As he spoke, Phil noticed Carter kept an eye on more important guests behind him. His wife wore a low cut gown exposing an upper thoracic midline tattoo, suggestive of more graffiti below. The conversation ended abruptly when the city's mayor entered the hall, prompting Carter to dismiss Phil.

Phil then eyed Rick Polk, assaulting a table loaded with food. In his hand was the championship trophy, an instant conversational piece.

"My first foul shot was nothing but net," said Rick to an elderly couple trying to get by for some crab cakes. "Swish-a-roo! Then came the second shot."

"Rick, how did you get here so fast?" said Phil freeing up the older couple from the play-by-play recap.

"I was the only one on the team without a pretty girl hanging on my arm after the game," said Polk. "It was just me and my trophy wife," said the resident with a hug of the silver cup in hand. "Isn't she beautiful?" He then kissed the coveted prize.

"Did you see Boyce walking out with Caroline?" asked Phil. "They looked like a married couple. Why am I always the last to know?"

"Come on Phil, they've been hot for each other for a few weeks now. Open your eyes. Jealous?"

"What? Don't be silly."

"They do make a striking couple," continued Polk. "Almost as good looking as you and Jenna. Somebody has to replace the "dream team" when you and Ms. Ranier are gone, Phil. Remember, we are set to graduate shortly."

"Where's the rest of the team?" asked Phil.

"Helping Stan set up in the Congo," said Polk. "They'll be over in a bit. Remember the ceremonial tapping of the keg is going off in about an hour."

"I've never seen Stan so excited," said Phil. "He even brought in an old accordion from home, the one he played growing up as a kid. He was practicing the *Beer Barrel Polka* last night."

"Ah Dr. Drummer," said a voice from behind. "All set for the speech?"

Phil turned about to see CEO Mitchell and his wife, both in formal wear, and looking very comfortable with the surroundings. Their lives were sprinkled with such events, hobnobbing with the elite of society. For the next five minutes Mitchell spoke only of the project and the wonderment of it all.

"How did you get involved with this project?" asked Phil, attempting to make conversation with Mitchell. Polk had vanished.

"I was CEO of a Boston hospital when a young Vic Fanicci approached me together with his former boss," said Mitchell with a glaze of nostalgia. "They needed permission to proceed with the prospective study and I helped them steer the project through the hospital's red tape. I've been closely involved with the project since day one."

"Do you remember that Mediterranean cruise they sent us on John?" interjected his wife with a warm smile. "I even got this pearl necklace as a gift," as she stroked the perk around her neck.

"He-hem," continued Mitchell while clearing his throat. "Actually dear that was a continuing medical education trip that met mandated requirements set by the state's hospital administration board. Don't you remember the lecture I went to?"

"No," said his wife with a shrug of her shoulders. "I do remember Italy though."

At that moment, Mr. and Mrs. Frederick Riles stepped into the mix, the chairman sporting a brand new tuxedo and his wife in a dark blue formal evening gown. She wore a brilliant pink corsage on her new dress, which sparkled of elegance. Phil had never seen his chairman so excited, a beaming smile across his face. They actually made a very nice couple, he thought.

"I can't believe it," said Riles, lifting upwards on his toes. "I just can't believe it. After all these years the day has finally arrived."

"Neither can I," said Mitchell while shaking hands with Riles. "I was just telling young Dr. Drummer here of our early days with the project. Congratulations Fred," said Mitchell while still holding his hand firmly. "All of this is in honor of you."

The flattery caused the head of chairman Riles to gyrate in an up and down fashion, similar to a bobblehead doll on a car dashboard. Phil momentarily thought he had gone into a seizure of joy, complete with a gurgling chuckle.

"Ah Dr. Drummer," said the voice of a photographer behind Phil. "Your presence is requested for a photo."

The photographer led Phil to a staged location in the lobby with a crisp mauve background symmetrically peppered with the names Union Park Biotech and Lysovage. Out of nowhere Stuart Greyson appeared at Phil's side. The photo-op was for future Union Park propaganda touting their "next generation of surgeons." Greyson wore an Armani tux and expensive smell with a perfectly gelled hair wave. It was the first time the two confronted each other since their brief clash at sea. Phil noticed Greyson's incisor tooth had been cosmetically repaired to its former excellence.

"No hard feelings?" asked Greyson with an extended handshake to Phil after the photo. "I mean, that was a cheap shot you hit me with."

"A cheap shot? You hit me twice before I threw one punch."

"No hard feelings my friend?"

"No," said Phil. "As long as you apologized to Vanessa."

"I did, I did," said Greyson quickly, now holding out his arm for his wife to enter the conversation.

Mia Greyson looked beautiful. She wore a sleek black dress with high heel shoes along with petite diamond earrings that sparkled in the light. Phil always thought highly of the chairman's daughter, wondering how she turned out so well.

"Dear, you've met Dr. Drummer before," said Greyson with an arm around his spouse's waist. "He is also one of the primary surgeons involved with the project."

"Yes, yes," said Mia with a smile and extended hand. "Isn't he also the man responsible for your tooth?"

"Well I can explain," backtracked Phil. "I didn't intend to knock out your husband's tooth, it was all…."

"No worries doctor. I've told Stuart a hundred times not to be playing basketball with you younger boys," said Mia Greyson with a smile. "He can't come to terms with the fact he's getting older."

"Ah," said Phil with hesitation. "I see."

"An incidental elbow between friends," said Greyson. "But we won the game dear. That's all that matters."

"Men," said Mia with a roll of her eyes.

Stuart laughed and hugged his wife while staring at Phil, a wink of the eye. Greyson then noticed a couple approaching Phil from behind and without warning spun Mia around and walked away.

"Dr. Drummer," said Nurse Hudson with her beau in tow. "I'm sure you remember the good captain."

Nurse Hudson looked marvelous with a tight one-piece red dress on and black high heel shoes. Beside her was the proud captain of the booze cruise vessel, dressed in full naval uniform, holding onto his catch. The skipper's outfit was white and covered with shiny military ribbons. He wore a matching hat with a polished black brim.

"Sure I do," said Phil with an extended hand to the captain. "You look beautiful Nurse Hudson. How did you get dressed so quickly? Where's the cheerleader outfit?"

"It's in the hotel room upstairs," said Hudson with a smile. "I plan on putting it back on late tonight after a few stiff drinks. It always brought me good luck after the big game."

"How's the hand?" asked the skipper.

"A bit swollen," said Phil while looking down at his extremity. It was turning black and blue from the game. "But we won, that's all that counts."

"Nurse Hudson," said a familiar voice from behind. "Good evening."

The group turned around to see Dr. Knight and his wife, Margaret. Despite the years they looked stunning together, the doctor still physically fit and commanding respect.

"Were you the captain of the trip up in Boston?" asked Knight with his right hand in a pocket. "The one that landed one of our doctors in the brig?"

"Yes sir," said the captain. "Is that gentleman here tonight?"

"No more shop talk," interrupted Mrs. Knight with a wave of her hand. "At least not tonight. Nurse Hudson, have you seen that gorgeous floral display near the ice carving? Please let me show you."

Hudson and her shipmate left with Mrs. Knight, leaving Phil alone with his mentor.

"Jen doesn't look good Phil, "said Knight. "I was just up in her room. Her vitals are all over the road."

"What's wrong?" asked Phil. "She was a bit short of breath this morning. I checked some of the labs from the Infectious Disease doctor and they were all negative. I ordered a venous Doppler and that was negative, no clot."

"Don't know but I ordered a bunch of stat tests," said Knight. "Should be back in about a half hour. It's not a pulmonary embolus... and besides she is on a blood thinner. Her breath sounds were a bit distant and she was anxious, her pulse a bit shoddy."

Just then a commotion broke out directly behind the two surgeons, with voices raised. Both Knight and Phil looked over the crowd at an entrance doorway, swarming with security personnel. Knight recognized the unwelcomed guest first.

"Looks like the woman in the cat fight video," said the surgeon to Phil. "They're roughing her up."

Phil broke away and quickly approached the area of concern to find Fanicci directing a bunch of burly sentries.

"Get your hands off me!" yelled Vanessa at the guards.

"Get her out of here gentlemen," said Fanicci with smile. "She's not on the A-list anymore." Fanicci wore a tacky blue suit with a yellow tie for the occasion, with matching handkerchief.

"Excuse me, excuse me," said Phil, pushing his way into the midst of the body builders. "She is with me."

"No, I'm sorry," said Fanicci. "She's not on the invite list. Not anymore."

"She's my date for the evening," said Phil.

"Don't make me laugh," said Fanicci. "She should be on Broad Street, hooking, where she belongs."

"At least I'm honest," said Vanessa. "Not like you."

"Get her the hell out of here before I call the police," said Fanicci. "Scram!"

The guards then grabbed both of Vanessa's arms and lifted her off the ground, turning her body around towards the exit. Some well-dressed guests behind her seemed inconvenienced by the whole matter.

"Get your hands off me," she screamed. "You're hurting me."

"Victor," said Phil in anger. "If she goes, I go. No speech. It's that simple."

"You're hurting me!"

"You're on the payroll now Drummer, so just go with it. She's nothing to us anymore," said Fanicci while turning away. "Don't waste your time. There are plenty of others waiting to take her place."

"I said she is my date. My personal invite!" said Phil. "You know the invitation that said Dr. Drummer and guest."

Fanicci just turned around and faced Phil with a smirk.

"No speech, I mean it," said Phil. "Let her in."

"You're naïve Drummer," said the Union Park representative. "She'll play you for everything your worth. Trust me. She's a real pro."

"She's my date."

"Let her in," said Fanicci with a shake of his head. "She's his problem now." He then walked away.

"Thank you Phil," said Vanessa while fixing her hair. "What's with that security team? A bunch of goons!"

"I noticed that too," said Phil. "They seem a little overpowering for the event."

The two looked at each other, some doubt in their eyes. For the first time since he met her, Phil sensed fear in Vanessa.

"You look absolutely gorgeous," said Phil to his newly found date. "Strawberry?"

"No, I'm going establishment," replied Vanessa in reference to her lipstick. "Time for some change. It's called Russian Red Rouge. Do you like it?"

"Love it."

The duo then blended into the crowd, comfortable in each other's presence, and casting a striking couple. They moved as one, a team, ready for the big game.

"Ladies and gentlemen, may I have your attention?" said the voice of Vic Fanicci from above. He was on a stage centered on the back wall of the lobby, decorated with banners and flowers. "May I have your attention, please?"

The guests turned in unison towards the stage with drinks in hand, a few reaching for some final hors d'oeuvres. All eyes fixated upon the salesman with the yellow tie. It was then that Phil noticed Stuart Greyson staring at Vanessa from across the room, a peculiar squint to his eyes, his wife staring upward in awe at the speaker.

"Ladies and gentlemen, thank you for your support and encouragement over the years," said Fanicci. "The project we're here to launch has been like a journey through the desert, the faithful having now reaching the Promised Land." Scattered rounds of applause broke out during the speech. Seated on stage was chairman Riles, showing the look of a kindergartener on his birthday, ready for some cake. Next to him was a beaming V.P. Joe Carter surveying the crowd and occasionally nodding his head in appreciation of Fanicci's comments. The vice president then arose to address the crowd.

"Thank you for all coming," said Carter. "We have an exciting program scheduled tonight followed by dinner, here in the lobby. It's a pleasure to see so many good friends and employees of Union Park," said the executive. "Everyone here is part of the team effort that brought Lysovage to market. You should all be exceptionally proud of your work." He clapped his hands in appreciation as the crowd joined him in applause.

Phil then spotted Dr. Knight staring at the ground, oblivious to the minister of propaganda. He knew the look on Knight's face well. He was distraught over Jennifer's progress, sensing something amiss. Nothing else mattered to Knight when such a frown appeared. Nothing. Phil doubted Knight would even make it through the evening without returning across the street to check up on Jennifer.

"Has anyone seen what happened to our Union Park Biotech stock today?" asked Carter with a raise of his right hand. "Anyone?" A round of applause erupted. "That's right, it jumped three fold today on Wall Street. That speaks volumes of our Lysovage product." A wild applause cut loose.

Phil looked discretely at the woman next to him, trying hard not to fall in love with her, if he hadn't already. Vanessa was much more than Union Park made her out to be–intelligent, sensitive and full of passion. He sensed how deeply Union Park hurt her, despite her denials, having served them so well over time. Crazy he thought, how the lives of two random people are thrown together in such short time.

"Now everyone, please join us together in the main auditorium where Dr. Riles and his world class research team will present the findings of the Lysovage project. I'm sure you will find the results captivating," said Joe Carter with a confident smile. "And again thank you for coming to join us tonight. We won't disappoint you. I guarantee it."

Suddenly the blare of a bagpipe troop erupted from the corner of the room, the crowd stepping aside. Six men in kilts led a procession into the main hall, their music loud and clear. Phil placed his hand on Vanessa's back as the duo turned towards the door, shifting in the surge. Phil looked back on the stage to see Dr. Riles standing in exaltation, scanning the crowd. The chairman looked like Moses parting the Red Sea and watching his people being led to freedom. His wife stood proudly at his side. They then stepped off the stage into the rear of the procession.

"I'm so proud of you dear," said Mrs. Riles. "So proud."

"Congratulations daddy," said Mia. "I love you."

Riles just smiled at the two most important women in his life, noticing his daughter had no glass of wine in hand. In due time he thought, in due time she would tell her mother the good news.

"Thanks again Fred," said a voice from behind Riles causing him to turn around. It was his old med school roommate, Dr. Stein from the department of obstetrics and gynecology. Stein had introduced him during Grand Rounds several months ago. Riles asked his friend to serve as emcee during the scientific portion of the ceremony, and Stein accepted the invitation without reservation.

"You're welcome Larry," said Riles stepping back to shake hands with his old classmate. "We've come a long way old friend. A long way."

"I'm very proud of you Fred, very proud. You deserve it."

"Thank you again," said Riles with a glance over his shoulder. He stopped the forward progress of Stein in order to allow some distance between them and his family. He continued to hold Stein's hand while smiling.

"What an event," said Stein. "First class. Congratulations. I love the bagpipes!"

"Larry, I heard the good news," said Riles in a low tone. "I just wanted to thank you personally for all the work you've done with Mia. Thank you from the bottom of my heart."

"Good news, what good news?"

"It's O.K. Larry, I know," said Riles, still holding his hand. "Stuart told me the good news. I hope you understand how elated we are. Your fertility clinic is a blessing to so many young men and women in the area."

"What are you talking about Fred?" asked Dr. Stein. "Are we on the same page, Fred? Or maybe I'm missing something?"

"Mia's pregnancy Larry. Stuart spilled the beans to me the other night. It's O.K., I know. I wanted to thank you for everything you've done. I'm finally going to be a grandfather Larry, and it's all because of you. Thank you. Thank you so very much. I just can't wait to tell Mrs. Riles. She'll be in heaven."

Dr. Stein just stared in disbelief at his old friend, the noise of the march starting to fade.

"Larry?"

Dr. Stein couldn't speak.

"Larry, what's wrong?" asked Riles sensing the physician's angst. "Is there a problem? You can tell me. What's wrong? Is everything alright with my Mia?"

"Fred, your daughter is not pregnant," said the chairman of obstetrics. "She was never pregnant. I'm so sorry if there has been a misunderstanding."

Riles stared in silent disbelief at his friend.

"I apologize for any misunderstanding," said Stein sadly.

"What? But Stuart... told me," stuttered Riles. "I don't understand."

"She and Stuart are infertile," said Stein. "It's just one of those things in life Fred. I've tried the best I can. I hope you understand that. Please tell me that you do. I've tried the best I can."

"Daddy hurry up," said Mia from behind. "We are all waiting for you."

Chapter Twenty Eight
ROLL OUT THE BARREL

At first Mo thought it was a gang of stray cats fighting, a strange sound echoing through the basement. The noise possessed an eerie inhalational tone reminding him of an asthmatic friend he grew up with on a hot summer day. The cacophony's rhythmic beat caused his head and shoulders to sway in unison. It was when the Liberty Bell came sprinting down a hallway in full escape mode with terror in her eyes, that Stan's voice could be heard.

"Roll out the barrel, we'll have a barrel of fun
Roll out the barrel, we've got the blues on the run"

He spotted the brew master walking towards him with the black and white monster strapped to his chest, his arms struggling to contain the clamor. Despite the obvious strife Stan continued to scream aloud.

"Zing boom tararrel, ring out a song of good cheer
Now's the time to roll the barrel, for the gang's all here"

Mo looked back for help but all of his mutinous teammates had evacuated the Congo, leaving the captain high and dry, to face the approaching creature alone. He decided to take a stand for the team, yet suddenly noticed a smile on Stan's face.

"Jak sie masz?" asked Stan, now stopping directly in front of Mo. Somehow he had soothed the beast, which was gasping for air and contracting.

"What the hell is that Stan?" yelled Mo.

"An accordion. I've had it since grade school. Do you like it?"

"No! You scattered the cat... and the team. The boys will never come back down here now. They'll think the place is haunted."

"Don't be silly," continued Stan while putting the accordion down. "You can't tap a keg without singing the *Beer Barrel Polka.* Now let's get some ice around that barrel Mo, it has to cool down for thirty minutes before we proceed with the ceremony. That's standard operational protocol for tapping a barrel of beer."

"Yes sir," said Mo, still trying to make sense of the instrument on the floor.

As the duo proceeded with preparations Stan noticed his friend to be whistling the catchy tune. He could taste the vintage brew already, knowing it was well worth the wait.

Da-da-da-da, da-da-da-da, da-da...

Things were not as cheery across the street. After some brief commotion the audience was informed of a slight change in the program. Instead of Dr. Riles speaking first the honor would now go to Dr. Greyson, followed by Dr. Drummer and then Riles. The chairman's bewildered face remained visibly ashen as he sat down next to the podium at the head table. His slow and unsteady movements prompted Phil to think he had a stroke.

"Thank you Dr. Stein," said Greyson while looking at the audience and cameras. "Thank you for that fine introduction." Behind the speaker several large screens transmitted his image.

What followed is exactly what Phil expected. A polished speech glorifying the pharmaceutical product at hand, paid for in full by Union Park Biotech. Greyson was at his best, soaking in the limelight and dazzling the crowd with medical hype. The audience was smitten by the command performance given by the physician with leading man looks. It would be a tough act to follow.

"I would like to conclude my discussion with some words from a patient of mine," said Greyson. "She wrote me this lovely letter after her abdominal pain completely resolved from a Lysovage treatment. Dear Dr. Greyson, I would like to thank you…"

Suddenly Phil's heart started to beat rapidly. He suddenly remembered his dad's parting advice prior to internship – "Work hard and mind your own business." And the dream, the dream – "No matter what you do, make a difference." He peered to the other side of the podium to see Dr. Riles, now regaining some color and crossing out some written lines on a paper before him. Anger replaced the dazed look upon his face. Phil looked out at the faces in the vast audience, staring at Greyson and his sob story. He then noticed Vanessa, whose attention was centered not on Greyson, but on the man she loved. Her arms remained crossed, her face devoid of emotion.

Suddenly Dr. Knight arose from his second row seat. He started to exit the aisle while stepping over the legs of guests, who responded with annoyance in their eyes. Several of the Union Park executives in the front row turned around, distracted by the commotion. Knight was staring down unapologetically at his cell phone. Jenna thought Phil, something is wrong with Jenna!

"Thank you," said Stuart Greyson to a hearty round of applause. "Thank you for coming out tonight. And I look forward to meeting you all after the presentation."

Knight was nearly out the rear exit when Dr. Stein took the podium, shaking Greyson's hand on the way.

"Amazing stuff," said the emcee. "Thank you very much Dr. Greyson, it's an honor to have you on staff here at the Philadelphia General Hospital. Thank you so very much for all your work. What a wonderful and informative speech."

Phil became short of breath. It's now or never he thought. He began to hyperventilate. His head began to spin.

"Our next speaker is a brilliant up and coming surgeon here in Philadelphia," said Stein. "One who we hope will continue his career at the PGH."

The vast arena began to whirl as his vision became blurred. He said a prayer to his mother asking for guidance, still unsure of his direction.

"Dr. Phillip Drummer is the Philadelphia General's chief surgical resident who over the past five years distinguished himself as one of the best," said Stein. "His inquisitive mind brought him to the Lysovage project, and everyone at Union Park is so happy to have him on board."

"Talk to me mom. Talk to me dad," said Phil aloud as he reflexively stood up, his legs unsteady. "I need help. Please talk to me."

"He will be talking about the future roll of young surgeons and their use of Lysovage," said Stein. "Ladies and Gentlemen, it gives me great pleasure to introduce our next speaker, Dr. Philip Drummer."

There was applause but Phil didn't hear it. A strange, silent tunnel vision led him to the soapbox, speechless. He almost passed out as his left hand grabbed the podium, steadying his frame. His posture caused Riles to stand up and shake his hand, the pain from the fracture shocking his senses back to reality.

"Philip," said Riles with his teeth shining and hand shaking. "Easy now, are you O.K.? Take a slow, deep breath."

"Yes," mumbled Phil regaining his sensorium. "I think so."

"Just stick to the script Philip," said Riles. "Take your time and read slowly from the teleprompter, just like we practiced."

"Yes... yes," said Phil.

"Just keep smiling and read the sentences," said Riles. "It's that simple."

"Yes, thank you."

Dr. Riles then leaned forward and whispered into his ear. "Make me proud son."

The simple comment caused Phil to stare back at his chairman in disbelief, squeezing down on his hand, despite the pain.

"Make me proud son," said the chairman again with a corny grin and bob of his head. "This is your moment."

"I'm not your son," said Phil sharply while releasing the chairman's hand. The two stared at each other briefly.

"Phillip, I just meant..."

"And you, are not my father."

The chairman just gawked back at Phil, stunned by his retort. He slowly retreated and sat down, without saying another word.

It was a message from above.

Phil slowly turned towards the audience with a newfound confidence, suddenly able to hear their applause. He looked out upon the gathering and took a deep breath, as a smile appeared on his face. There would be no turning back.

"Thank you very much Dr. Stein," said Phil with a charm that rivaled the previous speaker. "And thank you very much Union Park Biotech for allowing me the opportunity to speak."

Both Fanicci and V.P. Carter nodded their heads in appreciation, confident in their chosen spokesman. His boyish looks and overhead image was playing well to the audience.

"I'd also like to thank one of our honored guests here tonight in the audience," said Phil going off script. "She has been with Union Park for years and her hard work and selfless dedication needs to be recognized."

"Philip," said Riles beneath his breath. "What are you doing?"

"Ms. Vanessa Rose has worked faithfully behind the scenes for years," said Phil. "While traveling the world she has been a steadfast spokeswoman for the cause and deserves a big round of applause for her commitment to the program. Vanessa has played a major role in what you are about to hear and surely is the reason why so many of us are gathered here tonight in celebration. Please stand up Vanessa and accept a big thank you from everyone at Union Park Biotech."

"Stick to the script Phillip," said Riles a bit more clearly. "Stick to the script!"

"I'm sure I speak for everyone at Union Park when I say thank you Vanessa. Thank you for the energy that you brought to the project. Thank you for helping to uncover the truth."

Phil began to clap as Vanessa stood up in the middle of the arena. Her image was striking as she waved overhead to the adoring crowd, turning her frame in full circle, the cameras projecting her on the Jumbotron. During the applause Phil glanced at the front row where Fanicci was sharply moving his hand horizontally back and forth across the front of his neck, in a frantic signal for Phil to curb the antics.

As the applause eased, Phil paused, holding the audience with silence for a full five seconds. Sweat poured down the face of Dr. Riles, as his eyes pleaded for conformity.

"I had a canned speech ready for tonight," said Phil with a smile. "But who wants to hear a canned speech?"

A hesitant yet cordial light round of applause followed.

"What I thought instead would be an informative case presentation involving one of our Lysovage patients," said Phil. "In other words the story of one of our patients passing through the project, from beginning to the end."

Phil suddenly appreciated a kick in the shin from his chairman, who was smiling and looking outward. Fanicci loosened his vulgar tie and unbuttoned his top shirt collar, starting to look quite uncomfortable.

"Would everyone like to hear that?"

Applause broke out from the crowd.

"I thought so," said Phil. "The presentation was scheduled for earlier in the week but it was unfortunately cancelled, so here we go."

"Phil, don't do it," mumbled Riles "You will regret it for the rest of your life. Stop right now."

Phil hit the slide button before him, which projected the demographic information of Julia Rudenko on the main screen.

"J. R. is a pleasant thirty six year old healthy female who immigrated from the Ukraine several years ago. She is the mother of three beautiful girls with her most recent uncomplicated pregnancy three years ago. Her daughter was delivered by Cesarean section here at the PGH at that time. Post operatively J.R. developed painful abdominal adhesions which were refractory to traditional treatment programs."

Fanicci suddenly arose and scooted into an aisle, heading back towards the audiovisual room managing the slide show. His action prompted Riles to look upwards through the spotlights, squinting at the glass panel control room. There was some commotion outside the door to the right of the room. He couldn't make out the face of the lone occupant in the A.V. room but the portly silhouette next to a large trophy was all the information he needed. Polk had hijacked the high tech sideshow, now in full swing.

"Three weeks after receiving Lysovage, J.R. developed severe abdominal pain prompting one of our senior surgeons to emergently return her to the O.R." said Phil. "Her abdominal cavity showed a diffuse inflammatory process and a small perforation in her bowel that was repaired." Phil then reached forward and pressed the button on the podium to deliver another overhead slide.

Riles continued to look at the rear of the arena, where the door outside the A.V. room remained locked. Some arena employees and security were speaking to a very animated Fanicci.

"Multiple specimens were obtained at the time of the surgery," said Phil while looking backwards at the screen. "Her pathology showed a diffuse inflammatory process with widespread multi-organ cell destruction."

Riles looked upwards to see the first pathology report generated for Mrs. Rudenko on the screen, the one Phil had secured from floor clerk Wilma Williams. He stood up and leaned towards Phil while putting his hand over the microphone.

"What the hell are you doing?"

"Just presenting Mrs. Rudenko," said Phil. "Remember the case presentation that you cancelled earlier this week?"

"Stop right now," said Riles. "Do not show any more pathology reports young man or you will never graduate.

Do you understand? I will destroy your career as a surgeon, so help me god."

Phil defiantly clicked the next slide up on the screen while looking at Riles.

"Interestingly a second pathology report from the same surgical day showed slightly different findings," said Phil. "As you can see this report does not describe the destructive process seen in the original report. Our next speaker will explain this inconsistency."

"That's it Drummer, your career is over," said Riles who was still standing up. "Over! Do you hear me young man?"

Union Park was now in full damage control with Fanicci directing the actions of the heavily armed security team. Some members of the team were forcefully pushing their bodies against the A.V. room door, trying to bust it open. Hospital CEO Mitchell spoke outside the door to the head of security, his son-in-law. A rumble of excitement began to roll throughout the arena.

"Several months later the patient continued to have severe abdominal pain prompting a repeat surgery by one of our attending surgeons," said Phil rapidly, sensing the end was near. "Again, intra-operative findings suggested a diffuse inflammatory process at which time multiple tissue samples were obtained."

The chief resident then delivered the next overhead slide showing the most recent pathology report from Mrs. Rudenko. It was the report sent just days earlier by Doc Johnson, with the final impression stating – Borax.

Loud commotion erupted in the arena with everyone now sensing the speaker to be a renegade. The noise of the crowd grew heavy.

At that very moment, across the street in the Congo, everything was on schedule. Mo and Stan were singing

Roll Out the Barrel in preparation for the long anticipated tapping of the keg.

"That's thirty minutes, Stan," yelled Mo over the sound of the accordion. "Mr. Jankowski, tap this keg!"

"I agree Mo," said Stan while putting down his instrument. "Get me the rubber mallet my friend."

The last remaining keg of Schmidt's beer in the world was a vintage model, requiring the tap to be hammered inwards. Once the main spigot was driven into the barrel a second smaller breathing peg would be hammered into its side. Stan had done it a thousand times but this would be the most memorable. The keg itself was majestically perched atop an old steel table in the middle of the room.

The retired beer truck driver then raised the mallet in preparation for the first blow but then paused.

"Time goes by too fast Mo," said Stan. "I can remember rolling this baby into the back of my truck a quarter century ago. It's hard to believe we are here today, so many years later. Who would have guessed it Mo? You and I, alone in the subbasement of the Philadelphia General, about to travel back in time."

"Yea, yea, right Stan, tap the keg brother," said Mo. "I'm thirsty."

"Na Zdorovie," said Stan with a raise of his hand. "Na Zdorovie."

The Pole then began to rapidly hit the sharp end of the spigot into the barrel's spout hole causing a harsh echo throughout the basement. The hard plastic keg cap was however dry rotted, a product of too many steamy Philadelphia summers in the attic. Stan continued to hammer away, unable to penetrate the nozzle yet sending the already elevated internal barrel pressure to a new level.

"Come on Stan," said Mo. "Show me what you got."

After ten more blows the brew master was spent. The aged barrel's pressure critically high.

"Let me try," said Mo. "Step aside."

"No," said Stan while wiping the sweat from his brow. "No, it can be dangerous if you're not experienced."

"Stan, the team is going to be over here any minute now," said Mo. "We have to have this baby pouring out some Schmidt's by then."

"Get me the steel hammer," said Stan. "It may break the spigot but we have to take the chance."

"Where's it at?"

"Two rooms down, next to my cot," said Stan.

Back at the arena Riles was now shoving Phil away from the podium in a controlled manner. Stuart Greyson got involved and held Phil's right arm tightly at his side. A loud crash came from the rear of the auditorium, the A.V. room now breached by security. The bang sent a nervous quiver through the crowd, now starting to stand up.

"It's over Drummer," said Riles. "The show is over and your career is over."

"Are you nuts?" asked Greyson while continuing to subdue Phil. "She got into your head too?"

Phil began to struggle back, pushing Greyson in the chest. Chairman Riles reached towards the podium to remove the overhead borax report and clicked some panel buttons, inadvertently delivering the next slide to the audience, the security team not yet figuring out how to shut down the exposition. As the trio struggled a roar went out through the vast hall, causing all three combatants to look upwards at the screen.

There in full view was a text message that an inebriated Vic Fanicci had erroneously copied to Vanessa six weeks ago. It read as the following:

To: John Mitchell
Copy: Vanessa
From: Vic

Thanks for the quick work on J.R. report.
Mission accomplished.
I trust no e-trail on the chart.
Keep your eye on the prize.

–V

All three physicians looked to the rear of the auditorium, a shocked CEO Mitchell staring at the screen. The body of Rick Polk suddenly tumbled before him with the trophy airborne, prompting Mitchell to bolt into the room, trying to shut down the spectacle.

"Why so difficult?" asked Stanley softly to the keg before him. "I've adored you forever but our time has come my darling." He passionately stroked the keg. "No regrets my love."

"Yo, Stan," yelled Mo. "I don't see a hammer back here."

"Come to Stasiu precious, I've been waiting for you."

Then, with a raise of his hand, he delivered a mighty blow with the rubber mallet to the barrelhead, causing it to explode. The force of the blast was tremendous and sent Stan flying backwards. Metallic keg fragments became projectiles and penetrated several power lines in the room, setting off a shower of sparks. The thunder was heard throughout the hospital and even felt by those outside, wondering if an earthquake had struck. The main power grid just outside the hospital shorted out, cutting power to all buildings within a ten-block radius. Suddenly West Philadelphia went dark, a complete blackout.

Chaos ensued across the street in the Union Park convention center as emergency alarms and generator lights went on. Guests stampeded towards the exit thinking a terrorist plot was in progress. Phil shoved away his two assailants and jumped off the back stage. In the dim light he made out two burly security guards heading directly towards him, their path suddenly disrupted by Jackie Rhimes. Phil stumbled his way to the left, searching for an exit and wondering where Vanessa was, screams of terror now filling the hall. He fell over a metal rail as others trampled over him, quickly getting back up. To his right he spotted a set of double doors with an exit sign above, filtering people outside. He took three quick steps towards the door but was suddenly knocked down by a body hurling his way. The force of the ground's impact was tremendous as Phil felt a person on top of him. He cocked his head to the right to view the aggressor, suddenly shocked by the face.

"Get up," said Knight with a scowl. "His face beet red and hair across his forehead. Now!"

Knight arose and forcefully lifted Phil off the floor, his strength admirable. He held both hands on Phil's chest and brought his body close to his, the noise deafening.

"Jenna's dying Phil!" screamed Knight over the bedlam. "She's dying!"

"What?"

"She's on her way to the O.R. now and I need you!"

"Let's go," said Phil. "Let's go."

Chapter Twenty Nine
THE MONA LISA

THE TWO SURGEONS sprinted across the dark street with sirens blaring. Several city fire trucks had already arrived outside the hospital as white smoke billowed from a manhole. A pungent electrical burn smell was in the air. They darted up a hospital stairwell lit by emergency lights, dodging some workers running down towards the exit. Phil struggled to keep up with Knight as he approached speeds not seen since his Franklin Field football days. The duo burst into the operating theatre simultaneously with Jennifer's arrival. She was being rushed into the holding area on a gurney, with Nurse Caroline Ell at her side. A nurse anesthetist was at the head of the bed squeezing an Ambu bag, trying to keep her alive.

"She's crashing!" yelled Caroline. "Pressure non existent!"

Nurse Ell's unwavering attention to Jennifer brought the current situation to a head. She finished her work shift that day at three o'clock yet requested to stay overtime and monitor Jen with one-on-one nursing care. Throughout the day she became more concerned about her increasing shortness of breath and slight disorientation. When her blood pressure began to drop she immediately alerted Dr.

Knight, a maneuver that upset the hospitalist trailing the patient into the O.R.

"It's a classic tension pneumothorax," yelled the hospitalist. "She needs a chest tube." He was describing a spontaneous collapse of a patient's lung, which can affect the heart's function. The emergent placement of a chest tube into the patient's thorax would rapidly rectify the situation.

"Who the hell are you?" yelled Knight, having never seen the hospitalist in the past.

"Dr. Burke," said the young doctor, somewhat offended by the question. "I'm on duty for the SafetyNet medical group. This is my patient."

"She's my patient now," said Knight with a body language that all but excused the medical physician from the case.

"Jennifer!" yelled Phil while looking down at her. Her lips were blue and respirations shallow. A nurse rapidly placed a blood pressure cuff on as the team waited for a reading. The anesthesiologist on call suddenly appeared.

"Sixty over thirty," said the holding room nurse. "Oh my god!"

"Jen!" screamed Phil. "Open your eyes!"

She didn't respond.

"Open up all the I.V. fluids wide," yelled Phil. "Stat!"

Dr. Knight then calmly stepped up to the bedside and reached over the rail to hold her cool hand. He stroked it gently while keeping an eye on the overhead monitor. Next he took a stethoscope out of his side pocket and placed it upon Jennifer's chest, listening to her heart and breath sounds.

"Muffled heart sounds," said Knight while leaning forward, bringing his face close to her. "Interesting."

"It's a pneumothorax," said Dr. Burke. "You better hurry with the tube."

"Jennifer, it's Robert," he said loud and firmly. "Can you hear me?"

She didn't respond.

"Jennifer Ranier, squeeze my hand if you can hear me."

No response.

"C'mon young lady, squeeze my hand, just one time. I need to know if you can hear me."

Suddenly she clenched his hand, holding on firmly.

"That's it Jennifer," said Knight. "Very good. Now Jennifer, take one deep breath for me. As deep as you can." Knight then looked quickly back at Phil saying, "Watch her systolic pressure."

Jen struggled to expand her lungs and take a deep breath, the pressure on her chest turning it into a gasp. She began to weakly cough.

"See?" said Knight. "Arterial pressure dropped ten points with the breath."

"Pulsus paradoxus," said Phil. "I've never seen it before."

"What did her chest x-ray show?" asked the anesthesiologist.

"Equivocal," said Knight as he slowly tilted Jennifer's head to the left in order to inspect her neck.

"I saw a collapsed lung on the chest x-ray," said Dr. Burke defiantly. "I strongly recommend a chest tube be put in the patient right now. I'm going to write that in the chart."

"Look, look at her jugular vein," said Knight.

"It's grossly distended," said Nurse Ell. "It was the first thing I noticed."

"Excellent clinical pick up Nurse Ell," said Knight. "Thank you for calling me. You saved her life up until this point in time."

"Thank you," said Nurse Ell while brushing Jennifer's hair off her forehead. "Thank you doctor."

"Get her in the O.R. now Tony," said Knight to the anesthesiologist. "Were going to do a stat pericardial window."

"Yes, sir," said the gas passer. "Right away." He began to wheel Jennifer down the hall.

"Dr. Burke, do you still think it's a tension pneumothorax?"

"It's my leading diagnosis," said Burke with a bit of hesitation. "I'd like to order an echocardiogram first to rule out any other etiologies."

"The young lady is dying Dr. Burke, do you think we have time for a radiologist and ultrasound tech to get here on a Friday night? You may as well call in the coroner, young man."

Just then Rick Polk burst into the room, his face swollen and right eye nearly shut. There was some blood oozing out of his left nostril. His shirt was ripped around the right shoulder area.

"What's going on?" asked Polk.

"What's going on is we have a healthy female who just returned from Nepal with a bad case of amoebic dysentery," said Knight while continuing to stare at the hospitalist. "Over the past week she has been struggling to regain her strength and today took a turn for the worse. Her systolic pressure is dangerously low, she has muffled heart sounds and marked distension of her jugular vein."

Polk didn't speak while trying to digest the information.

"And our medical friend here thinks she has a tension pneumothorax," said Knight while pointing at the hospitalist. "So what's your call Dr. Burke? Is it a pneumothorax? Remember, the patient's life is in your hands."

"Ah, I'm not sure," said the doctor. "I'm going to have to look at the computer again, check her labs. I just picked her up on my shift this afternoon."

"It's not a pneumothorax," said Polk. "You just described Beck's triad. That's pathognomonic for cardiac tamponade. She has a cardiac tamponade."

Knight took three steps in the direction of Dr. Burke, his frame towering over the hospitalist.

"Dr. Burke, have you taken your medical board examination yet?" asked Knight. "You know, the little quiz permitting you to become a board certified medical physician?"

"No, no I haven't," said Burke. "But I am studying for them."

"Well you just failed," said Knight with a growl. "Missed it big time. Now get the hell out of here, because this patient is mine!"

Jennifer indeed was suffering from infectious cardiac tamponade, a condition in which fluid accumulates in the pericardium, or sac in which the heart is enclosed. The build up of excessive pressure from the fluid prevents the heart from working properly, resulting in not enough blood being sent to the body. Cardiac tamponade is a medical emergency whose treatment requires prompt decompression of the fluid surrounding the heart muscle. Otherwise, the result is lethal.

"Hurry up," said the anesthesiologist while sticking his head outside the operating room. He was talking to the three surgeons scrubbing their hands at the sink. "I don't know how much longer her heart is going to hold out!"

The surgeons tossed their scrub brushes into the metallic sink while staring through the window into operating room number four. The procedure would be Knight's first since his self-imposed exile several weeks earlier. On the table rested Jennifer with a breathing tube down her throat and nurses circling.

"Let's do this men," said Knight with a lead step towards the door. "Speed is of the essence."

"Stop!" yelled a voice from behind the trio. "What do you think you're doing?"

The threesome looked behind to see Chairman Riles standing there, his arms across his chest. His rented tuxedo was torn above the right knee and he had a deranged look on his face.

"Jenna's critical," said Knight. "Cardiac tamponade, needs an emergent window."

"Oh really," said Riles. "So where's the surgeon to do it?"

"I'm doing it," said Knight.

"No you're not," said Riles. "You're on medical leave, remember?"

"Don't give me that crap Fred," said Knight. "She's dying."

"But Robert you told me you're incapable of safely performing any operations," said Riles smugly. "So why should I, the chairman of the Department of Surgery, allow you to do surgery?"

"Hurry up," said the anesthesiologist again sticking his head outside the room. "I'm maxing the pressors and she is nearly asystolic."

"You pompous ass," said Knight. "A woman's life is a stake here!"

"I'll call in one of the heart surgeons right now," said Riles. "Will only take a minute."

"Drummer will do it," said Knight. "How's that? Good enough for you? Polk will first assist."

"These two hooligans at your side are no longer members of the residency staff," said Riles. "Not after the stunt they just pulled across the street. As of this moment they are officially discharged from the program."

"I'm doing the case!" said Knight turning back towards the room. "Nobody is going to stop me."

"I'm calling security right now," said Riles while reaching for a phone on the wall. "I'll have the three of you arrested and removed from the hospital proper."

The comment caused Knight to turn around and strike the phone with his right hand, sending it flying down the hall in multiple pieces. He next took one menacing step towards Riles who held his ground.

"You're no leader," said Knight. "Never have been. Why they crowned you chairman is beyond me."

"Robert, please," said Riles with attitude. "I've never understood why you don't liked me, ever since our training days together?"

"Maybe it's because you botched a case and killed a young woman way back when I was an intern Fred. Remember? You blamed everyone else–except yourself." Knight was referring to the case that resulted in the death of Jim Turner's mother, thus prompting his lethal revenge on the system four years earlier.

"I did not injure that patient," said Riles. "It was never proven."

"Gentlemen," said the anesthesiologist. "Now please, or she's dead."

"Screw you Fred," said Knight while turning back towards the room. "You dropped the scalpel into the patient's abdomen and she bled to death. Everyone saw it." Knight turned towards the room with his team, only to be blocked by Riles stepping in front of him.

"Get out of my way Fred," said Knight in anger. "Get the hell out of my way!"

"I will not," said Riles. "I forbid you to enter this room."

"Don't make me hurt you Fred, because I will."

"I dare you to touch me," said Riles. "What's right is right."

Knight cocked back his right arm to strike the chairman but the combined effort of Phil and Rick prevented any forward progress of his upper extremity, their action reflexively stopping the blow.

"Oh that was so nice," said Riles with a pathetic shake of his head. "You've always had more brawn than brains Richard, perhaps that's the reason why you're not chairman. Too bad you've seen your last day here at the PGH. We are all going to miss you," said Riles with a flash of his teeth. "And that goes for you two goons also."

Knight waited for the aristocratic jaw of Riles to rotate straight at him before delivering the knockout punch, a powerful unobstructed right hand jab. The chairman dropped like a sack of potatoes, his two front teeth sailing across the room. The gang then stepped over the crumpled body of their former chairman into the operating room.

"Finally!" yelled the anesthesiologist as the team burst into the room. "You're cutting it close gentlemen, way too close for me."

"Prep the field Phil!" said Knight while being gowned by the scrub nurse. "Neck to pelvis." He instructed the nurse to pour some alcohol over his swollen right hand.

Phil began to paint Jen's body with a sponge stick soaked with liquid betadine, realizing it was the first time Knight ever addressed him as "Phil." His broad arm strokes sent antiseptic liquid flying all over the floor.

"Do you remember the first line you every spoke to me?" asked Phil of Knight. "Here in this very room five years ago when I was prepping out a patient?"

"Sure I do," said Knight while stepping towards the field with Polk. They were holding sterile surgical sheets to begin placing over Jen.

"You're not painting the goddamn Mona Lisa," said Phil while stepping backwards, the prep complete. "I'll never forget that line."

"Hmmm," said Knight while covering up Jen. "Well I guess this is the only case where that is not true," said Knight sincerely. "If anything, the opposite."

"Oh my God," said a circulating nurse while holding her right arm across her chest in admiration. "That was so beautiful, Dr. Knight."

"Knife!" yelled Knight.

As the scalpel hit the skin there was a peculiar ambience in the room, the rest of West Philadelphia in darkness. Generators hummed to provide enough overhead light as the physicians coned down upon a tight surgical field. The only thing that mattered was Jennifer Ranier.

"I'm going subxiphoid," said Knight in reference to his surgical approach. His incision began at the tip of the lower sternum and extended vertically down towards Jennifer's abdomen.

"Look at that blood," said Knight. "It's dark."

"No oxygen," said Polk as he manned the suction to keep the field clear.

"Blood pressure dropping!" yelled the anesthesiologist. "Some S-T changes on the EKG. Hurry! She's gonna flatline!"

As Phil held some skin retractors he witnessed the pure skill of his mentor at his best. Knight rapidly developed an anatomic plane directly beneath Jen's breastbone and latched onto her swollen pericardium with a clamp. He took a scalpel and drove it into the distended sac, bursting purulent fluid all over the field. A collective sigh of relief followed, as everyone looked up at the monitors.

Phil said a prayer.

"C'mon Jen," said Knight. "Come on back."

Knight reached backwards to grab a set of defibrillator paddles and placed them on Jen's heart, but they were unnecessary as her vital signs rapidly improved.

"Thank God!" yelled the anesthesiologist. "Her numbers are rising!" Sweat was pouring down his face. "I'm getting too old for this stuff."

As Phil looked down into the wound Jen's heart came back to life. It began to beat rhythmically and strong, sending much needed oxygen to her body. Her blood began to turn bright red and her skin pink. She felt warm. He looked up at Knight who continued to stare at the monitors, not yet celebrating.

"How's the EKG Tony?" asked Knight. "Any changes?"

"No," said the anesthesiologist followed by a pause. "No. It looks good, no signs of cardiac damage. S-T changes have reversed, normal rhythm."

Knight continued to peer over the surgical sheets at the EKG monitor. While doing so he slowly put down the paddles.

"I think you did it Robert. You saved her life. Congratulations, you saved her life."

It was only then that Dr. Knight looked upwards at the heavens to quietly thank the gods, his steady hands still upon the field. No one spoke until he returned his gaze upon the two residents across the table.

"Wow," said Polk.

"Thank you gentlemen," said Knight. "Thank you very much. Mission accomplished."

"Not a second to spare," said Phil.

The team then irrigated out Jen's pericardial sac of any remaining fluid as her heart pounded away. With reliable hands Knight cut a rectangular window into her pericardium to allow any further fluid to decompress. They began to suture close the wound.

"Who should I put down as the head surgeon?" asked the circulating nurse completing some paperwork in the corner. She was quite aware of Dr. Knight's medical leave status.

"Good question," said the anesthesiologist. "I mean look at you three. One guy is on medical leave, the other has a broken hand and the third guy looks like the mob just roughed him up. It takes the three of you to make one full surgeon.

"The Holy Trinity," said Polk. "Put us down as the Holy Trinity."

"I'll go with the Trinity," said Knight with a laugh. He shook the hands of Phil and Rick. "Holy, I'm not so sure of."

The elder surgeon stepped back from the table and took off his gown, a look of satisfaction in his eyes.

"Ladies and gentlemen," said Knight. "I've said it before with sadness, but now I will say it with joy. You have just witnessed my final case."

"One we will never forget," interjected the anesthesiologist.

"No one here will ever forget it," added the scrub nurse.

The phone rang on the wall behind the anesthesiologist, prompting him to pick it up.

"What?" said the wide-eyed anesthesiologist. "When?"

Everyone stared at him in anticipation. Several more seconds passed in silence.

"Oh my God, I'll be right down." He hung up the phone, shock in his eyes.

"Who was that Tony?" asked Knight.

"The E.R.," said the shaken physician. "Someone just jumped off the hospital roof."

"What!"

"They think it was a suicide attempt. Security is rushing the body into the E.R. right now."

"Oh my goodness," said the nurse.

"I've got to get down there immediately," said the anesthesiologist to the nurse anesthetist. "Take over."

"Is he alive?" asked Knight. "Do they know who it was?"

"No," said the physician as he bolted towards the door. "I mean I hope they're alive, but I don't know who it was."

"Was it a male or female?" yelled Phil as the anesthesiologist left the room.

"I'm not sure, they didn't say," was his last line that echoed through the hallway.

As the operating room door slowly closed Dr. Knight tilted his frame to look outwards at the floor, where Dr. Riles had previously fallen. The chairman's body had disappeared.

Chapter Thirty
FINAL RESPECTS

It was a bleak, rainy Wednesday morning in North Philadelphia as Phil and Rick stepped off the Broad Street subway line. Once above ground they walked four blocks east in search of a funeral home situated on a cross street equally inaccessible from all directions. The narrow lane was blocked by a garbage truck trying to get by a parked hearse, refusing to move. The black hearse had seen better days.

"C'mon back!" yelled the city worker to the driver, attempting to reverse the refuse behemoth out of the alley. Piles of stinking garbage lined the cobblestone street, rotting from the summer heat. "C'mon back!"

"Why do they call it a funeral parlor?" asked Rick. "I mean I think of a parlor as a happy place to sit and read the Sunday paper." Rick's face was swollen beneath a set of raccoon eyes, a result of the convention center security team beat down.

"It sounds better than a mortuary," said Phil, the morning reminding him of his dad's funeral service.

Down the street from the funeral home rose a massive grey stone church complete with a rectory, convent and grade school. The complex was shoe horned into the surrounding blue-collar neighborhood, having served the populace for the past two hundred years. As the two approached the funeral parlor bells from the steeple above began to ring.

"Bong… bong… bong." The slow, solemn sound echoed down the street.

Two funeral attendants dressed in black garb welcomed Phil and Rick to the service. They were tall, gaunt retired men with white hair, trying to enjoy retirement with a part time job. One reeked of tobacco, the other with a bad case of dandruff across his shoulders.

"Good morning gentlemen," said the attendant on the right. "And welcome to the service." His voice was morbid. To their right in a small sitting room lined with pictures of the Sacred Heart of Jesus was an elderly woman in a dress playing the organ. She wore thick black shoes and a set of old fashioned cat winged glasses, squinting at a music sheet, serious in her roll. A few oversized chairs in need of new upholstery sat empty beside her. The turnout was sparse.

The duo signed the guest list and took a religious remembrance card from the desk. They saw Maurice first, dressed in a suit and tie, a cane in his right hand. He was last in line about ten people back from the coffin.

"Good morning gentlemen," said Maurice, his voice a bit off from a swollen jaw.

"Morning Mo," said Phil. "How are you doing?"

"I'm ah-right," said Mo.

"What did the doctor say?"

"He said I was lucky to be behind that concrete wall. Just nicked up a bit, some shrapnel in my leg."

"Get well soon Mo," said Phil.

To the left of the coffin stood a lone family member, also dressed in black. On the right were three flower bouquets, one from the local V.F.W., the second from a Rotary Club and the third complements of the funeral home. Scattered around the corpse was a collection of keepsakes along with Old Glory in the corner. There was a scuffed baseball signed by high school teammates after the city championship game. A Philadelphia Flyer's hockey puck sat next to a framed ticket stub from the November 20th, 1960 Eagles game that still reverberated through the northern section of town. A DVD case containing *The Bridge on the River Kwai* was set to accompany the deceased on their eternal journey.

Stan Jankowski was dressed in his Schmidt's uniform, a request he gave to his sister just months prior, his name embroidered on the left hand pocket. Beside him sat a single picture showing the beer truck man and his cronies in the factory taproom, raising a glass of suds on a hot summer day. He looked so young to Phil.

"I'm so very sorry," said Phil to his sister. "My deepest condolences."

Amelia Jankowski was the last remaining sister of Stan, the two having lived together for the past six years.

"Thank you for coming Dr. Drummer," said Amelia. "Thank you for bringing Stan back to life."

"Excuse me?" said Phil.

"You know, he was dying of cancer," said Amelia. "Doctor Johnson told him he only had a few more months to live."

"No I didn't," said Phil deftly, disguising his shock at the sudden revelation. "I knew Dr. Johnson and Dr. Polk operated on him, but had no idea he had a terminal disease."

"He didn't want to tell anyone," said the sister. "A stubborn Pole to the end."

"I'm so sorry," said Phil. "He was a wonderful man and it was a pleasure to have known him."

"I'm very sorry," said Rick Polk, now entering the conversation. There was no one behind the two in line. "He was family to us."

"You two men brought Stanley back to life," said Amelia with a warm smile. "He was just waiting to die... until he started to talk about the Torpedo Room. From that moment forward he was full of life and energy. It was the best thing that could have happened to him."

Phil and Rick smiled, aware of the inner peace in the family member's eyes.

"I'll never forget the day he rolled that old keg out of the attic," said Amelia. "I've never seen him more happy. Thank you."

"You're welcome ma'am," said the duo. "You're very welcome."

"He would have wanted to die that way," added Stan's sister. "I know it sounds crazy but I know my brother. He took so much pride in tapping a keg the correct way. He went to heaven in a blaze of old Schmidt's beer."

The funeral mass was held down the street in the old church, a visiting missionary from the Philippines running the service. In broken English he spoke of the simple life, one surrounded by friends and family as opposed to material goods, a lifestyle Stan knew well. A female soloist in the choir sang *Amazing Grace* to conclude the ceremony. Thirty minutes later Stan's casket was taken to a local cemetery on a hill, and lowered into the ground for all of eternity, next to his parents. Dr. Polk and Doc Johnson served as pallbearers.

Two hours later Phil and Rick were rushing back into the hospital to attend a meeting before the PGH Disciplinary Board, their futures very much at stake. While walking through the hospital lobby they ran into a visitor from the east.

"Dr. Drummer, so good to see you," said Dr. Albright with a set of flowers in his right hand. "How's she doing?"

"Great," said Phil. "Like a new woman since the surgery. When did you get into town?"

"Just got off the plane," said Albright, some balloons in his left hand. "Rushed right over here to see her."

Phil noticed an elevated sense of excitement in Albright's mannerisms. Peculiar he thought, wondering what may have transpired in Nepal.

"Believe it or not she may be going home tomorrow," said Phil. "I'm sure she'll be happy to see you."

"Thanks, have a wonderful day," said Albright. He then hurried down the congested corridor towards the elevator.

"Hmmm," said Polk. "I saw some deep, deep concern in his loving eyes, Philip."

Phil ignored the remark.

The hospital disciplinary board consisted of three administrative staff members and two physicians selected from the department involved in the matter. The setting was a dark, musty conference room in the Kirby building. The hospital vice president spoke first. He was a massive man whose jowls vibrated with each word.

"Good afternoon doctors," said the chairman of the committee. Phil and Rick stood before him, looking up at their elevated platform. "Today we are here to discuss a serious matter that occurred last Friday here in the hospital, and across the street in the Union Park center. A matter which has led to the death of at least one person and perhaps indirectly to another, while gaining national attention." The speaker looked over a set of glasses on his nose at the two. "Gentlemen, do you have an attorney present to represent you?" A female stenographer chewing gum typed away in the corner.

"Ah no," said Phil.

"We represent ourselves," said Polk.

"I see," said the speaker. "Gentlemen, to recap my knowledge of the event, you both helped to arrange a party in a section of our hospital without the appropriate consent from the administration. The party itself involved members of our maintenance staff and a former patient who bootlegged a keg of beer into the facility. Is that correct?"

"Yes sir," said Phil. "It all seemed very innocent at the time."

"Yes I see. What appears to have happened next, at least from the testimony of a Mr. Maurice Rhett, that's R-h-e-t-t, was that there was trouble tapping the keg." The chair spoke slowly as if trying to help the stenographer. "Mr. Rhett was then instructed to secure a metal hammer from a Mr. Jankowski, that's J-a-n-k-o...."

As the board member continued to recap the strange series of events Phil noticed a pensive Dr. Knight sitting towards the end of the table. He then thought of Jenna and Dr. Albright sitting at her bedside. Maybe she found her nirvana in Nepal? The tap-tap-tap of the stenographer continued.

"Dr. Drummer, hello, are you with us?"

"Yes, yes," said Phil, not having heard the last few lines.

"That's right," interjected Polk. "And that's when the keg exploded."

"Instantly killing Mr. Jankowski?"

"Yes," said Phil. "We just came back from his funeral."

Over the next twenty minutes the committee chair chastised the two residents for their poor judgment and blatant disregard for rules. Each board member categorically condemned their actions. It quickly became obvious to Phil and Rick that each member of the council was distancing their name from the debacle. Dr. Knight was the first member from the Department of Surgery asked to speak.

"There is no doubt that the party in the sub-basement of the hospital was wrong," said Knight. "Some high jinks from two chief residents, nothing we haven't seen before. However what happened after that was a truly unpredictable and tragic accident, a series of events not anticipated by any of the physicians standing before us."

An audible murmur emanated from the board members.

"Order, order," said the chairman. "Let the good doctor speak."

"We need to separate events within the control of these two residents, as opposed to actions outside of their control. Remember, their professional reputations and ultimate graduation from this training program is at stake," said Knight. "A most serious matter."

"Dr. Knight, charges are being filed by the city police and federal authorities bordering on terrorism. We have to hold someone accountable for this," said the chair.

"What transpired at the Union Park center in my opinion was an act of heroism," said Knight. "An action taken by several brave young…."

"That's outrageous!" screamed Dr. Riles, as he rose off his chair. It was the first time Phil and Rick saw him since the memorable night. The chairman's face was bloated from Knight's knockout punch a few days prior. "These two men along with the help of a local prostitute orchestrated a high tech act of terrorism that played out to a national audience. The subsequent suicide and death of my good friend, CEO John Mitchell, a person we all knew and respected, was a direct result of their careless disregard for authority. These two miscreants before us should be arrested immediately and prosecuted to the fullest extent of the law. At a minimum they should be immediately released from the surgical residency program. Their actions are a disgrace to the Philadelphia General Hospital."

"John Mitchell's suicide was a result of John Mitchell's decision process," said Knight. "These two men didn't push him off the roof of this building. At the time of his death they were with me saving the life of a young woman. Remember? You were trying to prevent us from operating on that woman."

"You assaulted me!" screamed Riles at Knight. "My attorneys are working on that matter."

"Order gentlemen, order please."

"Mr. Mitchell was embarrassed by the disclosure of his personal text messages to the general public!" screamed Riles. "Information displayed for public consumption by these two before us. His suicide was a direct result of Mr. Drummer's broadcast and the subsequent fallout."

"Fred, you're the one who hit the button to advance the slide show," said Knight.

"Don't play games with me Richard!" yelled Riles. "The A.V. room was commandeered by Dr. Polk. He was running the slide show!"

"Gentlemen order please," shouted the committee chairman. "Let's try to discuss this calmly."

"These two gentlemen along with the help of a courageous young woman exposed a despicable scheme, hatched by a pharmaceutical company and designed to dupe the public into believing a sham medicine actually works," said Knight. "They should be honored for their actions across the street. Who knows how many people were involved in this disgraceful cabal?"

"Don't insult me!" screamed Riles. "I'm a man of integrity!"

"How the greedy tentacles of such a company penetrated into the walls of this academic center, I'll never know," said Knight. "Who knows how many people are on their payroll."

"How dare you say such a thing!" screamed Riles, his face fire truck red. "I had no knowledge of their back-room dealings with pathology reports! None whatsoever."

"No one said you did Frederick," said Knight. "Is there something you would like to tell us?"

"Yes Richard there is," said Riles. "My attorneys have secured a signed affidavit from Mr. Fanicci stating I had no knowledge whatsoever of his actions in regards to altering pathology reports. None! I had no idea of what they were doing."

"But Dr. Drummer gave you a copy of both reports several days prior to the main event," said Knight. "Why no action then?"

"Ah, ah... er," mumbled Riles, stunned by Knight's implication.

"What wouldn't a man of such integrity look into this matter further?" asked Knight. "That's what I don't understand Fred. You had the warning signs in your hands and for some odd reason, didn't act on it. Why?"

Riles went silent, keenly aware that Phil gave him the reports prior to the convention. He tried to formulate a response but thought it best to simply remain silent.

"Doctors, the matter at hand involves the actions of the two residents before us," said the committee chair-person. "Not Dr. Riles." He paused to allow tensions to ease. "Let's try to concentrate on their actions, there will be plenty of time in the near future to calmly discuss the decision process of others involved."

"Understood," said Knight.

"Young men, is there anything you would like to say in your defense to the committee before we adjourn for private deliberation in this matter?" asked the chair. "Dr. Drummer, you may go first." For the first time the stenographer looked up at Phil in anticipation of a comment, her gum chewing stopped.

"Well I would first like to say that I meant no physical harm to anyone," said Phil. "The death of Mr. Jankowski was a horrible accident. We all loved Stan. What happened after that was a domino effect. I would like to apologize to everyone affected by my actions, which at the time seemed quite benign, but in retrospect were catastrophic."

"I see," said the chairman. "Anything else?"

"Yes," said Phil. "What happened across the street was a necessary exposure of irregularities in my opinion. I didn't volunteer to get involved with the Lysovage project, but was rather pulled in by their marketing team. Once on board it became obvious to me that distortions existed within and between data reports. I brought these inconsistencies to the attention of my mentor, but for some reason they were never addressed." Phil paused to gather some composure while looking at Riles. "I just had to do something," he said, now looking at each board member. "To remain silent was not an option."

"I see," said the chair, while jotting down some notes on a paper before him. "Mr. Polk, is there anything you would like to say to the committee?"

"Yes," said Rick. "Again, as Dr. Drummer stated, what happened in the hospital was an accident. I apologize for our actions. We were wrong to set up a party downstairs. What happened across the street was a friend helping a friend." He then looked to his right at Phil. "The man next to me is the most honest, trusting and reliable friend a person can have," said Polk. "He is a man of integrity, a true leader respected by every resident in this hospital. When he asked me for some help, there was no hesitation or question in my mind. I had to assist him. In my heart I believe what we did was right. Something had to be done."

"Thank you Dr. Polk," said the chair. "And thank you for coming down from your hospital room to discuss this matter. The board is aware of your need for hospitalization after the event, and respect your time and energy provided to us."

"That's a sham hospital admission!" yelled Riles. "He isn't suffering from post-concussion syndrome, but rather was admitted by Dr. Knight to the hospital in order to keep some bizarre streak alive. A streak that has allowed this former resident to reside within the walls of a hospital, free of charge for five years! It's a side show gentlemen, don't be fooled by their shenanigans."

Knight did not respond.

"Noted," said the chair while gathering up his papers. "Dr. Drummer and Dr. Polk, thank you for your time. The board will have a decision within forty-eight hours, this Friday, which to my understanding is your tentative graduation date. You are dismissed."

"Thank you sir," said Phil.

"Thank you," added Rick.

Later that evening Dr. Riles sat in his home library, still seething from the conference. He had lost so much over the past five days–large sums of money wagered on now worthless stock, two front teeth, and a good portion of his professional reputation. To make matters worse his close friend committed suicide, a product he had worked on for years was dead, and his daughter was not pregnant. While looking at a framed picture of his father he said out loud, "What else can go wrong, dad?"

The phone rang and he answered it. Vic Fanicci was on the line, calling from his brother's house in South Philadelphia. Riles was tempted to hang up on the salesman, but allowed him to speak.

"Listen Fred, I'm hurting too," said Fanicci. "No job, no apartment, no future, for Christ's sake I'm calling you from my brother's house on a rotary phone!" A television blasting a gaudy game show was heard in the background.

"What now? Make it quick," barked Riles.

"I'm in a heap of trouble with Union Park," said Fanicci. "They've released their attorneys on me, it's really ugly. They're like wolves out for my blood."

"Why Vic? Why did you and John do it?"

"It happened over a period of years," said Fanicci in between sips of beer. "It's not like we planned it. He knew the pathologist in Boston, and I knew the patient's names, once we got to Philadelphia it all just spiraled out of control."

"But Lysovage worked Victor, it really worked, and that's what makes it so tragic." There was another pause in the conversation. "Everyone loses on this one Victor, everyone."

"I know, I know Fred but listen, I need a favor from you," said Fanicci. "A little matter the lawyers want cleared up." Riles heard two dogs barking in the background, along with Victor's brother telling them to shut up.

"A favor? You have some nerve!"

"Listen Fred, I was prompt to sign that affidavit your legal team put in front of me, you know the one stating you had no knowledge of our doings with the path reports."

"I didn't have any knowledge Victor!" screamed Riles.

"I know, I know, but I still signed the paper."

"What do you need Victor? My patience is growing short with you. Don't waste any more of my time."

"O.K., O.K., take it easy," said Fanicci. "All I need is a short statement from you saying the remaining thirteen vials of Lysovage were appropriately destroyed by your department. That's it, a simple request, but I need it like pronto my friend."

Silence.

"Hello, Fred are you still there?" asked Fanicci.

"Can you please repeat that statement Victor," said Riles in a slow methodical manner. "Again, tell me exactly what you need from me?"

"A statement," said Fanicci. "Nothing fancy. You can even write it."

"Saying what?"

"That your department or a member of your staff appropriately disposed of the remaining vials, like you told me so. The lawyers just need it in writing."

"How many vials did you say?"

"Thirteen Fred, what are you deaf or something? Remember our conversation on the cruise? I told you a simple way to remember it was the lucky number thirteen, just like I was going to get lucky that night," said Fanicci. "Which by the way I did. Hoorah!"

Chairman Riles hung up the phone. He did not sleep well that night.

Chapter Thirty One
GRADUATION DAY

On Friday morning Phil woke up alone in his apartment staring out the window, the final day of his residency. It went by so fast, a blur of patients, surgeries, friendships and troubles. Five years ago he stepped out of the apartment a tentative intern, unsure of himself and the future. Now he was fully trained, confident and experienced, but the future remained uncertain. His parents were gone, his personal life a mess and in twenty-four hours he would be unemployed. He wasn't even sure about graduation that evening, the decision from the Disciplinary Board due in just a few hours. He was in no hurry to start the day.

Yesterday he helped transport Jennifer home, to a stately carriage house in Bryn Mawr on the estate of Stacy Ricketts. Stacy married into more money than Phil would ever make in his surgical career, her husband Princeton the grandson of a tycoon. The carriage house was tastefully built eighty years ago to house a cantankerous mother-in-law and sat on a slight slope near a stream, surrounded by tall oak trees. Jen was so happy to be out of the hospital as was Dr. Albright, another voluntary member of the transition team. Albright arranged for a series of oversized stuffed animals to be waiting for Jen, including a four feet high panda bear. Outside of the carriage house Albright unfurled a Tibetan prayer flag invoking peace and goodwill to everyone in the ritzy suburb. He stole the show by noticing the peculiar cut of Stacy's diamond earrings, a design Princeton personally selected for their recent wedding anniversary. In all the hoopla, Phil barely spoke to Jen, quietly placing his partially melted box of chocolates on the kitchen counter, and hoping she would find the note inside. He left a second-class citizen, still residing in the proverbial doghouse of Stacy Ricketts-Brown.

A ring of the doorbell broke Phil's musings and forced him out of bed.

"Good morning Philip," said Rick. "I have no home, no job and no future. Do you have room for the Liberty Bell and I?"

"Sure I do," said Phil. "I've been expecting you two. How are you feeling?"

"Honestly I don't know, with everything going on," said Polk. "Today worries me. I'm not sure what is going to happen."

"Me too," said Phil. "Rough time sleeping last night. I just sat in bed this morning listening to some pigeons. I believe I'm depressed."

"I'm not even excited about the streak," said Polk.

"Oh yea, congratulations," said Phil. "You made it. Immortality my friend, it's a PGH record that can never be broken."

"Anticlimactic," said Rick. "I thought I'd be carried out of the hospital on the shoulders of my classmates, instead a pinstriped volunteer rolled me out in a wheelchair. Her breath smelled like peppermint licorice."

"That's life," said Phil. "The journey trumps the destination, we are both living proof of that."

The two friends ate breakfast together while reading the *Philadelphia Chronicle*. The newspaper had a major article on the series of events involving Union Park and the Philadelphia General, with a major emphasis on Dr. Frederick Riles, whose life work was destroyed by a dastardly scheme involving Union Park officials and an unidentified lab in Boston. A photo of the dejected surgeon accompanied the piece as he explained his innocence in the whole mess, a victim of greedy forces working in clandestine fashion beneath the surface. The photo showed Riles holding an affidavit from Union Park stating he had no knowledge of the collusion leading to the convention center debacle. Out of respect the name of CEO John Mitchell was infrequently mentioned in the article, as was that of the PGH surgical residents involved.

"I actually feel sorry for the guy," said Phil. "I mean in reality he knew nothing about it. Years of work down the drain."

"When you sleep with dogs you're going to get fleas," said Polk. "And Riles was sleeping with a lot of dogs."

"When is the board decision coming out?" asked Phil while folding up the newspaper.

"Noon today," said Rick, stroking the cat.

"What's your guess?"

"We're dead men," said Polk. "Absolute dead men."

The phone in Phil's apartment rang at high noon. Both he and Rick were informed of the board's decision. Neither man would graduate that evening.

At exactly six o'clock in the evening Chairman Frederick Riles strolled to the podium to speak to the graduation class. The ceremony was being held on the top floor of the hospital's administrative wing, a cozy little area for intimate gatherings with a grand view of the city. Outside of the venue it was a cheap event, a fitting end to an archaic training system for surgeons. A buffet table sat along the back wall littered with finger foods and beverages, a smorgasbord fit for a child's birthday. Next to the window sat a set of shiny graduation chairs made entirely of solid maple hardwood, painted satin black with gold beading, their scrolled tops proudly displaying the seal of the Philadelphia General Hospital. Each graduate would receive a chair as a token of the hospital's appreciation for their hard work and dedication, a parting gift. Only two chairs sat in the room that evening, as did a somber tone among the honored guests.

"Good evening everyone," said Dr. Riles. "Welcome to this year's surgical residency graduation ceremony." Dr. Riles scanned the sparse crowd, consisting only of fifth year residents Cathy Finley and Jackie Rhimes. Thankfully the parents of Cathy Finley showed up along with two younger siblings, as none of Rhimes' family members attended. Noticeably absent was Stuart Greyson, despite his promise to be there. The three cafeteria workers manning the buffet table nearly outnumbered the gathering.

"We have a wonderful ceremony in store for you tonight," said Dr. Riles, standing alone in front of the crowd. Both Dr. Knight and Dr. Johnson were boycotting the event, in response to the Disciplinary Board's decision to banish Phil and Rick from the program, sending their two young lives adrift.

"Before us are two fine surgeons with a bright career ahead of them," said Riles, a cafeteria worker suddenly struggling with a coughing spell. "Over the past five years Dr. Rhimes and Dr. Finley have exhibited superior surgical skills along with a moral character reflective of the Philadelphia General. It's been my personal privilege to watch them mature not only as surgeons, but as individuals."

The youngest sister of Cathy Finley began to clap.

"Thank you, thank you," said Dr. Riles. "As expected, each young surgeon has already accepted a coveted position to continue their careers, Dr. Finley in New York City and Dr. Rhimes...ah, ah... let's see..."

"North Philly," said Rhimes with a shake of his head. "Just up the street. Temple."

"Yes, yes, I'm sorry," said Riles. "So much going on here. Yes, Dr. Rhimes in Philadelphia itself, our fine city."

There was no applause, the event somehow growing flatter, Riles sensing dismay.

"Now, without further ado, I'd like to invite each graduate to the microphone to say a few words, prior to the presentation of their beautiful academic chairs," said Riles. "The chair presentation ceremony will be followed by a buffet that our cafeteria staff has prepared for us."

The young Finley girl again began to clap wildly, her eye on a chocolate cupcake with rainbow sprinkles.

"It gives me great honor to first introduce Dr. Cathy Finley," said Riles while clapping. "Ladies and gentlemen, Dr. Cathy Finley." Some cafeteria members began to clap as Cathy stood up, along with Jackie Rhimes.

The two surgeons approached the podium without a smile, Jack suddenly strutting his Philly pimp roll. Cathy Finley spoke first, the only resident who avoided all the drama of the past five years.

"It's been a tremendous five years here Dr. Riles," said Cathy, her voice cracking a bit. "I would like to thank you and all the members of the surgical staff for your support and guidance, without you none of this would be possible."

"You're welcome," said Riles, realizing Finley was the only sane resident in the bunch. He wondered why Dr. Rhimes stood next to her, he being a wild card in the deck.

"However I cannot and will not accept my diploma without our full class being present," said Finley with conviction. "Missing tonight are Dr. Phillip Drummer and Dr.

Richard Polk, two of the most admirable men I've had the pleasure to know."

Cathy's parents shifted in their seats as the smile on Riles' face disappeared, his eyes expressing surprise at Finley's remarks. He had hoped the event would go off without a hitch.

"Simply put, they excelled here at the PGH over the past five years and without their support and trust, I don't think I would have made it." Her parents broke their silence and clapped loudly. "For four years we were a team, and I cannot graduate without my teammates. So Dr. Riles I thank you for your guidance and support, but I respectfully decline my graduation diploma. Thank you very much." She stepped back to allow Jackie Rhimes to speak.

"Just one minute here," said Riles approaching the podium.

"That goes for me too," said Rhimes. "We spilled our guts for this institution day in and day out, always available 24/7. It was hard but it was fun, because we had each other's backs, always looking out for one another. Now we are hurting because two team members are missing. We either graduate as one, or leave as none."

"Just a minute you two," said Riles. "I did not make the final decision regarding...."

Suddenly the rear room door opened and in walked Doctor Johnson, followed by Dr. Knight, wearing their white lab coats. Behind them paraded Phil and Rick, a serious look on their faces.

"Doctor Riles, good evening," said Doc Johnson. "Sorry we are late. Allow me to introduce the two remaining graduates of this year's class. Dr. Philip Drummer and Dr. Richard Polk. I believe you know them?"

"What the hell is going on!" said Riles. "The board's decision was final. Get out of here right now!"

"Listen Fred, there's been a change in plan," said Johnson. "These two boys are graduating tonight, whether you like it or not."

"I'm the chairman here," said Riles. "And that decision has already been made in conjunction with the hospital's Disciplinary Board."

"Fred these two men are the best residents we've seen come through her in the past thirty years," said Dr. Knight. "I'm sure you know that. I believe it fitting this group graduates together, tonight, in this very room. What do you say?"

"I say I'm going to call security right now," barked Riles. "Better yet, I'm going to call the Philadelphia police department, after last Friday's events they'll be here in a flash to handcuff you degenerates." Riles was irate as he reached for his cell phone. "These depraved scoundrels will never graduate as long as I'm the chairman here. Understand? Never!"

"Don't bother," said Knight.

"What did you say?" asked Riles while dialing the cell phone. "I'm calling the police."

"I said don't bother, they're already here."

Riles froze with the cell phone to his ear, staring at Knight.

"Hello, 911 is there an emergency?" said the voice over the phone. Phil noticed fear in the eyes of his chairman. He went to speak but said nothing. "Hello, this is 911, can I help you?"

The chairman slowly brought the phone down from his ear and terminated the call, while continuing to focus on his colleagues. The cell immediately chimed back.

"There is no emergency," said Riles slowly to the 911 operator. "My mistake, everything is O.K. on our end. Thank you." He continued to gawk at Johnson and Knight while returning the phone to his pocket. Then in a reluctant and methodical fashion his gaze drifted towards the rear of the room where several Philadelphia police officers stood still.

"Dr. Riles?" asked the elder policeman in a deep, commanding voice, his sleeve bearing a sergeant's rank. "Dr. Frederick Riles?"

Phil noticed his chairman to begin hyperventilating, his look rapidly scanning the face of every resident. Yet, he did not speak. A look of panic overtook his face.

"Mommy, look at the policemen," said the young Finley. "They have guns."

The chairman's eyes began to bulge as his face turned ash white. Phil thought Riles was going to vomit when the officer spoke again, now approaching the group.

"Dr. Riles, we would like to have a few words with you sir." The squeak of leather on the officer's body was loud.

"Yes officer," said Riles weakly, his voice dry. "What's this all about?" He looked beyond the sergeant to the two other officers in the room, the shorter one scratching his cheek and missing an index finger, a smirk on his face.

"The death of Mrs. Biddleton," said the policeman. "We just have a few questions for you sir," said the officer. "Downtown, that is."

"But, but, I'm in the middle of a graduation ceremony here officer, I'm sure you can understand that. I'm the chairman of the Department of Surgery, here...., here at the Philadelphia General."

"Now!" said the policeman, his two associates taking a menacing step forward.

Dr. Riles dropped his head down and began to cry, tears rolling down his cheeks. The two burly policemen then grabbed his arms and began to escort him out of the lounge. He looked to his associates for help, but there was none.

"Suspect in custody," said the sergeant into his shoulder radio. "In route to downtown station."

"Roger 251, in route to downtown station, over," was the garbled response.

The beleaguered chairman mumbled some faint gibberish on the way out. Phil thought he heard the words "I'm sorry" but was unsure. Then there was silence.

Doctor Johnson stepped up to the podium, a white hanky from his pocket wiping his brow. He took a deep breath while scanning the small crowd.

"I'm sorry for the disruption ladies and gentlemen, let me introduce myself. I'm Doctor Johnson, the senior surgeon here at the PGH and, by the letter of the hospital bylaws, the current acting chairman of the Department of Surgery." His smile brought a calm to the group.

"My first action as chairman is to step down from the position and appoint a new chairman," said Johnson. "The man I'm about to introduce has been a stalwart here for some time, a trusted friend and colleague more than deserving of the coveted chair. In my humble opinion he should have been the chairman some time ago. So, it gives me great pleasure to announce the new interim chairman of the Department of Surgery, Dr. Richard Knight."

Applause broke out in the room, louder than one would have expected considering the numbers. Knight accepted the new position with a shake of Johnson's hand. He then stepped to the podium.

"I am honored to accept this position Dr. Johnson, and I thank you for your guidance over the past several days. We all thank you for the many years of outstanding service as both a surgeon and educator."

Applause broke out as Johnson waved. Phil noticed several other residents filtering into the room, a result of Riles being paraded out of the hospital and social media.

"I am privileged to introduce our graduating class this year," said Knight with a smile. "I've served here for over three decades and can honestly say there has never been a stronger class of young physicians to pass through the Philadelphia General. We are all proud of you and your accomplishments."

The room continued to swell with guests and the applause grew louder. Phil noticed some members of the maintenance department, and nurses from the general surgery floor. Even clerk Wilma Williams ambled into the room, the first time Phil had ever seen her walk.

Dr. Knight then delivered a wonderful speech focused on integrity and the role of change in life. "Always be honest with your self," he said, and "never be afraid to change for the better." He individually asked each resident to stand up while reading a list of their accomplishments, followed by a few personal anecdotes from their years at the General Hospital. The chairman subsequently handed each resident a diploma, saving Phil Drummer for last.

"Our final resident is a young man who came to us five years ago from somewhere up north in coal country," said Knight with a smile. "We soon found out he was much more than a coal cracker, much more. Philip Michael Drummer has been an exemplary resident, possessing the mind of a scientist, the hands of a surgeon, and most importantly the heart of a champion."

A round of applause burst out in the room, Phil bowing his head in appreciation.

"During his years at the PGH he has gone through more hardships then most men do in a lifetime," said Knight. "Yet he always persevered and did the right thing, no matter what the consequences. Over time I've heard his fellow residents refer to him as a confidant, leader, trusted helper and most importantly, a friend. He is respected by everyone in the hospital, from the valet parking attendant to the department chairman. And from what I hear he's a darn good basketball player, recently bringing the coveted PGH league trophy back home to where it belongs."

A round of applause followed, interspersed by laughter and whistles, Mo Rhett and some of his team now in the room.

"Over the years he has developed a set of surgical skills that I can attest to," continued Knight with a smile. "I'm hoping that's why all the nurses in the O.R. tell me he has a good set of hands."

The crowd roared with laughter at the joke, Phil now noticing Nurse Hudson and Ell in the mix. With each passing minute the crowd pushed farther into the room. Cafeteria workers hurried to bring more food up to the celebration.

"From a personal standpoint our lives have crossed closely over the years," said Knight. "Close enough that each one of us have been deeply affected." Knight paused to look directly at Phil. "We have laughed, learned and at times cried together," said Knight in a serious tone. "Yet in the end, we learned one important lesson."

The crowd grew silent, sensing a big finish, aware of the history between Phil and the newly elected chair.

"That life is short," said Knight. "Way too short. And to love life and those people that truly matter in our lives, we have to be honest with ourselves and constantly change for the better. And Phil Drummer has taught this surgeon that lesson."

"Hurrah, Hurrah!" shouted the crowd, now standing.

"Oh yes, one more thing," said Dr. Knight. "It gives me great pleasure to announce that both Dr. Polk and Dr. Drummer have accepted associate professor positions here at the PGH. So don't worry, they're not going anywhere. Work starts next week! Welcome to the work force gentlemen, we've been waiting for you. And congratulations to all the graduates!"

A joyous celebration ensued, started by the youngest Finley girl sprinting toward the buffet and her cupcake. The cheering mob swarmed upon Phil and his colleagues.

"We made it, Rick!" said Phil. "We finally made it!"

Across the street at that very moment Stuart Greyson was preparing the Betsy Ross Room. It was a clear night as he drew back the shades, the city skyline beginning to sparkle. He knew from the start that medical student Kayla Lehigh was special, her initial shock and repulsion followed by a burning desire for more and more. A sense of urgency was in the air, as tomorrow the fourth year medical student was heading out west for a long rotation. The night's theme was her idea, the product of an insatiable appetite matching that of her mentor.

Three hours earlier Stuart promised his wife to "stay strong," ahead of a final attempt tomorrow morning in the fertility clinic. Two hours earlier he promised his shaken father-in-law to be present at the graduation ceremony. One hour earlier he had popped two small blue pills for good luck, the effects already in action. While staring out the window he saluted William Penn a top city hall, both men in full form.

At the ten minute mark came a knock on the door, right on schedule. He pictured Kayla and Kaylee sitting at the bar downstairs in the lobby, both women in tight skirts and high heels. They winked at him as he passed by while pouring some alcohol into their bodies. He couldn't believe it, a threesome. How Kayla pulled it off was beyond his wildest imagination. Nervous energy shook his body as he looked into the mirror, his hair perfect. He turned to the right to open the door, wondering which vixen would be first.

With a turn of the latch he opened the door, shocked by a man standing before him.

"Dr. Greyson," said Detective James while holding his I.D. badge out. "I'm Detective James from the Philadelphia Police Department." Behind him were three massive police officers. "You're under arrest for the murder of Mrs. Joyce Biddleton. Please put your hands behind your back."

The policemen swarmed past the detective and apprehended Greyson's shaking body.

"I'm calling my attorney," said Greyson in anger. "This is a big mistake!"

"Cuff the little man," quipped James, a befitting slur Greyson hadn't heard since his high school gym class days. "And for Christ's sake put a robe on him."

Greyson was read his Miranda rights and escorted out of the hotel lobby. He passed Kayla and Kaylee, both giving statements to a police sergeant, mascara streaking down their cheeks. Neither girl made eye contact with the doctor. Within thirty minutes Greyson was downtown in the police precinct, being approached by yet another detective. He sat alone in a room, his attorney on a bender and off the grid somewhere in Las Vegas.

The detective presented the facts. Borax found in two patients with one of them dead. A statement from Union Park Biotech and another from the operating room coordinator, saying only he and Riles had keys to the Lysovage samples. Lastly a hand written statement from a Professor Shoebottom recalling his phone call, the memory clear at least on that day.

"Do you have anything to say in your defense?" asked Detective O'Brien.

"Yes," said Greyson. "I'm innocent."

Detective O'Brien then placed some gloves on and pulled out a plastic bag with a glass vial inside. He carefully opened the bag and lifted the vial out with his right hand while showing it to Greyson.

"Recognize this?" asked the detective.

"Sure, it's a vial we used in the Lysovage project. Obviously empty now." Greyson slouched angrily in his chair, still upset over the aborted tryst.

"This vial had your fingerprints all over it," said O'Brien. "Including the inner side of the glass. Peculiar I thought. As if you were sticking your finger inside to clean it out."

"Big deal."

"It is a big deal Dr. Greyson because this vial was completely filled with borax. There was no Lysovage whatsoever inside. Imagine that?"

"Go figure," said Greyson. "Bad batch from the factory."

"Nah," said the detective while pulling out a piece of paper. "Here's the Union Park assay test specific to this vial's bar code. It left the factory with pure Lysovage in it."

"Have them recheck their machine," said Greyson while shifting in the chair.

"Dr. Knight brought this vial to our attention," said the lawman. "It was in his possession. He specifically said that you gave it to him."

"Knight's crazy, an angry old man. He's hated my father-in-law ever since he botched a surgery back in the day. I wouldn't trust him."

"So you didn't give him this vial, which was laced with borax?"

"That's right. Now if you would please let me go, I have some important business to take care of tonight."

The detective just shook his head in disgust while sliding a paper across the table to Greyson. It was littered with signatures, most in ink, a few in pencil.

"Recognize this list?"

"No. Never seen it before."

"It's a list of witnesses who saw you give the vial to Knight," said O'Brien. "Don't bother counting, since I've already done it. There are one hundred and forty seven names on the sheet, including your own."

"Are you mad? What are you talking about?"

"It's the sign-in attendance sheet from the last Grand Rounds conference at the PGH," said the detective with a smile. "I believe the lecture was titled "Post Surgical Abdominal Adhesions – The Science and Expanding Role of Lysovage." I'm sorry if I mispronounced a few of those words, science wasn't my forte."

Greyson just stared at the list, his memory still good. He thought the stunt was a good idea at the time, a bit of showmanship.

"Dr. Knight claims you tossed this vial to him during that conference," said O'Brien. "Across a few rows I believe, in front of the entire audience. He thought it a bit cocky by the way."

He didn't respond, cursing Knight beneath his breath. He should have asked for the vial back.

"At that meeting, you asked him how it felt to hold the future of medicine in his hands," said O'Brien, reading from Dr. Knight's statement. "Wow, pretty heavy stuff."

"No comment," said Greyson, running a hand through his hair.

"Unfortunately it was your future Dr. Knight held in his hand young man, which in my professional opinion doesn't look very promising. Do you have any other questions Dr. Greyson?"

"Yes, I want a new attorney. Get my father on the line."

"Get him outta here," said O'Brien to a policeman at the door. "Put him down in D-block!"

The physician was escorted to a holding cell in the basement of the facility, containing two local vagrants.

The cell was isolated, the mechanical clunk of the lock echoing through the hall.

"Look here Steven," said the larger of the two inmates to his friend. "We have a visitor." Tattoos littered his hairy arms. "I just love company."

"He's cute and he looks ready to go," said Steven while getting up off his cot and approaching Greyson. "I love his hair. Are those highlights?"

"What's your name precious?" asked the muscular one. "I'm Francis but you can call me Fanny." He wore some eye shadow.

"Stay away from me," said Greyson. "I'll scream. So help me God, I'll scream."

"Yippee!" yelled Steven on tiptoes with a nervous clap of his hands together. "What's the French word for a three way Francis? I can never remember it. Menage ah something?"

"I don't speak a lick of French," said Fanny with a loving step towards Greyson. "But he's a real smooch. So go ahead sweetheart, scream all you want. I kind of like it that way."

"Ahhhhhhhh......"

Chapter Thirty Two
A FINAL QUESTION

For the next three months Dr. Knight remained interim chairman, after which time he retired. During his tenure he restored stability to the storied program and chaired a search committee to select a permanent replacement. Once the transition was complete, he stepped down as Chairman Emeritus of the department. His urban medical outreach center morphed into a Women and Children's Wellness Center funded by a pharmaceutical giant trying to polish a tarnished image. Union Park Biotech poured millions of dollars into the center after the convention center debacle, turning Knight's brainchild into a state of the art facility soon the be a paragon for all intercity wellness centers. He looked forward to working there every day.

After hearing of her plight, Dr. Knight selected Ms. Vanessa Rose as the center's chairperson, a position she gladly accepted. She excelled in the new role, which unleashed a multitude of previously unrecognized talents. Her experience with exploitation provided a common ground for patient interaction, and her marketing and business skills tapped into a steady flow of cash into the facility. She became an outspoken advocate for women's health and a respected businesswoman in the community.

Dr. Riles never recovered from the negative impact of his actions, sentenced to a lengthy parole and community service program. He drifted down the academic ladder, exiled to a struggling community hospital just outside Camden, New Jersey. His cramped office featured a commanding view of the Philadelphia skyline across the river. His son-in-law pleaded guilty to involuntary manslaughter charges and received a minimum five-year prison sentence at Graterford Prison, his good looks condemning him to a punitive stay at the facility. His jail cell had a commode but no flat screen T.V. He despised prison life. His wife quietly filed for divorce.

Maurice Rhett remained out of work for months recovering from his work related injuries, yet was able to return to regular duty on the first day of the basketball season. He led his maintenance team to the Promised Land that year, regaining the championship trophy. His Congo was shut down by the hospital administration, yet its memory lived in infamy, as did that of Stan Jankowski. Maurice was often heard whistling The *Beer Barrel Polka* while going about his duties, bringing a smile to any hospital passerby.

Phil and Rick quickly adapted to their new roles, the two an instant hit with the house staff. Rick's in house quarters were exchanged for a small condo just up the street from the PGH. He would still spend an occasional night in the hospital for old times' sake, the comforting hum of the medical center putting him to sleep. Phil made rounds daily with Nurse Hudson at his side. She wore a wedding ring from a man previously in love with the sea.

Jennifer fully recovered and within three months regained all her lost weight, returning to ample form. Her brush with death gave her a new outlook on life, now free of hesitation and negative vibes. Energy and confidence exuded from her frame. It was soon October, one of her favorite months.

"Thanks for dinner," she said to her date across the table. "The wine was fantastic."

"My pleasure," said the handsome physician sitting across from her. "You look fantastic."

"I've never felt better," said Jen. "And that's because of you."

The couple walked through the streets of Philadelphia holding hands, an autumn nip in the air and leaves across the ground. Some Halloween decorations were scattered about the tightly packed row houses. A black cat began to dart across their path but suddenly reversed course. An acorn fell from a large oak tree and pinged off a garbage can.

"I love Philadelphia," said Jenna. "I couldn't imagine living anywhere else. It's magical."

"An enigma, abrasive but full of brotherly love," said her date.

They walked through the historic district with the sun setting over the horizon, a horse drawn carriage passed by with hooves clopping on the cobblestone street. Arm and arm they strolled past the Liberty Bell and Independence Hall, still bustling with visitors. Their route took them to Love Park, Jen's favorite spot in the city, the water fountain pink in October. City lights began to sparkle in the twilight, the two stopping in front of the *Love* sculpture.

Jennifer took a deep breath while looking up at the four simple letters that meant so much to so many, the crisp autumn air full of peace. She slowly pirouetted full circle with her eyes closed and mantra in mind, a move taught to her by a wise monk in Kathmandu. She opened her eyes to see the *L-O-V-E* letters still there, but not her date.

"Phil?" she said, looking about.

"Down here," came the nervous reply from her date, his voice cracking.

She looked down to see Dr. Phillip Drummer on one knee, a sparkling diamond in his hand. He had the most wonderful look on his face. The gem was a boulder.

"Hey, a proposal!" yelled a Philadelphian chomping on a pretzel, covered with yellow mustard. A car driving by tooted its horn.

"Jennifer Ranier, I love you," said Phil, now taking her hand. "I've loved you since the moment we first met."

"Oh look!" shouted a nearby woman.

Jen's head began to spin, caught off guard by the pending question. Suddenly she couldn't think, as Phil continued to kneel.

"Say yes! Say yes," yelled the crowd, their cell phones out.

"Phil, please get up," said Jennifer. "What are you doing? They're filming us, please get up."

"Never," said Phil.

Her heart began to beat rapidly as tears welled up in her eyes, the piercing sound of a fire engine nearby. Overcome with emotion, she began to cry.

"Jennifer Ranier, will you marry me?"

The beautiful woman from Baltimore took a deep breath before responding, her answer caught on a vid eo that went viral. Her reply was immediately broadcast around the world.

CHAPTER THIRTY THREE
EPILOGUE

ONE MORNING PHIL woke up on his birthday thinking of Nurse Hudson. She was right he thought – what just happened? He slept in that day, already mid-morning and the house empty, its occupants dispersed throughout the Delaware Valley. Eight years ago they all moved out to the suburbs, a quaint Victorian home in the Haverford area, befitting a surgeon and his crew. He sat up on the side of the bed and moaned from a backache, a present from father time. A cat on the bed ignored his presence while Belle, the Labrador retriever, licked his hand. Today was the big day. While shaving he practiced his speech in the mirror, wondering why the face of a twenty-five year wasn't staring back at him? He was up late last night in the operating room working on a young man stabbed in the stomach while in dispute over a woman, such fiery passion. He worried how fast the next fifteen years would go by.

While reading the newspaper some birds chirped outside on a feeder as squirrels scurried below. He tried to digest the sporting news, but too much was on his mind. Someone pressed the fast forward button on life and there was no slowing it down. He pictured his own father at age forty-five.

While pulling out of the driveway he noticed the inspection sticker on his car was nearly overdue. The gardener had failed to mulch the side bed, and the sprinkler system was not watering the front yard very well, a patch of brown grass. His son forgot to bring in the garbage cans, partially blocking the driveway needing to be resealed for the winter. Suddenly panic, was his daughter's field hockey game tonight or tomorrow night? He couldn't remember. He wondered if there was enough time to stop at the dry cleaners on the way to work, maybe his wife already did? Perhaps it was time for a vacation, the last one being six months ago, as Little League All-Stars consumed the summer. Work, work, work – "never be the richest man in the cemetery" his brother warned him.

He saw thirty clinic patients that morning, all with similar stories and complaints, trying to give each one comfort. Every step outside of an exam room brought more interruptions. A call from the E.R., a critical lab value, reports to sign off, another physician on the phone. It was endless. Several patients were happy, one was angry and another brought him baked cookies. In a flash it was lunchtime, a brown bag peanut butter and jelly sandwich lasting five minutes. Then it was time.

Phil squinted as he stepped outside, the autumn sun bright and directly overhead. The busy plaza was centrally located between several hospital wings, and a favorite spot for a break. Several trees were located in the commons, otherwise littered with benches and a central fountain. The gathering was to the right where a small stage had been erected and rows of chairs set, the crowd already waiting. It was Vanessa he ran into first, still beautiful and dressed in black. She never seemed to age.

"Ready Phil?" she asked.

"Let's do it," said Phil. "Just like old times. Am I first?"

"Yes," said Vanessa with a smile. "He would want it that way."

"Good afternoon ladies and gentlemen," said Phil. He was standing in front of a podium wearing a long white coat, his hair still full and frame athletic. "It's truly an honor to be standing before you on a day set aside to honor a man we all knew so well. A man whose actions affected the lives of so many, in such a positive way."

A round of applause followed from the now full seating area. A standing room only section began to swell.

"Dr. Richard Roman Knight was the distinguished Chairman Emeritus of the Department of Surgery here at the PGH," continued Phil. "But he was much more than that. He was a person of many talents and expertise. A maverick. A true Renaissance man."

A breeze whipped through the plaza followed by another round of applause. Seated on stage, Mrs. Knight acknowledged the crowd with a smile and nod of her head.

"He was a skilled surgeon, a mentor, tireless educator, and proud member of the PGH staff." Phil paused to again scan the crowd, seeing some old fellow residents and a lone woman wearing a deep pink dress in the back row, with dark sunglasses.

"Despite his progressive physical limitations Dr. Knight was a stalwart, a man who feared nothing. He was someone who up until his final day on earth, contributed to the betterment of society, which was his ultimate purpose. Such commitment brings us here today to pay tribute to his vision, his life's work, his magnum opus."

More applause. Phil noticed a camera crew from the local news channel filming the event. He thought of Doc Johnson, and how proud he would have been, the surgical program now among the nation's elite. Earlier in the day he telephoned Johnson, updating him on the planned event.

Phil continued on with the speech, offering personal anecdotes involving Knight over the years. His touched upon a love for classical music, especially Alexander Borodin, whose involvement in medical education affected his own life decisions. He recounted the story of Knight tossing everyone out of the operating room one by one, for various reasons including a cell phone, leaving only Nurse Ella Frey to help finish the case. He spoke of Knight's love for opera including Giacomo Puccini, frequently commenting on the statue honoring the composer in his hometown of Lucca–a lasting tribute to a life of excellence.

Rick Polk sat in the front row smiling, with Nurse Ella Frey at his side.

"Yet despite all his passions, Dr. Knight had only one true love in his life," continued Phil with a look towards Mrs. Knight. "And that was his beautiful wife of forty-four years, always at his side, enjoying all that life had to offer. Their contribution to the Philadelphia community cannot be measured in words, but hopefully today's dedication will provide an enduring tribute to a relationship that brought so much good, to so many people."

Louder applause broke out as Mrs. Knight stood up to wave, some flowers given to her by an attendant.

"And now it gives me great honor to introduce our next speaker," said Phil with an extended hand. "Mrs. Vanessa Templeton is the current chairwoman of the Richard Knight Women and Children's Wellness Center, which as you know, has recently relocated to the new building behind me. For many years she worked tirelessly along side Dr. Knight and helped build the Wellness Center literally from the ground up. Ladies and gentlemen, I introduce to you Mrs. Vanessa Templeton."

Vanessa approached the stage with confidence, hugging Phil at the podium.

"Thank you Phillip," she said in his ear. The two were best of friends.

During her speech Phil sat down to enjoy the moment–Dr. Knight's moment. He passed away just over a year ago, complications from a progressive neurologic condition that robbed him of his physical talents, yet never touched his heart, mind and soul. To the end he was a warrior, positive in every way. Ironic thought Phil, he would not be best remembered for his undeniable surgical skills and clinical prowess, but rather his humanitarian efforts, which became well known nationwide. He recalled the day Knight showed up in the Torpedo Room to discuss his idea for a grass roots clinic to help the less fortunate. At the time it was an odd plan. Fortunately, he lived long enough to witness the success of his enterprise.

Then it was time. He arose and accompanied Vanessa and Mrs. Knight to the corner of the stage where a single cord hung from a pulley. On the count of three they simultaneously pulled the rope while a group of children from the center released balloons into the air, a string quartet beginning to play Borodin's *Nocturne*. Their action lifted a drape just to the right of the stage, uncovering a bronze statue of Dr. Knight. As the balloons swirled their way out of the plaza applause broke out from the crowd.

The statue was one of strength and beauty, showing Knight amid women and children surrounding him on each side. It depicted a towering, yet welcoming man, with arms extended around those in need, the children looking upwards in appreciation. His body and arms were firm, forever without tremor. A plaque beneath the pedestal plainly read:

Richard Knight, M.D.
Chairman Emeritus, Department of Surgery
Founder of the Knight Wellness Center
Surgeon, Teacher, Husband, Father, Friend
Humanitarian

Pictures were taken in front of the statue as the crowd pressed forward in appreciation.

"He would just love it," said Phil to Vanessa, their gaze upon his face. "Finally, his statue. Look at the smile on his face."

"I told him we were going to put one in front of the new center," said Vanessa. "He didn't believe me, but I'm sure he's looking down now with a grin. I love the spot."

"He always joked a statue in his honor would be the favorite target of every pigeon in the city," said Phil.

"Thank you," said Mrs. Knight, now entering into the conversation, with tears in her eyes. "Richard would have just loved it, so beautiful. Richard and I thank you for all your hard work over the years."

"You're welcome Mrs. Knight."

Phil worked his way through the crowd, a slap on the back from Polk leaving some pastry powder on his shoulder from the luncheon. He high fived Maurice Rhett in appreciation of him coming out of retirement for the big day. Mo looked great.

"Hey Drummer, happy birthday!" said a voice from behind. Turning around he saw Nurse Hudson, having made the journey from Martha's Vineyard for the ceremony. They hugged each other.

"The birthday boy!" said Hudson still holding onto the surgeon. "Was I right?"

"You certainly were Lucy," said Phil. "I woke up one day and was forty-five. Honestly I don't know how it happened. How's the captain?"

"Great, great, I told him to stay home," said Hudson. "Out at sea whale watching or something. We'll talk later," said the nurse heading towards the statue and some old friends. "Will you be at the dinner tonight?"

"Yes," said Phil. "See you then."

"Great speech," said another female voice to the right of Phil. "He would have loved it."

"Caroline," said Phil with a warm smile. "I'm so happy..."

"Mommy, mommy!" yelled two little boys with freckles across their face, jumping into her arms, their weight causing her to moan.

"Where's the rest of the gang Mrs. Boyce?" asked Phil.

"School trip with dad to Baltimore, the aquarium again," said Caroline. "Never a dull moment."

"I've heard excitement always follows you around," said Phil with a smile. "Is that true?"

"Hey, that's my line," said Cara. "And you know Phil, that catfight video is still somewhere in cyberspace," said the nurse in a muted tone.

"Shhh," said Phil with a look behind his shoulder. "The kids still don't know about it."

"We want cake mommy," said the younger of the two. "Cake! Cake! Cake!" went the chant.

"Then cake it is!" said nurse Boyce. "Let's go. Hup, two, three, four..."

Phil stepped away to approach the woman in the rose pink dress, patiently waiting in the back row. She wore a set of dark sunglasses and black shoes, along with a designer purse. She stood up and stretched, her physique still shapely despite the years, some silver bangles across her wrist. While approaching she smiled and pursed her red lips with a subtle grin. The two hugged without speaking, her body always fitting perfectly into his, her scent intoxicating.

"How did I do Mrs. Drummer?" asked Phil while looking her in the face, the sun sparkling off her shades.

"Not bad," said Jennifer with a smile and squeeze. "Not bad. Was that Lucy Hudson?"

"Yes," said Phil.

"There they are," said the leader of a group of children heading towards Phil and Jenna. "Mom, Jack's class ran over, I'm sorry we are late."

"Don't be sorry," said Jennifer to her oldest daughter. "Thanks for rounding them all up."

"Children," said Phil to the gang. "What a surprise."

"Happy birthday," said the crew hugging their father.

There was Maya, from Nepal, the oldest of the four. She was a graduate student at Penn studying International Relations. Second in line stood Madison, a spitting image of her mom, currently a sophomore in high school, with plans to be a physician. Next in line was Anna, the oldest twin, a blend of beauty from both parents, tall and thin, the smartest of the bunch. Then there was Jack, the caboose by two minutes, a ball of fire with his dad's looks and mom's spirit, the straw that stirred the drink. The twins just turned thirteen years old.

"Thank you everyone," said Phil.

"I thought we would all take the afternoon off and do something special," said Jennifer, the family now beginning to stroll away from the plaza. Phil held Jennifer's hand as the children walked beside.

"It's your day dad," said Maya. "What do you want to do?"

"How about an old fashioned picnic in Fairmount Park?" said Phil. "Your mom and I always went there when we were young. Right honey?"

"The zoo, how about the zoo?" said Jack.

"We'll get dinner from our favorite food truck," said Phil. We always ate from one right near the art museum. Is it still there, Jen?"

"I doubt it," said Jennifer. "That's kind of greasy stuff anyway."

"I always got a Philly cheesesteak and pretzel," said Phil. "I can taste it now. Yellow mustard only."

"I've got practice at six," said Anna. "Who is going to drive me there?"

"I'd also like to stop by the Rocky statue and take a picture," said Phil. "That was my favorite movie."

"Dad, you have a million photos standing in front of that statue."

"Since it's my birthday we can even turn off all of our cell phones, and just talk," said Phil with a grin. "Now that would be special. You know–disconnect to reconnect."

"No way! Never! Don't be crazy!" was the combined cry.

"Honey, I know it's your birthday," said Jen. "But a walk down memory lane may be a little rough on us all. They've heard all of your stories a hundred times before. Sometimes you live in the past."

"I love the past," said Phil. "If only I could travel back in time. Wouldn't that be great? So what do you all say? The park?"

Just then an acorn fell down from an oak tree, hitting Phil on the shoulder and bouncing in front of the group. He reached down and picked it up.

"Hey, a lucky acorn! Who wants it?"

No one answered.

"Jen?"

"No thanks," said Jennifer with a squeeze of her husband's hand. "I already have one."

THE END

ABOUT THE AUTHOR

Dr. Michael Banas completed his undergraduate studies at the University of Scranton. He then attended the University of Pennsylvania School of Medicine followed by an Orthopedic residency at the University of Rochester. His final year of surgical training took him to Los Angeles where he completed a Sports Medicine Fellowship at the Southern California Orthopedic Institute. Dr. Banas currently resides in Dallas, PA with his wife and six children. He specializes in Orthopedic Surgery and Sports Medicine.

27448977R00194

Made in the USA
Middletown, DE
18 December 2015